THE
MAYAN
LEGACY

The Mayan Legacy

More books may be ordered through booksellers or by contacting:
JS Books Publishing
7301 Ranch Road 620 N Suite 155
Unit 300
Austin, TX 78726

info@jodysummersbooks.com

ISBN: 978-0-9891079-6-9 (sc)
ISBN: 978-0-98910779-7-6 (ebook)

Printed in the United States of America JS Books Publishing rev. date: 12/22/19

THE
MAYAN
LEGACY

JODY
SUMMERS

OTHER BOOKS BY JODY SUMMERS

A Brush with Death (Book 1 *Art of the Dead* series)

A Brush with Fire (Book 2 *Art of the Dead* series)

A Brush with Evil (Book 3 *Art of the Dead* series)

FOREWORD

An interesting note to this novel is the fact that not only are a number of the experiences related herein ones to which I am intimately familiar, one is particularly unusual.

I wracked my brain for quite some time to come up with a suitable near-death experience to use in the opening scene. As it turns out I had an "AHA" moment, or more appropriately a "DUH" moment when it occurred to me that I had actually survived the perfect experience to use. As a result, the first scene and the near-death experience described here was drawn, almost in its entirety from my OWN life, and I still retain the scar.

I guess sometimes truth really is stranger than fiction.

1.

*September 4th 2016
Labor Day Weekend*

There's an old joke that goes like this:

> *"Ninety percent of collegiate deaths are preceded by the words,
> "'Hey Man, watch this!'"*

Pretty funny, actually.

But in the case of Jeremy Andrews, the likelihood of someone dying from the deeds following his proclamation was probably more like 95 percent and had gone way beyond college: but his luck was still holding. Also, if it happened to him it was going to be on film. He was 28 years old, and the things he'd already done would have killed most people: collegiate gymnast, former diver, and trampolinist. Not to mention he was an accomplished sky diver with several hundred jumps in his log, a private pilot, a certified scuba diver, a martial artist—hell, he'd even tried his hand at a second-rate stunt school. He'd never been hired as a stuntman, he'd tell people, but he did have some great photos of him being beat up, burned up, blown up, jumping motorcycles over gasoline fires, and falling off four story buildings into a ten foot square, five foot thick mat. He'd been on a mission his whole life to try anything and everything. Adrenaline junky was the popular term. Except now, with new technology, he was getting the chance to get his adrenaline rush on video.

So maybe it wasn't so strange to find him on Labor Day weekend at the lake sitting in the front of an open-bow boat with his old Parasail parachute on, and a ski rope attached to the front of his harness stretching out in front of him to a small jet boat with a camera strapped to his wrist.

"Joel, you and Les need to hold that 'chute up higher," Jeremy yelled from up front. "It's not inflating yet and it should be."

Joel and Les nodded and tried to do as Jeremy directed.

"You know you're an idiot, Jeremy," His on-again, off-again, girlfriend Valerie Latham commented.

"Uh, huh. Lance, go ahead and ease up we can hook up everything right here."

Valerie just stared at him. His incessant need for adrenaline rushes unnerved her, and it had only gotten worse since he'd discovered video.

"No problem, Jer," Lance answered as he slowed the boat.

It took them just a few minutes to string the parachute up over the windows of the open-bow boat, and straighten the lines, while Jeremy double-checked his Go-Pro wrist camera attachment. The ski rope was already connected.

"Great," Jeremy said as he sat in the bow, "Now call Frank and tell him to slowly take up the slack while you match his speed."

Lance picked up his cell phone and called Frank, who was 175 feet away in the jet boat that the ski rope was attached to. "Ok, Frank, really easy now. Just start to take up the slack while I match your speed. As the slack uncoiled Lance began easing forward and Jeremy braced his feet in front of him on the inside of the bow and clicked the video camera on. It was turned to point out in front of him and should be picking up part of his legs and feet as well as the rope and the boat way out in front of him. Perfect.

~

Jeremy shifted his attention to Lance, the driver of the little runabout. Lance was just slipping his Captain and Coke back in the holder and grinning broadly. "Good job Lance, I think you have his speed matched."

"Yeah, for now," he answered, "As long as he doesn't try to gun that thing. This little rig was never meant to keep up with a jet boat, and at 175 feet away I can't call or signal him fast enough."

"You could phone him." Jeremy said, smiling broadly back at him.

"Yeah, right. And look back at you and keep the boat straight and hear something over the revving engines all while I try to steer with one hand. Your ideas just keep getting better and better, Jeremy."

The plan was to have the two boats go slowly in unison while the parachute inflated, then accelerate until the parachute lifted Jeremy out of the boat. Presto! They'd have homemade parasailing without a beach, or one of those giant reel things.

Maybe it won't come as too much of a surprise that a certain amount of alcohol was involved with this Darwin Award candidate of an idea, and though someone must have considered it ahead of time or the parachute and camera wouldn't be there, it's still pretty certain that the onset of this little adventure was preceded by something similar to the above mentioned collegiate death sentence:

"Hey man, watch this!"

Nevertheless, there he sat in the bow of that boat, his sole consideration for safety being an oversized ski vest strapped over his parachute harness.

At this point, the boats were going roughly ten miles per hour, and someone should have noticed by now that the parachute already had more than enough wind to inflate, but it hadn't, and never would. The turbulence of the airflow over that divided windshield would see to that.

Somewhere in this idiotic process, the jet boat in front eked out another mph or two, and Jeremy began to be crunched down into the bow causing him to call back over his shoulder.

"Hey Lance, could you inch it up a bit? That turkey has sped up some, and I'm getting compressed up here."

"Sure thing, Jeremy."

Now Lance was in fact the owner of the ski boat and an accomplished and normally safe boater, but, just like everyone else in this ill-conceived caper, he had been caught up in the excitement of the moment, and his normal judgment had been undermined by copious quantities of Captain Morgan. At this point, if Lance had been questioned, it wouldn't have been surprising for him to declare he *was* Captain Morgan. This, however, was better than the concoction the rest of them were drinking. Joel had invented a lethal mixture of Grape Juice, Red Bull and potato Vodka that he was calling a RipSnort and everyone but Lance was partaking, to their brain cells' detriment.

At any rate, Lance carefully matched velocities with Frank until the long ski rope just barely settled back onto the top of the water. Unfortunately, Frank perceived the change of tension on the ski rope as excessive slack and, to compensate, he hit the throttle a bit.

For those unfamiliar with small jet boats, there is really no such thing as "hitting the throttle a bit," those things *move,* and just a bit of gas causes more than just a bit of reaction. The resulting surge by the jet boat caused Jeremy to truly be compressed into the bow. He initially attempted to resist, but quickly realized the futility of the effort, so he did the only thing available to him: he took a deep breath and went limp, letting the ski rope yank him over the bow and deciding that his entire concentration should be on *not* panicking. He reasoned that the boats would stop shortly, and the vest he was wearing would then pop him to the surface.

What he couldn't have possibly calculated was chance.

Chance, which, in this case, took the form of one of the parachute lines behind him snapping like a whip due to the velocity of his departure, and incredibly managing to drop a loop around his neck prior to him being submerged. The parachute still remained in the ski boat, and he was being pulled by the ski rope attached to the jet boat, so basically, Jeremy was a second or two from having his head severed by a ¼ inch diameter, 550lb test, nylon parachute line. Except that chance interfered again, this time in Jeremy's favor. All of which Jeremy was blissfully unaware.

In those few seconds while he was being drug underwater, Jeremy had that experience that we have almost all heard of and next to none of us has ever experienced. Except his had a unique twist.

With his eyes closed, and water rushing by around him, Jeremy had his life flash before his eyes. Memories of playing army on the levees by Lake Pontchartrain,

marbles in the school yard in New Orleans,

his first snow fall and playing in the woods in Memphis,

the civil war haunted house he and friends had braved one night,

his first kiss,

neighborhood football,

summers at the pool where he started diving,

his uncle's dairy farm where he and his cousin had horses,

the heartbreaking move to Houston in high school,

becoming serious about gymnastics

meeting his first true love,

Elton John,

the Bee Gees,

In-A-Gadda-Da-Vida,

his second love, the one that had stayed with him into college until the miles ate them up . . .

The memories roared past, sights, smells, songs, feelings, emotions, all in an incredibly vivid blur of sensation. For several seconds, Jeremy was completely unaware of the increasing stress on his lungs from holding his breath, or the water blasting past his closed eyes in that murky lake, or the death that was so quickly closing in on him, then another memory of a pebble racing toward that deep spot on that big funny shaped rock and the rock beginning to . . .

Suddenly the rushing motion ceased, and like a cork Jeremy popped to the surface. He gasped. His shock was such that he was totally unaware of removing the loop of rope from around his neck. Only the burning sensation from that rope remained as he paddled back to the ski boat Lance was gingerly maneuvering toward him. His mind was reeling from the physical sensations as well as the extraordinary experience of truly having his life flash before his eyes right up to where that rock . . .

Wait a minute, he thought. *"what rock?"*

A scream jarred his thoughts as he pulled himself above the railing of the boat. He jerked his eyes up in time to see his friend, Jane, collapse in the boat and Valerie evincing a look reminiscent of someone watching a puppy being smashed by a car. Taking all this in, Jeremy smoothly pulled himself the rest of the way into the boat, not even noticing the parachute still draped along the length of its interior.

"What's wrong with her?" he asked, pointing to the unconscious Jane, "And for that matter, what are you looking at?" he directed to Valerie.

"It's your neck, Jer," Valerie answered. "Does it hurt?" Valerie was a dark-haired beauty with a sculpted face and a strong, slender form. Her emotional make up was much more akin to that of a man than a woman though, so the degree of concern in her voice caught his attention more than the words themselves.

Suddenly, the burning sensation he'd noticed while swimming back to the boat came to the fore, and he realized that it *did* hurt. It burned like hell as a matter of fact.

"Yeah. It burns. What is it?" He gingerly reached up to his throat and was shocked to feel raw and crusty flesh. His touch sent new twinges of pain along his already overloaded nerve endings, but he continued to slowly trace the path of the wound around his neck. "My God," he said, looking up at Valerie.

"You didn't notice?" Valerie responded.

"Notice what? I know that something has happened to my neck, and it burns like hell, but I haven't a clue why."

Valerie leaned closer to him. Putting her hands on his shoulders, she let her gaze go first around one side of his neck and then the other.

"This mark goes all the way around your neck, Jer, and crosses on the right. It looks like a rope was around it. Didn't you feel a rope around your neck? For that matter you must have taken it off. Don't you remember that?"

"Not a clue. I had no idea anything was around my neck, and I don't recall taking it off. Which rope was it? Is it bleeding?" Everyone else in the boat seemed speechless, and Jane was just beginning to rouse. Her boyfriend Joel, a talented musician and an annoying wit, was holding her. Lance just kept staring. So, again, it was Valerie that answered.

"Judging by the diameter of the wound, I'd say it had to be one of the parachute lines, and no, it's not bleeding. It looks like it burned into your neck so the whole wound is cauterized. It's pretty disgusting though." Her assessment was rather clinical, just what he would have expected of her.

"Great. Thanks for that. So that's why Jane fainted, I guess. I sure don't remember the rope around my neck, though. I can't even believe I took it off, but I do recall my life flashing before my eyes."

His comment brought a hint of a smile from Valerie. "Yeah, right, your near-death experience, huh?"

Jeremy riveted her eyes, staring intently, "Yeah, really, Val." His brow furrowed while details of the experience raced through his memory, especially the part about the . . . But he was interrupted again when Lance finally spoke.

"I think you must have been snapped over the bow so fast that one of the parachute lines behind you looped around your neck like a whip, but that would mean . . ."

Lance's voice trailed off as his mind rebuilt the scenario, but Jeremy finished it for him.

"That means that I was getting drug by the ski rope in front with a loop of parachute line from behind around my neck and . . . and . . . his eyes focused on the parachute lying deflated in the back of the boat. My God, why didn't my head . . ." Now it was Jeremy who couldn't finish his sentence as his mind pictured the gruesome decapitation that by all rights should have occurred.

"I gunned the boat," Lance interjected in a distant voice. "I didn't know why I was doing it, but I gunned the boat." Lance's unconscious reaction was, in fact, the second instance of incalculable chance that had saved Jeremy's life.

"But I was only a few feet out in front, Lance. How did you know you wouldn't . . ." Again, he didn't finish the sentence as his mind generated an image of the ski boat's propeller colliding with his body. All he had considered in the instant he was snapped over the bow was to not panic so he wouldn't drown. The other consequences had never crossed his mind or awareness. He really *had* been close to death this time.

As waves gently buffeted the boat, Joel and Les coiled up the lines and canopy of the parachute.

"Good thing we didn't give him enough rope," Joel quoted with a sly grin.

Les looked taken aback, "Looking at that mark around his neck, you really think that's funny, Joel?"

"Maybe if we'd just shown him the ropes first . . . "

"Enough, already," Les cut in now, suppressing a smile.

Joel glanced at Jeremy and Val who were sitting in the bow talking in low tones that didn't make it past the bow windows. While they talked, Jeremy coiled up the long rope that had been disconnected from the jet boat.

"That's about as tender as I've ever seen her," Joel offered.

"Isn't that the truth? How long have they been dating now? Six months?" Les wasn't given to offering personal comments about others, so his question caught Joel's attention.

"Yeah, if you want to call it that. I don't get it. Valerie seems so sweet to everyone, but when it comes to Jeremy, she seems to turn the deep-freeze on and off. It kind of makes me wonder what Jeremy sees in her."

"Well, she is damn attractive," Joel began. "I'd say he's in better hands than Allstate."

"Yeah, but it's not like Jeremy can't attract plenty of those, but I'll grant you he certainly seems to see *something*. And are you really making insurance puns now?"

"Well you know, fifteen minutes could save you . . ." Joel cut off at the scowl on Les' face. "OK, not funny," he finally conceded.

As they finished stuffing the parachute into a bag in the back of the boat, Jane sidled over and sat next to Joel.

"What are you two talking about? As if I didn't know. Jeremy and Val, right?"

"Guessed it in one," Joel said as he kissed her lightly on the cheek, "You feeling OK now?"

"Yeah. I can't believe I fainted. I've never done that before. It was just that . . ." She shuddered slightly, but then wasn't about to let Joel change the subject. "So, what do you think about Jeremy and Val? Strange, huh?"

"That's pretty much what we decided," Les answered.

"It only took Jeremy nearly dying to soften her up a bit. Did you notice?"

"Yeah, that's what we were just discussing," Joel said.

"I think something happened to her in the past," Jane offered, I've seen this before. Some guy probably did something and now she's afraid to open up. That's why Jeremy is the only one she shows her cold side to. It's because she likes him."

"You hardly even know her," Joel answered, "You figured all that out from the little you've talked to her? What are you, psychic?"

"No. Not talked to her. She didn't tell me a thing. It's what I've learned from watching."

"Yeah, right. You do think you're psychic."

Jane ignored Joel's look of skepticism, "I'm telling you. Hasn't Jeremy talked to you about her?"

"Not really, and it wasn't for my lack of trying either."

"Hmmm," Jane responded, "He likes her, too, then."

"So why wouldn't he talk to me?"

"Because she's being so damn aloof. I'd guess it's driving him nuts."

"Hmmm . . . that makes sense." Joel muttered

"If the two of you boys are through discussing our friends' love lives, I'd be glad to get you a beer. Besides they're coming back here."

"Hey," Jeremy said as he came up. "What are ya'll looking so secretive about?"

"Oh nothing, Joel answered. Before Jeremy could respond, Joel continued. I see you got that camera off your wrist. Has everyone forgotten we have a video to look at?"

The comment worked. Jeremy completely forgot their conversation as his eyes widened. "Oh man, you're right. Maybe we can see where I took the rope off my neck at least."

But the idea didn't last very long. As Lance guided the boat back across the lake to the dock Jeremy's injury exerted some influence on his decision. The air from the boat's cruise speed caused the burning in his neck to increase and as he gingerly touched the area, he could detect some swelling too. There were also the other people at the party to consider and how the wound looked.

Jeremy raised his voice of the noise of the wind and tapped Joel on the shoulder.

"Joel, I think we're going to have to put off looking at the video. I'm thinking I better get this looked at and I'm really not in the mood to explain this to all the others or deal with their reaction to seeing it."

Joel only hesitated for a moment, as everyone else turned to look at them. "I understand, Jer. We don't need anyone else fainting either. We can set up a time later to get together and watch it."

"Thanks, Joel."

Lance turned his attention back to steering the boat and everyone else who had been unconsciously leaning in to listen, tilted back into their seats. The boat sped on. Every jolt going over a wave reminded Jeremy that leaving quickly was a good decision.

* * *

Ninety minutes later the wound was really beginning to burn. Val was driving his car back toward the city. He had just about convinced her to take him home and skip the trip to a doctor but suddenly he changed his mind.

"I guess we'd better stop by the hospital," Jeremy offered unexpectedly.

"Why? What's wrong?" the concern in her voice was unmistakable, though she had continued to lobby for this choice the whole trip back.

"Well the muscles in my neck are swelling, and it's getting a little tough to swallow. If they keep this up it might make it difficult to breathe. I don't want to have to find out if you can perform an impromptu tracheotomy."

"Well, I don't know about that, but any excuse to take you by the doctor is fine with me."

From there on Valerie remained conspicuously quiet for miles, until she finally asked a question. "Jeremy, when you were swimming back to the boat, I found my attention divided between glimpses of the mark on your throat and the look on your face. What was going through your mind?"

Jeremy never ceased to be delighted with Val's thinking. Her physical beauty was merely a part of the allure; her bright wit and broad intellect were equally exciting, and he wished again that she could be more open with her feelings. What was holding her back? She was reticent to lay down her emotional armor to begin with, but when you combined that with her more natural protective proclivities, it definitely raised her 'aloofness' to a fine art. Jeremy felt certain she had serious feelings for him, but she would neither voice them herself, nor let him confess as much to her. Consequently, their relationship floated along on an enforced and, in Jeremy's opinion, fake veneer.

It stood in stark contrast to the relationship he had seen between his parents growing up in Memphis, Tennessee. Their relationship had been open, loving and mutually supportive. That example was possibly the reason Jeremy had been so slow to commit to relationships in his life and suffered so much from the one he had committed to. Most everything that came his way seemed to lack the possibility he'd seen in his own parents. If he was going to make a commitment of that depth, he wanted it to have the quality of relationship he had witnessed growing up. Valerie's question, though, reminded him of something else. His whole life had just flashed before his eyes, and as much as the phrase reeked of *cliché*, the reality of it was amazing. How could so many thoughts, so many sensations, flash so clearly through his mind in such a short space of time? Why do people's whole lives flash before their eyes when death is imminent, even if they don't know it's imminent?

He remembered, his last vision before he popped to the surface, that pebble and the boulder. What the hell was that about? That wasn't a life experience of his, and even if it had been, how could his view have been from that perspective? What was that rock anyway, and why was that particular part of the vision so fuzzy? What really mattered was that *that* event never happened! Everything else that raced through his mind was a sequential blur of life events he recognized. So, what was that last thing?

"Jeremy?"

He'd become so caught up in his train of thought that he'd forgotten to answer her.

"Oh ... uh ... sorry, Val. It's just that it was such a strange experience, having my entire life flash by me and well ..." He turned to stare at her, dragging her eyes momentarily away from the road. "Val, something really strange happened."

"Yeah, you almost got yourself killed, you idiot," she said smiling. She was well aware of his daredevil tendencies and to the extent possible, comfortable with them.

"No, it was something stranger than that. When I was underwater, my life did flash before my eyes. You know, just like everyone says it does. But there was...something else ... something that wasn't part of my life. It was like it was stuck right there at the end, just before I popped to the surface, and I can't imagine what it was."

Val slowly turned her head back toward the road then asked, "Well, what was it you saw?"

His voice took on a dreamy quality as he drew up the image,

"Something about a pebble, no, maybe a bullet and a big black boulder . . . I don't know...for some reason that part is really blurry." His voice trailed off.

"So? What's so strange about that?

"What's so strange is that it never happened."

"Oh," she said, apparently thinking. They both fell silent.

When Val pulled into the hospital parking lot 20 minutes later, she asked, "So how's the throat feeling?"

"About the same. This is probably a waste of time."

"Well, it may be a waste of time, but it's a smart waste of time. I'm not really up to trying to insert a Bic pen tube in your throat so you can breathe."

Jeremy turned to her and smiled as he opened the door, "Where did you hear about that? It would probably work."

"Hell yeah, it would work. I think. I'm pretty sure I saw it in a movie somewhere."

"You think you could do that?"

"If I had to, to save your life, yeah. Well, I'd need a sharp knife, too."

"Good grief. I'm dating a female MacGyver."

Walking into an emergency room is an unnerving experience, Jeremy thought. They usually wheel the worst cases out immediately so you're not sitting in the waiting room with people bleeding everywhere, but still, a bad one zooms by every now and then on a gurney. He felt silly for even being there. It could have waited till tomorrow.

For the second time in an hour, he was reminded of his youth. The first cut he had ever gotten that was bad enough to require stitches, from pulling up large cane reeds he remembered, had resulted in his first trip to the emergency room. He'd been 11 and absolutely scared to death. It was funny how some of those old feelings still lingered, even when he had far outgrown them.

As they approached the counter, Jeremy couldn't help but notice the look on the lady's face as she caught sight of his injury. He was certain that she viewed him as a suicide attempt, and he didn't feel like dealing with it.

"No, I'm not a suicide attempt OK? Could we just get in to see the doctor?"

She stared pointedly at his neck, squinted her eyes slightly, and turned her gaze to a small stack of clipboards beside her.

She didn't believe him, and he didn't care. She handed him the forms with a minimum of comment, and he and Val went and sat back down to fill them out.

Forty-five minutes later they were walking back to the car. Jeremy had some salve on his neck to show for his visit.

"I told you it was a waste of time." He was beginning to feel tired. The adrenaline he'd been functioning on had finally dissipated and exhaustion was closing in.

"It was worth it just to have him tell you the swelling was pretty much finished. And that cauterization thing . . . well it's a pretty neat trick to seal up your own wound right after you inflict it on yourself."

She paused for just a second then continued, "Jeremy, do you really have to take these stupid chances?"

Jeremy stopped walking and turned to her. "Oh, so now you care?"

"Oh, don't be an idiot. I've always cared. I don't have so many friends that I would relish losing one."

"Ah. Friends. I forgot." He started walking again and didn't try to hide the disappointment in his voice. Sometimes he couldn't fathom why he kept playing this game with her. Over and over he thought that the experience he was having with her must be exactly what most women went through with their men: loving someone who was never willing to commit and frequently not even able to admit to any feelings but knowing they were there anyway. It was frustrating to say the least and gave Jeremy a great deal of empathy for women. For the life of him he couldn't tell whether his relationship with her was ever really going to go anywhere or not, and it was difficult for him to continue to play like he didn't care. Pushing the issue wouldn't help, though. It was either wait and see or leave, and to her credit, Val had never tried to hold him back from that option. So why was he still here?

As usual, the train of thought ended with an unresolved mental sigh, just as they reached the car.

"Give me the keys. I can drive the rest of the way."

Val only paused a second before reaching in her purse. "Are you sure? I don't mind."

"Yeah, I'm fine. Just a bit tired. I'll have to drive home when I drop you off anyway." Jeremy saw her stiffen momentarily at his comment. She had apparently been expecting him to stay. Usually those suggestions, if any, were his. It gave him something else to think about. The hesitation was miniscule, though, as Val quickly caught herself.

It was enough to send memories of being with her flashing through his mind, causing his body to react slightly.

Damn her, he thought.

While Jeremy drove her home, Valerie couldn't help but speculate on her own reasons. It had never been her natural tendency to easily display emotions. Even as a little kid she had been struck with a feeling of vulnerability on any occasion where she let her emotions show.

She wondered if it was her mother's natural coldness that had been imparted to her. It was just too personal and felt too vulnerable. Feeling that way was at least one weakness she didn't have to live with or let others see. As the years had gone by, though, she had let her heart reach out to a couple of people and ultimately found what she expected: pain.

The truth was that for all her predilections to not display her feelings or in many cases even acknowledge them, she had tremendous feelings for Jeremy and had fantasized about marrying him, but she hadn't found the courage or the certainty within herself to risk the pain again. She hadn't yet realized that she never would have that certainty, and that relationships were a risk you either took or you didn't. If you took it, you risked pain, but if you didn't it was a certainty that you would experience the emptiness of never letting someone close to you.

It was a rather ignored yet prevalent example of the axiom that nothing in life is free.

Jeremy pulled into her driveway and turned to her. "Well, here we are." There was a weariness in his voice that touched Val, and he wasn't making a move to kiss her. She found that even more endearing and on a sudden urge, she leaned over and kissed him gently on the lips. It was more than just a peck, but quick enough that she had pulled back before Jeremy had a chance to respond.

"I'm glad you're OK," she said, realizing a depth of sincerity that she was amazed to be expressing.

Valerie could see Jeremy's face flush and found it gratifying. A momentary lowering of her armor was rewarded with a profound reaction from him. The tenderness it aroused surprised her.

"Thanks Val," was all he could muster as his fingers clenched around the steering wheel.

She paused, about to say something else, then smiled, opened the door, and was gone.

Her departure left Jeremy feeling even more exhausted, as though his last burst of energy had been to maintain appearances for her and now with her gone, the fatigue roared in. He knew he was going to struggle to stay awake on the half hour drive home.

The one thought that kept his eyes open was the recollection of the last strange event at the tail end of his aborted parasailing attempt. What was the deal with the pebble? Or was it a bullet? Letting that puzzle slide, he thought about the rest of the images and guessed it was a good thing when your life passes before your eyes and you have the sensation that it was a good one . . .

Once in his driveway, he put the car in park and absently reached up to touch his neck; his fingers encountered the sticky salve from the hospital. It still burned.

* * *

Valerie sat at her vanity removing makeup and trying to decide if she was angrier with herself for kissing Jeremy or for not kissing him a whole lot more. At age 27 she had already been married for four years, divorced for two, and unhappy about love for six. She knew she had a gentle and tender heart, but almost no one else was aware of it. Except her dad. He used to refer to it as her armor and her underbelly because he always knew of her soft spot underneath, the part she hid so well.

It was that soft spot that had led her to her first marriage and that same soft spot that had caused her heart to be nearly ripped from her chest when it had ended. The man had turned out to be insensitive and never really understood the depths of the woman he had married, so he let his eyes wander and where they wandered the rest of him followed. When Valerie found out, she tried to discuss it with him. He mouthed platitudes but didn't change his habits, and her self-image was strong enough that she couldn't remain tethered to such a demeaning situation for long. Still, she stayed longer than she should have out of love and hope, but in the end it didn't matter.

Since then she simply couldn't find enough of her heart or courage to let it go again, until Jeremy.

She opened the back door to the apartment that had been her home for about 18 months. It was in the Bee Caves Road area, and she loved it for a number of reasons. Living in Austin was like a dream to begin with, and she felt it a moral imperative to participate in the breath taking views the city provided.

Her apartment complex was built into a hillside that gave her an expansive view of the Texas Hill Country from her little upstairs deck. Sitting here in the evenings and watching the sun set was one of her favorite getaways. Even early evenings were picturesque with the lights from the homes in the hills seeming to reflect their counterparts in the sky. The panoramic view always provided solace for her self-imposed solitude.

Moving out of Kansas City had been a vocational requirement as a lobbyist for companies seeking the expansion of digital rights for artists, but she hadn't been prepared to take the step to D.C. yet, especially not during this difficult election year. She felt it better to start on the state government level, and her employers concurred.

She leaned back from the deck railing, took a seat in her wooden rocker, and looked up at the stars. A wave of emotion washed through her as she realized how close she'd come to losing him, followed by a bit of self-revelation at how much that meant to her. The realization at first filled her with a thrill of fear, but then it made her consider acting on her feelings for a change instead of just sitting on the sidelines. Maybe this time she'd found someone worth taking the chance on, if she could just bring herself to do it. A little shudder coursed through her as some darker memories, those of her last attempt to let her heart go, intruded. Then again, maybe she should keep waiting.

~

Jeremy tossed and turned. The dreams rolled over and over up to the instant he'd surfaced in the lake and noticed the burning around his neck. His hand absently drifted up to the injury.

Pain.

He bolted upright in bed removing his hand from his neck. His dream had led him to actually touch the wound and now, not only was his hand sticky from the salve, his pillow was stained and his whole neck was throbbing. He glanced over at the clock by his bed. 3:30a.m. He sighed. At least it was Labor Day weekend, and even though it was Monday morning, he'd be able to sleep in. He took a sip of water from the bottle he kept by his bed and lay back down. Images of Valerie danced before his closed eye lids. Damn! He thought. Why couldn't she just be a little less guarded?

He had been so naïve with his divorce two years ago. It was *stuff* that she ended up wanting, and it was stuff that she got. He didn't mind losing his belongings nearly as much as realizing that they were more important to her than he was. Now, it was the missing chunk of his heart that he resented the most. Hell, maybe he wasn't so different from Val after all.

His thoughts slowly eased their frantic pace and, with the help of a good novel, by 4:00a.m., he drifted back to sleep.

2

April 4ᵗʰ 2016

The sun would be rising in two hours, and if Chuck didn't get this damn telescope swung around in time, he was going to miss the opportunity.

The massive 200 inch diameter, 100-foot-long, Hale reflector telescope was slowly swinging into a new position as Chuck waited impatiently. It was another incredibly clear southern California evening. He had been staring at a brand new celestial body, one that someone had dubbed a cosmic ghost. It looked a lot like a nebula, but this was bright green and contained absolutely no stars, leaving it in a class by itself as a cosmic oddity. But what he was supposed to have been doing was focusing on the rings of Saturn for a project NASA was paying the observatory to undertake. Now the evening was slipping away, and if he didn't get the huge telescope swung around and refocused pretty soon, he'd have no data for the evening. That wasn't good. Even 45 minutes of data would suffice for tonight, but having nothing to show would highlight his unscheduled endeavors with the space ghost.

The gears continued to hum, but the small delay seemed to take forever. Finally swinging into position, Chuck swiveled his little seat closer to the optic and peered through the lens onto the great mirror and out into the not-so-far reaches of the solar system.

Charles Kohler had been working at the Mt. Palomar Observatory in California for over 20 years and had never tired of spending his evenings staring up at the heavens. It gave him a sense of connection to the universe.

He'd acquired enough tenure to be the chief operator of the Hale telescope, the oldest of the large reflectors in the US. It was a strange and lonely existence, being awake nights and sleeping during the day. On many evenings he was the only person there, especially when there were a number of minimally funded projects to be handled. Still, with an IQ topping 185, it had always seemed to Chuck that solitude was preferable to the company of others. With an insatiable desire to learn more about the universe around him, and a pervasive difficulty in relating to others, the job had fit him like a glove.

Saturn gently slid into the field of view as Chuck operated the controls and slowed the telescope's movement to a minute crawl. The image centered, and he stopped the movement altogether. As he fine-tuned the focus and readied the camera to begin its sequential shots, the only sound was the low whirr of the gears that kept the telescope in perfect sync with the movement of the earth, therefore providing the photographic clarity NASA wanted. The rings of Saturn stood out in glorious splendor, revealed in amazing detail in the view field of his tremendous telescope. For that was how he thought of the Hale telescope. It was, for all practical purposes, his only child and the center of his existence; it was his own personal eye into the vastness of the universe.

He smiled as he finished his adjustments. The giant reflector was locked onto its target. There was nothing for him to do now but wait, and if he chose, to do his own study of the surface and rings of Saturn while the attached camera did its work. He was in his element.

3

Jeremy opened his eyes. Aches and pains in every joint rivaled the burning sensation of his neck.

What an idiot he thought, remembering the numerous beers and rum drinks he'd consumed on the lake. It was one thing to drink like a fish, and another to try these stupid stunts, but to combine the two was absolute lunacy! One of these days his luck was going to run out. The more he thought about yesterday's little foray into idiocy, the more he wondered why his luck hadn't run out right then. It was nothing short of a miracle that he was still breathing. In the space of about thirty seconds, he'd had three separate methods of dying: drowning, getting decapitated with the parachute line, or getting run over by the ski boat. *God must really want me around for something,* he decided, as he threw the covers back.

He eased himself up in bed and slowly began to stretch. If there was one thing he'd learned over the years in gymnastics, it was how to stretch out the morning kinks. After rotating his head each direction to the sound of muted cracks from his vertebrae, he slid onto the floor in a wide straddled position. In fluid movements, he leaned to the left and right, touching his toes, then slowly slid his hands out in front of him until his face and chest were flat on the floor. Most people would wince just to watch the demonstration, but Jeremy gave it no more thought than breathing. He'd been doing this for years.

He lay there for a few moments letting his thoughts wander. He had a huge concert coming up later in the week, and the details niggled at his thoughts. All of the contracts had been signed and the people erecting the stage were already scheduled. At this point his biggest worry was that everyone would actually come through with what they'd been contracted to do. Last minute jitters he knew. They were part of the job description.

It was one of the first promotions Jeremy had done himself and he was lucky to be able to feature Willie Nelson. Willie didn't produce shows himself and actually didn't even book his own gigs, but Jeremy had made points with him when he had met Willie at a drop-zone one afternoon. Willie had decided that a tandem jump was on his bucket list and Jeremy just happened to be on the load he was going up on. They'd hit it off on the way up and when Willie found out he was producing a concert, he'd told him he'd put a word in with his agent and they could talk more on the ground if he survived. Willie had still been plying his trademark laugh when he and the jumper he was tethered to left the plane.

~

He'd stumbled into the concert producing, line of work six years ago when a friend had corralled him into helping at a charity concert. He'd proven to be so good at bringing details together that before he knew it, he had his own business going as a producer. It not only paid the bills in high fashion, but it supplemented his substantial real estate income and allowed him a varied and unusual schedule which suited Jeremy to a "T".

The upcoming event was originally scheduled to be at the Stubs Bar-B-Q and amphitheater until a hot-air balloon manufacturer asked to be a sponsor of the show and have a hot air balloon floating above the event. That wasn't something that could be done in downtown Austin, but the money was worth the effort so Jeremy had moved the venue to the Nutty Brown Café and amphitheater. It was a bit out of town on Hwy 290 and much better suited to tethered balloons. Now that he thought about it, he remembered that he needed to recheck the forecast. If the weather was still permitting, he needed to verify with the FAA to make sure there was no glitch with his pre-approved safety bulletins.

He pushed up off the floor and ambled toward the shower thinking again about Valerie. Were they headed anywhere? Did he want it to go somewhere? Jeremy was struggling to come to grips with one of his own foibles. Once he decided he had a real interest in a woman, he would catch himself making any amount of excuses to explain away flaws in her character. Nobody's perfect, he'd tell himself, and to his credit that was a good trait to a point, but taken too far it became a prescription for being taken advantage of and ultimately getting his heart broken. It had happened time and time again, to the extent that one day he'd had to make a conscious decision to either be willing to be hurt or to gravitate toward cynicism and give up trying altogether. He imagined the latter choice was the more popular one, and it explained the jaded perspective of so many of his friends. Still, he'd vowed not to go there. That was not who he wanted to become. The decision had cost him, though. It still did, for that matter, so now here he was with a woman whom he harbored quite a bit of feelings for but barring a few unguarded moments, he had no idea whether she really wanted to go there or just be friends. It was maddening.

Well, there was no better way to get his mind off events than a little exercise and he hadn't done his martial arts forms in days. He'd take a bike ride to the park and go through his forms. He warmed to the idea, then on impulse decided to go ahead and take a shower first. He'd have to take another one later, but this one would help loosen him up for his workout.

Twenty minutes later, he was on his bike wearing a black T-shirt, his black doh bohk uniform pants, his wooden practice sword strapped over his shoulder, and a baseball cap. He looked a bit like a refugee from a Chuck Norris movie, but he didn't care. Being outside was wonderful, and he was almost intoxicated with the prospect of both the workout he was anticipating and the Hill Country air. After all those years as a competing athlete, Jeremy never felt quite relaxed if his day didn't include some kind of exercise. The gym was always an option, but the commercial gyms seemed to be more about socializing these days than working out, which was all well and good on occasion, but it didn't fulfill his desire for some real cardio.

His home in Lakeway was a bit west of the Lake Travis dam, off of FM 620, and really just on the cusp of what the locals called "The Hill Country." The smell of the juniper wafted on the cool dry air as he glided east in the direction of the park by the dam.

The terrain frequently made Jeremy thankful for the 21 gears on his mountain bike. He'd need every one of them before he returned. The hills he would effortlessly speed down in one direction would be his nemesis on the return trip.

As he sped along on a relatively level patch with the wind in his face, Jeremy's mind gnawed again at the revelations from his near death images.

Really, why would your life flash before your eyes anyway? That question kept haunting him. Was there some purpose in it? Was there supposed to be some wisdom gleaned from all those images? Were they supposed to prepare you for something, or simply bid farewell to what had been? Was there significance in the particular images that appeared, versus the ones that didn't? Flashes from New Orleans, but next to nothing from Houston, his first girlfriend, but not his first wife, and interestingly enough, nothing from Valerie.

And then there was that strange image at the very last, the little bit with, what he was now certain, was a bullet and the rabbit-shaped rock. It was rabbit-shaped wasn't it? He hadn't thought about that at the time but seeing his memory of it now, he was certain that it was. Strange.

What the hell was that episode about anyway? He'd never shot a rock. As a matter of fact he could count on one hand the number of times in his life he'd ever even shot a gun. He hadn't seen any image of a weapon at all. As he began to pedal, finally at the bottom of the hill, he struggled to recall the image. It was all so vague. Besides not seeing any sort of gun, he hadn't seen any image of himself or a setting either, just the bullet speeding toward its target, a target he didn't recognize.

Traffic on 620 was thankfully light this morning. With the boom in Austin, the scenic highway had become more and more crowded. He hated it. The little park he was making for was adjacent to the west side of the Lake Travis Dam. The park was a blade of land with a boat launch ramp and picnic tables that provided a beautiful view of Lake Travis and the cliffs that rose up around it. Jeremy absolutely loved having that view while he worked out.

Reaching behind his back he felt for his Ipod. The headphones were already in his ears under his cap. With a practiced movement, he pushed the button and the familiar strains of Hall and Oates blocked out the wind noise. Eighties music. He loved it. It was going to be a great day.

* * *

Images of Jeremy were still dancing in her mind, even before her eyes opened. Had she been dreaming of him too? It was almost as though he had been with her all night long, being the last thing she remembered as she fell asleep and seemingly still there when she awoke.

She threw back the covers in a combination of frustration and determination. Who the hell was she kidding? Was it really worth losing someone she might have a great love with just because she was scared?

Hell, she'd almost lost him anyway. Maybe that was one reason she was shying away from this guy. Daredevils like him had a predictably short life span, didn't they? Her mind drew up the image of the burn around his neck. It was a damn miracle he was alive. Still, a part of her recognized her own idea as an excuse. Just another excuse to maintain a safe distance . . . far enough away that she couldn't get hurt. Again.

She moved into the kitchen to start her coffee and opened the sliding glass doors to her little deck. It was slightly cool outside and the dry air made it seem even cooler. As it percolated, she went back to her bedroom to retrieve her slippers, then briefly stood on the deck. It was the perfect place to drink her hot morning beverage. The brisk air and spectacular view made her wonder again why she hadn't yet bought a place. But she knew the answer was really two fold, one, she had been in a hurry when she'd first moved here and didn't want to take the time to look for a house, and two, she hadn't been sure at the time how long she'd stay. That question had been answered since then though, and it was probably time to actually start looking for a place.

She went back in, fetched her drink and came back out. It'd have to have a view like this though, she thought, which wasn't a difficult task in the Austin area. Sitting in her chair with her warm mug cupped in her hands, she let her eyes range out over the distant terrain and thought. Maybe she'd call him today. What could it hurt?

4.

April, 2016

The endless void of space stretched out before it. Millennia had passed as it roared through the plane of the Milky Way galaxy. The awesome ellipse of its original path was continually altered by intermittent proximity to myriad stars.

It gave off minute bits of itself as it rocketed silently through the vacuum of space, but still, after all these millennia it was counted large as such things were measured, and the fact that it had never collided with anything else after such a tremendous interval of travel was a mute testimony to the vastness and comparative emptiness of the universe.

Much as humans, on a molecular level, are comprised mostly of space not of matter, so the universe, for all its galaxies and solar systems, is comprised primarily of interconnecting emptiness.

Dark, colossal, mindless, and mighty in its mass and velocity, it came on and on through space. The great alignment had set it on a new path. Now, one last nudge from the Red Giant in the previous solar system had fixed its new course, on a fateful rendezvous. Though it was oblivious to its own destination and nothing in the universe with awareness had yet detected it . . . Its path was set.

* * *

Chuck awoke and the pain returned. No particular injury, just the general pain of waking up in the morning at age 67. Something always seemed to hurt. It was three in the afternoon. He'd been asleep since 8:00 a.m. Seven hours. That was more than he usually got, and frankly more than his old body needed. He lay there in his lonely bed a moment longer and stretched, listening to the creaking and cracking of his old joints.

Presently they began to feel a bit better, however, and he eased out from under the covers and trundled toward the kitchen. Thoughts of a hot cup of coffee thrust themselves to the forefront of his mind.

As he made it, he thought back on the previous evening. It had been typical, and, after a while, boring letting the camera take its endless shots of Saturn and its rings for the NASA project. But as the dawn had crept on him, he'd begun to move the telescope back to its *home* position in preparation to close the dome. Because he'd been a bit bored he'd stayed in his position at the optics while the big telescope moved.

That was the only reason he'd caught that glimpse of *something*. At least he'd thought it was something. Still, it had only been a glimpse as the telescope swung its prodigious girth around, and he wasn't at all sure what it was. His first thought was that it was a meteor, one he hadn't heard or read about, but the more he thought about it, the more curious he got. Something about its tail was bothering him. He couldn't put his finger on it but something struck him as unusual. Also, it didn't appear to move across his field of vision quickly enough to be a typical meteor, and if it had been far enough away to appear to move that slow, then it was orders of magnitude too bright for the average meteor. Almost unconsciously, Chuck had instructed the digital camera attached to the telescope to record the image he was seeing, but with an even higher magnification than the one he was viewing. This feature was a relatively new addition to the Palomar telescopes; they all had additional viewing ports attached to high-resolution cameras.

It was a puzzle, and Chuck's mind thrived on puzzles. So much so that he was blissfully unaware of the effort of his hands preparing the coffee he'd gotten up to fetch. Maybe it was something he could check into this evening. If it was still there. If he could find it again. If he wasn't too damn preoccupied with the stupid NASA project to get to it.

It was one of the few downsides to the job he loved so well. More than just occasionally the contract work the observatory accepted to keep it well funded was mundane and boring and, to make it worse, it occupied enough of Chuck's time to keep him from focusing on research projects that really meant something to him.

His brewing was underway now so he had a few minutes. He took the opportunity to turn on the TV and check the weather. The weather was wonderful on Mt Palomar in excess of 300 days out of the year, but on those days that it wasn't, Chuck found himself having a paid day off. To most people this would be a welcome respite, but to him it was a condition he actually found annoying, another of the peculiarities of the lifestyle he'd chosen.

He harrumphed as he watched the weather. It was going to be foul this evening. That was just great. He wondered whether his little anomaly would still be there when the weather afforded him another opportunity to search for it. Tonight would be a night to curl up with his latest book, a fiction thriller, one of his few vices.

5

September 6ᵗʰ, 2016

Jeremy sat back on his knees with his eyes closed. He was through with all of his forms except this one last sword form, since he couldn't carry his staff on his bike. It was a lacquered and carved oak practice sword he carried, similar in weight to the live one that sat in its cradle on the mantle. It was too valuable and too dangerous to be carried on his bike for a workout. He breathed slowly and deeply with his eyes closed, dividing his concentration between the form he was about to do and the breeze blowing through his hair. He loved these workouts, for more than just the physical exercise, but for the moment alone in the outdoors, especially when he could execute his forms on a promontory such as this with a view that was at once breathtaking and peaceful.

Slowly he opened his eyes and moved the sword from its position in front of him to its starting position parallel to his left thigh. He was crouched down on his left leg with his right arm across his body on the hilt of the resting sword. His next motion would simulate drawing the blade from its sheath and making an upward cut to the outside right. His pose at that moment was a classic one seen in many many photos of martial arts swordsmen. Rocking back on his left foot, more onto his toes, and extending his right leg in a slightly bent ready position out in front of him, he took one last breath and all other thoughts left his mind. For the next few moments it was only the form, his body and his sword. In one smooth motion the sword came up off the ground and across in the sweeping upward cut...

Several moments later he finished, brought the sword to its resting position beside him, mimicking a sheathing motion and sat back on his knees. He was in the exact position on the ground where he had begun. Several deep measured breaths later, Valerie rode into his mind. Damn! What was he going to have to do to keep that woman out of his thoughts?

Well, there were only two answers, and he knew what they were. He was either going to have to call her, or he was going to have to find someone else to occupy his time. At this moment he really had no desire to chase anyone else, so that really left him with just one option.

Picking up his sword and using the little string he used to strap it over his back, he got back on his bike and headed home. It was an easy ride . . . except for that last hill, and for those few grueling minutes at least, Valerie was again out of his mind. It was a truism athletes discovered, that you cannot hold other thoughts or worries in your mind while seriously taxing your body. The exertion exorcises any thought beyond bodily sensations, which was why it was such a wonderful stress reliever. When he returned he'd call Valerie, if he could even catch her. That in itself was usually a trick.

~

Valerie was tentatively reaching for the phone to call Jeremy. She had waited most of the day and even now her doubts were nagging at her. Her hand wasn't quite to the receiver when it rang, causing her to jump.

"Hello?"

"Hello there." It was Jeremy.

"I was just thinking of you." Valerie started to add that she'd been on the verge of calling him too but initially decided against it.

"Were you? Well I just got back from working out, and thought I'd call to see if you wanted to get a glass of wine this afternoon and then some dinner."

"That would be great. I was actually thinking about calling you to see how you were feeling." She decided it was ok to mention that she was about to call him as long as it referred to his neck. That wouldn't seem like excessive interest, just friendly concern.

Jeremy hadn't really thought much more about his neck while he was working out but, now that she mentioned it, he did recall the slight sting of the wind as he'd raced down that one long hill.

"It's doing fine. It's just strange looking in the mirror and realizing that I'm going to have a scar all the way around my neck for the rest of my life."

"Yeah, Jeremy. I can't even imagine how lucky you were."

"Kinda makes one figure we're here for a reason, doesn't it?"

"Sure would make me feel that way," she almost murmured.

"Well, great then. I'll pick you up around 3:00 and we can go grab a glass of wine up on the Lake, then figure some place for dinner. Maybe we can hit the Emerald Inn, if you're really feeling hungry."

"Sounds good to me."

"Alright then. I'll catch you later."

When Jeremy hung up the phone he was feeling like something had been left unsaid. Not by him though, by Val. He imagined that her thought to call him was more than just about his neck. The neck was just a good excuse to call without seeming too interested. It seemed like every nuance of tone or obvious comment left unsaid only underlined that she was trying to hide her feelings. Damn that woman!

He decided right then and there that he really was going to broach the topic of *them* tonight. To hell with it, at least he'd know something.

~

Val's thoughts were also in a whirl after she hung up the phone. She was no less sensitive than Jeremy, and she felt pretty sure he'd sensed her feelings for him. She was just afraid that he'd read too much into them, because she wasn't going to be more than friends with him. Was she? She couldn't even make that statement in her mind without second guessing herself. What *was* it with that guy?

What Val couldn't see about herself was the depth and breadth of her own barriers. She led herself to believe that she just hadn't found another guy that she really cared for, but the truth was, she couldn't open her walls long enough to even see one right in front of her.

* * *

When Val opened the door Jeremy almost had to catch his breath. She was in a quintessential "little black dress". This particular one left one shoulder bare and with her hair swept to the opposite side, the geometry of it gave the sensation of her being much more exposed than she actually was. Still, it wasn't even the flattering attire that nearly left Jeremy breathless. It was the look in her eyes. That sparkle of joy at seeing him was unmistakable, and truly the only clue Jeremy typically got of her feelings for him.

It was said that in ancient Egyptian times the peddlers in the market could determine a customer's interest in their wares by the eyes. When the eye beholds something it desires, the pupils dilate. On some level everyone knows this, but in the case of the peddlers, if the pupils dilated, the prices went up. And whether Jeremy knew it consciously or not, her pupils dilated as she beheld him. All he knew for sure was that that look told him Valerie was very glad to see him.

Then he saw her eyes slip down to his neck as she leaned out to give him a big hug, being extra careful not to let her face touch the cauterized skin.

"Hi there," she said in a low melodious tone before promptly leaning back.

"Hi there, yourself. Are you ready?"

"Not quite. Come on in for a second while I go pick out some shoes."

Jeremy was familiar with this drill and following her in, watched her tiptoe barefoot up the stairs before he took a seat on the couch.

Her two-story apartment was eclectically decorated with bits of memorabilia from places she'd been, but the whole thing gravitated toward the darker, warmer tones that a decorator would say were associated more with a man's tastes than a woman's. It felt warm and homey and was altogether neat and tidy.

He only had to wait a moment before she came back down wearing what he could only describe as casual pumps. She looked incredible, and Jeremy felt his heart accelerate a bit just looking at her again.

"So where are we going to go?"

"Well, since it's about midafternoon, I thought we might try the Iguana Grill. We can have a nice glass of wine there, watch the sunset, and then decide if we want to stay there or go to the Emerald Inn for dinner."

Valerie smiled, quickening Jeremy's pulse a bit more.

"That sounds wonderful."

Moments later they were headed back in the direction of Jeremy's home, up FM2222 to loop 620 and Lake Travis.

Lake Travis is part of the Highland Lake chain that winds through the Texas Hill country. The Lake is essentially formed by dams on the Colorado River, but it is augmented substantially by the confluence of the Pedernales River, both of which are purified by their mutual limestone bottoms. Owing to that limestone, Lake Travis is a beautiful clear-water lake with cliffs soaring intermittently on both sides; it's on top of one of those soaring cliffs, right off Loop 620, that the Iguana grill sits, presumably, but not necessarily, named for some of its former inhabitants.

There are several restaurants dotting the cliffs of Lake Travis, including the most famous, the multi-tiered Oasis, but it wasn't multi-tiers and crowds that Jeremy was seeking that evening, but the more laid back, gentler ambience of the Iguana. The Iguana grill has a nice, casual interior dining area, but its main draw is the outside dining with umbrella covered tables sitting out behind the restaurant and protected from the cliffs by a wrought iron fence that overlooks Lake Travis about 350 feet below. The view in three directions is spectacular and a perfect vantage point for watching the sun set over the Lake and the Texas Hill Country.

A cool front had passed through the area and though more warm weather was bound to be on the way before autumn could take hold, this afternoon was a perfect 72 with a light breeze and cloudless skies. They got there early enough to get a table in one of the premier spots right next to the railing and even sitting down, the drop off on the other side of the railing a few feet away was enough to give the sensation of vertigo. The entire setting was positively breathtaking.

"May I get you something from the bar?" The waitress asked, as she pulled out a chair for Valerie.

"Why don't you bring us a wine list," Jeremy volunteered seating himself beside Valerie, giving them both an unobstructed view of the panorama.

As she turned to walk away, Jeremy briefly caught the odd look the waitress was giving him, an unwelcome reminder of the ugly scar that was to be a permanent feature on his neck. He turned his gaze back to Valerie just in time to see her eyes too, quickly flicker away from his neck. Instead of dodging the obvious, she commented.

"Does it still hurt?"

With fingers gently floating up to his neck, Jeremy responded. "It stung a little when I slept, but otherwise, no."

"Why do you do these things, Jeremy? You're going to get yourself killed."

"I love the experiences, Val, and let me tell you, I'm not going to get myself killed. If there was one thing I learned from yesterday's little adventure, it's that God wants me around for something, and I'm not going anywhere until I do it. Come on, aren't you the least bit jealous at the things I've done?"

"Are you kidding? I can barely stand the idea of being around when *you* do them, much less do them myself."

Jeremy shook his head. From his perspective, other people who didn't crave adventure or adrenaline the way he did were at least as odd as they perceived him to be. To him, life was a chain of exciting moments strung together by the calm moments that consisted of planning and paying for more of the exciting ones. He couldn't understand people who saw it differently. He decided to change the subject.

"So what's new on the digital rights lobbying front? Any big legislation in the offing?"

Valerie smiled at the subject change. "I'll give you one thing, Jeremy Andrews, you're never boring, and in answer to your question, the major battle is still over whether or not it is fair and right for the government to mandate that copying restrictions be built into media devices. It's a prickly topic from any direction you look at it.

The biggest problem at the moment, though, is that most of the rhetoric these days is going toward the presidential election. No one really wants to talk about anything else unless it's that. I think everyone is scrambling to be a clear front runner since O'Rourke is finally done.

People are really confused, but this new guy, this Carl Iverson, is like a bolt from heaven. He's a Colorado rancher and a real live hero.

I haven't heard so much positive talk about a politician since Ronald Regan. I don't think I'm going to get much else done 'till after the election."

Jeremy stared briefly at that beautiful face and tried to imagine saying 'no' to her on a regular basis. It was little wonder she was such a success in the lobbying arena. Between her intellect, her beauty and her disarming smile, she was a difficult package to resist regardless of her objective. It crossed his mind then to wonder if most of the lobbyists in Washington weren't women. *Ha. And women swear that men have all the power. What a crock!*

"I'm sure you will, Val. I'm sure you will. So when is the next vote on anything?"

"Probably not until late October, or maybe not even until after the presidential election."

"About sixty days, huh? So are you just not that busy for a while or what?"

"It's hard to tell. Later this week things are going to start to pick up, and I'm probably going to end up in Washington for most of the latter part of next month."

"Washington's nice in the fall."

"The people aren't any nicer."

"So why do you do the work?"

With a quizzical tilt to her head she answered, "I've asked that question myself many times, and I think it's about hoping to accomplish some good. Trying to be a part of something bigger and attempting to make a difference in the world beyond myself. Of course, the money isn't bad either."

By the sly grin on her face Jeremy gleaned that her last comment was meant only for humor and to keep things light. She was in this, at least partially, for altruistic reasons, and it warmed him to see this facet of her heart.

Moments passed before the waitress finally returned with the wine list, and Jeremy noticed the delay in the service, but since he planned to be here for a while he let it slide. The waitress stood patiently as he perused the menu.

"White wine sound all right to you?" When he looked up he saw Valerie staring at the waitress with a rather spooky hard gaze, and as he followed it he noticed the waitress was again staring at him. This was already getting old.

"I'm sorry, sir, but I just have to ask; how did you get that wicked injury around your neck?"

Jeremy was more than a little surprised that she had the nerve to even ask the question, much less add in the word 'wicked', but he wasn't offended by it and tried to think of how to describe the incident in as few words as possible. In the meantime, he broke out in a brief laugh. "Well, I got yanked out of a boat by another boat with a parachute line wrapped around my neck and drug underwater for a hundred yards or so."

The waitress' response was quite gratifying. Her hand flew to her face accompanied by a sharp intake of breath. "Oh my God that's horrible. It's a miracle you're still alive."

"My thoughts exactly. I think we'll take a bottle of the white Bordeaux."

Unsure of how to take the abrupt change in topic, her answer was brief and flustered. "Uh, yes sir. I'll be right back."

Jeremy turned his attention out to the lake and Valerie mutely followed his gaze. The boats crisscrossing the blue water were a myriad of shapes and sizes. On any given day, the 60 plus mile long Lake Travis could have watercraft ranging from wave runners to 80 foot sail or motor yachts, to open sea racers. The radiating white "Vs" trailing behind them on the blue water collided, forming complex geometric shapes.

Lake Travis is one of the clearest in the country. Its crystal blue water, soaring white cliffs, and dark green cedars and junipers were always a captivating sight.

They sat there quietly, each lost in their own thoughts taking in the view, until the waitress returned, breaking the spell that was holding them.

"Your wine sir," she said as she held up the bottle for him to see.

Jeremy nodded and she proceeded to uncork the bottle and offer him the obligatory first taste.

"Fine, thank you," he said after a small thoughtful sip. He promptly redirected his attention back to Valerie as the waitress continued to fill their glasses.

"So how about you?" Val asked. "What have you got coming up on your calendar?"

Jeremy's thoughts had again drifted back to the succession of events that comprised his life flashing before his eyes. Somehow he couldn't seem to get those images out of his mind for long. He tried to imagine why they seemed to have a stronger presence in his thoughts than the near ripping off of his head. He was so engrossed that it took a moment for her words to register, and another moment to drag his mind back to actually think of the answer to her question. "I do have one big concert scheduled for this Thursday and two other tentative ones later this month, but actually it's a little slow at the moment."

Valerie seemed to lose interest in the question she had just asked and both of them returned their gazes to the panorama of the lake. A gentle breeze blew across their table, rustling the tablecloth and muting the sounds from the lake below.

Their shared silence felt warm and companionable. Val loved the outdoors as much as he did. The sensation melded into his other past experiences with her, causing a sudden surge of feelings to well up inside of him. Maybe this girl *could* be the one.

Jeremy turned his head and focused his gaze upon her, letting the emotions continue to rise. Maybe he should just tell her how he really felt. He'd allowed her forced barriers to deter him long enough. As he prepared to speak, Valerie turned her head and caught his eyes. He saw a split second of tenderness before it got smothered by something else. *Concern?*

"Valerie," he began, "don't you know that . . ."

"Stop, Jeremy. Don't say it."

"But I—"

"No, Don't."

The ferocity of her statement stopped him cold, and he felt shaken to the core. He was on the verge of baring his feelings for her and she, seeming to sense it, had harshly forestalled him. It was the emotional equivalent of a slap in the face. He drew a breath to say more, but couldn't summon a response.

But even Valerie couldn't let that void stand as it was— an emptiness that seemed to swallow all speech. Long seconds passed, however, before she finally added a tidbit to assuage his feelings, "It's not time . . . yet."

The "yet" was a three letter lifeline that left him with a modicum of hope. He almost resented it, but it did mitigate his growing embarrassment. It was a dichotomy he couldn't reconcile, and left him with the sensation that his emotions were being controlled by hers. Still, there seemed no reasonable way out. He couldn't voice his feelings now, after such a forceful demand not to hear them. If he did, he could only do so by assuming that she didn't really know what it was he was about to confess, and as much as he'd like to take that tact, he couldn't. He knew she knew what was coming. There was no doubt in his heart.

Clenching his teeth with a barely discernable nod, he forced his gaze back to the lake. His desire to be there vanished, smothered by embarrassment. The only thing that saved him was the waitress returning to refill their glasses. They both drank again in silence, using their gorgeous surroundings as an unspoken excuse not to talk. But their silence was no longer serene. It was strained.

The second glass of wine disappeared, and then the third. Jeremy watched Val's hair dance in the occasional breeze while she apparently engrossed herself in the aroma of her wine. He could feel the temperature drop as the sun sank low over the Hill Country landscape, and the golden glow that had warmed them for the last hour now turned a deepening red. The shadows stretched perceptibly across the other diners and for a brief moment Jeremy let the voices of the other diners into his awareness. Their words were just barely below his threshold to comprehend, so he let his eyes shift back to the darkness of the lake. The sun down there had already set, as it would for him and Val in the next few minutes.

The quiet between them seemed to almost turn into a contest, each non-verbally daring the other to break it. It was Valerie who finally ventured into the gap.

"Why don't we get something to eat here? Not only am I hungry, this wine is taking quite a toll on my empty stomach."

Jeremy considered briefly telling her that he was ready to leave. He felt like he was in the middle of an unsolvable conundrum; he was sure he didn't want to stay here, but as he looked up into Valerie's eyes and smiling face his ire faded. All the unspoken emotion lay there like a vast ocean behind her eyes pleading for his understanding and patience.

At the moment, with that look in her eyes, giving up on her wasn't an option. So, with a deep sigh, he said, "Sure. Let's eat." He began to swivel his head and look for the waitress who, by this time, was probably annoyed with them squatting at her table for so long. "At least, we can if I can find that waitress." It was 6:30 and the place was bustling, so it took him a few minutes to garner her attention.

By the time they finished their grilled salmon, the stars had come out and darkness had overtaken the lake. A gentle breeze gave a voice to the hills but not enough movement to chill them. The shore line was dotted with intermittent lights while the water itself was an inky black, broken only by the occasional passing of a boat. It was a different kind of beauty to behold from the daylight sights but no less captivating. The conversation, however, remained pointedly light, and both of them felt it. Jeremy thought about just taking her home but something occurred to him that would lessen the tension without having to actually end the evening.

"I have an idea," Jeremy ventured, "Why don't we go hear Joel play? His band, Avatar, is at The Hole in the Wall tonight and he'll get us a good seat if we show up."

Valerie's smile seemed to qualify for a yes even before she spoke. "That sounds like a great idea."

Jeremy found the waitress again who was most anxious to get their bill and free up her table.

The Hole in the Wall is a no-frills bar near the University of Texas campus just a bit north of downtown. No-frills is the colloquialism for "dive bar with great music" and is very popular with both the college crowd and the local bands. It was a 20 minute drive from the Iguana with no traffic and the conversation between Jeremy and Val in the interim was minimal, which was going to make their choice of destinations an even better idea. No one was going to be doing a lot of talking with the band playing in that small venue.

Jeremy opened the door for Val as he glanced at the sign in the window; "Avatar playing tonight" it read, and he felt the vibrations of the music through the doorframe as he pulled it back. Joel was wailing on stage with his new lead singer, Joan. It only took him a fraction of a second to recognize the song. "I Love Rock and Roll", by Joan Jett.

Jeremy had to snicker at the choice of music given the new singer's name. It occurred to Jeremy that there weren't any tough-girl-hard-rock females these days, and it was something he actually missed.

"Yep, this is The Hole in the Wall alright," Val ventured over the prevailing din. "Not fancy but the music's always good."

Jeremy's eyes took in the bare beam ceiling, vinyl covered metal stools, and picnic table or wood booth seating. It certainly had a down-home feel.

"Even better when Joel's band is playing," he offered.

The band was just finishing the song as they sat down and Joel promptly waved, announced that the band was going to take a break, and came over to sit with them.

"Hi guys," he said as he seated himself, "Your neck's still looking disgusting, I see."

"Thanks a lot...Beelie," Jeremy retorted, dragging out the name like Hugh Grant in Two Weeks' Notice. Joel's full name was Billy Joel Williams, and he hated it. His parents had been die-hard Billy Joel fans and none of it but the name had rubbed off on Joel; he hated Billy Joel's music, not because of the music itself but because his parents had played it so much when he was a kid. It was a cruel joke that Joel ended up being a musician himself. At any rate it was a fun point of irritation for him that Jeremy knew well and used often.

"Oh, that's a low blow even for you, Jer."

"You don't think you deserved it?"

"Well, maybe. You know, with Halloween coming up you have the perfect start for a Frankenstein costume there. Just stick a couple of thimbles on the side of your neck and turn a sportcoat around backwards . . . "

"Ok, Joel. Enough already." Val's interjection was a surprise to both of them, and Joel actually did stop in mid-sentence.

Jeremy's laughter followed on its heels. "Wow. She actually shut you up. That has to be a new experience for you."

"As a matter of fact it does feel new. What's up with you guys? I'm glad you came by. It's a little slow right after the holiday weekend."

"We were just out for dinner and remembered you were playing here so we decided to take in a little culture," Jeremy said. "But…uh…Joan Jett? Was that Joan's idea? And when did she join the group?"

"Actually, no, someone requested it. But it's the kind of music Joan likes anyway so, what the heck. I heard her singing at some place on 6th street last month and decided she'd make a great addition."

"Well she really is good at any rate," Val added.

"Hey did you guys hear about the new asteroid some guy at the Palomar observatory discovered?" Joel began, "They named it Kohler-Leporidae after the guy who found it and the fact that it looks a bit like a crouching rabbit."

Joel was not only a musician but an amateur astronomer and a space and sci-fi geek to boot. If he wasn't rattling off some dumb quote from some commercial he was updating everyone on the latest celestial happenings. Actually, Jeremy found it entertaining.

"No. I hadn't. Anything special about it?" Jeremy glanced at Val as he spoke and she seemed intent on hearing the answer to the question. He was glad she wasn't being bored.

"Not really. Well that's not true. There was some flap about him looking for something else when he found it by accident. What are the odds, huh? Kinda like 'Double your pleasure, double your fun.'"

"Ugh … And astronomical, I'd say."

"Ha ha," Valerie responded, sarcasm thick in her voice. "You two are hilarious."

"So is it going to hit the earth or something?" Val asked.

"Nah. Just passing through, is what I've heard."

"Well maybe we'll get to see some cool photos."

"Hopefully," Joel answered. "Hey it's too bad ya'll already ate. You haven't lived until you've had their Mickey D burger. It's two all-beef patties, special . . ."

"Stop," Jeremy interrupted actually putting his hand over Joel's mouth, and chuckling. "Go play some music and spare us."

"Good idea," Joel answered after removing Jeremy's hand from his face and grinning, "Before the crowd decides to lynch us for taking too long a break."

Joel sauntered back up on stage and the band started up again.

"Joel's jokes may be lame but his music certainly isn't."

They stayed for about two drinks before Jeremy's mood darkened again.

"You about ready to go?" He asked.

"Whenever you are," Val answered giving him an appraising look.

~

On the way home Jeremy's spirits continued to descend. He pulled up into her driveway, trying to decide if he was even going to walk her to her door. A kiss goodnight certainly didn't seem to be on the menu. At last he decided that not walking her was just plain rude, and regardless of his feelings, he wasn't going to resort to rude.

She exited her side of the car at the same time he did, forestalling any thoughts of him opening a door for her, and they walked somewhat separately up the short sidewalk to her apartment. When they arrived at the dim yellow light on her stoop, Jeremy turned to face her.

"Thank you for the evening. It was a beautiful night." The phrase was a bit cold and he knew it. He imagined she did too, but he didn't care.

With those words he broke eye contact and turned to go. He didn't even get his shoulders turned away from her, however, before he sensed her movement from the corner of his eye. He turned back just in time for her lips to close on his and her arms to flow around him. Without considering any other ramifications, he responded enthusiastically and the kiss lingered on and on, their hands and bodies drawing as close as they possibly could.

When Valerie finally drew back, it was with a dreamy look in her eyes and a visible unsteadiness from the ardor of the kiss. Jeremy just stood there. He hadn't a clue what would happen next, but he was in such shock after that kiss that her next words didn't even surprise him.

"I had a wonderful evening with you too, Jeremy. Please forgive me for my standoffishness. You know how I struggle with showing my feelings, and I didn't want you to leave tonight without knowing that I care."

Jeremy stared, increasingly dumfounded, considering how to possibly respond. The moment seemed to hang for an eternity before a hint of fear began to creep onto Valerie's features.

"Thank you for that." He finally managed to stammer out. A tentative smile illuminated her face making it even harder for Jeremy to concentrate. "It's uh, nice to hear something every once in a while." She seemed unabashed by his somewhat tentative reply.

They kissed again and Jeremy wondered if she was going to ask him in or if he even wanted her to. *Restraint might be a better idea*, he thought, *at least this time*. But as he got in the car a moment later, he was suddenly angry.

"Shit," he said out loud. "What the hell is the *deal* with that girl? One minute she plays cool and virtually forbids me to tell her my feelings, then the next she about attacks me on her front porch and volunteers hers! Shit!"

* * *

Valerie watched him pull away before turning to go inside. Her feelings were a painful contradiction. On the one hand, she was deathly afraid of a man whom she was so attracted to as to barely be able to maintain control when she was around him; on the other hand, that very attraction and loss of control signaled what she had longed for her whole life, someone she could fall irretrievably in love with. She was delicately balanced on the tightrope of some of her most basic personality traits and her deepest desires. It was a precarious trap for her, and one she wasn't going to be able to easily resolve. Unfortunately, the result for Jeremy was a seesaw of her reactions to him.

What the hell am I thinking, she asked herself as she slowly closed her apartment door. For now, her fears were winning the battle against her heart.

6

April 2016

From the top of the hill where the observatory sat, Chuck watched the sunset in his typical solitude. A low smattering of clouds broke the variegated hues of purple, orange, and pink into a tapestry of color to shame the likes of any Van Gogh. Chuck smiled as he beheld it. *Color therapy*, he thought. It was a phrase he had heard years ago, but one that had stuck.

The awesome aerial palette never failed to make him feel inspired and somehow more a part of the fabric of God's work. Every evening when the weather allowed, which was most every evening that he even came to work, he stood here to watch the setting of our own little star, and appreciate the variety of color it presented.

He was a bit of an unusual scientist, but part of a growing number that had ultimately found a faith in God through the study of what He had created. Time and time again, as his eyes beheld the cosmos through the lens of his giant telescope, he was struck by the perfection and complexity of the tiny fraction of the universe that was available to behold. In the evenings as he shifted his view around the cosmos, he observed galaxy after galaxy of every conceivable shape and size, each one with millions perhaps billions, of stars, and each one of *those* with the potential to capture one or fifty planets in its gravitational field, and each planet with the possibility to host life similar to, or wildly divergent from, that which Earth sustained. Just the mathematical possibility of other life, when viewed in terms of the sheer magnitude of potentials, seemed a virtual certainty. He didn't spend much time pondering over aliens. He just recognized the overwhelming likelihood of the existence of other life and moved on.

At nights, alone in his observatory, Chuck dreamed of the day man would finally achieve faster-than-light, or, more likely, quantum travel, and the door to those other galaxies would suddenly be open. Tonight, however, he had tasks at hand and wouldn't have much time to randomly gaze at the desires of his heart.

Tonight he was to focus the great lens of the Palomar telescope on the belt of Orion and the nebula there, to glean some data for a scientific project being conducted in Switzerland. Chuck didn't even know the nature of the experiment, but that wasn't unusual.

Any research that might conceivably yield financial or academic acclaim was closely guarded and when they depended on an outside source, like him, to aid in acquiring data, he was given only the minimum information required to accomplish the task. This didn't bother Chuck; on the contrary, it normally sparked his intellect to try to intuit the goal the gathered data was intended to support. It made for another interesting distraction to aid in the passage of the lonely hours of the night.

The moon was in the crescent phase this evening. Not as good as no moon at all, but better than trying to peer past the light of a full moon. He reread the notes on the task he was to perform and looked at his watch. Orion wouldn't be high enough in the sky for the necessary research for at least a couple of hours, so he had a little more time to play than he had originally thought. Smiling to himself, he climbed up into the little chair that was attached to the telescope frame. The adjustable seat was positioned just below the protuberance that accepted the lenses, so that he could easily peer through and swap out whatever lens he needed, with as much comfort as possible. He engaged the motor that swiveled the huge barrel housing the incredible 200 inch mirror, the heart of the Palomar telescope. The celestial eye proceeded in its stately pace across the heavens toward the crescent that appeared high in the evening sky while Chuck listened contentedly to the gentle, familiar hum of the machinery. He didn't spend too much time looking at the moon these days. He had done so much of that in years gone by that dear old Luna had lost most of her mystery for him, but this evening, on a whim, Chuck decided to give the old girl a gaze.

What he really wanted to do was to look at that comet he had seen ten days ago with the strange dot in her tail. Not that he had seen the dot himself, but the photo he'd taken and carried around in his pocket, had illuminated the little anomaly. By now, there was no telling where it might be. He'd had no way to gauge its trajectory in the brief time he'd had to observe it.

When the gantry came to rest, Chuck leaned into the lens to make minor adjustments then leaned back abruptly to change lenses. He'd forgotten he was using one of the higher power ones and with that one in, about all he could discern of the moon's surface would be the regolith everywhere and, frankly, staring at a close-up of rocky debris and dust wasn't what he'd had in mind.

After switching the lenses, he again peered through the telescope. His eyes fell on one of the prominent "seas" of the moon, The Sea of Tranquility. He couldn't gaze at that landmark without remembering July 20th, 1969, the day John Glen and Buzz Aldrin first set foot on the moon. It was the beginning of nine years of moon missions and the only foray man had attempted into space in his lifetime.

When he considered all that man had learned and all the inventions that resulted from that exploration, it baffled him why the world seemed to have completely dropped the ball on manned space flight. From microwaves to freeze-dried food, the litany of discoveries that were merely ancillary to the space exploration effort was myriad. He supposed it was because there wasn't really anything else in our solar system that man wanted to see badly enough to actually *go* there. Unmanned probes sufficed just fine, and as for anything beyond that, the distances were just too great for current vehicles to be practical. Someone was going to have to come up with some sort of faster travel before we were likely to go visit any other solar systems, much less other galaxies.

A quick glance at his watch reminded Chuck it was about time to get to work. He was reticent to give up his play time, though, so rather than quickly swinging the great telescope around, he set it on a slow path over to Orion's Belt, which allowed him to watch the universe slowly move through his field of vision.

Galaxies and stars uncounted flowed across the lens; their profusion alone was awe inspiring. The telescope was almost to the bottom of Orion's belt when Chuck noticed a bright spec with a tail in an area where he wasn't accustomed to seeing anything. It was extraordinarily unlikely for it to be the one he'd spied days before. The telescope had glided past the object before Chuck could halt its motion so he made it retrace its steps. Yes, there it was again. Chuck stopped the movement of the telescope; or rather he stopped its directed motion.

The machinery of the huge telescope was constantly in motion actively counteracting the movement of the earth. Without such action, objects moved immediately out of the telescope's field of view. Even close objects like the moon wouldn't stay long in the viewfinder deprived of that constant correction.

Once the object entered his field of view, he was surprised at how quickly it moved off. Even with the earth's motion counteracted the object moved away. That meant it had a substantial motion of its own, much more so than he had noticed before, assuming it was even the same body. A comet maybe? That was what he'd speculated before, but Chuck was unaware of any passing celestial bodies that were expected to be visible. He removed his eye from the lens and glanced up at the sky. The object wasn't visible to the naked eye, just through the telescope. When he looked back through the lens, it had almost moved completely out of the field of view again.

Intrigued, Chuck glanced down at the celestial coordinates that were visible in a window on the side of his chair then spent a moment recording its relative movement so he could easily find it again. Unlike the other evening, he didn't intend to let this little mystery slip away from him again, especially since it was virtually a miracle that he had stumbled on it a second time. Why hadn't he heard anything about this comet? Had he stumbled onto something new? He smiled. Another puzzle.

Reluctantly, Chuck moved the telescope up to the knife sheath hanging from the belt of Orion where the Nebula was located. His thoughts, however, remained in another part of the universe.

7

September 6th, 2016

Jeremy's neck burned. It felt as though a hemp, rather than nylon, rope was still wrapped around his neck, sawing back and forth, deeper and deeper. He reached up to touch it, and the instant his fingertips touched the raw skin, he jolted awake, sitting upright.

"Damn, that hurts!" He managed to avoid touching the scar around his neck during the daytime because it never accomplished anything besides pain, but when he was asleep his hands sometimes betrayed him. He realized he'd been dreaming about getting snapped out of the boat. He tried to imagine the parachute line snapping into a loop then around his neck, but it just seemed too far-fetched. He absolutely couldn't remember any sensation of it being around his neck, which struck him as strange in itself, as was his amazing lack of recollection of removing the thing when he surfaced.

As he got up to go to the bathroom, he stopped in front of the mirror to look at the scar. The waitress had called it wicked. He agreed. Most of the melted crusty flesh had sloughed off already. Looking at it, he thought that if it wasn't for that scar, he would have no proof that the incident ever happened. How could any details of such an extraordinary event leave such a minimal impression on his mind? All he could recall was how focused he'd been on not panicking or drowning. His focus had apparently been strong enough to block his awareness of a rope around his neck or a ski boat bearing down on him, things on which he could have no effect. It had apparently worked, too. He had remained calm and not drowned. Amazing what the mind could do.

An image had been in his mind just before he awoke. His fingers touching his scar had obliterated it. He had the vague sense of some kind of a dark rabbit, but he couldn't remember. Whatever it was, the image was gone. What was still there was the memory of Valerie's kiss and the effect it had had on him. *Damn*, he thought. There was just no getting her off his mind.

* * *

Valerie's eyes opened, and she was surprised to realize she was smiling. She couldn't understand why, until memories of Jeremy flooded into her mind. Some of them were from dinner last night, but she realized with a bit of a shock most of them were from her dreams. In her dreams the kiss at the door had been the beginning of the evening not the end. She blushed at the recollection then considered how absurd it was to be blushing at her own thoughts, in her own bedroom, by herself.

8

Closing the door on his Jaguar, David Coulson set off to work. From his five thousand square foot, two-story home at the end of Tortuga Trail, overlooking Lake Austin, to the sprawling medical building where he worked, took twenty minutes. Usually. Some days he liked to push it and see how fast he could negotiate the curves and steep hills of his surrounding neighborhood. In this endeavor it was important to disregard all the other less capable and annoying drivers that attempted to thwart his efforts. Anything short of running them off the road was fair game as far as he was concerned.

He didn't normally drive the Jag, only on occasions when he needed a little more excitement or to dissipate some frustration and test his skills. He couldn't drive it very often because he was too well-known, and his driving stunts could glean him negative publicity if people found out the identity of the maniac behind the wheel. Sure, he'd gotten a few calls from the Austin police about complaints against him, but nothing anyone felt inclined to prove or he couldn't shrug off with the weight of his social prominence.

Although his title sufficed to stifle minor traffic complaints, it hadn't stopped that idiot doctor in Kansas City from issuing a false diagnosis. "Previously undiagnosed bi-polar with sharp and disconcerting mood swings." That is what the moron had said, but it was crap even though the words continued to resonate with him. He was an accomplished surgeon and a recent owner of an existing cosmetic surgery clinic. Well, now he was in the Austin area; and Kansas City was behind him. He had heard once that men only moved for two reasons, work or women. He guessed he could vouch for that idea.

He seriously disliked being spurned and between his apparently affable exterior, his dapper looks, and his serious money, it certainly wasn't an experience he was familiar with, yet this one woman had turned him down. He had offered her everything, but when he asked her to marry him, she had asked him why.

The question had so caught him by surprise that he answered with an honesty he didn't intend. He said it would make it harder for her to leave him, but that she would be a millionaire so what did she care. Then she'd said no.

The acid of that single syllable still ate at his insides. She had told him no! How could she do that? He'd tried to change his tact and re-don his charm, but it was too late. He had been so furious he'd left her there in Jamaica by herself. Even the thought of that lovely setting now seemed to set off sparks. Then she'd moved away. No amount of money or alternate company had seemed to placate him since, so after spending a small fortune to glean her whereabouts he actually sold his practice and followed her.

If you'd asked him if he wanted revenge, he'd deny it vehemently, stating that such an emotion was beneath him. As a matter of fact, it had only taken him a couple of weeks to convince himself that he'd just moved to find a better city with more scenery and lucrative opportunities. He was now so convinced of his own lie that, to him, it was the truth.

David was easy on the gas pedal until he was out of his immediate neighborhood, but from there he conveyed his pent up rage through the steering wheel and accelerator of the 400 horse power engine. The Jag responded like the cat it was named after and hurtled through the winding streets and hills of the beautiful Austin suburbs with the sounds of tires screeching and tortured road surface lingering in its wake. Every chance he took and every death-defying curve he negotiated felt like he was doing battle with the source of his rejection. Somehow the fierce excitement and dangerous challenge always seemed to help purge thoughts of her from his system, at least for some interval of time.

When he arrived at the hospital fourteen minutes later, he was unscathed. The Jaguar seemed to pant briefly when he first pulled into the covered parking space, then slipped back into its normal purr. He'd only had one close call when some stupid woman tried to turn left on the yellow, and he'd had to swing into the oncoming lanes to avoid her. Fortunately, at that instant there hadn't been any cars coming, so the stunt had worked. He was exhilarated at the thought of it. The Jag had performed the slalom-like maneuver with ease. He glanced at his watch. Fourteen minutes. Better than usual. He was determined that someday he could make it in 11, but that would require extraordinary luck with the lights, or to run a few.

David took a deep breath, and slipped smoothly into his doctor persona. Effortlessly, he slowed his breathing, to help redirect his thoughts from the drive and that woman, to his work. The little squeak from the locks on his car followed him as he walked casually away, listening to the echo of his footsteps in the big underground garage. By the time he reached the elevator, the only residual from his Indy 500 commute was the feral grin that lingered on his face.

It was a grin that would have frightened most children.

9

April, 2016

Chuck awoke at two in the afternoon, early for him. He'd crawled into bed at 6:00a.m. but he'd had to read for quite a while to get to sleep. He was still thinking about the comet he'd seen, the one that wasn't supposed to be there.

He eased himself stiffly out of bed, feeling groggy. Even after working night shifts for years, his body was intractably, irrevocably, diurnal. It didn't seem to matter how long he slept during the day or how long he worked at night, his body would simply never quite adjust. He always felt a bit groggy upon waking, usually until after sunset or at least three cups of coffee. He wondered how the bats did it. But he loved his work and his work was the dark heavens with its billions of pinpricks of light.

The miracles of outer space never ceased to amaze him. One such revelation was that each light from a star was like travelling through time; by the time the light from a single star reached earth, so much time had passed that the star from which it originated may no longer exist.

The concept of travelling through time fascinated Chuck, and even though it wasn't truly his field, he had spent no small amount of time studying the branch of quantum physics that spoke of how every point in the universe was connected to every other. That one bit of knowledge intrigued him the most, for if that was true, all those stars he loved so much were really only a heartbeat away. Travel time no longer mattered. Distance no longer mattered. Someone just needed to decipher the code to do it. He wished for the thousandth time that it could happen in his lifetime.

His knees creaked as he slowly moved across his house to the kitchen. The automatic timer had done its job, and he could smell the coffee brewing. Two cups of his vanilla nut blend and his mind should begin to function a bit more normally.

Living in the hills outside of Escondido, California, Chuck was never more than a few steps away from a breathtaking view. The back of his house was mostly windows looking out over the drop-off that was his backyard and on toward the lights of the city. On the few evenings he was at home he loved to sit in the glass encased den and imagine those lights to be like the stars he so dearly loved, except each light represented not a star and possible planets but the microcosm of a family and its members. The family he never had. Now the stars and galaxies were his only family.

He had been married twenty years ago, but Louise couldn't have kids. When breast cancer took her only a few years into their marriage, Chuck had decided to give up on the family dream and pursue only what could never leave him. His only remaining family was his sister, Donna, and a grown niece who lived near DC, neither of whom he'd seen in years. Some days that lack of familial connections made the normally inspiring mountains seem to close in around him. On those rare days he would travel the thirty miles down to Oceanside and spend hours watching and listening to the endless motion of the waves. The ocean always impressed Chuck as the perfect distraction because it impinged on so many senses at once; the rhythmic pulse of the waves, the tangy salt smell, the feel of the sand between your toes and the sparkling of the sun off the airborne drops. It was a perfect place of peace to think, and some of his best ideas came from those seaside sessions.

Now, twelve years later, he was content, if not completely fulfilled, by the life he had chosen. The only social interactions he ever had were with the visitors to the observatory on the days he got in early, or with the students and post-docs from Cal Tech who ran the other four tele-scopes at the facility. They were pleasant enough, but more than once he'd caught a whispered comment from one to the other about how he was "such a strange old man". The usual response when he listened long enough to hear it was, "that's what happens when your IQ approaches 200". From the genius' point of view, it was very little consolation to be a genius when it left most people thinking you were nuts. Maybe that was the reason most geniuses held such disdain for people in general. He wondered why he didn't.

Driving up to the facility, he smiled as the awesome spectacle of the observatory revealed itself against the vast, dark firmament. The great white dome loomed like a giant egg being pushed up out of the ground into the starry night sky. Low evergreen trees stood around it, their night-faded green display lending a contrast to the starkly smooth surface of the dome. The large arch of the viewing panel was retracted when he arrived, letting light spill out, reminiscent of the pupil of a giant cat's eye. At any given time of the year Chuck could quickly locate whatever constellations might be hanging above and beside the dome as he rounded the last curve into the facility. Tonight, Orion and Cassiopeia were the first to greet his eyes, but they were such familiar old friends that he barely noticed them.

He pulled into the parking lot and quickly found his assigned spot. Tonight he was on a mission. The scheduled project he'd been working on the previous evening wasn't going to take him more than an hour or so this evening. After that he planned on using the free time to find his unusual comet again and maybe even recalculate its trajectory. Right now there were some students using the telescope under the direction of one of Cal Tech's professors, so he had some time to kill.

He went into the little snack room adjacent to the main viewing room and got himself a cup of coffee. Benjamin was already there.

"Hi, Ben," Chuck said, "Doing a little maintenance tonight?"

"Yes sir. There was a glitch in the tracking motor on the twenty-four inch and I thought I'd just take the opportunity to check on the others while I was here. It's fixed now."

"What was wrong with it?"

Ben looked a little sheepish as he answered. "Actually it was a field mouse, Sir. He got caught in the gears somehow and gummed up the motor. I had to back it up and clean everything out."

"A field mouse! How the heck did a field mouse get in there?"

"Beats me, Sir, but it's fixed now."

"Well good job finding it."

"Thank you, Sir."

Chuck left the room thinking how nice it was that a few young people still observed old-style manners. Ben was always quick with the "yes, sir" and "no-sir" polite replies, and he wondered in passing if it had any-thing to do with the boy's heritage or just parenting in general.

Chuck wandered back into the main telescope viewing room with his fresh cup of stale coffee, and on a whim decided to climb the catwalk ladder that ascended around and inside the viewing dome. It led 'round and 'round, all the way up to the spot where the retracting panel met the other side of the dome. This was meant to allow workers to access the door manually, if needed, and so it had a little platform that gave Chuck a great view through the top of the observatory at night. On evenings when he arrived early, he had utilized the platform to watch the sunset. This evening was one of those, and the view didn't disappoint. From that vantage point, Chuck watched as the sun dipped into a broken cloud bank lingering past the hills and over the Pacific. Those clouds proved to be fertile fodder for the sun to paint multi-colored tapestries across the sky. Hues of magenta, azure, and gold floated into his view with breathtaking brilliance. He didn't often watch the spectacular scene for two reasons. For starters, he didn't normally arrive at the observatory until well after sunset. Secondly, it left lingering feelings of the loneli-ness that permeated his life. Tonight, however, he was still excited about the prospect of viewing the meteor or comet he'd discovered last night, and so he'd arrived early.

He could see the Pacific Ocean in the distance beneath the amazing colors of the sunset, and sure enough a tiny wave of loneliness swept over him causing the vestiges of his romantic bone to twitch annoy-ingly. Another puzzle chased those thoughts away, however; the simple fact that he hadn't heard or read anything about the appearance of the comet he'd observed last night was extremely curious.

Usually, if anything interesting like that appeared in the sky, even if it could only be seen by powerful telescopes, it usually made some kind of blurb in the science journals or on the Internet. But for this one, there was nothing. How could it have just appeared in the night sky? Maybe this comet was one of the bodies trapped in the gravitational field of the Milky Way galaxy, and since the Earth had passed through the plane of that galaxy just a few years ago, that might explain its unexpected appearance.

He was still pondering as the sun winked out beneath the Pacific.

The thought that the Mayan culture managed to calculate the Earth's passing through the plane of the Milky Way galaxy never failed to fascinate Chuck. It was December of 2012 that had marked the end of the Mayan calendar and also saw the Earth pass through that plane; the winter equinox of 2012, to be precise. Of course that exact date had been disproved. The Mayans hadn't accounted for leap year.

How could an ancient culture have calculated such a complex 26,000 year celestial cycle yet not figure in leap year? Yet another puzzle. Maybe it *was* this rare event that accounted for the appearance of his comet. His comet. Maybe he could be the one to officially make the discovery. Somehow he couldn't buy that one, though; surely someone else had seen it. Nevertheless, the prospect excited him, and was more than ample reward for the otherwise unpaid for, and certainly unscheduled work for the evening.

The hours slipped by as Chuck patiently watched from his perch while Orion and Cassiopeia rose slowly in the sky. He was on his second cup of coffee and the students were just about done with their little introduction to viewing through Palomar's famous telescope. It was a moonless night and therefore everything else in the night sky looked that much brighter.

It was possible to stargaze with these telescopes even when the moon was full, but the clarity of the distant celestial objects was much diminished. Chuck was pleased that tonight, with the darkness of the new moon, his viewing would be at its best.

He glanced at his watch. He had another thirty minutes or so to kill so he eased down the winding stairs and slipped into the tiny office adjacent to the 200 inch mass of technology then seated himself comfortably in front of the computer terminal. His gaze locked on the screen as he brought the full weight of his extraordinary intellect to bear on the search. It proved fruitless. There was still nothing about a new comet in the sky, and again he couldn't shake the strangeness of the lack of corroboration.

Chuck padded out into the main viewing room for the huge reflector and gazed in familiar delight at the bright, bronze-colored precision metal of the telescope's gantry. He briefly glanced around at the students who were slowly filing out of the building for the evening, then moved up to the little seat just beneath the viewing optics and adjusted it. Turning to the small tray of different lenses on his left, Chuck selected one of medium power and slid it into the receptacle on the telescope. Next, he turned to the keypad and keyed in the coordinates he had recorded for the comet the night before. Instead of waiting for the telescope to swing into position to view, Chuck put his eye to the eyepiece and watched the sky seem to gallop by as it smoothly moved to its assigned position. It was moving relatively fast, but not so fast as to preclude viewing the objects along the path of its swing.

There. It slid into view as the telescope slowed on its final approach to the coordinates he'd entered. It was glorious. Its tail was much longer than his last view of it. He wondered how it had come to be and where it had been. Did this brilliant spectacle come from somewhere in our galaxy or had it entered in from somewhere else unimaginably far away? The former was the more likely, the latter more intriguing.

As he watched, he moved the telescope to the leading edge of its path, just ahead of the tail. Something caught his eye—. The little dark spot in the tail he had previously only seen in the photo he'd taken. Was it bigger than before? It seemed easier to discern now. What could cause that phenomenon? It looked like a tiny dark hole in the comet's tail. Chuck adjusted the focus, then noticed that the hole seemed to be changing position in the comet's tail.

It couldn't be moving. He realized that this object, whatever it was, was moving at an oblique angle to the path of the comet, therefore it had to have motion of its own. If it *was* moving then it had to be some sort of celestial body. A possibility occurred to him, but one that was so remote he could barely give it credence. Could it be an asteroid? One that was visible within the tail of a comet, actually visible *because* of the tail of the comet? His concentration on the eyepiece redoubled as he stared at the mystery unfolding in the heavens before him. An asteroid should be recognized as a double spot, one blue and one yellow close together. The dark spot could easily be the blue one, but the comet's tail was yellowish itself so he couldn't see a yellow spot. He was stock still, riveted to the eyepiece for several minutes. Then . . . there it was: a yellow spot that was tracking the blue one . . . An asteroid then. It was incredible. He had just found an asteroid nobody else had seen, and in the same field of view with an unreported comet.

The odds against this experience were mounting by the second, yet it was there before his eyes. Spotting an asteroid in the tail of a comet was virtually impossible. Since asteroids were composed mostly of rock and metal rather than dust and ice, they didn't give off a tail, and the tiny double spots of light were hard enough to spot by themselves let alone hiding in the brilliant tail of a comet, not to mention the miniscule chances of them occupying virtually the same point in outer space, or at least the same point from Earth's perspective.

Chuck pulled his eye back from the eyepiece and reached to the little tray beside him. He replaced the 9.9mm lens and selected a substantially more powerful 30.9mm lens. When he looked again, the diverging paths of the comet and the asteroid began to be more evident, and now he could tell that the asteroid wasn't round, but a slightly elongated shape. Judging by the relative motion he was seeing, the two objects would no longer be in the same field of view in a matter of hours. If he had picked a higher magnification for his choice of lenses earlier on, he might have missed the asteroid altogether. He felt certain that this was the same anomaly he'd seen on his last two work nights, which could only mean that they had been travelling at the same relative angles until tonight. Something had changed the paths of one or the other, and he'd spotted it just in time. The whole situation was way beyond extraordinary.

Almost without thinking, Chuck adjusted the motion of the great telescope to track the asteroid rather than the comet. Chuck's mind kept trying to fathom the calculation of the odds of him seeing a comet and an asteroid, both unreported, in the same field of view at the same time. The odds of it happening were multiplied by the odds of anyone seeing it, even with the right equipment, both of which were miniscule from the beginning. Astronomical, seemed much too diminutive of an adjective to express it. Unfathomable was closer. Winning five consecutive Powerballs would seem almost typical by comparison.

At the very least this extraordinary phenomenon wasn't going to go unreported for any longer, he decided.

Leaving the great telescope to automatically track the asteroid, Chuck slipped down from his perch in the viewing seat and grabbed his cell phone. He had at least two phone calls to make. The first was to the

Sentry project at NASA to have them engage the Hubble telescope; the second was to his old friend Robert Haynes at the W.M. Keck observatory in Hawaii. That facility had a pair of twin 10 meter telescopes that were some of the most powerful on the planet. It was definitely time to engage a bit of serious viewing power.

* * *

For the second morning in a row Chuck woke up earlier than usual. His phone calls to his colleagues the night before had initially been met with skepticism, but after further explanation, the skepticism changed to awe, then excitement. It looked as though Chuck would finally have a celestial body named after him. Whoopee, he thought sarcastically.

He was still struggling with the odds against his extraordinary discovery. Asteroids had never been a focus of any particular interest for him, but he *had* been interested in comets, and now with this new puzzle, he decided it was time to expand his knowledge on both fronts.

With a cup of coffee in hand, he went straight to his computer. Research sure had changed over the years. He remembered sitting in dusty, narrow passageways for hours on end when he had done his research for his doctorate on quantum physics and its potential relevance to intergalactic travel. In many ways he missed the peaceful solitude of the library environment, the sensation of being lost in the catacombs of knowledge as he negotiated the constricted isles of the stacks, where back alleys of books upon books surrounded him, and the tiny sequestered nooks where he might sit for hours and pour over chapters from a seldom seen volume. These days it was so much faster to sit in your own little study and let your fingers race across the keyboard to drag up the nearly infinite amount of information available across the World Wide Web. It was more convenient and efficient, yes, but still lacked that quality of romance and adventure a majestic old library could invoke; the aura of delving back through time and through the minds of great men to uncover new knowledge. On the other hand, he was older now and driving across town to sit on hard wooden chairs or tramp through narrow aisles amid dusty volumes for hours, had much more appeal for him as a memory than as an actual deed. These days it was much better to work from the comfort of his own chair in his own home.

So it was with a serious gusto that Chuck focused his awesome intellect on the information available about asteroids in the cosmos. What he found first surprised him, then, the more he read, the more his surprise turned to fear and from simple fear to a swelling sensation of foreboding.

He began with a flip to a National Geographic website to get some general information. One article did a fine job of delineating the differences between asteroids and comets. It read:

"Comets consist of compressed ice and dust whereas asteroids are made of rock and metal. That difference in composition allows comets to emit tremendous tails when they passed close enough to a star to generate the heat necessary to allow some of its particles to stream out ahead of it. The term 'tail', in fact, is actually a misnomer. The glowing stream emitted from a comet always precedes the comet itself and is both produced and propelled by the radiation from a star. These beautiful streamers can stretch for thousands of miles ahead of the comet and make them much easier to detect.

What people think of as the tail is more like an arrow pointing out the comet's direction of travel."

Chuck thought about that for a moment. It was true enough, and he'd read it before, but still, for earthbound viewers it was nearly impossible to gaze at a comet and hold that concept in your mind. On Earth, tails *always* followed the object, and somehow that truth continued to intrude on one's thinking while viewing celestial objects. He turned back to the article:

"Asteroids, on the other hand, being made of rock or metal, do not contain any particles that can vaporize and glow. Consequently they are much more difficult to spot. The primary source of asteroids in our solar system is the tremendous asteroid belt that dwells between the orbits of Mars and Jupiter, but that doesn't preclude the possibility of asteroids coming into the sphere of our sun's influence from outside our solar system or even outside of our galaxy. As a matter of fact, with the extraordinary galactic alignment that occurred a couple of years ago, the one made famous by the Mayan calendar-predicted apocalypse, the opportunity of extragalactic celestial bodies became significantly more likely."

That last gave Chuck pause. He was very familiar with the end of the Mayan Calendar and the celestial alignment it represented, but he had never really considered all of the potential ramifications of it. This was something he was going to have to look into again.

He browsed a number of sites that were focused on the outcome of "Planet Killer" asteroids striking earth, but those doomsday predictions were not the kind of information he needed. He finally found a NASA article about the numerous "close calls" that had happened since we began paying attention and some notable strikes that scientists had documented from Earth's distant past. These began:

"The strike estimated to have struck Earth in the neighborhood of 10 million years ago hit the Yucatan peninsula creating the giant oval of the Gulf of Mexico. Another, estimated at 300 million years ago, is believed to have struck the earth producing enough debris and dust in the air to wipe out the dinosaurs."

These few prehistoric strikes were based on theories and were the only mentions of asteroids from the distant past.

It struck Chuck as strange that there had been no other significant effort to identify potential asteroid or comet strikes on Earth until fairly recently. Chuck found another NASA article detailing it:

"In 1992, a group of scientists from various universities and NASA formed a workshop to study the topic of recent and potential asteroid strikes. They produced the Spaceguard Survey Report which led the House Committee on Science and Technology in 1994 to direct NASA to begin work with space agencies around the globe to identify and catalogue any celestial bodies that were larger than one kilometer in diameter and crossed the path of Earth's orbit."

Chuck skipped through the rest of the preamble to the actual examples Spaceguard had chronicled:

"On March 23rd, 1989 an asteroid designated Asteroid 1989FC missed hitting the Earth by six hours. This little jewel packed the energy of roughly a thousand of the most powerful nuclear bombs, and the human race became aware of it shortly after its closest approach. Had this celestial baseball been only six hours later most of the population of the Earth would have been eliminated with zero warning."

"In October of 1990, an asteroid that would have been considered very small, struck the Pacific Ocean. This little fellow only packed the energy of a small atomic bomb, about the same as the one that flattened Hiroshima, and if it had arrived a few hours later or earlier it could have easily struck a city rather than making a relatively harmless splash into the center of the ocean. Remember, relatively here, is just a comparative term."

"In 1908 an even smaller asteroid, one that never even made it to the ground, exploded in mid-air, in Tunguska, Siberia and just the blast concussion flattened some 60 million trees. Even though this explosion also happened to miss a populated area, the dust from the detonation of this tiny celestial speedster still lit up the European skies for days. Another one of roughly the same size struck the Brazilian rain forest on August 13th , 1930."

The article went on to point out that it's not just Earth that gets singled out for these impacts; the Shoemaker Levy 9 comet slammed into Jupiter in July of 1994. This one apparently broke up into about 20 large chunks before hitting the surface, but even so, they caused a line of tremendous explosions that are still visible to our telescopes as dark spots on the planet's surface.

Chuck found this data extremely interesting and even a bit unnerving in light of his new discoveries, but the one quote that caught and held his attention was linked to a website with the unimaginative name of "Orbits and Trajectories.com" that gave a succinct explanation of how to determine asteroid trajectory. It read:

"We live in an enormous cosmic shooting gallery."

Now that his fears were being aroused, Chuck looked for more documentation of anything that was being done about these potential strikes. He finally found another article from "Operation Lifeboat" a website devoted to the possibility of a lethal planetary strike. It read:

"The Spaceguard Survey Report has since evolved into a more formal and comprehensive effort called Sentry. This program has developed into a massive undertaking to identify and catalogue all potential asteroid strikes of a size greater than one meter in diameter."

Chuck felt that this type of project was the very minimum we should be doing. After a miraculous multi-thousand year major-strike-free window to develop our technology, the human race now had the ability to defend itself against such onslaughts, but only if we learn of the impending danger in time. That amount of time, to some extent, depends on the size of the approaching killer. The larger it is, the more time we would need to act with any hope of success.

Satisfied for the moment with some of his new knowledge on a previously neglected topic, Chuck got up from the computer and strolled back toward the kitchen. Studying made him hungry, and unlike in his library forays of years gone past, he didn't have to wait.

10

July 2016

Chuck drew his face back from the eyepiece. He'd spent a good many evenings watching his new-found asteroid. Asteroid Kohler Leporidae, they had named it. The name consisted of his last name and the biological family name for the variety of animals that included rabbits. Some imaginative astronomer had noticed the elongated rounded hump on one side of the asteroid and the shorter one on the front. A striation near the top of the smaller hump looked remarkably like the laid back ears of a rabbit. At any rate, he finally had a celestial body named after him. It was now in the history books. The unusual circumstances that had surrounded its discovery had led to discussions about its path through the solar system and then the recording of data about its size, shape and composition. That buzz had barely made a news blurb and had died down completely two days after the announcement of the discovery, except in scientific circles such as the International Astronomers Alliance, and of course Sentry itself. Still, even that had died down in a few weeks.

The initial elation he'd experienced at his discovery and being permanently listed in the history books had also faded. Now he was feeling a kind of foreboding. There was something about this asteroid. For starters, it wasn't rotating. It presented the same "crouching rabbit" aspect to them at every attempt to view it. A non-rotating asteroid wasn't unheard of, but it was unusual. It also thwarted the scientific community's attempts to measure it. Without being able to see the back side of the thing, they could not truly measure its mass or its real size. It could be like looking down on a cylinder, all you saw was a circle unless you changed your perspective. Asteroid Kohler Leporidae could be many times more or less massive than it appeared from the single surface they could see.

He stepped down off the viewing seat, and headed for the computer. He'd been taking trajectory readings again tonight and wanted to compare them with the ones from three months ago. Normally, there was no reason to take such measurements like this; once you calculate the thing's path that was it.

So, there wasn't usually a reason to do it again. The path he had calculated for the asteroid was going to take it on a course to the far side of the sun from the earth's regular route, and therefore of no concern other than the tremendous scientific value of knowing about it so far ahead of such close proximity. In a few more days it would disappear behind the sun relative to Earth's view and be invisible for almost another two months. Chuck was given to errors in calculations but this time he decided to check his figures again. He wanted to be absolutely certain when and where Kohler Leporidae would reappear from behind the sun.

11

September 12th 2016

Valerie had been driving around for hours. She hadn't seen Jeremy in days. It was partially due to their schedules but also, at least on her part, due to a reticence to move things along any faster. Jeremy had called twice this morning and after his second call, she had turned her phone off, but she couldn't get him out of her mind. Mulling in her home was driving her crazy, so she hopped in her car and pointed her nose toward the lake. She loved to drive the curvy, hilly roads around Lake Travis. It was scenic, quite, and peaceful, just the combination she needed to think. With a little luck maybe she could resolve something about where to go with Jeremy.

She'd spent her life with her emotional armor on to one degree or another, but it was finally occurring to her that it had never seemed to be this bad before. Now she was struggling to understand it. Everything she'd learned about Jeremy only served to heighten her feelings for him. He was a wonderful man. So why did it seem that every time he made any overture toward her, all she could think about was running, and then later feeling stupid and lonely for doing it? They'd only made love once, and while that had involved all the awkwardness of a new couple, it had still been wonderful. Just the memory of it sent tingles through her midsection.

As she thought about, she knew the answer. David. Her last relationship with the doctor from Kansas City had really thrown her for a loop. She'd never experienced a situation with a man who started off seeming so wonderful, only to later reveal himself as a level-one whacko. It had left her shaken, and now she realized that included doubting not only her own judgment, but the character of everyone who might show any interest in her. It was like a light had come on. Why hadn't she seen it before? It explained her reaction to Jeremy, especially since he had the great misfortune to be the very next man in her life with any potential.

Valerie felt like a huge weight had been lifted off her chest. She was on the north side of the lake, but it was time to circle back around to the south side. She had a boy-friend to visit if it wasn't too late.

* * *

"Lakeway traffic, this is Saratoga 2887Mike entering left downwind for runway one-six, full stop."

Jeremy looked for any other traffic in the area as he settled into the pattern altitude of 1,900 feet, 1,000 feet above the runway of the little fly-in community. Larger airports have a Unicom or even a tower to give pilots airport information and direct traffic, but this little community on Lake Travis had neither, so it was up to the pilots to make sure of their own separation from other traffic, and determine the winds from the wind sock on the ground. Fortunately, that wasn't much of an issue because the airstrip was private and only property owners in the community utilized its 4300 foot concrete strip.

"Lakeway traffic this is Saratoga 2887Mike turning left base for runway one-six, Lakeway."

Jeremy had already lowered his landing gear, pulled the power back and lowered the flaps about a quarter of the way. Now he reached down and pulled the flap lever up another notch which pointed the nose at more of a down angle while further slowing his approach. He was 700 feet above the ground and had slowed to 100 knots. He was grinning furiously at his own picture-perfect approach.

A sharp gust buffeted the small six-passenger single engine Piper aircraft, but Jeremy barely noticed it. Gusts off of Lake Travis were common, and he was too busy preparing the plane for landing and trying not to get caught up in the gorgeous scenery of the azure lake and surrounding green hills to even notice the tiny jolt.

"Lakeway traffic, Saratoga 87Mike turning final for one-six Lakeway, full stop."

Jeremy pulled up the last notch of flaps. The increased nose down attitude gave him a perfect view of the runway as the small plane slowed even further. He was 400 feet above the runway and slowing to 80 knots now, right at landing speed. He glanced up one more time into the cloudless sky to scan for other traffic. Not that he expected any, and if they were there they should have heard his continuous position reports, but it never hurts to be extra careful.

Refocusing his gaze on the rapidly approaching runway surface, Jeremy gently began to pull the nose up.

78kts.

He felt he was sinking a wee bit too fast so he unconsciously added back a touch of power on the throttle. The sturdy little plane drifted into ground effect, the slight cushioning of air between the lower wing surface and the ground, and he pulled the nose up just a bit more—

He heard a squeak and imagined the puff of smoke wisping up from the main landing gear—

—Perfect.

The two main landing gear wheels squawked simultaneously as they gently kissed the concrete. Just for fun Jeremy pulled the yoke back a touch more to see how long he could keep the nose gear from touching the ground. It was a procedure that was taught as a technique for landing on a soft field, but Jeremy did it just to see how well he could. He finally let the nose wheel touch, making its own muted squeak and pulled the power all the way back to idle, then pushed with his toes on the top of the rudder pedals to engage the brakes.

A satisfied grin decorated his face as he taxied slowly off the active runway to his personal hangar adjoining his house. His attempts in the real estate industry had paid off intermittently but handsomely. He'd bought the place a couple of years ago as a distressed sale for around 300,000, and since then the value had skyrocketed. He hadn't even owned a plane at the time.

His thoughts didn't stay on his home though, or on his airplane. They turned to Valerie. He hadn't talked to her in days. He'd called her a couple of times this morning only to get voice mails and no return calls. It was perplexing. Over and over again he wondered why he stayed yoked to this woman. It wasn't as though he couldn't find someone willing to date him and certainly most any of those would exhibit more overt interest than she ever exhibited. So why did he continue to hang around? Maybe it was some latent masochistic tendencies coming out.

Once he was close enough, he clicked the garage door opener to the hangar and listened to the comforting rumble of the big Continental 300hp engine, while he wondered whether he should even call her again. He eased the throttles forward and stood on the left brake to slowly swing the Saratoga around. He would use the little tow bar on the nose wheel and push the plane back into the hangar. It still surprised him how easy the aircraft was to push. Being light for its size was an inherent characteristic of aircraft, but after flying in the sturdy Piper it always seemed too substantial to be so easily moved by hand.

Jeremy ran quickly through the shutdown checklist before pulling back the fuel lever and killing the engine. The propeller had barely stopped its last rotation before his mind was back on Valerie.

He'd wanted her to go flying with him today. He knew she loved it, but she hadn't returned his call. The frustration was like being on an accelerating merry go round. The faster it went, the queasier he became.

When he was young he had been guilty of falling for women who had either been only moderately interested in him or were intent on leading him on for some other benefit. In many ways this little extended foray with Valerie felt just like that but there was something else there. It was something about her spirit, and something about the way her eyes lit up when she saw him. If she ever voiced what he was certain he saw in her eyes at those moments, his heart would probably burst with joy.

He sighed. She wasn't voicing anything though, and what he thought he saw in her eyes was probably just a reflection of his own desires. He finished pushing his plane back into the hangar and pressed the close button on the door.

The echo of the huge door closing was still reverberating in the hangar when he felt the cell phone in his pocket vibrate. He pulled it out, but by the time he got it in his hand the ringing had stopped. Jeremy looked at the display and was surprised to see that, not only was it Valerie, but she had called him three times. This was a new event. In the eight or nine months since he'd known her, she had never called him more than one unanswered time when she called at all. His curiosity was piqued and excitement trickled through him. Wasting no more time, he pushed the redial button and called her back.

Valerie answered on the second ring.

"Jeremy, it's you. I've been trying to reach you."

"I was out flying like I said I would when I left the message inviting you to come along," he couldn't resist the little dig, then hated himself for it.

"I'm sorry. I got caught up in conversations with a couple of senators. They're really pushing me to go to DC."

Jeremy had kind of been expecting this. He knew her job had ties to Washington and was afraid that someday it would drag her there. "So are you going to go?" He asked the question with as much nonchalance as he could muster, but he suspected that she could glean the tension beneath his words. She paused before answering. He hoped her tension-enhancing teaser wasn't for his benefit.

"Uh, I don't know. I don't want to. Listen what are you doing?"

"Nothing yet, I just closed my hangar door from my flight."

"Would you like some company?"

This was another curve ball. Val had been famous in his experience for her aloofness. Now she was taking the initiative. What had changed? "Yeah, sure. When did you have in mind?"

"Now. I'm in your driveway."

"What?"

"Well, I was driving around thinking about you, and the next thing I knew I ended up here. I watched you land by the way. Nice soft-field technique."

"Why thank you. I'm surprised you noticed."

"I may not have my license yet, but I've got a few hours flying. Besides, I always notice things about you. Speaking of which, how is the neck?"

"Look, come on in, and I'll meet you in the den and show you."

"Sure."

Jeremy slowly pulled his phone away from his ear and stared at it as though it were some kind of an alien. Was this the same Valerie he had been trying to get close to for the last six months? Where was all this newfound forthrightness coming from? His curiosity was piqued as he left the hangar. Unconsciously, he reached up to touch the scar around his neck. The sharp pain of his touch caused him to jerk his hand away. When he reached the den Valerie was already standing there.

"To answer your question, it's still tender to the touch, but if I just keep my hands and clothes off of it, I don't notice it."

There was a slight tightening around Val's eyes as she moved closer and let them slide from side to side, inspecting the scar. "Man, I still can't believe you did that. You can even see on the right side there where the lines crossed. It's like a pale 'X.' When I saw it on the boat I thought it would fade out."

"Yeah. I noticed that in the mirror this morning, actually."

Without any warning Valerie stepped in, and Jeremy lifted up his eyes to meet hers. The motion put him in the perfect position to receive the kiss that Valerie planted on his shocked face. Flabbergasted gave way to passion as he responded.

When she finally eased back, the look of desire in her eyes was a reflection of the sensations coursing through him. He struggled to mutter a sound.

"Wow . . . I . . ."

Her next kiss smothered whatever he might have said. When they came up for air, Jeremy was torn between wanting more from her body and wanting an explanation for the sudden change. But he got neither as Valerie abruptly disengaged, her eyes remaining fixed on his.

"Valerie, what the . . ."

"Not now, Jeremy. Can we please just be together for a while? There'll be time enough for explanations later."

It occurred to Jeremy that he wasn't having much luck getting over that "dumfounded" feeling, but he was pretty sure of the sincerity in her eyes, and since he'd already waited this long, he could tolerate a little while longer. "Sure Val. What would you like to do?"

She looked pensive for just a brief second before answering. "Do you have any wine?"

"Cabernet sound alright?"

"Perfect."

"I'll be right back."

When he returned, she was already seated on the couch with the TV on. He walked around the couch a little disappointed set the glasses down on the coffee table, and slipped out the cork he'd already opened in the kitchen.

"BV Tapestry?" She said, nodding her head in appreciation as she saw the label. "Is this a special occasion?"

Jeremy evinced a sly smile. "I don't know, Valerie. Is it?" He saw the blush rise in her cheeks before she answered.

"I don't know. Maybe." She grabbed the remote and looked away from him while he poured for them both.

As the rich aroma of the wine wafted up to him, he wasn't quite sure how to react. The Valerie Latham he knew was cool, confident, and typically in command of any situation. Frequently, she even bordered on distant and aloof. This woman next to him was warm, affectionate, tentative, and exhibiting a vulnerability he'd never seen from her before. He could barely take it all in much less decide what he felt about it. He merely sat down beside her, offered her a glass, and with a steady gaze into her eyes said, "Cheers then. Here's to maybe."

"To maybe," she answered, smiling broadly.

So, with the bottle of wine on the table and glasses in hand, they both turned their attention to the TV. The Discovery Channel was airing a re-run about the end of the world predictions for the Winter Solstice of 2012. Even though the most-dire of those predictions had proven unfounded, the show intended to explain and illuminate the great accomplishment of the Mayans in even creating such a precise calendar.

Jeremy's interest was piqued, but he figured it wasn't a topic Valerie would care to watch. He had already switched to another channel when Valerie spoke up.

"Wait a sec. Go back to that, would you?"

"Are you interested in space exploration, Val?"

She turned to him sharply with a broad grin and nearly sloshing wine from her glass. "I am when they include things that might affect good old planet Earth. Besides, all my life I've heard so much about the end of the Mayan Calendar, and it occurs to me now that I don't really know what it was. Can we watch for just a few minutes? If I'm going to watch this stuff, I'd rather do it with you."

Surprised, Jeremy smiled as he turned back to the TV. "OK," he said, and switched the channel back.

A view of the Earth from outer space appeared on the large flat screen in front of them and was quickly replaced by a drawing of a partially opened book with a pencil sticking up from it. In seconds he and Valerie were completely absorbed.

> "As a place to start, let us use a model to explain precisely what this 'Great Year' actually is. The year 2012 is the year that marked the end of a 26,000 year cycle, ending in a great galactic alignment that was calculated on the Mayan calendar and results in the calendar ending on the winter solstice (December 21st) of 2012. But what exactly is this galactic alignment?

> To understand exactly what is happening, it is useful to think of an image with three different parts. The first two parts consist of an open book on a table and the third part is a pencil sticking up out of the crease of that book. Imagine one side of the book lying flat on the table and the other side lifted up to a 60 °angle. The side of the book still resting on the table represents the plane created by earth's orbit around the sun and the side that is lifted up represents the plane of the Milky Way galaxy. This 60 °angle never changes. What does change, however, is the angle of the pencil."

As they watched, a small arrow moved from area to area depicting which item the narrator was referring to. It was confusing at first, but Jeremy felt like he was getting it as the narrator continued.

> "The pencil represents the tilt of the earth's axis as it rotates around the sun and that does change. If the point of the pencil remains stationary, then the eraser representing that axis would make a circle creating the shape of a cone above the crease in the book once every 26,000 years and this is the "Great Year" that is referred to in the Mayan calendar. The result of this alignment is that the earth will pass basically from the top to the bottom of the Milky Way galaxy and so at one point it must pass through the plane of the galaxy.

According to a quote from the Mayan text on that day a 'fiery dragon' would breathe upon the earth: 'The fire will flow from the serpent's mouth when the tree of life, sun, moon, and earth align in December of 2012.'

There was some speculation within the scientific community that when this galactic alignment occurred and the Earth passed through that plane, three new conditions, each with their own potential for world-wide destruction, would be present:

First, the Earth would be exposed to a concentrated beam of Gamma radiation emanating from the galactic center, which had only recently been discovered to consist of a vast black hole. This beam would be perceived from Earth as a great mystical light. The danger being that direct exposure to the immense radiation of the galactic center might drastically alter life on Earth.

Second, the Earth would potentially be exposed to all the celestial bodies that are trapped in the gravitational field of the Galactic plane including meteors, comets and asteroids. This meant that one of the celestial bodies already orbiting through the Milky Way's galactic plane could impact Earth.

And the third was that the earth would be, for a brief time, exposed to the same gravitational field that holds the Milky Way galaxy itself in place. This could result in a sudden shift of the Earth's magnetic poles causing violent geologic upheavals such as earthquakes, volcanoes, tsunamis, and even dramatic climactic shifts.

Well, as we all know that time came and went and whether it was off by a year due to the miscalculation of leap year or not, none of those things happened. But what might yet have happened, what the Mayans might have been referring to, is that their calendar, marking that great alignment, could have spelled the beginning of the end. There has been a substantial increase in NEOs or near earth objects passing through our solar system since the end of the Mayan calendar. The theory is that it was in fact our system's interjection into that galactic plane that allowed other space debris to be redirected and some of it apparently toward us.

Regardless of the effect, or lack thereof, of the Mayan alignment, the presence of NEOs has been on the increase for quite some time, leading the government, headed by NASA, to form an initiative called Sentry. The program evolved several years ago from the original Spaceguard Survey Report and grew into a massive undertaking to identify and catalogue all potential asteroid strikes of a size greater than a meter in diameter. This effort has recently been undermined, however, and nearly abandoned by the slashing budget cuts of our current president who feels that all monies spent on space exploration are a waste of valuable resources.

Some scientists suggest that we have already felt some of the effects of that celestial alignment in the form of climate changes, earthquakes, hurricanes and other geological and meteorological disturbances that have been on the increase for years."

"My God," Valerie breathed. "That's all pretty incredible."

Jeremy's eyes were glued to the TV, "No kidding. I hadn't heard the scientific explanation before, just the ones referring to the predictions of the event. I'm glad I didn't see it before the event. This makes it seem so much more real."

They both paused to have another sip of wine in unison, and Jeremy realized that Valerie had slid closer to him on the couch. He subtly responded to her gesture and smiled.

Valerie picked up the remote and muted the TV before turning to Jeremy. She was so close that facing him almost begged for another round of kissing, but she didn't. She just stared at him with a look of wonder.

"How could a culture that ancient have ever come up with such an accurate and long reaching calendar? Hell, a thousand years after them the Europeans still thought the world was flat."

Jeremy thought a minute, then kissed her gently on the mouth before replying. "It's another of the great mysteries of life." His grin was positively roguish.

"What if the world really was going to end in a few months? I mean, I wonder if some kind of asteroid strike might not be what was referred to in Revelations as the seven years of the tribulation where the world experiences tremendous upheavals and billions of people die. You know just like the one Joel was talking about last night."

"You're not the first one to come up with that theory, Val, but I'm a Christian. God can have me whenever he wants. And as far as the one that Joel was talking about, that's not coming anywhere near us. It's apparently a miracle that we spotted at all."

"I feel the same way, but still . . ."

"Kind of makes you want to appreciate the moments you have, doesn't it?"

"I'll say." As those words left her mouth, Jeremy watched the expression change on her face. He tried to decide whether he thought it was a look of sadness or shame. The sudden change certainly sparked his curiosity and though he wasn't sure what was coming next, he was pretty sure it wasn't about the end of the world.

"Speaking of which, I have a story I need to tell you. It will, in part at least, explain my behavior over the last six months, and it's something I just realized today was still having a tremendous effect on me," Valerie paused briefly, staring into his eyes, "On us."

Those last two words riveted Jeremy's attention, and he leaned back slightly from her so he could better take in her face.

"OK. You have my attention."

A touch of hesitation seemed to mingle with embarrassment in her expression as she glanced down to collect her thoughts. Jeremy was almost afraid to hear whatever it was she was about to tell him.

"Well, it started over a year ago when I was still in Kansas City. I met a man on an Internet dating site, and it started out pretty much like all the others, you know…small talk…, but right up front there was a twist. I had been talking to this guy and finally gave him my phone number.

"Is this 'Adventuresome' from Match dot com?"

"Yes. DoctorDave?"

"That's me. David will be just fine. What's your real name, if you don't mind?"

"Valerie."

"Well, it's nice to talk to you Valerie. I liked your profile and I must say you're quite photogenic."

"Thank you very much. So, I see that you're a doctor. What kind of medicine do you practice?

"I own a cosmetic surgery clinic in the area."

"Oh. Well, I bet it keeps you busy."

"It keeps me as busy as I let it. I usually can make time for the things I want to do."

"And what would that be?"

"Well, go out with you for one. Will you let me take you to dinner tomorrow night? I promise to make it memorable."

"I'm not sure if that sounds scary or wonderful. What do you mean by memorable?"

"You said you like adventure. Have you ever been in a small airplane?"

"Yes, a time or two. How small is it?"

"It's a twin engine Beech called a Baron. It seats six."

"So you're proposing to take us somewhere for dinner in your plane?"

"That's what I was thinking. An early dinner though, say 5:00?"

"Where?"

"There's a little place in southern Oklahoma that has the best *catfish in the world and it has its own runway."*

"Has its own runway?"

"Yep. You fly right in and taxi up to the restaurant to park."

"OK. That does sound like adventure. Count me in."

"So, there I was, sucked in from the very beginning. I hadn't done much Internet dating before, and here was this guy. He was polite, wealthy, handsome, and adventurous. I guess I shouldn't be surprised that I got involved. But even that first date ended in a rather big surprise."

"I do believe that was the best catfish I've ever had, Dave. Thank you very much."

The place was quaint and rustic, but it sat secluded at the end of a dead end road and the entire back of the restaurant was a window overlooking a great northern loop of the Red River."

"Wait until dessert gets here," he replied with a sly grin.

"Oh, I couldn't possibly eat anything else."

"You won't want to miss this, Valerie. It'll be here in a moment."

"But . . ."

"No buts. It's already ordered and will be here shortly."

"As if on cue, the waitress came flowing out of the kitchen with a tray on her shoulder. A folding stand seemed to appear from nowhere and she set the big tray on it. She managed just a hint of a flourish as she touched a lighter to the large skillet which burst into a lovely blue flame."

"I must have leaned back from the flames because Dave chuckled slightly before speaking.

"Startled you, did it? The taste is even more surprising than the show. I get especially tickled that a quaint little catfish place serves this dish at all, but I guess the owner enjoys making it, so believe it or not, you get to have an exotic dessert with your fried catfish."

"David's laugh was rich and sincere as we watched the server. Turns out it was bananas foster she was preparing, and I hadn't ever had them before. Jeremy, that dessert is simply a delight to the senses. Flames for the eyes, aroma for the nose, and a heavenly sweetness as the piece-de-re-sistance for the tongue.

"David had brought some white wine that the restaurant opened and served with the appetizers and through dinner. But when they brought cognac with the dessert I started thinking about the trip home."

"How are you going to fly us home after all this alcohol."

"I'm not."

"He said it with a sly smile on his face. Thinking back, I'm certain he let that linger as he did just to let all the different possibilities, run through my mind before giving me an explanation."

"I'm having a car pick us up."

"What about your plane?"

"I'm having someone come to pick it up, too."

"But then where are we going?"

"I was almost afraid to hear his answer. This was moving pretty quickly, and all of sudden I wasn't comfortable with that much money being thrown around. I mean on the one hand, I was used to being around senators and congressmen who were being wooed by companies and even countries, so it wasn't totally out of the realm of my experi-ence, but I wasn't used to having this kind of money thrown specifically at *me*. It was more than a little unnerving, and I felt that some sort of expectations were being laid before me that I hadn't had the chance to agree to ahead of time.

"This new line of thought even permeated the cognac buzz to a small degree, so it was with more than a modicum of trepidation that I followed him outside of the little restaurant toward the stretched Cadillac limo that was waiting for us in the parking lot."

"I thought we might take a drive through the country. We have a few hours of daylight left and I think we can find a scenic back road to enjoy. It's a beautiful evening and flying would have been over too quick."

"So, he had assumed that I wouldn't have any desire to abbreviate this first date. Though, I must admit, the entire experience was as entrancing as I'm sure he intended it to be. What woman wouldn't be pulled in, to one degree or another? Still, a couple of unwelcome thoughts about being a high priced hooker slithered through my mind before I could banish them."

"That sounds nice,"

"I replied, but the words sounded cold even to my ears. David just smiled and opened the door. As I slid across the rich, soft, black leather my eyes were drawn immediately to a large, beautifully wrapped present on the seat diagonally across from me. My mind was dancing at the possibilities when the door opened and David slid in from the other side. He caught my eyes, immediately noticing where my gaze had been, then smiled even bigger."

"Yes. It's for you."

"I recall the sensations that passed through me at that point being an interesting montage. I was intensely delighted, truly surprised, slightly giddy, and overlaying it all was a thick blanket of suspicion. I barely knew this man. This was a first date, for heaven's sake. He had picked me up in his airplane, flown me to a unique and remote wonderful dinner, had a limo pick us up to take a meandering route back home, (at least I assumed he was planning to take me home) and now there was a large wrapped present on the seat in front of me.

The different sensations competed with one another for a voice, the result of which was a bit of a nondescript croaking sound escaping my lips that might have been the word "I," but finally coalesced into . . ."

"uh—why thank you, but you shouldn't have.

"Well you're welcome. Go ahead and open it."

"My shock and surprise apparently delighted him. I hesitated but finally reached across the seat and began to open the package. As I gently undid the bow and slid the ribbon off the box, I sensed a soft shuffling sound coming from within that made me surmise there was clothing inside. At that point, however, I had the strangest sensation. A thin sliver of fear crept into my mind and seemed to burst into ice chips inside my whole body. The train of thought produced a hesitation of my hands which David noticed."

"What's wrong, Valerie? Go ahead and open it. It's OK."

"At that point I couldn't imagine why I would have such a powerful sense of foreboding over a simple gift, so I forced myself to smile and smoothly continued to open the present. The last piece of meticulously applied tape came free and I slid the cardboard top off. My mouth dropped. It was a full length silver sable fur.

"My first thought was of the price of the thing. Many, many thousands of dollars. The second thought was that I was being bought.

"Somehow I managed to let my intuition be overridden by the rush of the moment. The only thing I can say in my defense is that, much to my surprise, the rest of the evening passed with him being a perfect gentleman."

Jeremy shifted in his seat and quietly poured them both another glass of wine. All she could do was smile and continue.

"In retrospect, I should have known better. Anyone with his wealth and intelligence would know not to make overt moves on a woman you've barely met, yet lavished with gifts. That would be too transparent, or maybe redundant would be a better description.

"Anyway, things did move along, and in many ways he seemed like a wonderful man: a gentleman, a witty conversationalist, and a professed Christian. He flew me out to see my mother and father early on and did a wonderful sales job on my mom. From that point on she was couldn't quit trying to convince me to marry the guy if he asked. Between her, the money, and the man's overt culture and manners, I must admit I was falling into what I would now refer to as his web.

"The first inkling I had that things might not be as they seem was when he finally took me to meet his children. His two sons had a house of their own. They were all smiles when we met, but I sensed some tension in the room and when his oldest son, Brian, had the chance he got me alone."

> *"Valerie, I have to tell you, you seem like such a nice woman and I don't want you to get hurt. My dad is not what he seems."*
>
> *"What? What do you mean, not what he seems?"*
>
> *"He's not the nice guy he portrays to the public. You may not have seen it yet, but you will. I just don't want you to be in a place where you feel stuck when you finally find out who you're really dealing with."*
>
> *"But what do you . . ."*

"That was as far as I got before David appeared, and I would have sworn I caught the slimmest of daggers escape his eyes in the direction of his son before turning to face me. The dagger I thought I'd seen vanished immediately, replaced by his winning smile."

> *"Would you care for a glass of wine, Valerie? I believe I left a few good bottles here the last time I passed through. Maybe they saved one or two."*

"Somehow his innocuous question seemed to have a hidden blade of accusation sliding through it. It sent a light little shiver through me, and when we left his sons' home about forty-five minutes later, I had another speckle of doubt darkening my thoughts.

"More hints seemed to gather as we continued to date, but they were never from him. It was just, a word here, or an anxious look there, or some other intangible I could never quite put my finger on.

Then there was always the allure of the money. Well, it was more than just the money really . . . more like, the lifestyle. As I thought about it, I decided money was to lifestyle what a smile was to happiness, just one element, but it was an intoxicating one, and when my doubts threatened to crescendo, I would tell myself that surely I was falling in love with this man. I nearly had myself convinced.

"It all came to a head when he took me to Jamaica for a romantic getaway and asked me to marry him."

"Really, David, why do you want to marry me?"

"The whole scene was just surreal. We were standing there in this gorgeous hotel room with drinks in our hands and the ocean stretching out below us through a set of panoramic windows. All of a sudden the look on his face was an interesting combination of dumfounded and calculating. Apparently, the dumfounded won, because I got an honest answer from him I don't believe he intended to give."

"So it will be harder for you to leave me. What do you care, anyway? You'll be a millionaire."

"My heart froze. At that point it was my turn to be dumfounded, and in an instant it all came crashing down.

"My mouth must have sagged open as I realized that my initial thought on the very first night had been right on. I was simply being bought. Some sort of a hooker with a golden cage. For some reason I felt afraid to tell him no. I mean there I was in another country with a man I now understood to be someone I didn't know at all. So, with as much gentleness as I could muster in the situation, I told him no. It was then that I finally got a glimpse into the darker side of his personality. Something I'd never seen. He exploded."

"What do you mean, no?"

"No, David. I'm sorry. I don't want to marry you."

"What do you mean you don't want to marry me you crazy bitch!

"At this point he hurled the glass he was holding across the room. It shattered against the wall and I jumped.

"Do you have any idea what you're turning down? You'll never find a man to give you what I can. Do you understand me?"

"I'm beginning to."

"For a brief moment I saw his hand flinch from his side and I thought he was going to hit me. His face flushed and contorted into a mask of anger and frustration. I think I must have held my breath until he whirled and left.

"I just stood there in shock at that beach house, listening to the ocean waves for ten minutes. I couldn't believe it. How could I have been so stupid? How could I have known this guy for months and not seen this side of him? And when I say he left, I mean left— left the room, left the hotel, left the island completely. So, there I was in Jamaica by myself. It was the first time I had ever been out of the country, and now I needed to get myself home. I remember thinking that I had never had such a cacophony of emotions roaring through me at once. I was shocked, crushed, scared, and somewhere overlaying it all, immensely relieved. I felt like a downed deer who had just watched the lion above me turn and walk away.

"It took me a couple of days to get home. I hadn't brought much in the way of money and David took my ticket with him when he left. At least I still had my passport. It was scary to say the least, and having to call my parents to help me only added humiliation to my growing feelings of stupidity.

"When I got back to the states he only waited a day or two before he started calling and emailing me, wanting me back and apologizing profusely. Knowing what I did now, it felt disgusting to have to live through this renewed set of lies.

"As I continued to be steadfast in my refusal to give him another chance, his demeanor turned more and more ugly, and he began to turn his attention to the gifts he had given me: the fur, a small plane, a ring, a tennis bracelet. The list went on, and once he was convinced I wasn't going to change my mind, his calls became increasingly rude and vaguely threatening. I kept thinking he must have to hide in his office or go somewhere to make those calls, because surely he couldn't let anyone on his staff at the clinic or the hospital hear him talking to anyone like that.

"There was a part of me that didn't really want the things he had given me, but there was another part that felt like they were a small price for him to pay for the deceptions he had so deftly foisted on me. I gave him the ring back promptly, but refused to return the other things, and then refused to take his calls. This seemed to send him over the edge. He would call me fifty times in a morning. Seriously, fifty. And when I'd finally answer, his comment was: "Good. I just wanted to make you answer." Then he'd hang up. When this tactic didn't produce results, he sued me. Once I was faced with the prospect of high legal bills or giving him back his stuff, I relented. I negotiated and gave him the plane back and kept some of the other items. It began to be more about getting this loon out of my life and not living in fear."

Valerie stopped there. It was as if she had run out of will to go on with the story rather than run out of story to tell. Her heart was pounding and a miasma of embarrassment hung in the air as she looked up at Jeremy.

Jeremy had sat perfectly still and almost unnaturally quiet through the whole story. There could be no doubt that she had his complete attention. The air-conditioner blowing in the background suddenly seemed loud. The look in his eyes was one of compassion, and it almost made her even more uncomfortable, so she abruptly continued.

"I haven't dated anyone seriously since then, Jeremy. I couldn't begin to tell you whether it's a lingering distrust of the opposite sex or simply me distrusting me. Really, I have tried so hard to be careful who I let into my life, and this shyster fooling me, made me feel so incredibly stupid, I don't know what to do."

~

The light had come on in Jeremy's mind. This explained so much about why their not-quite-relationship had been puttering along. He wasn't sure exactly where he wanted to jump in. There were too many things he wanted to say, and too many emotions flooding through him. He finally decided to go with his gut.

"Anyone can be fooled, Val. I would venture to guess that if you talked long enough to anyone who has had any life experiences at all, you would find a similar story.

It may not be laced with the money that this guy was throwing around or the extent to which he was willing to carry the deception, but the general plot line would be there. It's happened to me too."

This last comment struck a nerve. Her eyes widened ever so slightly, and a look of relief and curiosity flowed across her face. She virtually dove across the couch and into Jeremy's arms. He was so delighted that when she reached a hand up to his neck accidentally touching the back part of his scar, he didn't even feel the pain.

12

September 7th, 2012

Chuck had been fidgeting for days. Uncharacteristically ignoring the beautiful sunset, he drove the windy road up to Mt. Palomar, with his eyes focused on the road and his mind racing. He knew his calculations had been accurate and the KL asteroid, as he had come to call it, should have reappeared from behind the sun three days, fourteen hours and thirty-five minutes ago. He was anxious for the sun to set so he could check the night sky again. Where was his little mystery?

Two hours later, with his eye glued to the lens of Palomar's mightiest eye, he had his answer. Kohler Leporidae had reappeared. Its path had changed. Chuck couldn't believe his eyes. He set the telescope to continue tracking on this new path and went back down to his computer to check these new figures. *It must have been the sun's gravity,* he thought, as he eased back from the computer. There was just enough force to bend the asteroid into a path that curved around the sun, and now it looked as though its new path had a much greater significance.

For now, instead of Kohler Leporidae passing between Mars and Jupiter at the winter solstice, its new path intersected with the Earth's orbit around the sun. A couple of additional calculations on the timing of the asteroid and the blood drained from his face.

Unless something changed again, Earth was on a collision course with a 25 mile wide asteroid.

Chuck could feel his pulse racing faster. He had to check the figures again. Surely he hadn't just discovered the first planet-killer asteroid painting a target on Earth. He had to check his figures again. He had to be sure.

And then he was.

Kohler Leporidae was travelling at roughly 50,000 miles an hour; at that pace, once it passed the sun on its way toward Earth, they had a little over 74 days to stop it. Or else Armageddon was about to be unleashed in truly biblical proportions.

It was 3:00a.m., but for the second time in three months he had phone calls to make that couldn't wait. The first was going to be again to the NASA Sentry program. Someone had to know. Fast.

* * *

Bill Mathers put the receiver down slowly. His hands trembled and his face was pale. He'd been working with the Sentry project now for 10 years. The whole purpose of the program was to identify and track celestial bodies that might impact the Earth, but now, as he thought about it, he realized that he'd never really believed it could happen.

Suddenly, he was facing a different reality, one he truly wasn't prepared for. *Son of a bitch*, he thought.

Bill had known Chuck for at least five years, and in all that time he'd never known Chuck to be mistaken about anything to do with his beloved astronomy. If Chuck said it was a fact, then it was a fact, and Chuck had just told him this new asteroid had shifted course to strike Earth.

Oh my God!

A planet killer!

That's what they called an asteroid of this size. Two quick phone calls generated twenty more and twice that many e-mails. Before the clock had struck another hour the whole world knew. A chunk of rock at least the size of several mountains was hurtling in our direction, and Earth had a bull's-eye painted on it.

The media had picked up the story by the early morning news and millions, if not billions, of viewers were watching the wild headlines:

"Planet Killer Looms in The Evening Sky"

"Mayan Calendar Only Off By Four Years!"

"Planetoid Takes Aim At Earth. Impact Just Months Away!"

Finally some journalistic genius deciphered the asteroid's name,

Kohler Leporidae, recognizing the second part as the scientific name for the class of animals commonly known as rabbits. The Hubble Space Telescope had been repositioned to remain focused on the incoming menace, allowing the world at large to view it on any number of media outlets. Kohler Leporidae was indeed shaped like a crouching rabbit with its ears pinned back. The ensuing headlines were predictable.

"Rabbit's Revenge Streaks Toward Earth."

Unfortunately, that is the title that stuck, in the minds of millions throughout the media, and, to the dismay of the entire scientific community, the common term for this giant asteroid abruptly became, Rabbit's Revenge.

13

September 8th, 2012

"Oh my God!" Valerie exclaimed from down the hall. The tone in her voice garnered Jeremy's attention immediately, much more than the words themselves.

He was in the kitchen making them some breakfast— thinking more about their wonderful evening than what he was doing. He'd told her to make herself comfortable while he handled the meal, and she'd turned on the television.

"What is it?" He called from where he stood at the stove.

"Hurry! You have to come in here and see this. Hurry!"

Jeremy found his legs moving without his conscious thought; her tone was having that effect. Whatever she was watching, it was obviously scaring her.

"What is it, Val? What are you watch . . ." His word trailed off as his eyes landed on the TV screen. The headline looming at the bottom of the screen said it all—

"Planet Killer Aimed At Earth"

Wordlessly, Jeremy moved around the couch and plopped down beside Valerie, whose eyes were glued to the screen. After moments of watching, he turned to look at her, and her mouth was sagging open. It was only then he realized his was too. He closed it with an audible click, returning his attention to the screen. The narrator continued on about the details of the new discovery until he got to the scientific name for the asteroid and the new media moniker; Rabbit's Revenge. Something clicked in the back of his mind. Some little sensation of recognition sparked at the name, but for the life of him Jeremy couldn't place why. He let his mind sink back into the broadcast:

"Scientists are even now being called upon to offer possible solutions to the impending disaster. The President, himself, is slated to address the nation in an hour. Inside sources inform us that his speech will be to calm the populace and solidify the scientific community's resolve to find a solution . . ."

"This can't be happening," Valerie offered in a distant voice, "I can't believe we are listening to them discussing the end of Earth."

Jeremy was having a hard time reconciling the irony of their choice of viewing the evening before with what they were seeing now. In just the space of a few hours, one of the end-of-the-world scenarios that the Discovery channel had been speculating on was now looming before their eyes. It was too bizarre to accept. Jeremy kept waiting for someone to admit to the joke.

At the same moment, Valerie slid closer to him and was now hanging on his arm. He was still trying to take it all in when something the announcer said snagged his attention again.

"This just in. Scientists are now estimating that the Rabbit's Revenge Asteroid should impact the Earth around the third week in December. The exact date can be determined after some more observation. One scientist was quoted . . . "

"The winter solstice," Jeremy muttered, his tone taking on the same far-away sound as Valerie's.

"What?"

"The winter solstice. Just like they said on the Discovery Channel last night. The end of the Mayan calendar is on the winter solstice of 2012. December 21st."

"Yeah but that was four years ago less the three months we have left," Valerie breathed. Her voice had the detached timbre of a man walking to the gallows.

Jeremy just nodded. He felt like he was living some kind of dream. All his life he'd had a tiny feeling deep down inside that he would live to see the end of civilization. He'd never questioned it, and it wasn't something he was fanatic about. Neither was it a feeling he felt the need to share with people, but it had subtly directed many of his pursuits throughout his life; it was one of the reasons he was a pilot, a motorcycle enthusiast, a fisherman and so many other things. He could handle most any machine he might encounter from any type of automobile or truck to a plane, a boat, even a forklift or crane wouldn't slow him down. He also imagined it was at least one of the underlying reasons for his interest in martial arts. If he was forced to only own a single vehicle, it was invariably a four-wheel drive. In his home were books on survival in the wild and encyclopedias on how to *do* most anything. He had a crossbow, a compound bow, a shotgun and a .357 magnum. They were all items he was competent with, but they mostly remained tucked away in the back of a closet. He didn't think much about his choices to accumulate such things, he just enjoyed having them, but at the same time he had casually prepared himself for . . . anything.

Of course if this asteroid really *was* a planet killer, then it didn't matter what he knew, but that was not something Jeremy was willing to accept. Accepting that certainty would mean crawling in a hole and waiting to die, and *that* was something Jeremy simply couldn't do.

As he watched the news broadcasters illuminate the potential consequences of the impact of Rabbit's Revenge, Jeremy began to categorize what would be necessary to maximize his chances of survival—and now Valerie's, too.

"Maybe their calendar just marked the event that represented the beginning of the end, not the end itself," Jeremy heard himself say quietly.

A change in the announcer's tone brought him back to the moment.

"And now I'd like to introduce the man who discovered Rabbit's Revenge, or more appropriately the Kohler Leporidae asteroid and gave Earth the opportunity to save itself from this impending disaster, Doctor Charles Kohler."

The camera panned to the left onto an older looking gentleman with bulging grey eyes and a long, weathered face bearing a mixture of sadness and knowledge. He didn't seem at all excited about being there. When he spoke, however, his voice was deep and rich, immediately commanding attention.

"Jeremy, I know this guy! I met him in D.C. one time. He was trying to lay out the case to some senators for additional funding for space exploration."

"Really. That's a coincidence," he responded absently.

"Man, talk about a genius. This guy has to be the smartest man I've ever met. I got to talk to him briefly, and he can talk on any subject."

"Well, let's listen to him."

"Good evening. I have to say, I'm not particularly glad to be here sharing this information. I spotted this asteroid rather by accident; I was tracking an unreported comet and the Kohler Leporidae asteroid became visible in the tail of an unreported comet I had been tracking. Were it not for that comet I would have completely missed the discovery. This struck me as such an unusual phenomenon that I began tracking the asteroid instead, until it disappeared from view behind our sun two months ago. I made the calculations as to when it would reappear in view and didn't give the experience much more thought. Last night, it reappeared in view three days later than I was expecting. I was sure of my calculations, so I recalculated its path based on its tardiness.

It became apparent that its course changed no doubt due to the sun's gravitational field. Kohler Leporidae is 25 miles across, and is travelling in the neighborhood of 50 thousand miles an hour. If it continues with its current course and speed, it is due to strike Earth on the 21st of December. To say that the devastation caused by such an impact would be catastrophic is like saying that a steamroller rolling over a motorcycle might damage it.

There are some reasons for hope, however. First, as Kohler L. approaches us, it will continue to be exposed to the gravitational field of the sun and that might be enough to shift its course yet again. It's hard to imagine how minute a shift in course would be required to cause this mass to miss us entirely. As to any action we might take, I've already heard the military bantering around the idea of using some sort of a nuclear detonation to destroy it, and there are two problems with that. The first is the fact that if you explode a nuclear device against such a body in space, with no atmosphere to push against, nothing would happen. To accomplish anything the device would have to be planted inside the asteroid, and even if that were accomplished, it would merely split it in two. At that point the asteroid's own gravitation would drag the pieces right back together. The other problem is that if the explosion instead breaks the asteroid into many pieces, there would be an asteroid shower that would strike the Earth rather than a single body.

In the absence of any better alternative, however, this might be our fall-back position because as bad as the devastation of such a shower might be, it should be much less catastrophic than a single massive strike concentrated on one spot. At least the multiple smaller strikes wouldn't be likely to literally change the shape of the Earth or its orbit.

"As a better alternative, I am currently working with NASA to find a means of hitting the asteroid with something involving a continuing propulsion stream; striking the asteroid with an object of that sort should force the asteroid into a new trajectory, thus causing it to miss Earth altogether. My inadvertent finding of Kohler L. this far in advance of a strike allows such an opportunity. One of the biggest difficulties, however, will be finding just the right spot to impact the asteroid to maximize the effect of the propulsion. Delivering this propulsion source to the exact spot is crucial if the proper deflection is to occur.

Any other spot and a portion of the force could be spent pushing the asteroid in a slightly wrong direction. The amount of force necessary to accomplish this is going to be tremendous and will tax our abilities to deliver to the asteroid, therefore we must be accurate.

This is the path to which I intend to devote all my efforts. I am sorry to have to be the bearer of such bad news. Thank you."

And with no more fanfare he turned and walked off camera. The action apparently took the television crew by surprise, and there was an awkward moment of hesitation before the picture jumped back to the announcer who was visibly pale. His demeanor was almost more frightening than Dr. Kohler's words.

* * *

David punched the button on the remote to turn off the TV that stretched across half of his den wall. "Bullshit," he muttered, "What crap will they come up with next to frighten the public?" He glanced at the woman beside him in bed. She'd been pretty fun . . . as far as stupid sluts go. He didn't have much respect for women, certainly not those that he picked up in some high-dollar bar. He was in a foul mood and had a horrible urge to throw the remote but managed to resist it. He'd had to replace enough of those already, and it was getting annoying.

Surprisingly, it wasn't the news on the television that had him upset, but the news from his private investigator. Apparently, he had followed Valerie over to that man's house last night. What was his name? Jeremy something?

Who gave a shit what the little prick's name was anyway? But if she did screw the guy (and he really had no reason to doubt his PI), it was the first time she'd spent the night with a man since moving here from Kansas City. Or at least he was pretty sure it was. He had only been having her followed continuously for the last few months. Before that, his attempts had been pretty hit or miss. At the very least this was the first one he knew about, and he didn't like it. If the bitch wouldn't marry him, he was going to see to it that she never had anyone.

David glanced at his watch, and ran his fingers through his thick dark hair. His shift at the clinic began in forty-five minutes. He looked over at the blonde beauty beside him in the bed.

"Hey," he said, "Good morning." His tone conveyed a bare modicum of warmth to it and even that was a major effort.

"I've got to get to work, but I called a cab for you."

The girl's eyes were just beginning to focus while she stretched luxuriously. "Ah, David. I thought we were going to get to play some more today."

"Nope. I've got too much to do. The cab will be here in about fifteen minutes so you better get dressed."

A look of disgust blossomed on the girl's face. "Fine," she said as she threw back the sheet.

David gave her no more thought as he headed for the shower.

He still had some plans to make regarding Valerie, specifically what he was going to do with his new information and when.

* * *

Chuck strolled slowly out of the television station building, still thinking about the news he had just delivered to the world. He felt guilty, as if his discovery of the asteroid was somehow the cause of the world's problem

95

rather than the forewarning it needed to save itself.

If that was even possible.

He slowly and deliberately rehashed through the information. The asteroid couldn't be vaporized; splitting it wouldn't work; blasting it into smaller pieces would still produce a certain amount of catastrophe that could be just as bad in the long run. So that only left deflection. But how? Without any rotation, how was he to measure the mass and the distribution of that mass from a speeding asteroid? Without mass calculations, how could he determine the amount of force needed to deflect it, and how could he determine just where to place it even if he could get it there in time?

Ideas and possibilities danced through his mind as he posed the questions to himself. He was so engrossed in his train of thought that he barely noticed his route of travel until he was two-thirds of the way back to the observatory. Going home never even crossed his mind. He had a lot of work to do, and a finite amount of time to do it. If there was a way to solve this problem, he was going to find it. His motivation was more connected to his unwarranted sensation of guilt than his concern about dying. Or maybe it was just the simple reason that this was a challenge, and since he had been confronted with it, he was going to solve it, no matter what it took.

There was a vague hint of a smile as he closed the door to his Jeep, and an air of determination in his stride.

If anyone on the planet could solve the problem, it was Chuck.

14

September 25ᵗʰ, 2016

Since that night a couple of weeks ago when Valerie had stayed with him, they had barely separated. The stories of Rabbit's Revenge droned on and on talking of the impending doom of the planet and the international scientific community's various attempts to determine a course of action to prevent it.

For Jeremy, however, each passing day left him feeling more and more certain he was missing something. It was just a nagging little sensation that lingered like an itch on the back of his neck. With Valerie now firmly implanted in his life, it was a wonder he even thought about it at all, but during his quiet moments and when he awoke in the mornings or even during his more intense workouts, the sensation crept back up on him. It seemed to center around the experience of having his life pass before his eyes, but beyond that it was just nebulous.

And annoying.

* * *

With a gasp, Jeremy sat upright in bed, scaring Valerie awake.

"Oh my gosh!" he exclaimed.

"What?"

"I have it," he said.

"Have what?" she answered, her voice still thick with sleep.

"The answer to what it was I saw that day at the lake when I got my scar." Jeremy didn't like to refer to his 'scar.' It reminded him that his stupidity had left him with a mark for life.

Valerie's eyes widened as she sat up in bed, too. "What do you mean, 'what you saw'? You saw your life flash before your eyes. You told me so."

"Yeah. Right up till the very end, when I saw something that never was part of my life—until now. Remember?"

Valerie's change in position caused the covers to fall from her breasts. The sight distracted Jeremy, but only for a second. "What *are* you talking about?" She asked.

"The boulder and the pebble, Valerie. Remember I told you about the boulder and the pebble I saw right before I popped to the surface? I decided the pebble was maybe a bullet."

Jeremy turned to look at her in time to see the light come on in her eyes.

"Oh yeah. I remember now. What's so important about that?"

"Come on. Let's go turn on the TV. I want to double check something while it's still fresh in my memory."

Valerie slipped on some sweats and a T-shirt while Jeremy glided out of the room. "Slow down. I'm coming."

When she walked in Jeremy already had the TV on, tuned to one of the broadcasts about the Rabbit's Revenge asteroid. "That *is* it. Damn, that's unbelievable."

"What's unbelievable?" She asked as she plopped down on the couch next to him and crossed her legs.

On the screen a news reporter was interviewing a scientist from the Kohler Leporidae Summit's group of scientists, discussing the latest theory on how best to avert the upcoming disaster:

~

"Really, the only viable alternative is to send a missile up there to act as a thruster to effect a change of its trajectory. Any other option either won't work or will cause us a whole different set of problems. The problem is deciding what to send up there and where to place it, but we have to make the decision in the next two weeks if we are going to have any chance of it working."

Valerie's eyes were glued to the set, her question nearly forgotten.

She and Jeremy hadn't been watching any TV of late. It was amazing that anyone could get complacent about the impending end of the world, but this had been the main topic on virtually all the media venues for the last couple of weeks. Even something as permanent as dying was susceptible to a modicum of desensitization when you were constantly inundated with it.

"That, Valerie. That is what I saw. The boulder in my vision that day was the Rabbit's Revenge asteroid. And the pebble was . . . " His voice trailed off as his mind raced ahead. His next words were a nearly inaudible murmur, "I don't remember where the pebble struck."

Valerie was finally catching up. "You're saying that the image you saw that day was this asteroid? That's impossible."

Jeremy turned to face her. "Is it? Come on, me surviving that day was impossible." Silence hung between them for a moment as they both stared again at the TV broadcast.

"Not only that, but I think the pebble I saw was the missile or whatever we need to send up there to change its course. What if I saw the necessary point of impact?"

"You have to be kidding me. You don't really believe that, do you?"

He turned back to her. "Actually, I think I do. Why else would I have had a glimpse of something so random if it wasn't for a reason?"

"So, you think you can tell them where to aim the thing?"

"Like I said—I can't remember that part. As a matter of fact the more I think about it, the more I realize that the whole experience from the time I was yanked out of the boat is becoming increasingly fuzzy. Do you know I never felt that rope loop around my neck? And you know I have no recollection of taking it off my neck when I popped to the surface either, but I must have. The whole incident including my life flashing before my eyes and the RR vision all took place in a few seconds

"RR vision?" She smiled and paused. "Well then, what good is it? If you don't know the spot, then what good was having the vision?"

Jeremy considered for a moment. "I have to see it again, Valerie. I have to have that vision again so I can see the exact spot to tell them."

Valerie just stared at him.

She was caught between astonished and incredulous. "What are you saying? That you need to *try* to have a near-death experience again?"

The sarcasm in her voice was completely lost on him as he answered, "That's exactly what I'm thinking."

"You can't do that! You can't go try to kill yourself so you can see the vision again. It's called *near-death* for a reason. What if you succeed in doing it? There's no guarantee you'd survive the experience, and then what would you have accomplished?"

"If I don't try, there's no guarantee any of us are going to be around for Christmas," he answered deliberately.

Valerie was silent for a moment. "How can you do this, Jeremy? If you know you're trying to have a near-death experience, but you don't actually intend to commit suicide, then you'll know it's not really a near-death experience. Right? Won't that defeat the whole purpose?"

"I don't know. It might. But I'm going to find a way to try."

* * *

It had been an effort to tear herself away from Jeremy's house, but she had a meeting with Congressman Levin this afternoon, and she had to get prepared. Even though it was Saturday, Congressman Levin said this was the only time he had free. Part of her thought it was ludicrous— not the meeting on Saturday part, but the part about doing anything that seemed remotely normal with a planet-killer asteroid heading toward Earth. Still, chasing normalcy was a way to pretend that the world wasn't really about to end, and in that sense, routines were the perfect catharsis.

Jeremy was scaring her. Now that she had admitted to herself how much she cared for him, his new idea of intentionally pursuing another near-death experience to try to see a glimpse of that asteroid was frightening in the extreme. But was it useless? Is that really what he saw in the lake that afternoon, trailing after images of his life passing before him? He certainly believed it, and she believed in him, so maybe that was enough. But what was he hoping to see anyway? What information was there to gain from that vision that would do the world any good? Nobody had confirmed anything about sending something up in space to move the asteroid, much less needing some location. So far it was just speculation. She wondered if Jeremy had even asked himself that question, or if he was simply too taken with the idea of verifying that the asteroid was what he saw that day. Maybe she could ask him that question at least.

The traffic on 620 distracted her as she passed over the bridge beside the dam. It forced her to slow down, and that gave her a moment to look around, an opportunity she seldom got when she crossed the bridge. It was such a beautiful setting. One of millions, she thought, that made up planet Earth. Ever since the announcement of Kohler Leporidae, Valerie had been noticing what a beautiful world it was. Surely it wasn't about to end in three more months.

Focus. She had to focus. As the days moved on and the media coverage of the asteroid intensified, Valerie was finding it increasingly difficult to wrangle her thoughts into any cohesive order. Right now she should be thinking about her meeting with Congressman Levin, but her thoughts kept floating back to either Jeremy or the impending disaster, both of which seemed tremendously more important than any simple work issue.

The traffic picked back up, as she picked up the phone to call Jeremy.

"Long time no talk," Jeremy said.

"Ha, ha. Jeremy, I'm afraid for you to do this," She could hear the tension in her own voice.

"Do what? You mean a little thing like a near-death experience? I do it all the time."

Suddenly, she found his cavalier attitude annoying. "No. You take chances all the time, and that's bad enough. You don't intentionally try to get yourself killed."

"Nearly killed," he corrected, "Getting myself *actually* killed would defeat the purpose."

"That's a good point. What exactly *is* the purpose?"

"To see the asteroid again; I told you that already."

"Yeah, but why?"

There was a silence on the phone, and she knew she'd hit her mark. His next words were much more tentative.

"I don't really know for sure, Val. I just know that it's important somehow."

"You're going to try to kill yourself, okay nearly kill yourself, and you're not even sure what the purpose is? Doesn't this logic sound a bit off to you?"

"Haven't you ever done anything in your life that you knew was important, but at the time you did it you weren't sure why it was important?"

Now it was her turn to pause. Hadn't she just gone through doing this same thing with him? She didn't need to tell him the story about David. She could have opened up to him without the necessity of that admission. Couldn't she? But it had been important, though she wasn't sure why.

"I think we usually find out later why those things are important, but we don't know that when we make the decision," Jeremy said.

"That's not too comforting in this situation," she said. In the ensuing silence she would have sworn that Jeremy was smiling at her. "Are you grinning?" She asked with just a touch of annoyance.

"As a matter of fact, I am."

"Why?"

"I'm finding your concern rather touching and more to the point, I'm liking the fact that you're showing it. It's still a bit of a new sensation for me."

"Very funny. But seriously, please don't do anything stupid," She paused, "I'm not ready to lose you, yet."

"I wish I could tell you I'll be careful, but I can't. If it makes any difference though, I now have an even better reason not to die."

Valerie pointedly ignored his reference to them, leaping instead on a point of intuition. "You already have an idea in mind don't you?"

"Maybe."

"OK. Don't tell me about it until afterwards. I'll talk to you later."

She got off the phone rather abruptly, not too surprised to find that she was angry. Her thoughts churned:

Why was she angry? Because Jeremy was taking chances with his life? Yes. Dammit! She had meant what she said. She'd finally decided to open up to someone who was about to go flirt with suicide. Great. At least maybe there is a good reason. If saving the planet wasn't good enough, then she guessed maybe her selfishness had just gone off the scale.

15

Chuck sat back in his chair. Notepad scribbles, pencils, and calculators littered the space in front of him. Why wasn't that damn asteroid spinning? He kept focusing on that puzzle. But the "why" didn't really matter at this point. The real question was how he would ever get the data he needed if he couldn't accurately calculate its mass? Without rotation he couldn't calculate mass, unless he could somehow view the back side? Maybe orbit the asteroid first with the correct equipment to read its shape and composition? Without that data, there were just too many assumptions, and the chances for success went down exponentially with each one. For instance, regardless of what material the asteroid was made of, could its composition remain homogenous across the entire body? And without knowing the composition, how do you determine how much thrust would be needed and where to apply it?

They were only going to get one shot at this, so he had to get it right. Somehow.

NASA had been in constant contact with him. They were launching a space shuttle next week. The cargo bay area was going to be loaded to the gills with fuel. It would have all the thrust potential they could possibly provide, but they still needed to figure out how much to use and where to plant the shuttle when it came time later. Remote guidance wasn't a problem; they could adjust its path along the way as their data improved. Right now they had to get the shuttle enroute, or they would miss the opportunity to even try. As he considered this scenario, it occurred to him they might be better off taking out some of the fuel and adding a bit more sensing equipment. But if they were going to orbit the asteroid, there would be a point in time when their communication would be cut off by the asteroid itself. And since they didn't know what the back side of the thing looked like, they couldn't preprogram it to an orbit. Someone was going to have to go.

Chuck reached for the phone. NASA had been doing their own calculations and keeping him abreast of developments. He, in return, was offering anything he came up with. And this was urgent. The plans had to be changed. Launch was scheduled for five days from now, and there were a lot of alterations and recalculations to consider if the shuttle was going to carry a person and more sensing equipment. He'd call Bill Mathers again. Bill would put him through to the right people. *Jesus*, he thought, *how many other details are we forgetting?*

"Bill, this is Chuck again."

"Hi Chuck. What's up?"

Nobody thought of Chuck as much of a people person, but his observational skills didn't stop with inanimate objects. He could hear the tension in Bill's voice clearly.

"I've been doing some thinking Bill, and we're going to have to reconfigure the shuttle." There was silence on the line while Chuck explained.

"Damn, Chuck. That's a lot of recalculating to be done in such a short space of time, not to mention finding and preparing someone to be the pilot."

"I know, Bill. I don't see any other way though. If someone has a better idea, I'd be glad to listen to it."

16

Jeremy *did* already have an idea. There was a little skydiving place up north of town, not too far off I-35, and he didn't feel like waiting. He had a much newer parachute than the one he'd used in his aborted parasailing attempt that day, so he grabbed it and made for the door. No time like the present. Valerie's words haunted him though. What did he hope to accomplish? There was no way of knowing. He only knew that this was something he had to do. Ten minutes later he was pulling out of his driveway.

Jeremy smiled when he saw the sign: Central Texas Skydiving. He hadn't been here in quite a while, and he loved the feel of the place. A Cessna 182 was taking off as he drove up. How many jumps had he made out of one of those? Usually it had been with three other people planning to do what they called RW, Relative Work, where you and some others practice falling together and changing formations relative to each other. Non-skydivers thought of this as making a "star," but that was only one formation. There were many more, and it was tremendous fun going from one to the other in freefall.

The sky was a clear blue with only a few puffy clouds to break up the solid azure. The breeze was light and steady out of the south; all in all, a perfect day for skydiving.

"Hey, Jeremy," Jeff Sanders called as Jeremy parked the truck. Jeff ran the drop zone and had been the one to train Jeremy. Now Jeremy called him a friend.

"Hi, Jeff. How's it going today? Got any space?"

"The manifest is pretty full on all the planes, but we can fit you in. This end of the world stuff has got everyone wanting to jump. I have two classes running every day on weekends. Are you looking for a 182 load or something bigger?"

"Actually, I was looking for a solo today, maybe something on a bigger load where they already have the folks for their formation." Jeff gave Jeremy a quizzical look.

"Solo, huh? OK, I think we might be able to arrange that. I'll be right back." Jeff paused and glanced back, his eyes focusing on Jeremy's neck. "Dude. What the hell did you do to your neck?"

"It's a long story, Jeff. I'll tell you over a beer after the jump."

Jeremy was feeling kind of guilty. He knew that what he had in mind would put a strain on his friendship with Jeff, but he wasn't about to begin trying to explain it. And he was pretty sure Jeff wouldn't be interested in that beer afterwards.

"Yep, we have a Beech 18 load going up in about 20 minutes. They have a 12 man team, but there's room in the plane for one more. They'll be going up to twelve-five instead of 7,500 feet though. Does that work for you?"

"Perfectly, Jeff. Thanks." Jeremy's guilt waxed under Jeff's persistent curious stare.

"You going for a relaxing free fall, or you going to hop and pop and have a nice long canopy ride? It's a great day for a canopy ride."

"I haven't decided yet," he lied, "I just need to clear my head." Fill his head was more like what he had in mind, hopefully with a particular vision.

"Cool, man. Well, I'll let you suit up and check your gear. I have to go check on that class. Sometimes these newbies give me the willies."

Yeah, us old timers can too, Jeremy thought, turning back toward his car. He glanced up in time to see a rainbow of parachutes sprout in the sky. The old Beech 18 twin engine tail-dragger had just loosed a load, and since he hadn't been watching, he hadn't had a chance to see what formation they tried, just a star most likely, but it was hard to miss twelve parachutes converging on the same place.

He watched the chutes glide back and forth for a moment while he reminisced. Rectangular chutes had come into service about thirty years ago and quickly replaced the older round ones. They were much more maneuverable, had a greater forward speed, which was a big plus in stronger winds, and if flared properly, could set someone down on sharp gravel, barefoot without so much as a scratch. They were also available in a variety of sizes for different uses: five cells for lighter people, seven for the average male and nine for the tandem jumpers.

It had been many months since Jeremy had jumped, and even though what he was planning had nothing to do with fun, the thrill of it tickled him. He had no idea how this was all going to work, but he knew what he was going to try, and just that was enough to send a little lance of fear through him. He really wasn't ready to die, especially now that the possibilities with Valerie were blossoming.

He pulled his rig from the back of the car. It was hunter green and black, and looked like it was all straps and cords. Both parachutes were mounted on his back, one beneath the other, and it went on like a back-pack, except for the straps that went under his legs and across his chest. He'd repacked the main chute recently, and the reserve was still cur-rent. Reserve chutes were required to be repacked every ninety days by a licensed packer and inspected. Jeremy had had his repacked sixty days ago.

Hauling his gear closer to the landing target, parachute rig slung over one shoulder and helmet in hand, he had nothing else to do until it was time for his load. He probably had a forty-five minute wait or so even though Jeff had put him on the manifest right away. Waiting at a drop zone, though, was just plain fun. He had no sooner sat down when a brilliant orange and black seven cell swooped in, and the jumper touched his foot down on the three-inch flat rubber bulls-eye in the middle of a ten-foot circle of pea gravel.

"Nice," Jeremy said. He didn't really want to attract too much atten-tion today, but when another skydiver nailed a bulls-eye right in front of him, it was hard to keep his mouth shut.

"Thanks, man," the guy replied even as he twisted to begin hauling in the parachute that had floated past him. On a windy day, a very fast ver-sion of this maneuver was a necessity if a jumper didn't want his chute to re-inflate in front of him and start dragging him face first.

Jeremy was afraid the guy would come over to talk, but he seemed to be in a rush to get packed and back on the manifest, which he couldn't do until his chute was repacked. It was just as well. Fear was beginning to raise its ugly head as Jeremy continued to contemplate what he was going to try. He just hoped it worked, in more ways than one.

The moments passed quickly while Jeremy watched the other

skydivers and remained, unlike his typical demeanor, conspicuously quiet. When they finally called his load, he donned his jumpsuit, which went on like overalls, pulled the chute over his shoulders and cinched up the straps. His goggles hung from his neck and he carried his helmet as he walked toward the plane.

The starboard side engine on the big old Beechcraft was shut down while the jumpers loaded, but the other one still rumbled loudly. The characteristic sound of the huge rotary engine was a comforting memory. Jeremy had jumped many times from this old plane or another just like it, and the memories greeted him as he followed the other jumpers into its hollow, metal belly. He got an odd look from a couple of them. He could guess what they were thinking.

One jumper with a skull and cross-bones painted on his helmet in a glow-in-the-dark orange finally asked.

"Hey man, you're not with our formation are you? I thought we just had twelve."

No one really wanted 13 on their jump formation. It was hard to get away from superstition completely. Jeremy couldn't help but chuckle at the thought, given what he had in mind. They would *really* see that as a bad omen.

"No, I'm just going up for a solo."

"Oh cool. It's a great day for a canopy ride."

Everyone kept assuming that he was planning a long canopy ride since he was going by himself, which was fine with him.

"Yeah," he said, smiling half-heartedly as he made his way toward the back. He wanted the other formation out and gone before he made his jump, and positioning himself at the rear of the aircraft would pretty much assure that without words.

A few moments later Jeremy heard and felt the other engine firing up. The deep throaty radial engine sent tremors through the entire aircraft. It finally settled into a steady rhythm and the oversized front wheels began to roll. There was no taxiway, and the runway was made of hard-packed earth and grass, so the slow roll to the far end of it was more than just a little jarring, especially being in the rear. Jeremy hardly noticed.

He was busy going over details in his mind. Not only was he

concerned about trying this stupid idea, but in the event it worked, he was concerned about remembering what he saw this time. He had to try to remember everything he saw.

At the far end of the runway the pilot swung the tail around in a quick sweeping circle, causing even more air to swoosh into the big oval doorway just behind the cockpit. There were a few moments of hesitation while the pilot checked instruments with the big engines idling, then another brief hesitation while he checked engine gauges with the engines wound up. The bass roar from the engines wound up to deafening levels as the pilot shoved the throttles to their stops, and they quickly began to move down the bumpy turf. The ride smoothed out for Jeremy as the pilot lifted the tail wheel off the ground. The front half of the aircraft shook for a few seconds longer until the pilot lifted the big old bird's main gear off the turf as well. Their speed promptly increased as the vibrations faded. They were airborne. The pilot hauled back on the yoke and the vintage Beechcraft clawed its way into the sky.

The other jumpers were busy checking each other's gear for the first few minutes of the climb. Almost no one tried to talk over the roar of the engines and the wind noise blasting through the open door. Many of the smaller planes had doors that remained closed then opened in flight, but not the Beech 18. As they neared their jump altitude, the jumpers gradually became still in anticipation. This suited Jeremy just fine. His trepidation over his intended action was mushrooming. Skydiving itself was plenty exciting, but he was planning a little deviation to enhance the danger, so it bordered on down-right petrifying. Jeremy could feel a nervous sweat forming on his forehead. It was cool in the plane, but in another moment, he would have beads of sweat trickling down his cheek. Fortunately, the other jumpers were too preoccupied with their own thoughts to notice him. Even if they did, a nervous sweat wasn't exactly unusual on a jump plane, even with the blast of air coming through the open door. Jeremy felt the plane begin to level off before he heard the engines take on a lower pitch. The pilot must be lining up for the jump run.

At a signal he didn't see, the twelve jumpers ahead of him began to crowd up toward the door. They had compressed themselves into a pretty tight bunch by the time the pilot hauled the power back.

They were over the drop zone. Even though Jeremy had seen the sight a hundred times, he watched in fascination as the last jumper, on a shout from the lead one, pushed the compact group toward the open door. The first guy fell out backwards intentionally, so he could keep his eyes on the fellow jumpers behind him as they left the plane. They were all gone in a whoosh, and he felt the plane jump up abruptly at the sudden loss of weight. A second later and the pilot was banking sharply and adding power back to the engines. He would make a tight circle back to the jump run trying to conserve as much fuel as possible, while lining up for Jeremy.

During the bank, Jeremy watched the jumpers fall away and immediately gravitate back toward each other as they maneuvered their bodies, coaxing the relative wind to direct them back to their companions. This particular group was good. They had nearly assembled into a basic circle or "star" formation even before the pilot completed the bank.

Jeremy leaned back against the bare metal wall and considered again what was coming. How was this going to work? He had a sneaking suspicion it wasn't, but that wasn't going to stop him from trying.

The pilot had leveled and slowed again, and Jeremy could tell he was about to cut the engines. It was almost time to go. When the pilot actually did cut the power, Jeremy froze for a second in a quandary of indecision, but only for a second. He crouch-walked carefully up to the open door. The hole into space seemed like the great maw of a whale preparing to swallow him. He wasn't sure if he had ever been so terrified as he grabbed the sides of the door and hesitated another second with the wind blasting his face.

"You have to go now, or you'll never make it back the drop zone," the pilot yelled from the cockpit.

The unexpected voice over the wind jarred Jeremy into action. He looked up at the pilot, smiled along with a thumbs-up gesture, and dove through the hole. Tumbling for perhaps 500 feet he waited until the increasing velocity reacted to his arched back position which finally delivered him into a belly-to-the-earth, stable fall. He now had an extraordinary view of the world below him.

The last of the parachutes from the previous jumpers was just touching down and the world spread beneath him like a gigantic map.

Within a hundred feet he had reached what jumpers call terminal velocity, 120 miles an hour, and the wind blasting against his goggles gave him the sensation of floating rather than falling. Free falling never felt like falling actually, unless he passed by something to compare his velocity to— like a small cloud. Even when he had another person next to him pull their ripcord, the sensation was of them going *up* suddenly in relation to you, not that they were suddenly slowing down.

Jeremy looked down at the altimeter hooked to his chest, its dial unwinding quickly. His rate of fall was roughly 1,000 feet every five seconds making his normal freefall from 12,500 feet about a minute, but it was a long minute, and today he was going to stretch that minute to the limit. For safety's sake, jumpers normally pull their ripcord at 3,000 feet allowing them not only time to slow down, but also giving them a margin of error to deploy a reserve parachute should it become necessary. This was a precaution Jeremy intended to ignore today.

Seven thousand feet. He had been falling for a little over twenty-five seconds, his thoughts floating through the memory, the boat, the beer, the sensation of water rushing over his head.

Five thousand feet. He could see the people on the ground with their parachutes stretched out, repacking, loading into the next jump plane, even looking up at him. There were a few cars moving out of the parking lot.

Four thousand feet. A few wispy clouds floated around at this altitude. Little puffs of cotton he was supposed to avoid, but that reminded him of the speed of his descent.

Three thousand feet. He was now at normal pull altitude and his gaze shifted to the ground which now seemed to be rushing up at him. He swiveled his eyes around to look at the people. Many were now staring up at him intently. The vision should start any second now if he was going to have a chance to see anything. He was fifteen seconds from impact with the ground.

Two thousand feet. He rigidly held his arched position. He would have sworn he could see concern on the faces of those looking up at him. He even imagined them yelling at him to pull his ripcord; of course he couldn't hear anything but the wind. No vision yet. Dammit!

Twelve hundred feet. He was out of time. No vision and no time to see it even if it arrived. He moved his right hand quickly into his body and yanked the ripcord, praying he hadn't waited too long and that the parachute's deployment wouldn't make an unexpected hesitation.

The sudden impact of the chute opening felt welcome, but he had little time to consider it. It would still take another few seconds to get completely slowed down, and he barely had the time. He bent his knees, reached up for the toggles to flare the chute to stop his forward speed, if he even had time to do that before landing. This was going to hurt.

He was a hundred yards from the center of the drop zone when he hit the ground, the jolt rattling his entire skeleton, and immediately rolled at an angle to his side, letting the remaining velocity transfer as smoothly as possible into motion across the ground. His thick cushioned soles and his near perfect roll probably saved him from at least one broken bone. He rolled smoothly back to his feet and was already hauling in lines. The breeze was stiff, and he didn't want it to re-inflate his chute and drag him. As he pulled it swiftly to him, he saw from the corner of his eye several people running in his direction. *Damn*, he thought, *this isn't going to be any fun trying to explain, and to make it worse, it was for nothing.*

He didn't even have his whole chute in his hands when the first person reached him. Unsurprisingly, it was Jeff and he was yelling as he approached.

"What the hell do you think you were doing man? Are you crazy? I don't need any psycho's committing suicide at my drop zone. What the hell were you thinking?"

"I'll explain it to you in a minute Jeff. I'm sorry."

"Hey man, are you all right? That was way too close. What happened?" This voice was from another jumper that Jeremy barely recognized. It certainly wasn't anyone he felt he owed an explanation to, so he just kept walking with his double armload of bunched up parachute. Jeremy could feel Jeff still fuming, but for the moment he just walked beside him in silence.

No vision. That was all Jeremy could think about. There had been no vision. He was just a few seconds from death, but he hadn't seen a thing? Disappointment turned to deep frustration as he marched back toward the hangar. It was then he realized . . . he hadn't thought he was going to die.

Maybe that was the problem. Even though he had pushed it to the limit, a part of him had never really believed that he was going to die. He believed his chute would open, and he knew that he would pull before he hit the ground. Maybe there was a chance his chute would hesitate or not open, but he didn't really believe it. Maybe the problem was the control. He'd have to try something with an element that was beyond his control.

"So, are you going to explain to me why you were trying to give my drop zone a bad name or what?"

Jeff was still in lockstep beside him, and while Jeremy had been analyzing his failure, Jeff had continued fuming. Jeremy tried to imagine himself speaking the words to explain what he was attempting, but all he could think of was the incredulous look Jeff would give him. Still, he had to tell him something.

"Jeff, I'm really sorry. I guess I just zoned out. I was enjoying the freefall so much that I started thinking about all the jumps I'd done, and I guess I just forgot to keep an eye on my altimeter." Jeremy tried to give Jeff his best contrite look as he finished, but all he could see from Jeff was anger and disbelief.

"Just forgot to look at your altimeter? Seven hundred plus jumps and you forgot to look at your altimeter? You have to be kidding me. Look, Jeremy, I don't know what really happened up there, but I hope you weren't planning to jump again today because that just isn't happening."

"That's fine, Jeff. I completely understand, and I don't really want to jump again anyway. And once again, I'm really sorry I scared everyone."

Jeremy could see that Jeff wanted to say more, but there really wasn't anything else to say.

As they approached the trailer at the center of the drop zone, more people drifted over to Jeremy, a few asking what had happened, a few more asking if he was all right, and a few just staring. Jeremy ignored them all and did something skydivers typically never do. He simply carried his unpacked chute back to his truck and threw it into the back without any thought of repacking it. The action produced a few more murmurs from the crowd behind him, but Jeremy ignored them too as he jumped in the front seat and fired up the truck.

* * *

"Skydiving! What do you mean he was skydiving?" David listened to the telephone for another few minutes, the scowl twisting on his face. "He did what? Is this guy suicidal or something?" The murmur in his ear was low and steady.

"So she's not with him? Hmmm . . . Well, she will be, and I don't care what he does, you stay on him and keep me informed." He slammed down the phone without so much as a goodbye.

When it came to Valerie, David had a very difficult time keeping his temper. She was the first person to ever reject him, and it only made it worse that he actually cared for her, which was also a first. Usually, he was in perfect control of both his emotions and his expression. With Valerie, he just couldn't. The first woman he couldn't buy would be more accurate, but that was not a fact he was willing to admit, even to himself, assuming the thought had ever even occurred to him.

The image of her face when she refused him in Jamaica still burned in his memory. That was a mistake she was going to pay for, and he couldn't think of any better way to make her suffer than to take something from her that she desperately wanted just like she had done to him, but not too soon. It was important that she become very involved with this man. He actually hoped she was falling in love with him. As much as the idea galled him, it was an important part of his plan.

It had only been a week since he had wandered down to 6th Street and hung around until the wee hours of the morning, following the instructions of some guy his PI had recommended. He hoped his shabby clothes, hat, and fake facial hair were sufficient to disguise him. He couldn't afford to be associated with the business he was initiating. It could destroy his career. It *had* crossed his mind to accomplish this transaction through an intermediary, but after thinking it through, he finally decided that having someone else know what he was doing was riskier than doing it himself. This person would never know his name or hopefully anything about him. Everything would be handled with cash, and he would only contact this person through the disposable prepaid cell phone that he had purchased for the purpose.

David was feeling particularly jittery sitting there in that sleazy strip bar and jumped slightly when he was tapped on the shoulder.

"Are you John Johnson?" He heard a gruff voice ask even before he could turn his head. He'd wanted to use John Smith but it sounded too cliché even for these circumstances. Besides, with this little variation the guy might actually believe it was his real name.

"Yes. I'm John Johnson," he said, trying to add a little gravel to his voice and lower it at the same time. David was a bit taken aback by the man's appearance. He was a big man, easily 6' 3", and built like a tank. He wore dark green cargo pants, some kind of a tight black shirt, and some sort of military-looking jacket covered with pockets. His hair was brown, long, scraggly, and he had an unkempt beard. In addition, he had an odor of dirt, sweat, and something else nasty that David couldn't place wafting off him. The smell caused David to lean further back even more than the man's imposing size.

Being a doctor made David unusually sensitive to personal hygiene, and the combination of this man's smell, his size and the fact that David was unused to this type of skullduggery made him extremely uncomfortable. He realized he had been staring when the man spoke next.

"My friend told me you might want to do some business," he said, his voice seeming to go even lower and more ominous than before. "Let's go for a walk."

David reluctantly followed the man's slow gait out of the bar, feeling more vulnerable by the second.

"Uh, yes. You must be Cecil." David was certain that wasn't this man's real name either, but it didn't matter. He was much more concerned that his voice didn't sound as scared as he felt.

"Yeah, that's right. Let's get a little further away from people, and you can tell me what it was you wanted."

The idea of getting away from other people while in the company of this monster was the last thing David wanted to do, but he assumed it was necessary. The man walked a few paces away from the bar and took a step around a corner to a narrow alley between two buildings. There he turned, leaned against the wall, and simply stared at David. When David remained quiet, the man who called himself Cecil said, "Well?"

David nearly jumped but then answered, "Umm, I need to have

someone uh . . . taken out." Actually, saying the words out loud seemed dramatically more incriminating than merely thinking or planning them. David could feel his pulse accelerating further. How dangerous was it to even be talking with a man who did this for a living?

"You do, huh? Do you need it to look like an accident?"

"Uh, no, not really. Actually, a gun would be fine."

"Did Grant tell you what I charge?"

From there the conversation ranged off into directions that were so bewildering to David that he almost changed his mind. But not quite.

The entire interaction had taken less than five minutes and ended with David parting with five thousand in cash and leaving the 6th street area wondering if he was being stupid. But it didn't matter. If this deal didn't work, he'd find another. The money didn't mean anything. The only thing that was important was that one way or another, this Jeremy guy was going to die, and he was going to find a way to be there when Valerie found out about it.

17

September 28th, 2016

It was five in the morning and Chuck was pacing the floor at the Observatory. There were just too many things that could go wrong and too little he could do to prevent them. First, he still didn't know the mass of the damn asteroid, so it was going to require a pilot. Second, there was the issue of how to deliver the shuttle's thrust down to the surface without crashing it and losing the ability to utilize that thrust. Then there were the little things like how much was enough. Was there such a thing as too much thrust in this instance? Could they even deliver enough thrust to the asteroid to move it in time? And how much time was that?

Without knowing the mass, he couldn't calculate the thrust or the duration needed to accomplish the course change. From an engineering point of view, it was an impossible nightmare. Without the data he couldn't affect calculations and without calculations the best he could do was give the thing a push and pray. *Great. And oh, by the way, the fate of the world is riding on your best guess.* His pacing accelerated.

Chuck had already made two suggestions that were being acted on, but no matter what good ideas he had, he still remained plagued by all the details that were unknown, and at this point, unknowable. Chuck's stomach churned, and his headache was returning. The amount of sleep he'd been getting was barely worth mentioning and was the probable cause of the fierce headaches that had begun to beleaguer him a week ago. He wasn't a young man anymore, and this sort of abuse to his body was taking its toll.

His phone rang. The Chief engineer of NASA had been calling him five times a day for the last two weeks. They were preparing to launch the first shuttle, which was stuffed with every possible drop of fuel. The engineers were sweating the possibility of an accidental combustion of such a payload. If that shuttle exploded on the launch pad, it would wipe out a ten square mile swath, which would include the space center itself.

The launch date was scheduled for the day after tomorrow and was to rendezvous with the International Space Station to begin its retrofit and refueling. The NASA engineers had been calling with questions about various details of the mission, but most importantly, they were begging him to come up with some specific fuel requirements and particular mission specs. With the time frame being what it was they had no choice but to ready everything they could, pending more detailed instructions, hence the first shuttle launch. The second launch was tentatively scheduled for two weeks later if Lockheed Martin could get the additional external boost tanks finished in that time.

"Dammit, Daniel, I already told you that I'm not going to be able to figure it exactly until we get those readings from the back side of the asteroid. Just fill both shuttles with all the fuel they can possibly carry, and we'll figure the burn duration and location once the shuttles get there." Chuck was getting exasperated.

He hadn't had much interaction with this particular engineer, and he had answered these questions before. To make it worse, the guy kept telling Chuck stuff he already knew. It was a foible for which he had little patience.

"But Chuck we've never done anything like this before. The fuel requirements for this mission are orders of magnitude above anything else we've ever tried. If any of these liquid hydrogen or oxygen tanks rupture, or even the solid propellant for that matter, the explosion could wipe out the space center."

"No shit, Daniel. Do you really think this is news to me?" At this point Chuck couldn't resist telling Daniel something he already knew as well. "But we either have enough fuel to escape Earth's gravity, match the asteroid's 50 thousand mile per hour velocity and have enough left over for the required shove, or we don't. Let me just remind you, Daniel. If we don't make this work, any fuel explosion on the launch pad will be a spit in the ocean compared to the one that happens when Kohler-Leporidae strikes Earth."

There was silence on the other end of the line for a few seconds before Daniel answered.

"Yes, Sir," Daniel began, "I understand. I'd probably be better off harassing the manufacturers to step up the fuel production than bother you."

"Now you're thinking," Chuck answered simply.

"Have the other engineers figured how to link the shuttles yet?"

This was their planned resolution to carrying extra fuel. Both shuttles would be refueled at the International Space Station and linked together. The idea was to have one shuttle act as the command module while the second was to be sacrificed to the asteroid's surface to generate the required thrust.

"Yes, Sir. They have the link figured out and have determined that with the extra fuel in the cargo bay they can achieve the necessary escape velocity without having to jettison the external fuel tanks. Refilling them again at the space station they say is no problem. One thing they are fretting over though is determining the angle of the shuttle for maximum thrust once it's sacrificed, and also how to set it down at a particular angle on the asteroid with the remote controls. If the shuttle needs to be nose-in to the asteroid we're not sure if the terrain will allow that until we see it up close.

Also, if they have to crash it to get the angle, there's no guarantee that the remote controls for the thrust will still function correctly."

Seeing it up close again. Why was it that everything was being forced to hinge on last minute observations? It was a horrible way to execute a plan, at best. Still, there seemed to be no other way.

"So, no matter what we do, we basically have half a plan until we reach the asteroid."

"It sounds like it, Sir."

Chuck rubbed his eyebrows as he listened. This was not helping his headache. This wasn't even his area of expertise. These were thrust dynamics questions not astrophysics.

The truth was the entire planet was utilizing every resource they had and anyone with an IQ as high as Chuck's was being leaned on heavily. Furthermore, Chuck had a rare talent for seeing problems from unique angles. Improvisation was an invaluable asset to this project since none of it had ever been done before.

"Daniel, did they get the first two internal fuel tanks fabricated?"

"Yes, Sir. That's done. They fit in the cargo bay perfectly, and they are sure they'll have the other two ready for the second shuttle in time."

"Good. One less thing to worry about. Any other updates?"

"Yes, Sir. There is one. NASA got the word about an hour ago that the Russians, Japanese, Chinese and Germans have all managed to retrofit their own rockets to carry whatever supplies are needed to the space station, including the extra fuel."

"Great, Daniel. That's just great. If that's it then let me get back to my calculations."

"Yes, Sir. Bye."

Chuck fretted that in addition to the unknowns once they got to the asteroid, the entire process was something NASA had never done before. Launching two shuttles in such a short space of time, having to modify them extensively to allow them to be linked together once they were in space, and shoving them both so full of fuel, were all new tasks. From experience Chuck knew that every new facet entailed another opportunity for a mistake.

As a diversion, Chuck switched on his TV, but the newscaster seemed to be speaking directly to his fears:

> "... It is far and away the largest international collaborative effort ever undertaken and to at least some people's surprise, the entire venture has been affected without any politics. Every country having anything to offer has simply offered it to help the effort, no questions asked. Skeptics, who might propound that international cooperation isn't a viable goal to shoot for, are being forced to change their tune. Apparently, when the entire planet is threatened, the earth can cooperate. No doubt if Earth gets through this crisis, the political beating of chests will inevitably follow.
>
> In other news ... "

Chuck switched it back off. He had better things to consider than humanity showing good sense for a change.

* * *

Jeremy was feeling depressed. He'd put a call into Valerie but only gotten her voice mail, and as of yet she hadn't returned his call. After leaving the drop zone in a hurry, he had gone back home and repacked his chute in the hangar almost under the wing of his plane. All the while he thought about what had happened or more importantly, what hadn't happened.

He was struggling with whether or not to tell Valerie, but in the end, there would be no hiding it from her, especially since he was intent on trying something again. He had already come up with the idea on his drive back from the drop zone.

The thought caused him to look up from the packing of his chute and gaze wistfully at his airplane beside him in the hangar.

He was just closing up the backpack when the far door to the hangar opened.

"Anyone home?" A female voice called from the other side of the plane.

"Hey there," Jeremy yelled back, standing up. "I tried calling you," Valerie was looking especially devastating in her tight jeans and halter top. And she was giving him an appraising look as she walked over to him.

"Yeah. That's why I came over. Going skydiving?"

"Already been."

She moved directly toward him and pinned him with a fierce hug and a determined kiss, nearly causing him to drop the parachute pack. He decided right then that he was going to tell her and get it over with, "Hey, you want to go for a walk down to the docks?" His expression stopped her cold. There was a moment of hesitation before she responded trying to sound casual.

"Great day for it. Sure." Jeremy could tell from the curious look in her eyes what was coming next. "So, did you just wake up and decide to go skydiving? You haven't been in quite a while, have you?" There was more than just a hint of concern in her voice, and he was certain she hadn't forgotten their previous conversation about him trying to see the vision again.

"No, I haven't. Come on, let's walk, and I'll tell you about it."

It was a short walk through the subdivision and down the long steps to the community's boat docks. The expansive view of the blue water on Lake Travis was breathtaking, but Jeremy was so familiar with it, he barely noticed. He had other things on his mind.

A warm breeze picked up off the lake just as they stepped onto the docks.

"I thought we were going for a walk," Valerie said.

"I changed my mind. How about a little boat ride instead?"

Valerie unleashed a mischievous smile, "But I didn't bring my bathing suit."

"Neither did I. If we decide to get in the water, we can always find a cove to skinny dip in."

"Yum," she said, following him.

Jeremy's boat wasn't the flashy type. It was an understated 24' Wellcraft with a small cuddy cabin under the bow. The cabin was big enough for two to sleep in, if they were cozy, and had a little propane refrigerator and stove in it. It also sported a little porta-potty under a seat that Jeremy had never let anyone use and was probably only included in the design to allow someone to classify the craft as a houseboat for tax reasons. The medium electric blue was an eye-catching color and the black accents on the side merely added to the effect.

Jeremy stepped aboard, then turned to help Valerie before moving over to the captain's chair. With a turn of the key he had hidden on board, the big V-8 engine roared to life. The Wellcraft had plenty of speed but nothing to match the racers that regularly plied the lake.

"Could you untie those ropes for me?" He asked.

"Sure. Don't you worry about keeping that key on board?"

"Not really. For starters, it's not a typical practice and secondly, unless you approach from the water, you have to come through this community to get to these boats. Lakeway's not that busy and so many homes command a view of the docks that a stranger walking down here and getting on a boat would almost certainly attract attention. Besides, it's insured."

Valerie smiled and sidled up beside him as the sleek craft rumbled its way out of the covered slip. Jeremy's hand was smooth and sure on the controls as he cleared the dock area and reached for the throttle.

"Hold on," he said.

"Definitely," she answered, hooking one hand on his arm and the other around his waist.

The bow tried to reach for the sky before slowly lowering to plane out as the boat accelerated. The lake-flavored wind in their faces felt wonderful, and neither tried to talk over it or the engine noise as the boat sliced through the water.

Ten minutes later, true to his word, Jeremy rounded two bends then slowed and entered a quiet little secluded cove with high rock walls. He dropped the boat to idle and went to the stern to retrieve the anchor, one end of which was already tied to the cleat. Casually tossing it over the side, he returned to his chair to wait for it to catch. It did on the first try, and he killed the engine.

"Is this where we skinny dip?" Valerie had already taken her top off and was sitting on the backbench basking in the sun. Jeremy was caught a bit by surprise with her surprising show of immodesty, but he managed not to react.

"You bet it is, but can we talk a little first?"

She immediately fixed a serious gaze on him. "Sure Jer. What's up?"

He rose from the driver seat and went to sit beside her, "I want to tell you about what I did today."

Jeremy watched her brows furrow into a combination of concern and curiosity, and he almost wished he hadn't decided to tell her.

"Great. I'm all ears."

He almost pointed out that from his perspective she definitely wasn't *all* ears but decided that probably wasn't good timing. Instead, he started into the story, leaving out his intent to deviate from safe skydiving practices and his reasoning until near the end.

"You did what? Are you out of your mind?"

"Well, that was exactly what I was hoping to do. Be out of my mind like I was the day I got the scar on my neck, but it didn't work. I didn't see the vision again."

Valerie was suddenly livid. She sat up straight and leaned toward him. "Why would you do that, Jeremy? That's crazy. And even if you saw the vision again what are you hoping to learn? And even if you learned something useful, who do you think you could get to believe you?"

There was something in the intensity of her concern that warmed him, but he couldn't let it go there. Somehow, he had to make her understand. Gently but firmly, he grabbed her bare shoulders, trying desperately not to think about how soft they felt and with great effort, stared only into her eyes. "Valerie, there is a real possibility that our world could come to an end here in a couple of months, and if I can come up with information that might help avert that disaster, how could I not try?"

"But how can you be so sure you could help? What makes you the world's savior?"

"Val, that shape I saw was exactly like Rabbit's Revenge. I think it *was* Rabbit's Revenge, and that rock or bullet or whatever I saw heading toward it *must* be important. I feel it. Really, I don't have some kind of a death wish, especially not now . . . I just know I have to do this."

Valerie's tone abruptly changed as did the intensity of her gaze. "What do you mean, 'especially not now'?"

Jeremy was deathly afraid of verbalizing what he was thinking. A part of him was afraid it would break the spell or something, and he remembered his last attempt to express his feelings for her.

Maybe she would even revert to her old elusive self, but he was caught by his own words, and he couldn't really back out now. Any lie he fabricated would sound just like what it was, a lie. Still, when he tried to speak, he stammered.

"Well, uh . . . because of you, Valerie, because you finally seem interested in really being with me." It was all he could manage to spit out, and as he finished, he cringed inside as he awaited her response.

The intensity of her gaze softened, and she threw her arms around him. He returned the hug and waited for her to say something, but she didn't. She merely pushed back from the hug, stared into his eyes and kissed him. Passionately. The tension and fear drained from him like last year's nightmare as he lost himself returning her kiss.

The embrace lasted for minutes before they slowly pulled apart.

"Will you promise not to get yourself killed?"

Her voice was thick with emotion, but Jeremy took the statement for what it was: her assent to what he had to do. If possible, it made him feel even closer to her.

"I promise," he answered, knowing that she knew it wasn't something he could guarantee.

"Great. Then how about we go for that swim?" She didn't wait for his answer. She had her shorts off before he had time to react, but when her slender naked form hit the clear water, he was just seconds behind her.

* * *

Grant lowered his high-powered camera. He was an average sort of guy, medium build, brown hair, brown eyes. There wasn't one remarkable feature on his whole body, and that's what made him so good at his PI work. He could stand in a crowd and no one noticed. Ever.

They were just coming out of the cove and the girl had her mouth glued to the guy's face while he drove. Geez. They were both wet as if they'd been swimming but neither had on suits.

The girl might have had her top off but was clutching a towel over her shoulders and the guy was still wearing jeans but no shirt. His client would appreciate these shots; although why the wacko kept wanting pictures of this woman hanging all over this crazy guy was beyond him. It didn't matter as long as he didn't have to be around when the guy saw the pics.

Grant had been working for David for months. It had been a good gig, following the girl around, until recently when she started shacking up with this guy. Since then, his client had turned into a lunatic, and he had wanted to quit at least twenty times, but the money was just too good. The guy was supposed to be some sort of high-brow doctor, but as far as Grant was concerned, he was just a hyper jealous nut case. Twice he'd been around the guy when he actually saw some of the pictures he'd taken, and the tantrum he'd thrown with that wild look in his eyes would have done a Tasmanian devil justice. It gave him the chills to think about it. And now this guy he was following was starting to act weird too. Ever since the girl had started staying over at his house, Grant had been asked to follow the guy, too. He'd followed him to the skydiving place and photographed him nearly killing himself, then followed him back to his place where the girl showed up and they went for a boat ride.

Grant walked back to his car, shaking his head. *Damn*, he thought. Maybe he should warn this girl. Or maybe he would just quit. With this asteroid thing coming he really wanted to bolt for the mountains anyway. He was already packed. Maybe he'd just do that when he got his next check. Too bad he didn't have a girl to take with him, he thought as he slipped back into his white van.

* * *

Valerie felt like she was in some form of shock. She was still tingling from the warmth of Jeremy's arms, but she had been forced to leave earlier than she would have liked because she had a client to meet downtown this morning.

It seemed too strange that she had remained aloof from everyone, especially Jeremy, for so long, and now that she had confronted her feelings about her previous relationship, she could let go.

Not only that— she *had* let go. Abruptly. And here she was, letting herself fall for a man who was trying to have a near-death experience? To save the world? It all seemed like some sort of plot from a cartoon superhero movie.

Save the world. What a thought. Was this asteroid really speeding toward Earth on a collision course? Would it really wipe out everything? Could humans really do anything to stop it? It was just too incredible. As she considered the circumstances of her life right now, she felt like she'd just stuck her face into the middle of a tornado. But Jeremy wasn't the tornado. He was an anchor for her heart, and a piece of her she knew she had been missing all her life. He was the kind of guy little girls dream of when they wish to grow up and marry a wonderful prince— strong, sensitive, smart, kind, the list just went on.

She smiled at herself. *It seems that it's difficult to focus on the end of the world when you've just found love.*

That thought brought her up short. It surprised her so much that she almost missed her turn off of 620 onto 2222. Was she really in love? It suddenly felt a little bit scary. But why? It didn't change her feelings or his. Did it? Did he feel the same thing? A quivery sensation started deep down inside her. What if he didn't feel the same? Of course he did, but he hadn't said it, but then again neither had she. Did the coming asteroid have something to do with her feelings? She couldn't help but wonder if a lot of people weren't pairing up around the world as a result of the impending doom. Kind of like finding out you only have a few months to live as a result of some disease.

She almost missed another turn and decided she had better get her mind into her work. She had to convince a man to vote her way today, and she had better be thinking about that.

18

Jeremy watched the weather. A thunderstorm was developing about 150 miles away over the Hill Country to the west, but his mind was on Valerie. He could still smell her scent on him and feel the touch of her lips on his. He shook his head. Not now, he thought. He had to focus. This thunderstorm looked like just the ticket. It would provide the element of unpredictability that his last attempt had lacked.

The storm was moving slowly. There was plenty of time, so he switched to the news to see the latest on the asteroid.

"NASA today said that the launch of the first shuttle to the space station was on schedule for tomorrow and would be followed by the second one next week. Scientists are still trying to puzzle out the necessary fuel requirements but are running into some snags. The lead scientist on the project, Chuck Kohler, was quoted yesterday as saying that the main problem now was the lack of spin on the asteroid which confounded their attempts to determine the mass of Rabbit's Revenge. He said that without that data . . . "

Jeremy had tuned out the TV. He was already making alternate plans to leave the city with Valerie if the asteroid was going to hit. He'd considered the mountains, but it occurred to him that the Texas Hill country might be just as good a refuge and one hell of a lot closer, maybe less crowded, too. He glanced over at the old Range Rover and the repainted U-Haul trailer he was storing in his garage. Sometime soon he needed to get those two ready to go.

Turning back to the weather station, Jeremy watched as the thunder cell he had been tracking began to dissipate. *Damn*, he thought. *Not today.* But maybe that was a good thing. He could use a little more rest. Besides, it was September; there would be another cell in striking distance soon enough.

19

October 3rd, 2016

Chuck put his pencil down. It was ten in the morning, and he hadn't been to sleep yet. His shift had ended at the observatory at 6:00AM, but he was still working on some calculations, and he wanted to watch the second shuttle lift off.

The first one had gone without a hitch and was now docked with the International Space Station. The refitting of the brackets on its belly to allow it to mount to the other shuttle was well underway, and its fuel tanks were awaiting the rockets from the other countries that arrived later this week. So far everything was going according to plan except for that one small detail. Where to put the thrust and how much was enough?

Sure. Small detail.

Chuck's scientific mind couldn't quit gnawing on the fact that they were attempting something on a hope and a prayer. He had spent countless hours trying to come up with an alternative method of diverting Kohler Leporidae but nothing of any value had surfaced. The option they were taking was still the best one he could devise. Except for that gaping hole in it. There *had* to be a way; there had to be some method to discern the proper spot to plant the shuttle for the diversion. Unconsciously he had picked up his pencil again and was now grinding its point into his desk. The noise finally snagged his attention and he ceased destroying it. Just because the mission had never been done before didn't mean that it couldn't be done. He'd certainly proven that to himself and others many times over in his life.

Suddenly Chuck felt extraordinarily alone. Images of Louise floated into his mind. She had such beautiful eyes. Usually he managed to keep himself occupied enough to keep his mind off her, but even after all these years he'd never completely recovered from the loss. She had been smart, kind, and gentle, and more than patient enough to deal with his many eccentricities. She had been a breath of fresh air into a life full of turmoil, even when he had been a young man, after a childhood of being labeled by peers and parents alike as an "odd little boy."

How many times had he overheard that phrase? All it took was hearing it once to counteract all the good feelings he had about his academic accomplishments, and he had heard it so many, many times.

His love of knowledge and his devotion to golden gloves boxing had carried him through school. The boxing gave him a constructive physical outlet to deal with all the taunts from kids who resented his intelligence. His whole life had been like that; other people never understanding him...until Louise. But it had been for too short a time, a few wonderful years, and she was gone. The cancer that had taken her had acted fast and left no options for treatment. He thought that at least she wasn't cursed with a painful, lingering death. The memories brought tears to his eyes, and suddenly his resolve was renewed. Now, being alone was a way of life. His parents were long gone, and his only brother had died years ago in a farm accident. The only family left to him was his niece, Susan, whom he rarely saw.

Either he would find a way to save the Earth, or he would soon be able to join Louise. Chuck smiled and wiped the tears from his cheeks. When he thought about it like that, it seemed like a no-lose situation. He lit up a cigarette, leaned back in his chair, and while the smoke curled up around his head, his mind pondered issues of mass, thrust and placement. The rest of the world slipped away.

20

Grant was now replaced by Cecil watching the house. He'd been stalking Jeremy for a week now, trying to get a feel for his schedule and the best opportunity to get at him when he was alone. It had been a frustrating exercise, because the guy didn't keep a schedule. It was also difficult for Cecil to hang around and just observe because he tended to stand out in a crowd. When people saw his massive 6'3" frame they were hard pressed to forget it. Not that he gave a damn about where he shot the guy, but he did give a damn about getting caught.

He didn't have a silencer, and this neighborhood was too twisty to make a hasty retreat. He definitely had to get this guy somewhere away from home. Feeling exasperated, he leaned back in the seat of his car. He'd find his moment.

* * *

The two shuttles were coming along nicely. Numerous space walks had finally accomplished the retrofitting of the special brackets that allowed the two ships to be linked together, and every rocket from the other countries had docked with the space station and off-loaded their fuel. They would launch in two days.

The pilot of the double shuttle, named Prometheus, was a veteran by the name of Eric Jenson. He had been on four shuttle missions and had been hailed by his peers as having the steadiest hand in the business. He was almost too old at 38 to be going on this mission, but it had been on a volunteer basis as the return trip could be dicey, especially if the RR asteroid hit Earth. If that happened, there most likely wouldn't be a place to land, much less someone to retrieve him. For that matter, there was still some question as to how much fuel he'd have left once he deployed the other shuttle. The problem was still the inability to calculate exactly how much fuel it would take to match RR's velocity and do the deployment.

While he sat peering out the viewport at Earth beneath them Henri walked into the room. The station's spin was engaged so there was simulated gravity allowing him to walk.

"I don't think anything's going to change, mon ami," Henri was one of the astronauts from France who had hitched a ride on one of their supply rockets to help with the station operation.

"Yeah, but I never get tired of staring. It's beautiful."

"Oui, let us hope it stays that way. Haven't you been inactive enough? Why don't you come help me with the refitting of some of the fuel lines in the command shuttle's interior fuel tanks?"

Eric turned to look at Henri's deep-set dark eyes and the concern there. "That's a good idea, Henri. Let me send a message to my family, and I'll meet you there in ten minutes."

"Bon. See you there."

He had been relaxing in the Space Station now for days and a little work would do him good. He moved to the communication screen to record a message to send to the media. "Hi Mom and Dad and Junior and Marie. I love you," he said to the camera recording him, "I'll get this job done. I promise."

It was the typical media platitude, but it was all he was willing to say with the whole world listening, and he knew his parents and kids would understand. Platitudes were *not* his forte.

There was another factor in favor of choosing Eric for this mission. He was single and his two children were already grown. It was a detail that Eric hadn't missed, but it still puzzled him. Being picked for a doomsday mission wasn't a dreaded thing when the consequence of failure was death for Earth anyway. The only difference was with whom you spent your last days.

He banished those dark thoughts and moved to the door, silently thanking Henri again for the distraction.

* * *

Two days later, the whole world cheered as they watched the film of the double shuttle launch from the International Space Station. It was almost ironic that the very space station for which so many people had fought and lobbied to build was now the platform that gave Earth its only chance of survival. If the space station hadn't been orbiting Earth, this plan could have never been executed. The best hope for Earth's survival was on its way.

Shortly after blast-off, Captain Jensen was allowed a relatively private conversation with his son:

"I'm scared for you, Dad. This mission is nuts. When are they going to tell you where you're supposed to plant that other shuttle and come home?"

Eric made a sarcastic snort into his helmet microphone. "I'm thinking they're going to have to tell me before I get there. What do you think?"

"Very funny, Dad," There was a brief pause then a more somber tone. "I'm proud of you, though."

"Junior, no matter what happens I want you to know that I love you, and I'm proud of you, too." As each of them struggled with what to say next, silence stretched. Each passing minute increased their separation by hundreds of miles. Junior finally spoke.

"Can you quit calling me Junior now?"

Eric laughed into his microphone, "Yes, Eric, I can quit calling you Junior now. Remember to take care of your mom, and tell your sister I love her, too." The connection was thick with emotion, but neither could think of any more words to fill the emptiness.

"I will, Dad. Hurry home."

"I'll do my best, Eric."

The connection broke and Eric senior sat perfectly still for a moment. There was still a mild crackling in his ear from the radio, and the displays in front of him were busy with information about his speed, course and the status of the double shuttle. He slowly glanced over to the other seat. Empty. No time or need to have a second pilot on such a risky mission. For that matter there was barely a need for him either. Most of this mission was automated. His main function was to pilot the shuttle around the back side of Rabbit's Revenge where it could not be piloted remotely and send back the data on its composition and shape so that the location of the other shuttle's deployment could be determined. Beyond that, he was pretty much here for the ride.

And what a ride it was—fast and utterly lonely. The shuttle was still accelerating to its designated 50 thousand miles per hour. At that speed it would approach the asteroid a little before it was halfway between the sun and Earth, circle the back side of the asteroid, then match its path. But that was still forty days away. *Forty days and forty nights*, Eric thought. *His very own journey into the desert—the desert of space.*

Eric moved his gaze to the front windshield. Nothing but stars. As a sailor he had spent a number of nights out on the open ocean and enjoyed the panorama of a star-filled sky, but none of it compared to the wonder of the view before him. The stars truly were limitless, and the vastness before him took him under its wing as the double shuttle named Enterprise II, blasted its way into the endless vacuum and a date with destiny.

21

Jeremy and Valerie lay on his couch watching the news report.

"Rabbit's Revenge has now passed the sun. It is seventy-two days away from earth, and the Enterprise II is thirty-seven days away from reaching the asteroid. Scientists say that they are cutting it very close with the time needed to affect the trajectory of Rabbit's Revenge, and they are still unsure as to exactly how to place the thrust shuttle once they reach it, or if they even have enough fuel to do so. The hopes of the world may well hang on chance."

"Wow," Jeremy said, with raised eyebrows and wide eyes. The two had been spending most of their time together and all of it at his house. Valerie had brought a suitcase over and simply not gone home. With circumstances as they were, being apart just seemed stupid.

"Wow, what? It's not like any of this broadcast is news. They just keep blathering about the same old things."

"I know, but the more I hear them, the more determined I am to try to do something about it."

"Jeremy, the hero, eh?" Valerie had not heard him talk about his vision in days, and she was beginning to hope that maybe he was going to let that crazy idea go. In a tired voice she asked the question she didn't expect an answer to, "So what are you going to try next?"

"I'm not sure," Jeremy lied. In truth he knew exactly what he was going to try, but he didn't see any profit in having Valerie worry about it. It was troublesome enough for the two of them that she knew he was bent on doing this at all.

"Right," she said, skepticism heavy in her voice. She didn't believe him, but she knew better than to pursue it. She simply turned her attention back to the TV and put her head on his shoulder.

The topics had turned from specific information about Rabbit's Revenge to speculations from scientists about the different sorts of disasters that could befall Earth as a result of the impact.

Then they spoke of churches holding mass prayer sessions both for survival and the saving of their souls, and the upsurge of end-of-the-earth cult groups that were advocating the cessation of all superfluous activities in lieu of enjoying each other's company for Earth's last days.

Jeremy spoke up abruptly, "The last one sounded like a tremendous excuse to quit work and not worry about the future, that is, if you didn't mind spending your last days with a bunch of weak willed lemmings, who would rather let someone else think for them than attempt to figure out anything for themselves." The disgust was thick in his voice as he continued, "Why does it seem that so many people feel the need follow someone?"

Valerie ignored the comment, since she was pretty sure that Jeremy wasn't listening to himself either. She was debating what to tell him and what not to; the more she thought about what he was hoping to do by trying to see his vision again, the more she felt like she shouldn't interfere, but it scared her horribly. It had finally dawned on her that her feelings for him weren't even something new, just something she was finally willing to acknowledge to herself. Should she tell him? Was it too soon? She finally considered the scope of circumstances and just laughed out loud.

Jeremy's attention was jarred from the television, "What's so funny?"

Valerie snagged his gaze and held it intently for a second. "I was sitting here trying to decide whether to tell you I loved you or not and then remembered the state of the world at the moment and your current intentions, and it struck me as absurd to consider waiting. So, I laughed." The whole sentence had come out so matter-of-factly that it even surprised her, but she instantly felt better regardless of his reaction.

Jeremy froze at the abrupt admission. He just sat there for a moment with his mouth sagging slightly and stared, "Did you just say you loved me?"

"Yes. I did." Silence hung heavy in the air for a long few seconds.

"Well, that's a relief."

"A relief?"

"Yeah. I was getting tired of feeling like the only one of us who knew that we were in love."

She started to lean in to kiss him, but Jeremy met her halfway. She would have sworn that the temperature in the room rose a few degrees in the next couple of minutes. When they came up for air, she put her hands on his neck, which was healing nicely, and looked up into his eyes. "Is that really how you want to tell me you love me?"

"It wasn't any more abrupt than your outburst. And anyway, I thought that last part was pretty good."

She punched him playfully on the shoulder.

"Ow! OK, I love you, Valerie, but it's not a new thing for me. I have been in love with you for months."

"Really?"

"You mean you seriously didn't know?"

"No, I didn't."

"Well, all I can say is that your powers of denial and selective perception are second to none."

She started to respond to the affront but thought better of it, deciding instead to focus on the positive aspects of the whole situation.

Only a smile preceded the next kiss and the warmth of his lips on hers sent chills all the way down her abdomen. He was right. How could she have missed it?

22

October 17ᵗʰ, 2016

"Finally," Jeremy exclaimed as he watched the weather radar. He had been waiting for weeks for another storm system to develop somewhere within a couple of hundred miles or so.

He wasn't quite sure why he wanted it to be that close, certainly his plane could get him hundreds of miles or so in any direction in just a couple of hours, but for some reason he didn't want to be that far away from home when he made this next attempt.

Valerie had left for an appointment downtown a couple of hours ago, saying it would be late afternoon before she could get back.

It was going to be the perfect chance. On his computer screen, the band of weather was tracking west to east across the northwestern edge of the Texas Hill Country and seemed to be gathering strength as it approached. At the moment it was just west of Big Spring. It would pass a bit south of Abilene in another hour or so. He could almost catch up with it right there if he hurried.

Perfect, he thought, and made for the hangar. He looked lovingly at his 1988 Piper Turbo Saratoga. It was the same model aircraft that John Kennedy Jr. had died in, and every time Jeremy remembered that little detail, he got mad all over again. There was no reason for young Kennedy to have died that way. It was stupid, and it wasn't just one mistake he'd made. It had been several in succession, not the least of which was the lack of pilot-in-command time in his own airplane. More than half of his entire flying time had included an instructor in the right-hand seat, and that was definitely not the type of flying that would encourage a night time solo flight over water, even without impaired visibility . . . Jeremy actually shook his head. Too many times his mind had turned to that fruitless train of thought. The only positive thing he could reason about his fixation with that particular death of a celebrity was the reminder that, not rushing to go somewhere or *having* to go somewhere, could save your life.

It was ironic, considering what he was about to attempt. He walked slowly around the aircraft checking tires, control surfaces, and all the other little details that comprised the preflight "walk around" of an aircraft. He checked the oil last before going around to the tail and pushing his weight down on the fuselage to allow the nose wheel to come up. Once it was off the ground, swinging the entire aircraft around to face the entrance was an easy task.

From there he clambered up the single step on the right-hand side and onto the wing to reach the door into the aircraft. In a side pocket was the hangar door opener. He smiled as he watched the massive door rise. He loved flying and had always had a love for pretty much any conveyance that would carry him free of the ground.

Moments later, he was at the end of the runway. He had done the engine run-up to check engine operations at takeoff power, and he was now about to get on the radio prior to departure.

"Lakeway traffic this is Saratoga 2887 Mike departing runway one-six to the northwest."

Since there wasn't a Unicom or tower at Lakeway, Jeremy didn't expect a reply. He simply moved the throttle to the forward stop as he finished his announcement. Racing down the runway, he divided his attention between the foot pedals controlling his nose wheel, his engine instruments, and his speed indicator. At 85 miles an hour he pulled the wheel back and launched into the sky.

His hands were sweating a bit though it was cool outside. This was an entirely different proposition from his try at the drop zone. He had reasoned that since he was ultimately the one in control while he was skydiving, he had never truly believed he was about to die. That must have been the reason that he hadn't had the vision. After giving it some serious consideration, he decided that there must be an element that was out of his control for him to actually believe he was near death and thereby initiate the vision again.

He was hoping this thunderstorm would be that element . . . He was also hoping that it didn't actually kill him.

Jeremy was flying VFR (visual flight rules) so unless he got into some high traffic area, which he was intentionally avoiding, he wasn't required to talk to anyone. The sky was clear at the moment. The reassuring rumble of the 300hp Continental engine soothed him as he continued to climb. His intention was to climb to 6,500 feet before leveling off. If necessary, he could adjust that altitude when he got closer to the storm.

It was difficult to try to imagine exactly how he wanted to accomplish this stunt, but it wasn't like he hadn't given it a lot of thought. He couldn't predict the storm, which of course was the point, so in the absence of any other brilliant ideas he simply intended to fly through the storm and see what happened.

Through all his years of daredevil activities, one thing he had learned was that if you want to survive a particular stunt, it was imperative to plan. Plan, plan, and plan again. People who tried dangerous activities and didn't live by their plan typically died by the lack of them. And he didn't have a plan. How could he?

How the hell was he supposed to find the middle ground between doing something dangerous enough to kill him yet managing to survive it? There wasn't an answer other than to just try. The only reason he could find to continue this ridiculous endeavor was the simple fact that he truly believed that the fate of the world might well depend on his success. But it certainly didn't preclude doubt. He couldn't even bring himself to say those words to Valerie, because they sounded too ludicrous. As she had so succinctly put it, "This is crazy," and she was right. Jeremy had decided, though, that crazy was something a reasonable person did when that person felt there was no other option.

When he leveled off, he was just beginning to feel the first stirrings of the air from the storm ahead. His ground speed was a bit over 200 mph, and the storm was still about 100 miles away. Thirty minutes. It was just thirty minutes away. The fact that he was already getting a bit of turbulence from the storm at this distance told him that this was one mother of a storm.

There was a good reason for the cardinal rule of never flying into a thunderstorm. They could be too powerful and unpredictable. Not only did the turbulence rattle your brain, it could potentially rip the wings off, although that was highly unlikely. A much more real threat was not lightning, as many might think, but downdrafts. They were not something you could see or predict. All you could really be sure of was that lurking somewhere in the vicinity of a building storm was a serious downdraft. If a pilot got caught in one, his only two choices were to try to climb or to try to turn and find a way out. Jeremy had heard of many cases where downdrafts overcame the plane's ability to climb, rapidly plunging them into the ground. That's why avoidance was the path of choice for any reasonable pilot.

But not today.

Today he was going to try it.

Jeremy racked his brain trying to decide if it was better to go straight through the middle of the storm or merely skirt the fringes. He wasn't really sure which one might be safer. Underlying all his concentration was Valerie. Images of her smile and her eyes kept floating through his mind. He really didn't want to die.

He was about fifteen minutes away when the turbulence began to approach severe. He tightened his seat belt a bit. This wasn't in preparation for a potential crash, he told himself, it was the only method of keeping his rump firmly placed in his seat. It is very difficult to control an aircraft if you're floating helplessly around in the cabin.

Five minutes later, his entire plane began to shake violently. The shaking was interlaced with sudden drops and rises as the raindrops began to pound the windshield. The force of the drops was so profound that Jeremy briefly thought he had found a patch of hail. The storm ahead of him was a behemoth of black and gray swirling clouds. It was easy to visualize a giant maw forming in the clouds to consume him and his tiny craft. In the absence of any better ideas, Jeremy decided to split the difference between the center of the storm and its outer fringes.

In the last few minutes before entering into the heart of the storm, Jeremy had to begin descending. He was loath to give up the altitude, but he could not bring himself to actually penetrate the clouds of this angry beast. Not only did it seem suicidal, but it was also illegal without contacting someone on the ground, and he couldn't do that. They would tell him to turn around.

No sooner had the thought crossed his mind than his radio crackled and came to life.

"Aircraft flying a northwest course south of Abilene. Be advised a dangerous thunderstorm is continuing to build in the area. It is strongly recommended to turn due west to skirt its fringes."

Jeremy didn't answer. By now the turbulence was getting severe enough to give him five to seven-foot jarring drops. Each one felt like it was going to either crack his spine or rip the wings off the plane. He glanced out the window at the wings, thinking fondly of the substantial "Hershey Bar" shape that this model of aircraft *used* to have. He would feel a lot better if he was in one of those models at the moment. The wings on the newer versions were just as substantial as the older ones; they just didn't *look* that way.

Another jolt rocked his train of thought, and his attention reverted to the instrument cluster in front of him. The engine gauges were all registering normal, but he was descending. Quickly. He wanted to haul back on the yoke to point the nose up, but that instinct was deadly.

It wouldn't help against this downdraft, and it would slow his forward speed dramatically. That was a prescription for a stall, and stalling his aircraft, especially right now was definitely not on the menu. Instead he gave the throttle a healthy push forward. The big Continental roared reassuringly, and the altimeter began to register a positive rate of climb. But just barely. Any additional downdraft, and he wouldn't have the power to compensate.

When Jeremy suddenly decided this was a very bad idea, it was too late. He could turn around but the path out of the storm behind him was about the same distance as the one before him, and he was not real keen on the idea of pulling the little plane into a sharp bank under these conditions. No. There was nothing for it; he was committed, and like it or not he was going to have to stay his course and fly his way out of this mess.

The rain pounded with an increased vengeance, and even though he wasn't technically in the clouds, he may as well have been for all he could see. Once he decided his visual references were useless, he reverted to his instrument flying skills and riveted his attention on the attitude indicator. He had no sooner shifted his gaze than he sensed he was descending again. He looked at his gauge and it said he was level but his altimeter told him he was losing altitude quickly. He was nearly at max power already, but he pushed the throttle to its stop anyway and heard the whine of the turbocharger kick in. The altimeter told him he was now losing 1,000 feet per minute and the aircraft was giving him everything it had. He pulled the yoke back a bit more, now willing to trade at least some of his airspeed for a little more altitude, if he could get it. The rate of descent reduced to 700 feet per minute, but he was already below 4,000 feet, and he was running out of time. His altitude readings were in feet above sea level and the ground level in this area was 1,700 feet, which meant he was 2,300 feet above the ground. That meant he had a little more than three minutes before he impacted mother earth.

Jeremy felt the cold sweat on his brow and unconsciously wiped his damp palms on his jeans one at a time. If he was going to have some sort of a vision, it would have to happen pretty quick. The thought crossed his mind that if his life did pass before his eyes right now it might well be the distraction that caused his demise.

The absurdity of it actually made him smile briefly. How ironic if the event he was trying to trigger ended up being the very thing that caused him to die. What a useless endeavor that would be and exactly the concern Valerie had voiced. He was beyond worrying about it now, though. All he really wanted was to escape this mess and get back to her.

3,700 feet.

Jeremy looked as his gauges again. The descent had dwindled to 400 feet per minute. Better but still deadly.

2,900 feet.

The ground loomed beneath him. Jeremy's grip on the yoke was cramping his hands and beads of sweat were trickling into his eyes. He had to force himself to lighten his touch. The rain was slacking, and he was thinking he could finally see the end of the line of storms. He took a deep breath and realized he had been holding it, as more cold sweat gathered on his brow.

2,400 feet.

Ground rush is a sensation normally ascribed to the last few seconds of free fall in skydiving, but Jeremy was experiencing it now. In this case it was due to proximity, not velocity. Some of the hills in the distance were higher than he was, and the cold sweat now poured off him. He risked pulling the yoke back even a little further and listened as the big engine whined, clawing desperately for some altitude as his airspeed decreased. Unable to do more than he was already doing, Jeremy couldn't help but wonder if he may have made his last mistake with this endeavor, yet he still felt strangely calm. Maybe unnaturally calm. A rivulet of sweat trickled into the scar on his neck, and though it didn't burn any more, the skin was still sensitive enough to make him jump from the salty moisture. The distraction was almost welcome. It reminded him of what he'd already survived and why he was here. He wasn't going to give up yet.

His pulse pounded in his ears. He focused on the cadence for a moment, then pointedly ignored it. At that instant the stall warning horn began to squeal, forcing him to glance at his airspeed again. 75knots. He was too close.

1,950 feet.

Jeremy glanced up from his instruments to spy the tree line in his path of flight. It was quite long, and if something didn't change quickly, he'd never clear it.

A sensation in his stomach told him something had changed. It was a sudden lightness, as though some great weight had been lifted from the aircraft and from his shoulders personally. He pulled his gaze from the looming tree line, but he knew he was climbing even before the truth registered on his gauges. In his very bones he felt the little aircraft struggle. The hands on his altimeter seemed to freeze for a moment, time itself seemed to take a deep breath then, amazingly, the needles on the gauge began to wind in the opposite direction.

2,000 feet.

He eased pressure on the yoke, letting the plane gather a little more speed.

2,300.

The stall warning horn desisted and even with the roar of the wind and the engine, it seemed silent in the cockpit.

2,800.

As he realized he'd clear the tree line, he pulled the throttle back slightly and lowered the nose to regain some welcome airspeed. The rain abruptly stopped, and Jeremy noticed a few more clouds dead ahead. He banked to his left into the clear blue sky off to the west, catching a glimpse of a small herd of buffalo on the hills beneath him. Several scampered away from the noise of his engine. He could almost see the fear on their furry faces.

That was way too close.

The minute he cleared the clouds of the racing storm, the turbulence stopped. One minute he was getting bounced all over the place, and the next it was so smooth he wouldn't have known he was in the air with his eyes closed but for the steady roar of his engine. He took a deep breath. Then realized: no vision. Damn! He had just risked his life for nothing. Again.

He stared for a moment at the trembling of his hand, then pounded the yoke in frustration, and almost absently corrected his course. He stayed very low, below normal radar for a few minutes before finally leveling off at 5,500 feet. He was going home. He hoped the FAA didn't send out a search party . . .

* * *

Valerie sat on the couch in Jeremy's den. The TV was on, but she wasn't really paying attention. Her stomach was churning. She'd been sitting there worrying for over an hour now.

Her appointment had gone well except that the guy kept dropping hints about getting into her pants. Not that that was anything new. It was just a part of the territory, and once she had learned that, she realized it was just another tool. Whenever any of her business contacts tried that tack, she quickly used it against them—led them on a bit to get what she wanted, then turned it off like a light switch. It usually worked amazingly well, and since the majority of them were married, they couldn't afford to express their anger at being used. The scandal of admitting improper advances in a business situation was simply not worth the risk. They were politicians after all, and the press was often not their friend.

Jeremy was weighing heavily on her mind. She hadn't been able to reach him on the phone, and when she had arrived at his house, the first thing she did was check the hangar. His plane was gone.

He hadn't mentioned to her that he was going to fly anywhere, so she had a pretty strong suspicion that wherever he went, had something to do with trying to have his damn vision again. If he got himself killed, she'd never forgive him. She plopped down on the couch, reached for the remote and fumed

A dull roar in the distance quashed her musings, and she bolted off the couch. All anger vanished as she raced to the hangar. She hit the opener button as she flew by, her footsteps echoing across the huge expanse to the door. She didn't slow there, though, not until she was far enough out on the pavement to see the source of the roar.

"Lakeway traffic, Saratoga 2887-Mike crossing midfield to enter left downwind for runway one-six." Valerie heard Jeremy's voice crackle from the radio he always left on in the hangar even before she saw Jeremy's plane

She let out a huge sigh. She hated this.

Her abrupt relaxation told her how tense she'd really been. She hated worrying about the man she had just fallen in love with, getting himself killed. But it didn't matter, she knew why he was doing it, and she couldn't argue with his reasons regardless of the fact that she didn't subscribe to the possibility of their success.

She watched Jeremy jockey the plane for a landing. Somehow the concept of the world ending in December just wouldn't take root in her mind. No matter how much they kept repeating it on TV, some part of her refused to believe it. It was difficult to decide whether her feelings on that were advanced denial or impressive intuition.

Jeremy was on final now, and she watched until his wheels gently kissed the pavement. He really was an excellent pilot, and Valerie always felt safe in the air with him. She moved over to the side as he slowed, knowing he'd make the first turn off the runway to avoid back-taxiing down the active runway. She didn't want to hamper his approach to the hangar.

Her relief sprouted a wide smile and that along with the wind in her face drained the tension from her body like a floodgate.

The roar of the engine had diminished once he landed, but as the plane taxied closer, the volume increased. She crossed her arms under her breasts as the tail swung around so it was almost under the eaves of the hangar. Fifteen seconds later he cut the engine, and a heavy quiet descended on the airport, leaving only the sound of the light breeze. It took a few more minutes, though, for Jeremy to crawl out of the cockpit.

"So how was the suicide run?" She asked, disapproval thick in her voice.

"Death defying . . . and Fruitless."

"What did you try?" Her tone softened markedly when she saw the pallor of his face. Something had scared him badly, and she couldn't remember *ever* seeing him scared.

"I flew through a thunderstorm."

"Oh my God!" Even though she had known that whatever he tried needed to be life threatening, she suddenly felt nauseated at the thought.

"It got pretty dicey too, but still no vision." He barely looked at her as he busied himself with securing the plane in the hangar.

"So, what are you going to do now?"

"I don't know, Valerie, I really don't, but I have to think of something."

He was barely looking at her, busying himself with the mechanics of getting his plane back into the hangar.

She could sense his disappointment, but his pale countenance was what riveted her attention. In the air Jeremy was a cool and confident customer, and she wasn't sure she wanted to hear what it had taken to shake him up like that.

"Come on," she said ratcheting up her smile a notch and grabbing his arm "Let's go inside and you can tell me about it." Jeremy's wan smile was all the reward she needed for her bravery. He took her hand and walked back into the house closing the huge hangar doors as he passed.

* * *

Cecil put his binoculars back down. *Damn. Why is one guy with a lot of money so worried about some girl being with another guy with money? He could get any girl he wanted.* It was stupid...but it paid well. This guy was tough to track, though. Cecil had just watched him land his airplane and taxi into his very own hangar off the runway. The girl had been waiting there for him. She was there all the time now—a little fact that had made his client simply bat-shit crazy.

It had been several weeks now, and the phone calls on his disposable cell phone were getting more frequent. His client was in a hurry. Cecil didn't really give a damn. He wasn't going to get himself caught because of some crazy rich guy's impatience. As a matter of fact, if the asshole didn't back off, he might be next in line to get bumped. But it *was* frustrating trying to find a time when the guy was alone somewhere other than his home. If he only kept some sort of schedule it would be so much easier.

Fortunately, there was one thing he did fairly consistently.

* * *

Chuck awoke in the middle of the night. His head was full of dreams of Louise, and the moment he remembered it was just a dream, a wave of sadness took him, but that wasn't what had awakened him.

He'd taken the evening off from the observatory to try to sleep in the darkness for a change. It wasn't working very well. Not only was his body rebelling at the attempted internal clock change, but his mind was still hovering in overdrive. It seemed no matter what he did or how tired he became, his brain wouldn't let go of the problem that he, so far, hadn't been able to solve. There had to be a way to be certain that the shuttle mission would be successful. He had attempted to come at the problem from every angle he could think of—both conventional and outrageous—but nothing brought any more certainty to the equation than his original best-guess method.

The plan was that once the shuttle reached the asteroid and made the orbit around it, the new information derived from its back side would give them the data they needed to plant the other shuttle, but having to wait that long to decide was making him increasingly nervous. Cutting it that close was too risky. Changing trajectories, refiguring deployment techniques, matching velocities yet again, burning more much needed fuel . . . it was all too chancy. He wanted these decisions made now so that preparations could be made before the shuttle rendezvoused with the asteroid. There *had* to be a way.

He turned on the light and grabbed his remote. Maybe something on the TV could distract him. The first thing he heard when the picture snapped on was a talk show host hailing the virtues of the surprising new republican candidate for president.

The entire presidential race, as important as it was, had taken a back seat to the news about the asteroid. Still, this new guy was a pleasant surprise. His name was Carl Iverson. He was a second-generation immigrant and a Colorado cattle rancher. He talked plainly, and honesty rang in every word he spoke. Even the factions of the press that backed the democrats couldn't find any dirt on this man.

The story in the limelight now was how he'd saved the life of one of his farmhand's five years ago when the man had been attacked by wolves. The farmhand had been hunting for stray cattle when his horse threw him and broke his leg. When the man didn't return, Carl had set off to find him. He's arrived just in time to see the injured man fending off one wolf with a stick.

The others were closing in when Carl shot three and had taken out a fourth with a knife when it attacked after he had dismounted his horse. The man had been black, and it had been that farmhand who'd leaked the story to the press. Carl merely looked embarrassed when it was brought up.

What a refreshing change, Chuck thought, *someone running for office that people could really look up to.* It was a change the US desperately needed. A man like that could do the country some good.

As quickly as it had started the political foray subsided and the host turned his attention back to tired opinions about the asteroid diversion attempt. So much for distraction.

In a funk of frustration, he reached for the remote, turned off the TV, and grabbed a Dean Koontz novel from the bedside table. He was reading Brother Odd, and as usual, Mr. Koontz thoroughly engaged him in mere moments. He leaned back against the headboard and let the story take him away.

23

October 25th, 2016

It had been an incredible experience to watch the moon virtually flash past him. That had been a little over two weeks ago. Eric was now accelerating past 40,000 miles per hour. If he were to turn around now, at this velocity, once he reached the moon, the trip from there to Earth would only take a few hours. He was already travelling faster and farther than any man had ever gone, and the shuttle was still accelerating. The double shuttle was functioning smoothly. The brackets holding them together had worked perfectly, and both shuttles were absolutely brimming with fuel.

There had been precious little for him to do with all the automated systems on board, especially since his course for the next few weeks was simply a straight line toward the sun. His biggest challenge had been to fight off the boredom that clung to the passing of days.

He was keeping an on-line journal that got regularly transmitted back to his computer on Earth, not only cataloguing his feelings but his observations regarding going "faster and farther" than any man in history. The 'faster' part wasn't really so disturbing. He couldn't really feel the acceleration or the velocity itself, but the 'farther' part was a different matter altogether. Even though being in space had been his dream his entire lifetime, he'd never considered how lonely it could be. NASA hadn't sent up solo missions in decades, so every other mission he had flown had been with crewmates. He had to believe it was a whole new experience of being alone, something people on earth could never imagine, and he had written as much in his journal. All those years as a boy with dreams of going into space somehow never included the possibility of doing it alone. He'd tried to imagine any other situation that might generate this same sort of feeling of solitude, and the only thing he could come up with was the idea of a single person in a deep diving bell—first going slowly down thousands of feet then ascending in even slower stages to avoid the bends. For him that would be worse. At least in space he felt immensely free, which was funny, as he was just as confined in a space shuttle as he would be in the diving bell with only slightly more living space. The disparity made him smile. Mental machinations.

The sun glared relentlessly through his front view screen and would continue to do so until he began to orbit the asteroid. It would have made it difficult to sleep if the flight deck had been the only place to close his eyes. Relatively speaking, there was a lot of room for him on this flight as the crew module had been designed to accommodate up to four people. It hadn't, however, been designed for the extended period of time he was going to be using it, but the extra space provided by being the only crew member left more than enough for the additional supplies.

The scientists had calculated the amount of heat the shuttles would have to absorb as they approached the sun and came to the conclusion that the heat tiles that were already installed to absorb the heat of reentry into the Earth's atmosphere would suffice for what he was supposed to do. Since there was no resistance from atmosphere Eric could simply angle the shuttle up to face his heat-absorbing belly toward the sun.

This maneuver would point the other shuttle's top surface toward the sun, but the engineers had collectively decided that the heat at the range they were anticipating would be insufficient to ignite any of the fuel in the other shuttle, and if it did damage to the surface of the other shuttle, it didn't really matter since that one was never intended to come back anyway.

Eric dreamed of his ex-wife and their life together, and of his children. He had had a wonderful life already, and he felt grateful for it. The little headache that had been plaguing him returned, causing him to automatically check the gauges for the oxygen flow. Everything was normal.

The kernel of worry that floated persistently just below the surface of his thoughts, he wrote off to the loneliness and boredom. This mission *had* to succeed. He reached for one of the many books he had brought and after one more lingering gaze at the infinity of stars around him, and a pleasant thought about how he was living a famous story, he immersed himself in another one.

* * *

David's general composure had been slowly disintegrating. The demands at the hospital seemed to be increasing in direct proportion to the continuing news about that damn asteroid. How could people believe that crap anyway? The news had been filled with stories of people leaving the cities in droves and taking their possessions with them in search of a place to "survive" the upcoming holocaust. It also seemed that that same sentiment had led others to steal and loot things they needed. This, in turn, was causing a dramatic increase in fights, car wrecks, and shootings so that the hospital was getting inundated.

Sometimes David had a difficult time remembering why he stayed in medicine. Money was the obvious reason he had gone into it and that part had been good to him, but he had a serious lack of mercy for humans in general. He found the majority of the population to be stupid and erratic, and he had little use for company other than his own or that of the women he used so wantonly and discarded.

Except for Valerie; but when she had refused to marry him, his use for people as a whole had taken a nosedive from its resident position at the bottom of the pool. He was bitter and angry, which was not a wonderful sentiment for a medical professional to use as a starting place. It colored every single judgment about the treatment of his patients. His hate had grown like a cancer, and it had all been channeled into his attempts to control Valerie from a distance, or at least monitor her life.

As the days passed, and her intentions with this guy seemed more and more permanent, David's logic and common sense had steadily declined. At this point David was acting more like an enraged bull in a bullfight. From his perspective he had been wronged and betrayed. All he wanted now was to lash out at the cause of his pain. Regardless of the outcome, his primary concern was to destroy the bringer of his pain, even if it killed him.

He chaffed daily over the delays from Cecil. Why couldn't that buffoon just shoot the guy and be done with it already? What was taking him so long? He'd tried calling him to coax him to hurry, but Cecil had just told him that if he was in such a damn rush why didn't he just go shoot the guy himself? The remark had upset him so that he had hung up the phone actually considering doing just what Cecil had suggested. But no. He wasn't good with weapons to begin with, and it would defeat his desire for vengeance if killing her damned lover ruined his life in the process. It was only supposed to ruin hers. She had no right to be happy after what she had done to him, and if his life was going to be a torture of loneliness, then hers would be, too.

There was a little part of him that was beginning to fantasize that once the other man was out of the picture, he would have another chance to win her back. The idea had crept into his mind a few weeks ago, and now he was beginning to actually believe that the possibility was there—of being with her again, having her on his arm . . . the image made him smile.

24

October 28th, 2016

Jeremy opened his eyes to Valerie's head nestled between his shoulder and his neck. The feel of her soft skin and the smell of her dark hair sent a little thrill through him. He felt caught right in between the desires to make love to her and to just keep holding on to this sensation as long as he could. He decided to do neither. He wanted to let her sleep, and he wanted to go workout. With each passing morning he felt more and more grateful to have her in his life. It was so much more than just her physical presence. Everything about her seemed to speak to his soul. Her feelings about her faith, her political stance, her desire to help other people, all spoke to his soul on different levels, and collectively they drew him to her in a fashion he'd never dreamed possible. The fact that the world may have scant few weeks to survive seemed to him the cruelest joke of all. How many people around the world had just fallen in love only to have their dreams cut short by a cosmic coincidence? There had to be a way to stop it, and with each passing day he was more and more certain that his vision was the answer. Still he hadn't been able to come up with another idea of how to accomplish that beyond what he'd already tried. Maybe he'd come up with another idea while he worked out.

As delicately as possible, Jeremy slipped out from under Valerie's head, taking care to slip a pillow in the spot his shoulder had been. Maybe she could sleep some more. Her sleep had been disturbed last night, apparently with some bad dreams. He'd heard her say the name David more than once in fear, and the sound had made his blood run cold. What a bastard that guy had been. Jeremy had had dreams of his own after that about getting his hands on that fool, but he'd never do it.

For all his martial arts training, he was a gentle soul, and the only circumstance that could provoke him to violence was protecting himself or someone he loved or some other form of righteous indignation. He almost hoped the idiot would try to harm her physically when he was around.

He was nearly out of bed when Valerie stirred.

"Good morning, sweetie," she said in a husky sleepy voice. She began to stretch as he stood up.

"Good morning to you, too, sleepy head."

She turned her head back toward him. "Where are you going?"

"I thought I might go for a bike ride and go through my martial arts forms. It seems like I haven't worked out in weeks, and it's bugging me. Do you want to come?"

"No, I think I'll pass. But why don't you have a cup of coffee with me first?"

Jeremy hesitated but the look in her eyes brooked no denial. "Sure. Just as long as I get my workout in sometime today."

Before the coffee was finished Valerie stood up from the table in her tiny pink negligée, walked around to Jeremy's side of the table and straddled him. He barely had time to get his coffee cup set down before she grabbed his face and began kissing him. Moments later he was carrying her back to the bedroom and the hours slipped away. It was early afternoon when Jeremy's eyes opened again. Valerie's eyes were open already.

"Does that count for exercise?" Valerie's expression was positively adorable.

"Well, yes. But no. I'd still like to go for a bike ride."

"OK. Come on with me to the kitchen then before you go."

"I might not make it out of here if I do that."

"Would that be so bad?"

Valerie eased out of bed and walked out of the room with Jeremy not too far behind. By the time he reached the kitchen she was looking in the refrigerator.

"What's this?" She asked. She was holding an opaque pitcher and sniffing. Before Jeremy could answer she had poured herself a cup and sipped.

"Oh wow this is that RipSnort stuff Joel concocted."

"Oh my gosh. You don't want that for breakfast."

"Who says? Have some with me before you go."

"You want me to drink some of that before I go on a bike ride?"

"Why not?"

Jeremy ended up having a glass and a half with her against his better judgment. He was finding that telling her no was easier said than done.

"OK Val. Now I'm going for a ride. Really."

"How long do you think you'll be gone?"

"Probably a couple of hours."

"OK. I think I'll just nap for another hour or so and we can go get something to eat when you come back."

"Sounds great." The small smattering of conversation made him smile. She was so easy to be around now that he had finally made it past her fear. It never ceased to amaze him to think of her change. To think he had been prepared to give up on her altogether.

Jeremy's mountain bike was in the hangar, and he went straight there after changing into his martial arts pants and a black T-shirt. He had his practice sword strung over his shoulder and through the band of his fanny pack. He would prefer to take his real sword but riding a bike with that thing strapped to your back was a little too suicidal even for him. It was probably illegal, too. Not to mention the slight buzz he was feeling from that damn concoction of Joel's.

He pulled out of the hangar and started down the hill. It was a clear blue afternoon— one of those special days that seem to come only in the fall. The sky attained an azure that made every other color in the world stand out in stark relief. He could see the lake off on his left. It was calm this afternoon. Boat traffic was typically heavy on summer week-day mornings, but this time of year it was very light, and without all those crisscrossing wakes, the surface of Lake Travis took on a pristine and stately peace. It was Jeremy's favorite time to be on or even near the lake. He almost wished he was going for a ride on his boat rather than his bike, but he really wanted the exercise. It was going to be a wonderful day.

* * *

Cecil smiled. "Finally," he muttered to himself. He had been staying away from the neighborhood for a few days because he was beginning to fear recognition from some of the neighbors. On a whim he decided to swap cars with a friend and come back this morning. It looked like the urge was going to pay off. Jeremy was leaving on a bike. He finally had a name, but only because he had done a little research on his own; it was the same research that had given him his boss's real name. Was that a sword strapped over his shoulder?

A martial artist, huh?

Well, he wasn't going to karate chop the bullet Cecil had in mind, though it was a reminder not to get too close to the guy. Still, it was another interesting little fact that David had neglected to tell him. He wondered if the guy even knew himself. It didn't matter much anymore, but the more he had talked to David, the more he disliked him. It would serve him right if Cecil only grazed this guy, Jeremy with a bullet, and then told him who had sent him. The thought made him smile.

Cecil climbed into his friend's SUV. He was going to have to figure out how to follow this guy without making him suspicious, which was going to be a nifty trick with the guy riding a bike . . . especially when he took it uphill.

* * *

The breeze in Jeremy's face and the rhythmic pumping of his legs helped him focus his thoughts. A brief image of the Rabbit's Revenge asteroid racing toward Earth through the great void of space greeted him along with the newscaster's continual descriptions of the world's attempt to change the outcome of the impending impact.

The days were passing and, as the disaster approached, he was feeling increasingly antsy about getting out of town and away from the city. Jeremy knew that as the event got closer, increasing numbers of people were going to begin to panic.

Probably the only reason that panic hadn't already taken hold was because such a huge catastrophe tended to breed its own denial. No one really wanted to believe it, so they just didn't; but they would, and when they did, hysteria was going to be the ruling emotion everywhere. He intended for he and Valerie to be long gone before that happened. The only problem was trying to decide how long to wait before he left. He had mentioned this idea to Valerie and his desire to head for the hills, literally. She had greeted the notion with a bit of a condescending smile and a simple admission that if he was going, she'd be with him. But he wasn't sure if she understood that he really meant it, and how she would react when he actually looked her in the eye and told her it was time to go.

There was almost a primal sensation of peace about the idea of taking his mate and running away from civilization to find some cave in the hills to survive. A mate. Jeremy's legs stopped in mid-stroke. He loved the idea of really having a mate for the rest of his life, however long that might end up being. His parents had always been so happy together, a wonderful model of what he wanted his married life to be. Nothing he had ever found before was even close.

How many times had he been prepared to give up on her before her sudden change of heart? Since it had been so sporadic for so long before that change, Jeremy couldn't help but wonder if another sudden change of heart might not be possible. That was the only downside to this new relationship. His legs pumped many revolutions while he considered that uncomfortable possibility, but he couldn't hold on to those doubts. Her explanation of her reasons for being so standoffish, and her reasons for the change, made sense to him, and short of something catastrophic, he didn't believe she would change again.

Jeremy was going up an incline now, and he could feel the growing burn in his thigh muscles. He down-shifted two gears and kept pumping, sensing a vehicle moving up on his left. He disliked having to ride on streets without sidewalks, but in some areas, there was just no choice, and this little stretch wasn't very long. His ears told him the car was close when it occurred to Jeremy that it was moving slower than it should be. Instinctively he crowded the edge of the pavement to give it more room to pass, but he eyed the edge warily. This particular section of road presented a rather nasty little drop-off down a rocky slope, and it was a tumble he wasn't interested in making.

He was just reaching the crest of this hill when the black Grand Cherokee pulled up beside him. Rather than looking at it, Jeremy focused on the edge of the pavement until a sound changed, causing him to glance left. An electric window was rolling down. Suddenly Jeremy was absolutely certain that this guy was going unreasonably slow. The realization caused him to jerk his head up.

By the time he saw the gun it was too late.

Jeremy hit the brakes and swung his head milliseconds before he heard the explosion, but by that time he was already feeling the searing sensation on the side of his skull.

The slight residual buzz from Joel's drink probably made the difference in his reaction time. All at once he felt like he was viewing himself from a distance. He barely noticed the wet sticky sensation on the side of his face as he stared in shock at his body catapulting over the handlebars and down the jagged incline. He instinctively prepared to roll and had the vague realization that he must not be dead yet.

Mere inches before impact his life began to flash before his eyes. The whole scene blazed through his mind just like it had before and right there at the end was the pebble—no, it was Rabbit's Revenge. He was certain of it, and there was that one spot on its surface . . . now if he could just live to tell someone.

All of this blasted through his mind as his body was still hurtling through the air; it must have lasted less than a second. Then, just as his body struck the rocks, Jeremy's world exploded to black . . .

* * *

Dammit! Cecil thought. The guy had flinched just as he'd fired; but there had been a lot of blood, and then he took that dive down the hill onto the rocks. Surely that would kill him. Maybe not. *Dammit!* He thought again. Cecil's adrenaline enhanced fury ignited like a land mine. All of a sudden, he didn't want to be around here anymore, and he didn't care about the rest of the money, but he did want a bit of revenge before he bolted town. He stomped the brakes.

It took him about 30 seconds to pen a little note and impale it on the brake handle of the bike before he got back in the truck and took off.

There, blowing in the breeze was the little white piece of paper with just two words on it. David Coulson.

Cecil laughed as he took off. Screw the rest of the money. He was out of here.

* * *

Valerie was getting a nervous, edgy feeling in the pit of her stomach. Jeremy had been gone now for over two hours, and he wasn't answering his phone. She had already dressed, stretched, done a bit of yoga, made herself breakfast, and vacuumed the den. He said he would just be an hour and a half or so. She forced herself to relax and went to turn off the TV she had left on in the den just to have a little background noise in the room. Maybe that was what was making her so tense.

The news was now constantly droning on about either the progress of the double shuttle, the progress of the asteroid, or the rising fever pitch of the population of the world. Politics was taking a seriously atypical back seat, even in the wake of an amazing new candidate. She guessed it only made sense. After all, the end of the world did sort of trump a presidential election.

Grocery stores were intermittently running out of bottled water, canned goods, and other storable staples, but the worst was the sporting goods stores. You couldn't find a tent, a camp stove, a sleeping bag or much of anything else on the shelves. They continued to sell out as fast as the stores could get them in, and now it was taking longer and longer for the stores to refill their shelves. In many cases they just weren't.

Just as she reached for the remote a picture of a helicopter flashed on the screen.

"Breaking news on the local front: A Life Flight helicopter was dispatched just moments ago to a biking accident on FM 620. No details have been released yet, but police believe that a possible shooting was . . ."

The news shook her. A biking accident on 620? The blood drained from her face. That was where Jeremy should have been. But a shooting? It couldn't be him. She dismissed the idea with a touch of foreboding nagging at her. But her hands were still shaking, as she dialed his cell phone. It went straight to voicemail.

Once the TV was off, the weight of the silence grew heavy in the room. Valerie's foreboding about Jeremy grew along with it. Something had to be wrong. Panic set in. In a sudden flurry of action, she grabbed her phone and speed-dialed his number again. The answer on the fourth ring was at first a relief.

"Hello. Who is this?" A deep voice began on the other end of the line. It wasn't Jeremy, and suddenly Valerie was shaking.

"You're not Jeremy. Who is this?" She replied with a mixture of fear and belligerence. Instead of answering, however, the voice asked her another question in a somewhat commanding tone.

"Ma'am, how do you know Mr. Andrews?"

Mr. Andrews? Valerie had a sinking feeling she knew who this person might be just from the tone he was taking, and the idea sent her anxiety meter into the red zone. "Who are you and what are you doing with Jeremy's phone?" She answered in a demanding tone of her own.

"Ma'am, this is Officer Mays, with the Sheriff's office. I need to know who you are before I can tell you anything else."

Something bad *had* happened, and it must be really bad to have a police officer answering Jeremy's phone. The heat in her voice crumbled, "I'm his girlfriend," she answered, with a tremble in her voice. "I was here at his house waiting for him to come back from his bike ride." She was also struck with how inadequate the word 'girlfriend' sounded coming out of her mouth. Wasn't she much more than just that?

"What happened?"

"Uh, Ma'am, there has been a shooting here. Jeremy has been rushed to the hospital, and we are going to need to ask you a few questions."

"That Life Flight was for him?" Valerie felt as if her heart had turned to ice and the cold was radiating out from there. She shivered. For a moment she couldn't even speak, and to his credit, the officer seemed to sense this, waiting patiently on the other end of the line while she desperately tried to find her voice.

"Is he all right?" She only realized she was asking the question when her ears registered what her voice was uttering. And she was deathly afraid of the answer. The brief moment before the officer answered almost sent her over the edge. Valerie felt as if the ice shard had exploded, and cold radiated out through her entire body.

"Well, Ma'am, he was in critical condition when Life Flight left with him. We can come to where you are if you like, to ask the questions, or if you prefer, we can meet you at the hospital."

"So that Life Flight was him. Oh, my God. Where did they take him?"

"St. David's Ma'am, but . . . "

Valerie hung up the phone and raced to her car.

The drive to the hospital was a blur. Images of a bloody Jeremy lying there alone in a hospital bed tortured her. By the time she arrived, she would have been hard pressed to even tell you which route she had taken.

She stopped at hospital admissions, breathless.

"Where is Jeremy Andrews?"

The nurse took in her mental state with a smooth practiced glance and seemed almost reluctant to ask the perfunctory question.

"Are you related to him, Ma'am?"

"I'm his fiancée," she answered abruptly. Although she was familiar with hospital rules and knew the required answer to stop this woman from hindering her progress, a part of her still couldn't help but notice how easy that particular lie slid from her lips. Somehow saying it out loud seemed to lend truth to the statement, and, she realized, it did characterize her feelings for him. It was a tiny kernel of pleasure nestled in a growing panorama of horror.

She felt as though she was moving through a dream as the nurse gave her a room number and directions. Fortunately, those directions included the pointing of a finger in the correct direction, or Valerie, in her haze, might have continued to stand there stupidly for a moment prior to getting her bearings. Memories of her father invaded her mind. He had died from a car crash so many years ago, but the last she had seen of him was in a hospital bed. Her pulse raced.

She streamed down the hallways following the various signs. When she reached his room she almost burst through the door, but then remembered at the last second that there might be a need for quiet. She managed to flow into the room as quietly as possible.

Her heart nearly stopped as her eyes fell on Jeremy. For a brief second she thought she was seeing her father and spots danced before her eyes. She leaned against the wall until the moment passed, then opened her eyes and assessed Jeremy.

The entire top of his head was bandaged above his eyes, and there was a bandage on his right arm with a sling holding it that hung from his neck. His face was swollen in a number of areas and already beginning to blacken. His closed eyes were beginning to blacken, too. She scanned the rest of him for any other signs of injury, but nothing else was visible, at least not with the sheet pulled over him. Still, it seemed as though nothing else was broken. There was an IV hanging beside the bed with a tube running to his arm.

Valerie had a moment of severe trepidation at the thought of calling to him, so she pulled a chair over to the bed and gently took his left hand in hers, holding it to her chest as she sat down.

"Jeremy?" Her voice was a tentative whisper that elicited no response. "Jeremy," she repeated a bit louder. Still nothing.

"I'm afraid he can't hear you."

The steady, even voice behind her made her jump, dropping Jeremy's hand in the process. It was a doctor.

"You scared me," she gushed out breathlessly.

"I'm sorry Miss—"

"Valerie. You can call me Valerie. I'm his fiancée."

Valerie didn't miss the quick shift of the doctor's eyes to her left hand which bore no ring, but they shifted away almost as quickly as he stepped forward.

"Nice to meet you, Valerie. I'm afraid your fiancée is in rather bad condition."

Valerie was used to reading people. In her business it was a necessity, so she didn't miss the extra emphasis he put on the word 'fiancée', but she chose to ignore it.

"What's wrong with him?"

"Well, there was a gunshot to the head," The doctor paused briefly at her sharp intake of breath then hurried on, "But as it turns out that was only a graze. It caused a lot of bleeding though, and a very slight fracture to his skull. The worse injury I'm afraid is from the fall off his bike and tumble down onto the rocks. It was a good thing he had a helmet on because it shattered. I imagine it took the worst of the blow. Still, he has a worse concussion on the other side of his head, and he hasn't regained consciousness. He's also suffering from a cracked collar bone and a cracked humerus."

"When will he regain consciousness?" Even as she asked, she knew the answer to this one, but her mouth was running ahead of her thinking processes.

"It's hard to tell. We have done an MRI of his head, and there is some swelling which we are treating, but as to when he will actually regain consciousness . . . that's anyone's guess."

Valerie's gaze shifted back to Jeremy, and tears gathered in her eyes.

A soft knock at the door drew Valerie's and the doctor's eyes. It was a police officer. When he spoke, Valerie immediately recognized the voice from her earlier phone call.

"I'm sorry Doctor, but I need to speak with Ms. Latham."

"Fine. But not in here." The doctor turned to Valerie, a look of compassion in his eyes. "It will be better if you two talk outside. I'm going to examine Mr. Andrews a little further, before I continue my rounds."

"Thank you, Doctor," Valerie said as she moved toward the door.

The moment she stepped outside; the officer smiled at her. The gesture seemed out of place in this context, but she found it relaxing anyway.

"I'm a little surprised you beat me here, Ms. Latham. I don't even want to guess how fast you must have been driving."

"Valerie, please." She managed a wan little smile back at the officer and ignored his implied question.

"So, you told the desk nurse that you were Mr. Andrews' fiancée. You told me girlfriend. Which is it?"

"Girlfriend at the moment," she answered, completely unabashed with his pointing out her lie.

"And how long have you been seeing Mr. Andrews?"

"About eight months now."

"Do you know of anyone who might have wanted him dead?"

That question shook her, and it made her wonder briefly if there was more to his past than he had shared with her. It was a disconcerting little doubt that she could have done without. "No. I don't."

"Do you know anyone by the name of David Coulson?"

Valerie stiffened abruptly as though receiving an electric shock. She had neither heard nor thought of that name since her admission to Jeremy and hearing it now from a police officer could be nothing but bad.

Officer Hays didn't miss her body's reaction but waited patiently.

"Yes, I do. He was a man I dated for a while before I moved here. Why are you asking that?"

"Well, there was a note stuck on Jeremy's bike with that name on it."

Valerie's heart began to race. Just hearing that name coming from someone else's lips was enough to cause her body to react with fear. "But how could that be? He's in Kansas City."

"We don't know, ma'am. Was your boyfriend a doctor? Because we ran his name through our database and there is a Doctor David Coulson here in Austin."

"In Austin?"

"Yes Ma'm. Right down the street at the Austin cosmetic surgery clinic."

The revelation of David's proximity set off a flash back of bad memories and caused her to shudder, another reaction that didn't go unnoticed by the officer. Still he held his tongue and waited.

Valerie turned and looked in the officer's eyes. "He's not a very nice man," she said, but her tone spoke volumes beyond her simple statement.

"You didn't know he was living here?"

"No, Officer. The last I ever saw him was when he left me alone in Jamaica, though I talked to him a few times after that. He was the main reason I decided to move to Austin from Kansas City."

"Do you think he could be jealous enough to try to kill your new boyfriend?"

"Not with his own hands, but yes, that would be something he might be capable of." How could this be possible? If David was living here, how long had he been here? How had he found out about her and Jeremy? Was he having her followed? It wouldn't surprise her. She remembered his bouts of rage.

"Thank you very much, Ma'am. This is some good information to go on. If the doctor did it, or paid for it, we'll get him."

"Thank you, Officer." A wave of nausea gripped her, as she opened the door to Jeremy's room. The doctor eased out as she entered. The emotional overload was almost too much. Having the greatest love of her life in jeopardy, dying, and finding that the nemesis of her love life might well have been the cause, *and* that that evil man was so close, threatened to tip her over the edge. She pulled up a chair, grabbed Jeremy's hand, bowed her head and began to sob. "Jeremy, what have I done?" She mumbled between her tears.

* * *

The police officer was waiting in his private office when David walked in. His secretary had informed him that the Sergeant wanted to see him. It was hugely embarrassing to have the guy show up at his place of work, but the embarrassment had quickly turned to anger, then to fear. His office was the most secluded place he could think of to hustle this guy off.

"How can I help you officer?" David said, as he casually closed the door to his office.

"We have had an attempted murder, and I was hoping you could answer some questions for me."

"Certainly. Is there something medically unusual about the case? Surgically altered appearance, perhaps?" The officer hesitated and David could feel the weight of his glare as the cop tried to decide what he thought of David.

"No. Actually you were implicated directly in the incident."

The officer paused again, and David felt the man's stare intensify even more.

"Really. How so?"

"Your name was stuck to the bike the victim was riding."

The surprise David exhibited was not in the least bit contrived and the concern was sincere as well. Just not for the reason the officer suspected. "Why would anyone do that?"

"That was what we were hoping you could tell us."

"I'm sorry, but I don't have any idea."

"So, you don't know Jeremy Andrews at all?"

"I've never met him before in my life."

The officer stared hard at him for another moment.

"Is that all, officer? I have patients waiting for me."

"Yes, Dr. Coulson, that's all for now. I hope you weren't planning on doing any travelling in the near future, were you?"

"I wish," he said, "I'm afraid I'm too busy for that."

"Good. Please don't. Thank you, Doctor."

The officer turned and left; David couldn't decide which emotion was more prominent—anger or fear.

Damn that woman. And damn Cecil.

25

Jeremy looked at his throbbing fingers again. The light coming down, combined with his adjusted night vision, was just enough to allow him to see the blood and torn fingernails. He was climbing up rough cobblestones, and it felt as though he had been climbing forever in this semi-darkness. When he looked up, he could see the small round circle of light in the distance. He must be in some kind of well, but he couldn't recall hitting the bottom. As a matter of fact, he couldn't remember the bottom at all. Shouldn't he be wet? All he could remember was climbing, and that there was something important he had to do.

He couldn't recall what it was, but he somehow knew that if he just kept climbing, he would remember when he reached the light. But how long had he been climbing? He had vague memories of falling back, but clearer memories of looking up again and seeing that the little circle of light was farther away than it had been before.

Now it looked closer but still far away. The sides of the well afforded plenty of hand holds, but he had been climbing forever. His arms ached and his legs burned, and when he looked up again, he couldn't tell that he had moved at all. But he had to! He had to do something, and whatever it was, it was very, very important. Reach up with one more hand, find the crevasse, grip again and pull. Ignore the pain. One more inch, one more foot. Push with his toes. Don't give up. He had to get out. He had to!

26

November 3rd, 2016

"This is a good sign," the doctor said in a matter-of-fact tone.

"What's a good sign?" Valerie had barely left Jeremy's side in days, and she hadn't left the hospital for more than thirty minutes. The doctor entering the room had awakened her from a stiff semi-sleep, and as always, she had watched his actions intently. If there was anything she could do, she was prepared to do it. Whatever that might be.

"His EEG is showing some slightly increased brain activity. There have been a bare few instances of this over the last several days, but the frequency seems to be increasing. That would suggest some improvement. The cranial swelling is virtually gone so really it's up to Jeremy to find his way out of the coma, and I would say he's trying."

Valerie sat still for a moment absorbing the doctor's words, but when he seemed on the verge of turning to leave, she spoke up, "Doctor, is there anything I can do?"

He gave her a fatherly smile. "Valerie, I'd say that you are already doing it. If I were him, I'd certainly be making every effort to make my way back to you. Also, I believe your presence here helps. I'm one of the proponents of the belief that coma patients do react to their environment on some level or another. If that is true, then your presence here is doing its part to speed his recovery."

Valerie smiled back at him. She wasn't sure if that little lecture bore any truth or not, but his willingness to offer it was all he could do, and regardless of her level of belief, it provided hope to mitigate her feelings of helplessness to some degree. "Thank you so much."

"Sure thing. Now why don't you try to get a little more sleep yourself? You look exhausted."

"I will, thanks again."

The doctor had barely left when she heard a soft knock at the door.

"Come in," she whispered, expecting a nurse.

"Hi there," Joel said with a huge grin. "Is our little buddy at the corner of happy and healthy yet?"

Valerie couldn't help but grin. "Do you ever tire of reciting TV commercials? And no, he's not quite there yet, but he's improving."

The boyish grin vanished from his face, "That's good to hear," Joel responded, "and no I don't get tired of it. I think it helps with my song writing."

"What, you plagiarize their lyrics and jingles?"

"No. It just gets me in the right frame of mind."

Joel's eyes shifted to Jeremy. "Has he even woken up, yet?"

"No, but the doctor says he is healing and his brain activity is ticking up."

"I'm sorry I didn't get here sooner, but I don't watch the news much, and I just now found out he was in the hospital."

Valerie turned to him, feeling a bit embarrassed. "It hasn't really occurred to me to call anyone, sorry." Her gaze slid back down to Jeremy.

"That's OK. I wouldn't have expected you to call me anyway, but I did want to come by and at least check on him."

Valerie simply smiled up at the concern on his face.

Joel stared at Jeremy for a moment. "Do they have any idea who might have done it?"

She paused for a few bleeps of the monitors then, without turning to face him, answered, "I'm afraid it was an ex-boyfriend of mine that I thought was still in Kansas City. He apparently followed me here."

"Wow," Joel breathed, "Not my idea of doubling your pleasure or your fun . . ."

Valerie made a soft chuckle. "You really can't stop, can you?"

"What? Oh. Sorry. No, I guess I can't." Joel reached into his pocket and pulled out one of his business cards. Valerie finally shifted her gaze to Joel as she accepted his card.

"Let me know if anything changes. I really do care for this idiot, but I've got a gig starting up in about forty-five minutes."

Valerie took the card gently then spared him a tender look.

"I will, Joel. Thanks for coming by."

"No problem. Say hi for me when he wakes up, OK? Also, as soon as he can function, I have some stuff to talk to him about with regard to the asteroid thing, OK?"

"OK," she answered, looking a little mystified.

"See you soon, Val," he said, already moving toward the door.

"Bye."

She watched him leave before turning her gaze back to Jeremy. He looked so peaceful lying there. Some of the bandages were off, though he still bore the sling for his collarbone. She took his free hand as she leaned forward over the bed.

"Please, Jeremy. Please come back to me."

27

November 8th, 2016
Election Day.

Chuck stared out the windows of the observatory. As the media continued to track all the events surrounding the attempted deflection of Rabbit's Revenge, Chuck's name got repeated frequently, causing a crowd to steadily ebb and flow around the observatory. They all wanted to ask questions in search of a little hope, but he didn't have anything for them that they hadn't already heard. They had started following him home in ever-increasing numbers until it had reached the point where he no longer felt comfortable there anymore. Since then the observatory had been his only refuge.

In a few more days it would be time to start the shuttles into the huge arc that would end with them reversing direction and matching course and velocity with Kohler Leporidae, which was now forty-three days from Earth. Once that was accomplished, the pilot would have to make the maneuver to orbit the asteroid and acquire the data Chuck so desperately needed.

It had been an interesting few weeks, when he wasn't suffering from frustration over his own ineffectiveness. He had found himself spending a lot of time contemplating the end of Earth and reflecting on Louise. Chuck was an avid if unconventional Christian, and he had spent a certain amount of his time lately rereading Revelations to see if any of what was happening matched the predictions there.

Mostly, it didn't, and he found that reassuring. Not that he had any trepidation about dying; in many ways it would be a relief, but he still felt like he had more to do in this life. He was interested in seeing those things through before moving on to the next one.

There had been a certain amount of fascination connected with observing the world's response to its potential demise. An hour in front of the TV could update anyone on all the anticipated reactions: runs on sporting goods and hardware stores, gun stores emptied of weapons and ammunition, cults popping up to huddle in remote spots and pray as the disaster approached, churches filling and people packing the highways in droves to get away from the cities.

That last one caught his attention. Surely people weren't thinking that through. Leaving the cities was a normal and reasonable reaction to a nuclear attack since most of those were likely to be targeting large cities, but in the case of the asteroid wouldn't it be better to linger in or near the cities where all the repositories of supplies were? Sure, there would be a lot more emphasis on self-defense in the urban areas, but there would be a lot more resources to draw from also. If a family were to flee the city, someone in that group had best be adept at hunting, fishing and gardening, and what about all the tiny little necessities that were so easy to overlook? Things like needles, matches, non-power tools, hand pumps for liquids, buttons, nails, screws, nuts and bolts. Many such small manufactured items would be impossible to replace once civilization was decimated. Of course, technology would be the first to go, and people's ability to communicate with each other would break down almost immediately. On the other hand, maybe he was underestimating the self-defense aspect. In this instance self-defense was more likely synonymous with self-preservation. As supplies continued to dwindle many people would, no doubt, be willing to kill to get them. All in all, maybe taking to the hills with all you could carry wouldn't be such a bad idea. At least for a while, however long a while might be.

Chuck physically shook his head to try and clear it. His eyes refocused on the TV, and they were actually spending a moment covering the presidential election.

What an interesting juxtaposition of events. Maybe one of the best candidates in political history running for President, and the entire election was stuck as almost a blurb between reports of the approaching asteroid. If the world survived, it would need strong leaders, and this Carl Iverson guy sounded like just the ticket. He wondered briefly if he could sneak out long enough to vote.

* * *

It didn't bode well that the officer had asked to see him again and David was nervous as he walked the hall back to his private office.

"Can I help you, Officer?" he said as he walked briskly to his desk. It was the same Officer as before, a sergeant Hays.

"Yes. Thank you. I just had a couple more questions for you."

"Sure," David said as he shuffled some papers on his desk. "Anything I can do to help."

"Thank you, Dr. Coulson, can you tell me where you were on October 28th? David hesitated as if he needed a moment to think, which he certainly didn't. "Yes, Officer, I was at the hospital all that day with numerous witnesses."

"So why did you move to Austin, Dr. Coulson?"

That question took him by surprise and he nearly flinched before he answered. He could only hope the Hays missed his reaction. David looked the officer in the eye and added a bit of iron to his voice.

"I was tired of the cold and the hospital made me an offer I couldn't refuse, then I found the clinic for sale. Why did you move here, Officer?" It was all David could do not to scream at this idiot.

"I'm the one asking the questions, Doctor." Hays countenance hardened visibly, and David could read expressions well enough to know that he'd better back off.

"Yes, Officer. Sorry." David managed to squeeze a bit of contrition into his expression even though rage was his primary emotion.

"Do you know a Valerie Latham?"

David hesitated as his mind ran ahead. The police must have already talked to Valerie. That's why they were here.

"My, I haven't heard that name in a while. Yes, I do know her. She is an ex-girlfriend from Kansas City."

"Did you know she had moved to Austin?"

This time David didn't hesitate, and he even managed some passable surprise.

"Why no, I didn't. So, she's here in Austin?"

"Yes," Hays replied coldly. "That's all for now Doctor, but we'll be back in touch. Please don't do any travelling for the time being."

"No problem, Officer. Oh, and Officer, how is the boy?"

"Still unconscious," he said as he closed the door behind him.

~

David breathed a heavy sigh as the officer left. The only bright spot to the whole experience was finding out that Andrews hadn't regained consciousness. With any luck the son-of-a-bitch would still die.

Thinking about it made David fume all over again. Not only did that lame brain manage to botch the job and not kill the boyfriend, but he'd left a damn note with his name on it.

He assumed that meant the fool wouldn't be coming to collect the rest of his money. It was just as well. At this point David might have considered trying to kill the idiot himself.

So far, he'd been able to use his reputation as a doctor and the mouth of an expensive attorney to adequately fend them off, but just the fact that he needed to do so was infuriating him further. In the meantime, *she* was spending her time at the hospital by his side. David shook with rage.

28

November 9th, 2016

It was the day after Election Day and Carl Iverson had won the presidency by a landslide. He was a war hero of amazing character, and it was a tremendous coup for the United States in general but in the flow of current events it was barely remarked upon.

~

"How are you feeling, Eric?" Arnie asked.

Eric thought for a moment, actually taking mental inventory rather than simply giving Arnie a generic answer. He knew that's what the man wanted. Arnie didn't waste time with pleasantries and though the question might seem simple enough, under these circumstances, at roughly twenty-nine million miles from Earth, it was anything but.

"I'm feeling good, Arnie." And at that moment he meant it. It was comforting to hear a voice. Different people from the shuttle staff made it their mission to talk to him whenever he felt like conversation. It was one of the little things they could do to help stave off the intense loneliness he experienced from travelling so far away from Earth alone.

Eric settled in to wait for Arnie's response. At the current distance from Earth it was going to take about four minutes for his words to reach Arnie's ears and another four for Arnie's response to get back to him. It was one of the reasons he was having so few conversations these days. What would normally be a five-minute conversation could, at this distance, take hours.

"No headaches?" Arnie asked.

"No, Sir. Not since yesterday. Did Iverson win?" Eric could picture the gray-haired man's bushy eyebrows furrowing as he asked the question.

He had seen it so many times. There were few people he would trust with his health as implicitly as he trusted Arnie. The man was not only a genius, but the personification of dedication. His thoughts wandered as he awaited the reply.

"All right, then. That's good, Eric. Let me know if anything changes. And yes, Iverson did win. Oh, and by the way, drink another quart or so of fluid; you're showing to be a bit dehydrated."

"Yes, Sir. That's good about Iverson, The U.S. needed someone with integrity for a change." Eric grinned. Nearly halfway to the sun and someone on Earth could tell he was a bit dehydrated. It was amazing.

He leaned back in his seat and raked his fingers through his graying black hair. It felt oily. Trying to keep it as clean as he did on Earth was just not an option, so oily was what he was used to. The break from normal society almost made him smile.

The weeks in the shuttle had been boring and tedious, but now he was just a few days away from what he'd come here to do and the anticipation of the activity ahead of him gave him a much-needed jolt of excitement.

* * *

Arnold Whitman had been the head medical mission specialist for all manned space missions for the last twenty years, and he had been monitoring Eric Jensen personally since the launch.

It had been decades since anyone had sent an astronaut up in space alone for any length of time, and that caused problems not only from a psychological point of view but also from a practical one. Even with their new advances, it was nearly impossible for a doctor to adequately diagnose someone else in outer space, and even when they could, self-treatment regimens were often difficult.

Arnie looked up from the screen of the new AAHMS (Advanced Astronaut Health Monitoring System). The brand new wireless system connected to its myriad of sensors inside Eric's flight suit was a miracle of monitoring technology and was adequate to record body temperature, blood pressure, heart function, hydration, muscle tone and even skin condition, but what it couldn't tell him was what was going on inside Eric's head. Not the psychological stuff. That was a whole realm all its own. Eric had been complaining intermittently of headaches throughout the mission, and Arnold couldn't determine any reason for it. The few ibuprofens that Eric had taken had relieved the symptoms, but they had continued to recur. The frequency wasn't increasing but the duration seemed to be.

~

Eric's part in the mission so far had been mostly that of passenger, but in a few days he was going to be called on to bring the double shuttle into a close orbit around an asteroid that was moving at 50,000 miles per hour and to strategically photograph and measure the back side of that asteroid.

This information would be the final piece of the puzzle to the placement of the second shuttle with its full complement of thrust. It was true that the shuttle could normally be commanded to make those movements without Eric, but in this case, there were two problems with that. First, the asteroid wasn't spinning so no one really knew what the shape of the back side of the asteroid was. It could be anything. Secondly, at the distance they were going to be when those commands were needed and the speeds at which they were moving, the eight minute round trip of the signal would be too slow, even without the brief blackout time when the shadow of the asteroid eclipsed the shuttle from Earth. And if they wasted too much fuel or time trying to make corrections, the window of opportunity to plant the shuttle and still have its thrust be effective would close. So, at that point the pilot became indispensable, and that was the moment that was rapidly approaching for Eric. Three days away.

Eric sat stone still in the cockpit. The soft humming of all the equipment had long since faded into the background of his consciousness, but now he took a moment to focus on everything. It was a game he played with himself to help occupy the time. Periodically he would stop, sit as still as possible, and count the different sensations he could perceive. First his hearing; the low hum he was now focusing on must be coming from some piece of machinery or maybe some combination of pieces. It was a soft low pitch, and he wondered what could be making the noise. There weren't any parts moving inside the cockpit that he was aware of, and he had a hard time imagining an electrical hum coming from such modern electronics, yet there it was. He turned his head to try to pinpoint the location, but as it had when he tried before, the sound seemed to be coming from everywhere with him in the center. Even when he closed his eyes and concentrated, he couldn't determine anything new and was reminded of the perpetual quiet of outer space. That was a thought he could have done without.

He decided to focus on something else. Taking a deep breath, he registered the smell. It was so strange. Astronauts over the years described something they call "the smell of space". It's most apparent to anyone who has been inside the cabin of a spaceship when someone returns from space walking, and they have described it as "strongly metallic and unique". Nothing else seems to fit, and it lingers in the shuttle for months after it returns from space. Eric remembered reading that one astronaut guessed that the smell was from "atomic oxygen clinging to your spacesuit". He didn't know about that, but sometimes he could catch a whiff of the "burnt gunpowder" or "ozone smell of electrical equipment" that he had heard others mention on their flights. He remembered it himself. But the most prevalent odor to accost him was the perpetual plastic smell of his spacesuit, or his own body. It seemed to him that smell was everywhere, all the time, and though he had learned to block out his awareness of it, when he stopped to concentrate, it again seemed overwhelming.

Next, Eric turned to sensations from his body. He felt *odd*. In the weightlessness of space, he most often felt swollen, as though the lack of external pressure on his body was allowing his insides to expand. Even with his attempts to do resistance exercises on a regular basis, his muscles felt strange. He often imagined that he could feel them atrophy as a result of the perpetual absence of gravity. In general, he felt swollen and limp, which disgusted him. Eric decided to turn his thoughts to something a little richer.

He centered his concentration on his eyes. He always did his eyes last because they were the easiest and actually the busiest of his senses, but today they were even more than that. They were the panacea to the sensation of emptiness that focusing on his other senses had brought into sharp relief.

As long as he didn't mind looking at the plethora of technological gizmos laid out in front of him in a panoramic view, he could be entertained for hours. There seemed to be no end to the dials, gauges, and electronic readouts that he could peruse. The technology of man did lose its interest, though, after weeks on end of staring at it.

He shifted his gaze to the windows. The front window was darkened by an electric current to make the constant, ever-increasing blaze of the sun bearable. Through that darkened glass the great ball of gas appeared like a thick greenish cloud. At times he was sure he could see swirls on its surface like a cauldron of animated smoke with darker spots that represented some miniscule change of temperature to its nuclear heat. But it was his side windows that most often held his gaze. Through them he could see the stars. Ever since he was young, he had loved to gaze at the stars and look for the constellations or wait patiently in hopes of catching sight of a meteor. That thought tickled him now as he raced to try to divert an asteroid. No view of the stars from the mountains or oceans of Earth could compare to the glory of light he saw through the shuttle's side windows.

From his current angle, he couldn't recognize any of the usual constellations, but just like watching the sky on a cloudy day, he could visualize shapes in those stars more readily than he ever could with clouds. Taking a moment to try to count a few always amazed him even more.

The universe was filled with untold billions of stars and each of those had the possibility of many planets around it and of all those billions of billions of planets, there were bound to be more out there with life that humans had simply not found yet. He finally found a thought that didn't leave him feeling so alone, but infinitely more connected to a piece of a larger tapestry. The immense expanse of outer space was just a larger scale version of the human body, made up of billions of molecules; each molecule consisting more of space than of matter . . . just like outer space. It was absolutely...

A fiery lance of pain shot through Eric's brain. He groaned loudly as one hand went to his head and the other automatically reached for the communications console.

"Houston! Something's wrong I—" At that moment the tiny vessel in his brain finally gave out. It was a little time bomb that must have been sitting there since birth. A miniscule, weakened wall of a small capillary, invisible to any of his myriad medical tests, and it chose that instant in outer space to fail.

Eric saw a brief flash of his wife's face just before his world went dark. If there had been any gravity, Eric's head would have slumped heavily down onto the console in front of him. Instead, his body simply became still. He floated, just like the other inanimate objects that floated in the cabin with him.

~

Eight minutes later the radio crackled to life again. "Eric, what is it! Eric! Oh my God!" Arnie said as he looked back down at his monitor. Eric's heart had just stopped. Arnie stood there in shocked silence before turning to the rest of the crew in the command center. "Eric Jensen has just died." For a few seconds the quiet in that room could have matched the silence of space.

* * *

Ten minutes later Chuck's phone rang.

"Good morning, Chuck. This is Arnie over at the command center. We have a situation here."

Chuck's head was a little fuzzy, but it wasn't from sleep. It was from the lack of it. The tone in Arnie's voice, however, jarred him into sharp focus.

"What is it, Arnie?"

"Eric Jensen is dead."

Instead of a sharp outbreak from Chuck, there was a heavy silence on the line for a moment.

"What happened?" Chuck finally asked in an oddly calm voice.

"We don't know, Chuck. If I had to hazard a guess though, I would say he had an aneurism. He died suddenly, and there were no preceding heart fluctuations and no reports of discomfort beyond his increasing headaches."

Chuck didn't waste any time on emotions. He was already calculating alternatives, possibilities, consequences, and more alternatives. Arnie waited patiently on the line during the silence. "Arnie, I would say our chances of saving Earth just dropped from about 70percent down to about 15percent at best. Let me do some thinking, and I'll call you back."

"OK, Chuck. I'll call everyone else and let them know the situation. I just thought you should know first."

"Thanks, Arnie." Chuck slowly put the receiver down, barely aware of the movement of his hand. Chuck was vaguely aware that he should have some emotion for the dead pilot but, like a soldier in battle, any emotion he might have felt for the pilot he barely knew was sharply overshadowed by his concerns for the mission and the fate of the rest of the world. The shuttle couldn't be piloted in the tight arc around the asteroid that Chuck was hoping for to determine its mass and shape. It could make the arc and match the asteroid's path by remote control, but the commands could not be affected quickly enough for anything more detailed than that.

With the pilot dead, due to a one-in-a-million flaw in a human body, the entire population of Earth was about to be forced to resign the fate of its existence to one stupendous guess.

29

November 10th, 2016

Jeremy opened his eyes, but he was still in the dark with only a circle of light far above him. He had just been dreaming, of a giant rock in the shape of a crouching rabbit with one dark eye looking right into him and a little arrow headed straight for that eye. It was his vision again, and it jarred him awake. Why was he in this well? He vaguely remembered trying to climb his way out of it only to fall back, over and over again.

It was time to try again. This time he was getting out of here. He *had* to tell someone what he'd seen. It was that important. With a renewed determination, he decided to try a new avenue. Each time before he had attempted to scale the sides of the well as though it were some colossal rock wall challenge, and each time he had fallen just short of reaching the top.

The diameter of the well was narrower than the length of his body with his arms extended, so he decided that this time he'd try a little wall-walking.

Putting his hands against one wall, Jeremy reached back with his foot to brace himself against the other one. He had to put his second foot up very quickly to keep from falling and once his body was spanning the diameter of the well, he began to *walk* backwards up the wall. The surface was slippery, and with every placement of his hands or feet, he faced the threat of falling back. At least with his hands he could place his grip on the rocky or less muddy surfaces. He didn't have the luxury of giving his feet the same advantage, and more than once a foot slipped. Each time, though, he managed to hold on long enough to regain purchase on the slippery sides.

The climb was inexorably slow, but he couldn't quit. Halfway up, his muscles began to shake from the strain, and he began to wonder if determination was going to be adequate to overcome the challenge. It seemed that he could feel the light and warmth on his back as he got closer and closer to the rim. Then there was a soothing sensation on his shoulders. Not just the warmth, but actually a feeling of being soothed somehow.

When Jeremy got to the point where he could just see the lip of the well above him, the flaw in his plan finally occurred to him. How do you let go of the top of the well and propel your body over the edge?

A wave of despair was just beginning to take him when his shoulders began to shake more violently, but not from the strain. It was an exaggeration of the warm sensation he had experienced earlier in his climb, and it was increasing. Somehow it felt welcome, and he focused on it . . .

* * *

"Jeremy? Jeremy!" Valerie's hands gently shook his shoulders as she called to him. She had been sitting there for hours and had seen Jeremy twitch and then seem to tense. She blinked her eyes to clear her head. Days had passed with her sitting in his room with him. She had only left when her job absolutely demanded it. It felt like she hadn't truly slept in days.

She had never been good at sleeping in the sitting position and Jeremy's little room only offered chairs. And to make it worse, every twitch, every murmur that escaped him in those days, had caused a surge of adrenaline and a hope of his waking. But this time was different.

After watching for several moments, it occurred to her that maybe she could help. He hadn't moved or twitched or muttered this much at once since she had begun her vigil, so maybe it was time she did more. All of a sudden it seemed important to shake him, and though she was almost afraid a nurse would come in and catch her, she did it anyway.

"Jeremy?"

~

Jeremy opened his eyes, but this time it was to the real world and the smiling face of Valerie gently shaking his shoulders. "Hi there. So, you

184

were the one shaking me?"

"Well of course I was. Who else could it have been?"

"I wasn't sure. I was trying to get out of this well, and I'd wall-walked all the way to the top then realized I had no way of getting over the edge. That's when I noticed my shoulders shaking."

Valerie smiled. "So, I saved you, huh?"

"Yeah, you did." Jeremy's eyes scanned his surroundings. "Hospital?"

"Yeah."

The memories came flooding back to him. "How long have I been out? The last thing I remember is that guy in the van having a gun. I flinched, felt something hit my head, then saw the rocks coming up."

"You've been out for a little over two weeks."

"My God." Jeremy's brain was racing trying to put together what had happened to him. "Did they catch the guy who shot me?"

Before Valerie could answer, the hospital room door burst open, and a nurse and the doctor flowed inside.

"Hi there, Sleeping Beauty," the doctor said; with an unmistakable look of satisfaction on his face. "I'm Doctor Lawrence, and we're awful glad to have you back with us."

"Yeah, I understand I've been out for a while."

The Doctor's eyes flickered momentarily to Valerie and then returned to Jeremy. "How do you feel?"

"Like I've been hit in the head, actually."

"That's reasonable," he said, "Since you were." His focus shifted from Jeremy's eyes to the machine on the table beside him, and he began to take notes. "It wasn't the bullet that caused the coma. It was the fall afterward onto the rocks. All your other vitals look normal though, and everything else is healing nicely. If nothing changes in the next 24 hours, I think we can let you out of here tomorrow afternoon."

"Thanks, Doc." Jeremy sensed that the doctor's attention was already shifting to his next patient, so he didn't bother to ask anything else. If the Doc said he was ok, he didn't see any reason to prolong the visit. He wanted to get back to talking to Valerie. He had a lot to tell her.

A moment later, Jeremy watched the doctor leave with the nurse in tow, then refocused his attention on Valerie. She looked embarrassed. He struggled for a second to recall what his last question to her had been, but she picked it right back up.

"No. They didn't catch the guy that shot you. He got away, but we think we know who might have paid for you to be shot."

Jeremy stared at her eyes as she paused. His head was aching, but that was almost a pleasant sensation from where he'd been. It at least verified he was in the land of the living. "What is it, Valerie?" he finally asked.

"Remember I told you about David?"

"The guy in Kansas City?"

Valerie nodded her head. "Not anymore. Apparently, he moved here about six months ago, shortly after I did. I had no idea."

The pleading look in her eyes made him feel sad. "This isn't your fault, so get that look out of your eyes. I'm certainly not mad at you."

"The police think that he has been having me watched and saw I had moved in with you. They don't have any hard evidence though, so they haven't been able to arrest him."

"It doesn't matter, Val. As a matter of fact, he might have done us all a favor."

"What do you mean?"

"I had the vision again, and now I know what it means. I think I can help with the shuttle mission. If I've been out for a couple of weeks, they must be getting close." Instead of the look of excitement he anticipated, Valerie suddenly looked sad all over again.

"I'm afraid it's too late for that, too."

"What? What do you mean?"

"The shuttle pilot died yesterday. The shuttle is on autopilot now, and the news is saying they have no way of piloting the shuttle around the asteroid to get in close enough to gather the data they need to deploy the second shuttle."

Jeremy smiled at Valerie's consternation, confusing her momentarily.

"But don't you see? That's why I had the vision. They don't need to pilot the shuttle to the back of the asteroid. That's what my vision meant. The shuttle needs to be placed in the indentation on the asteroid that looks like the eye of the rabbit!"

The look of incredulity on Valerie's face didn't daunt Jeremy at all. "Come on Valerie. This is it! This is why I had the vision, and why I had

186

to see it again. David's jealousy might have just saved the whole world." Jeremy got a pensive look on his face for a second. "Well, David's jealousy and Joel's concoction. That may have made a difference as well. Who knows?"

Jeremy could see that she wanted to believe him, but the information he was giving her was too incredible to digest. "Think about it, Valerie. I had my first vision before anyone had even discovered Rabbit's Revenge. How is that possible if not for some purpose? It *has* to be the reason I had the vision!"

Valerie's response was tentative at best. Jeremy could see the struggle in her eyes. "Jeremy, even if I do believe you, how are we going to get anyone else to?"

That comment brought him up short. It was a valid point. The story he had to tell was almost too incredible for him to believe, and he had lived it. How was he ever going to convince anyone else to bet the fate of the world on one man's unusual vision?

"I have no idea, Valerie, but we are going to have to find a way. I guess we could start by calling NASA."

"Maybe we should wait until you get out of here."

"Valerie, there is an asteroid streaking toward Earth. I'm thinking we don't have time to wait. Can you turn on the news?"

"Sure." Valerie picked up the remote to the ceiling-mounted TV and clicked the button. A news flash was up on the screen and Jeremy and Valerie were instantly engrossed.

". . . ago NASA released word that the untimely death of the shuttle pilot, Eric Jensen, was most likely due to an aneurysm, but there is no way to confirm. Scientists are still scrambling for ways to collect the data that Eric was meant to collect when he piloted the shuttle in close orbit around Rabbit's Revenge. So far, no new ideas have come to light though the shuttle continues on course and . . ."

Jeremy turned to Valerie. "So, it was an aneurysm. I guess I woke up just in time, don't you think?"

Valerie just managed to get her mouth closed as she turned to face Jeremy. "Oh my God, Jeremy! What are we going to do?"

"By 'we' do you mean, you and I, or are you referring to 'we' as in the whole world?"

"Both, I guess."

"I don't know about the whole world but *we*," he said gesturing to the two of them, "are going to drive to NASA and tell them a little story."

Valerie's eyebrows shot up. "Drive to NASA?"

"Yeah. It's not that far. You don't think they're going to listen to the wild-ass story I'm about to tell them on the phone, do you?"

"Well I . . ."

"Of course they're not," Jeremy smiled, "When was the last time you took a drive to the coast?"

After a moment's hesitation, Valerie smiled back.

30

Valerie spent Jeremy's last night in the hospital in the chair beside his bed watching him as he fell asleep. She was laboring with an unreasonable fear that when he fell asleep, he may not wake up again.

That fear kept her awake long after Jeremy was snoring softly, but the gentle sound finally lulled her into slumber, and she awoke to an aching back, and a smiling Jeremy staring at her from the bed above her.

"I love you," he said.

"I love you, too." She felt like a school kid grinning at his shining eyes. The fears from the previous night melted into a distant memory. It almost made her forget her aching back.

"Let's get out of here. We have a road trip to make. Buzz someone and let's get the paperwork moving."

It took almost three hours to talk the doctor into releasing him and then to actually get it done. Jeremy sat with uncharacteristic patience as the nurse wheeled him out of the hospital in the wheel-chair, still sporting a sling for his collarbone. When they arrived at the curb, Valerie was already waiting with the car, and he thanked the nurse, eased up out of the chair, ignoring the wave of dizziness and managed to slide gracefully into the car.

"Let's go to my house first, Val. I want to take my truck instead of yours."

"Why? Mine gets better mileage."

"Yeah, but mine doesn't need roads."

"Are we off-roading to Houston?"

"No. I'd just feel better if we could if we needed to. OK?"

She hesitated, considered arguing the point, then decided it wasn't worth it. "Sure," she said, "Or, we could take your plane."

"I thought about that already, but then we'd have to rent a car, and I not only don't want to fool with that, I'd rather have mine. We might be there awhile."

Valerie gave him a puzzled look. "How long do you think it will take to tell them your story?"

"Not as long as it's going to take me to convince someone to believe it, or for that matter to convince someone to actually *listen* to it."

Valerie read the look of determination on Jeremy's face. She'd seen it before. She merely nodded her head and returned her attention to the route back to his house.

"Oh, by the way," she began, "Joel came by the hospital to check on you. He wanted you to call him when you were...how did he put it? Oh yeah, at the corner of happy and healthy."

"I should have guessed. Man, I bet he's been glued to the TV. This entire situation is probably like a dream for...hey wait a minute. He's been studying this stuff for years. We should give him a call as soon as we get to my house. Maybe he'll have an idea for convincing someone."

"Worth a try," she answered.

Silence reigned as they were both lost in thought during the uneventful drive.

Once they were back at his house Valerie asked, "What's the gun for?" She watched as Jeremy hurriedly packed the black pistol into the 2002 Range Rover, along with a fair amount of camping equipment and some gasoline cans. Her voice echoed in the big hangar.

"If I'm not mistaken, someone just tried to kill me. I'm not giving them a second chance. Why don't you go in and pack? I'll be done here in a few minutes, and then I can call Joel. But I want to get there as soon as we can."

"What about the camping equipment and the gas cans?"

"I haven't ventured out of town lately, and I'm not sure how crazy it's getting. It might be hard to find gas."

"But even if the Rabbit's Revenge is coming, that's still over a month away."

"So? How long would you want to prepare for a world ending disaster, Val?" She sighed. He had a point.

"How long will we be there?"

Jeremy stopped and gave her an intent look. "As long as it takes. A few days maybe? A week? I really don't know."

Jeremy picked up the phone and dialed; Joel answered on the second ring.

"Jeremy! Good to hear your voice. I guess you're out of the hospital."

"The corner of happy and healthy."

"Ha. See? I'm contagious. Have you heard the news? Sounds like Earth is screwed. Too bad too, we were about to release a few new songs. Joan's written a couple of really cool ones."

"Well, maybe not. That's why I was calling you. Remember me talking about what I saw during my near-death experience?"

"Yeah. Val was telling me something about your dumbass idea about seeing it again."

"Yeah, well, I did. And it concerns the asteroid."

"What the hell are you talking about?"

Jeremy related the experience, what he saw before, what he thought it might mean and then the final piece falling into place while he was in the coma.

"Holy shit! Jeremy that's incredible. And you really think that what you saw is the truth?"

"What else could it mean?

Pretty damn random if there's no meaning, don't you think? And for that matter, from what I'm hearing, what better chance do we have?"

"Good point."

"So, with that in mind the question becomes, how the hell do we convince anyone at NASA that we're not crazy."

"Hmm...Let me think about that one, Jer. What are you doing now?"

"Packing to go to NASA."

"Not wasting any time huh? I guess talking to anyone in person would be better than sounding like a crackpot on the phone. Hey, you should tell them the asteroid is Mayhem and you are their insurance."

"Ha, ha. You really think this is a time for jokes?"

Joel's tone changed abruptly. "Jeremy, I have read a lot about this Chuck guy on the newscasts. I even went to a seminar of his out in California years ago. He is a possibility thinker and he has clout with the space program."

"You think we could get in to see him? Is he still in California?" Jeremy was getting excited at this news.

"Maybe, let me call a few friends and see what I can find out," Joel answered, remaining uncharacteristically serious.

"Sounds good. Call me when you know something. You know where we'll be."

"Will do . . . Good luck, Jeremy."

"Thanks."

~

Jeremy walked back into the house to see Valerie finishing packing her clothes. There was an air of frustration surrounding her.

"What's wrong?" Jeremy asked.

"I don't have any idea how long we're going to be. It makes it hard to pack."

"You'll be fine," he said as he left the room. "I'll meet you at the car."

When she came back out to the hangar, Jeremy was in the Rover waiting for her. His sling was gone.

"Ready?" He asked.

"As I'll ever be. Are you OK without the sling?"

"Sure it was just cracked anyway. Joel had some good info."

"Really? What?"

"Plenty of time to tell you on the road."

* * *

By the time they reached highway 183, it was already apparent to Jeremy that something was very different. For starters, the traffic was unusually light; for another thing, he saw an unusual amount of smaller trucks and trailers being pulled.

Jeremy wasn't nearly as certain about his odds as he projected. The story he had to tell was outrageous, and he had no idea what it was going to take to convince anyone to take him seriously. It didn't matter though, he had to try. He still felt that some possibility would present itself. It was unthinkable to him that he could have this vision, then, through a set of circumstances beyond his control, have it again, and then still not be able to use it. Something would definitely present itself.

He continued south. Jeremy was still struggling with how best to approach the people at NASA once he arrived there. No matter how he phrased the words in his mind, all he could hear was what sounded like the ravings of a lunatic. He sure hoped Joel came up with something.

They were already on the southern outskirts of town before Valerie ventured some conversation.

"Are you noticing all these trucks and trailers on the road?"

"Yeah, I am."

"Where are they all going?"

"I imagine to whatever place will make them feel safe in the event of a disaster." It was still odd to imagine the asteroid barreling toward Earth.

It was a beautiful, sunny day in the high 50s. Surely doom wasn't racing through the heavens on a collision course with their little planet.

But it was. And all these people were going and doing whatever it was that made them feel a bit safer. As if there was such a thing as safe.

Jeremy began to rethink his plans. After convincing someone at NASA, he'd intended to take Valerie and go into the Hill Country somewhere. Maybe find a cave or some shelter that wasn't in a city but that wasn't too far away from one either. It seemed to him that that would be the best combination of both worlds, the resources of the city with the solitude and security of the country. But now he wasn't so sure.

He felt an overwhelming responsibility to do something with the information he possessed about the asteroid. If not, he would have already taken Valerie and headed for the hills. There was an added danger to the path he was taking, but with each passing mile he was more and more certain it was the right path.

Once they passed the airport south of town and continued toward I-10, Jeremy looked over at Valerie and took a deep breath.

"Valerie, there's something that is worrying me." Her eyes were not only beautiful, but they glinted with the spark of intelligence, and now that intelligence was bent on him, awaiting his next words. He wasn't sure whether it was the beauty or the intelligence that attracted him more at that moment. He really did love her.

"I was planning on taking us into the hills to find whatever safety there was in the event of the asteroid strike, but now I think I'm going to be spending these last weeks trying to help avert it." He paused looking for a reaction, but all he saw in her eyes was anticipation of his next remark. "I'm struggling with the idea of not protecting you as best as I can. Maybe you should . . ." He couldn't finish and when he glanced up at her, the fire illuminating her eyes hovered between fierce anger and solid determination.

"Let me save you all that worry. If you think you're considering leaving me somewhere that might be safer, forget it. I'm in love with you, and I want to stay with you, and if that means I might be increasing my chances of dying, then so be it. If we're going to die, I'd much rather do it with you than somewhere by myself. Does that solve your conundrum?"

There was no denying the steel in her voice even if he'd wanted to. "Uh, well, yes it does," He paused, "And thank you. There's no one else I'd rather live or die with than you, either. For what it's worth, I think we at least have an adventure in front of us."

"Everything with you is an adventure, Jeremy Andrews. And yes, I think we do have an adventure ahead of us. I'd prefer to survive it, though, if that's OK with you."

"Yep. That was definitely heading up my list of desires," He smiled.

A comfortable silence ensued with both of them watching the countryside pass. The further south they went, the more desolate everything became. It felt like the people had already left and gone somewhere, which surely must be a foreshadowing of things to come.

They reached Columbus an hour later, the point at which the road they were on intersected I-10. Jeremy decided to stop for gas. The first gas station they passed had "sold out" signs on the pump, but the next one was fine. It was starting.

"Don't you think it's a bit early for gas stations to be running low?" Valerie exited the Rover to stretch her legs and stand beside Jeremy, who was watching the numbers on the pump spin.

"Not really. I'm guessing people are already stocking up. And remember, Val, the truck drivers who drive those refill tankers are people too, and a number of them are surely considering some things that are more important than driving the next load somewhere. So, it's the distribution that will break down first, not the actual supply of gas. Hmmm, with that thought in mind . . ." Jeremy opened the back of the Rover and pulled out two five-gallon gas cans. "I think I'm going to stock up myself."

He filled the two cans and mounted them in the bracket that was attached to the back of the Rover, then pulled two heavy locks from a little bag in the back and locked them.

"Whatever possessed you to get a bracket to mount extra gas on the back of the truck?" Valerie had a teasing lilt to her voice that Jeremy didn't miss.

"Just manly stuff. You never know when you might need a little extra go-juice."

"Yeah, right. Is this where you pound on your chest?"

Jeremy made an exaggerated survey of his surroundings, "Maybe later. It looks cool too."

The giggle escaped her before she could stop it, and she got back into the car.

Hours passed quickly.

The fact that it was a gorgeous clear blue Sunday afternoon made the persistent lack of traffic as they entered the outskirts of Houston both apparent and unnerving. The persistent sensation of a foreshadowing kept rippling through Jeremy's mind.

His entire life, Jeremy had felt the possibility of a future such as this. Step by inexorable step, he had prepared. If civilization took a one-way trip back to primitive, he would survive, and so would Valerie, of that he felt certain. Except that future would only come to pass if he couldn't avert it, and he fully intended to do just that. His vision wasn't a coincidence, nor was the timing. This was a blessing and a responsibility that had been laid in his lap.

The skyline of downtown Houston grew quickly in their front windshield as I-10 took them straight to its heart. Valerie was staring up at the looming structures while Jeremy took the exit to I-45 South, toward NASA. When Valerie finally spoke, it was as if she was reading his mind.

"This is eerie. It's like the world has already come to an end," She said, shivering slightly as she spoke.

"Except with everything intact," he added.

"Where is everyone, you think?"

"I'm guessing they're either staying in their homes or have already left."

"But to where?"

Jeremy glanced over at her and saw the tinge of fear in her eyes. All he could do was shrug.

* * *

Chuck leaned back from his computer screen. He hadn't been able to find any way around the problem. No matter how he tried, it boiled back down to one simple conclusion. Without the data he needed, the deployment of the booster shuttle was going to be a wild ass guess. Damn!

He'd been sitting in his house now for days trying to avoid the press that aggressively tried to interview him. It was even worse at the observatory. He felt lonelier and more useless than he could ever recall, and it was time to do something about it. Maybe if he was closer to the problem, he might have some better ideas.

Leaning back into his computer, Chuck began to search flights to Houston. He'd also give Bill Mathers another call.

31

"Houston control to commence Shuttle course change in two hours and twenty-five minutes and counting."

The alerts were coming regularly at 15-minute intervals, and each new one sent a little jolt through Bill.

He'd been called in to this project because of his affiliation with the Sentry Program and probably also because of his close relationship with Chuck Kohler, but beyond these simple connections he felt about as useless as a dust mote in the corner. To make it worse his introverted personality wasn't doing so well with the constant buzz of action that accompanied the maintaining of any space flight. When the news had come about the pilot, Eric, Bill had nearly had a cardiac.

"Bill, there's a phone call for you." He turned a little too sharply toward the female voice that had hailed him, and subsequently fretted that he might seem to her like a nervous little mouse.

"Thanks, Erin. Where's the best place to take it?"

"You can pick up the phone on any desk you like. Line two"

Bill looked around. There were plenty to choose from. This mission, for all its earth shattering (no pun intended) importance, was actually pretty simple and the number of staff needed to support it was minimal.

As Bill reached for the phone, he considered that many of these stations would fill later this afternoon when Houston Control would be called on to remotely swing the double shuttle in the giant arc that would circle Kohler Leporidae and put it on a matching course and velocity with the asteroid.

"Bill Mathers here," Bill felt better about the confident tone he heard in his voice as he answered.

"Bill, this is Chuck."

"Oh, hi, Chuck."

Chuck had neither the time nor the disposition for chit chat, and although he liked Bill, he was well aware of his propensity to babble. This was something he couldn't tolerate at the moment, "Listen, I was wondering if you could pick me up at the airport this afternoon."

Surprised, Bill stammered, "Uh, well, yes, I guess. What airport are you coming into?"

"Hobby."

"Well sure. That's close. What time?"

"I'm in at 3:40."

"OK. No problem but why are you . . ."

"I'll fill you in when I see you, if that's all right with you."

"Sure. I . . ."

"Great. Thanks, Bill. See you then."

Chuck was off the phone and gone before he could get another word out. Bill fumed briefly then remembered that this had always been Chuck's demeanor, and it certainly wasn't a reflection on him. *But why is he coming in?* Well, he'd find out soon enough and at any rate, going to the airport would get him out of the pressure cooker at the control center.

* * *

Valerie's eyes opened and her first sensation was the warmth of Jeremy spooning her and his arm around her chest. Her second was the light on the clock. It was 6:00 a.m., and it took her foggy mind a brief second to remember where she was. A Holiday Inn Express in NASA. Almost across the street from the Space Center.

"Yes, I'm awake, too," Jeremy said from behind her.

His voice startled her, but then she smiled as the pressure of his caress increased.

"So, what's on the agenda, vision boy?"

"Breakfast, I think, and then maybe a little planning."

"What kind of planning are you figuring on doing?" The mischievous grin on his face alerted her before his response.

"Most likely how to make use of your pretty face to get us an audience with someone that might listen."

She couldn't help but grin back at him. Her pretty face, as he put it, was actually the same technique she frequently used in her business, and her track record was good.

When they left the room, the air was thick and damp with the salty, fishy tang of the ocean. The sky was clear, and a gentle breeze kept the coastal smells filling their nostrils. Jeremy paused to look at the antique space vehicles perched on display at the Space Center across the street. Examples of the Mercury, Gemini, and Apollo rockets were on display on the grounds for anyone to see as they passed. Jeremy paused briefly then began to move again, but he didn't move toward their car. Instead he made a beeline to the Waffle House in the adjacent parking lot.

"Feeling like a waffle, are we?" Valerie asked as she realized his destination.

"Feeling like an idiot is more like it. Valerie, how the hell am I going to get anyone to listen to this crazy story I have to tell? I wouldn't believe it myself if it hadn't happened to me."

"Second thoughts, huh? Look, Jeremy, all we can do is go over there and do the very best we can."

His response was delayed as they strolled in the front door of the Waffle House, taking in the aromas of waffles baking and flat grill cooking. The place was busy, and the waitresses looked harried.

"Sit anywhere you like," One of the waitresses behind the counter called, as the door closed behind them.

After a brief glance around, Jeremy picked a table close to the grill. He had worked as a short order cook in college and he liked to watch the cooks work. It brought back memories of a simpler time.

"I know. It's just that I keep hearing myself reciting this story to some in-charge-engineer type, and I see that look on his face."

"What look?"

"That 'get this lunatic out of my face' look that he's going to give me when he realizes that I'm wanting him to change the course of the mission he's responsible for, on the word of a stranger who's telling him he's had a vision of what needs to happen. How are we going to get around the reality of that?"

"What can I get you folks?" The waitress had a surprising economy of teeth that she was apparently completely unselfconscious about, judging by the breadth of her smile.

"A pecan waffle, ham, hash browns and a cup of coffee please," Jeremy promptly volunteered.

Valerie tilted her head and cast him a bit of a surprised glance, "Come here much?"

Jeremy just smiled, "I love Waffle House."

The waitress was already registering a hint of annoyance when Valerie glanced up at her, "I'll have the same without the hash browns."

The waitress scribbled briefly. "Be back in just a moment," she said as she turned to leave.

"I think for starters we are going to have to come up with a more believable story to get in to talk to someone important."

Jeremy gave her a bit of a startled look. "You mean lie?"

Valerie smiled hugely. "Don't be such a Boy Scout. You're really not much into politics, are you? I use that technique all the time. I call it creative reality. It works like a charm."

"I knew I had some untapped resources in you, but I guess I didn't know the extent. I was just counting on your pretty face."

"Don't make me hit you."

"I wouldn't dream of it. It's just that I'm impressed with your suggestion, but don't stop now, help me dream up the *creative reality* we could use."

The waitress abruptly set the coffee on the table with a little bowl of creamers and was gone just as quickly. Her brevity caused Jeremy to look around. The place was packed.

"Maybe I should go into the restaurant business. This place is knocking 'em dead."

"Have you ever even been a waiter? You'd hate it, trust me. And waiting tables is one of the better jobs in a restaurant. You couldn't pay me enough to own one."

"You've been in the restaurant business, I'm guessing?" he asked.

"Waited tables and tended bar is all. That was enough."

"I was a short order cook for a while, so I understand what you mean."

Valerie looked a bit surprised.

"So?" Jeremy asked after a few seconds.

"So what?" she responded, "Oh, the lie. I'm working on it. Did you ever take astronomy?"

"One class in college— about enough to tell a meteor from a planet. Why?"

"Well, if neither of us knows anything about astronomy or physics this is going to be tough to pull off. Wait a minute, wasn't that pilot from Houston?"

"Eric Jensen? Yeah, I think so. Why?"

"Great. Let me think a minute."

"You know maybe Joel could help?" He offered.

Before Jeremy could question her anymore, the waitress conveniently arrived with their food.

* * *

Chuck wasn't particularly thrilled about the plane ride. It wasn't the plane itself he minded; it was the crowds he had no tolerance for. He had his own pilot's license, and would much prefer to fly himself, but his license wasn't current and hadn't been for years.

Chuck was a big man, and airline seats were notoriously ill equipped to deal comfort out to people beyond a middling size. As he excused himself into a seat by the window, since all the aisle seats were taken, he recalled his first trip with Louise to California. It seemed that memories of her were surfacing more and more frequently these days, and he couldn't understand why. She'd been gone for many years now, and he hadn't thought this much about her since her first birthday after her death. Maybe it was the potential cataclysm the world was facing. Maybe he would be getting to see her soon.

He picked up his book for a distraction. Dean Koontz. He loved Dean Koontz. The man's stories never failed to take him away. His only beef with the author after reading more than forty of his books was that they were never long enough. He always wanted more. Louise had liked him, too. *Dammit.* There she was again stalking his thoughts.

Forcing his concentration onto the page by sheer will, Chuck sank into the story as the plane soared across the southwestern sky.

* * *

"OK. I've got it. We need to get back to the room and fire up your laptop."

Jeremy looked up at her with a mouth full of waffle, unable to answer. He chewed quickly while she stared at him. Finally, he got out. "Got what?"

"The answer to how we're going to get in, you goof."

"Oh. OK. How?" Surprise was written all over his face, even with one cheek full of food.

"I'm going to call and tell them I'm his daughter, if he's got a daughter...which I think he does, and I want to get something out of his locker."

He was still looking a bit confused, so she added, "Eric's."

"The pilot?"

"Well, *yeah*," she said, "Who were we just talking about?"

"Oh. Look, Valerie, they're not going to let you into his locker even if they do believe you." Actually, he liked the way she was thinking and was a bit surprised that she could be so devious, but it just seemed so futile.

"Yeah, but we don't need to get into his locker, do we? All we need is to get close enough to someone important and get them to listen."

"That's true, but I still have to come up with some ruse that sounds more plausible than the 'vision' story or they'll never take me seriously."

"But it's the truth."

The indignation in her voice made him smile, but it didn't solve the problem. "So?"

Valerie started to respond then checked herself, "OK. You're right. So then, what are you going to say?"

"I don't know yet, but I need to spend some time on that laptop, too. I'll come up with something, because if I don't, I'm afraid that even heading for the hills isn't going to save us." He hadn't meant to let slip the plans he'd been making to leave with her, but he was so focused on the immediate problem that it just slipped out.

"Head for the hills?"

Jeremy's head popped up from another bite of food and saw the quizzical look on her face. "Uh, yeah, just a figure of speech, you know?"

But she wasn't buying it. "Did you have some plans in mind for us you haven't shared with me yet?"

All of the sudden Jeremy felt embarrassed. "Well, sort of. I just thought that once we'd done what we could here, we might head for a little camping spot I know in the hill country. It belongs to a friend of mine. Part of his thousand-acre ranch and it has some great little caves and streams and . . ." He stopped in mid-sentence when he looked up at her. She was regaling him with the loveliest smile he had ever seen on her face. It was so full of emotion that he completely lost his train of thought.

"So, you were thinking of whisking me away to the wild, eh?"

There was just enough iron in her voice that Jeremy couldn't tell whether she was teasing him or not. He decided it was best to answer as simply as possible and rely on that expression, "I just thought it might be safer there. Easier to defend."

"So, you were planning on defending me, too?"

Jeremy was surprised to feel his face flush. For a moment he couldn't think of anything to say, but he didn't have to, she wasn't through with him yet.

"Is this one of those Tarzan and Jane complexes?"

"More like Jeremiah Johnson and his squaw."

"His squaw?"

"Well, you do have some Indian in you, don't you?"

"I . . . How do you know that?"

"You told me one night over some wine."

"I've got to remember not to drink and chat," she said, bowing her head and shaking it in mock concern.

"Why don't we get back to the hotel and get to work? Maybe we can try storming the Space Center after lunch."

The humor promptly left her features as she looked up at him, "Sounds like a great idea. Let's get going. And by the way, I rather like the Tarzan and Jane metaphor."

Jeremy's grin was huge as they left the restaurant hand in hand.

~

It was almost noon and Jeremy was still pouring over his laptop when Valerie popped back in with a couple of sandwiches and sodas. She'd taken her turn on the computer for a couple of hours before she turned it over to Jeremy, then showered and left. By now his head and shoulders were aching, and the scar around his neck was vacillating between burning and itching. It was healing fine, but it had been so deep it was taking longer than he had expected.

She set the food down and began talking. Jeremy didn't even look up.

"OK, here's the idea. Forget the pilot's daughter thing. I'm going to pose as a research assistant to Linda Spinner from her Jet Propulsion Laboratory. My name is Amanda Hanson. It should be a name they'll recognize, and hopefully, haven't met.

You can simply be my companion and driver. I'm going to claim to have a radical new concept to divert the asteroid, and I want to share it with the director. That should get us in the door. From there it's going to be your baby."

"Wow. How did you come up with all of this? Just a couple of hours on the Internet?"

She smiled, "That's about right. What do you think?"

"I think you're going to get me a chance to talk. I'm just wondering how many sentences I'm going to get out before they order up the straitjacket. I have been giving it some thought, though, and I think I have an angle. Let's give it a try."

"You going to tell me your angle?"

His impish grin following her question was absolutely adorable, and she couldn't help but smile back.

"Nope. I think I'll let the surprise on your face be real when I tell the director."

"Fine. Then let's eat and get going."

~

It was almost 2:00 before they got in the car and drove across the street to NASA's Johnson Space Center. The sound of the gulls in the sky and the renewed tang of ocean air lifted Jeremy's spirits and provided a bit of much needed, albeit unwarranted, hope.

* * *

Chuck was one of the last to step off the plane. He'd sat near the back because it was the only place he could get a window seat, and he wasn't in such a huge rush to exit anyway. He'd still have to wait on his bag downstairs.

As he left security, he searched the crowd for a familiar face. He would have missed Bill altogether if the rotund little fellow hadn't recognized him first and waved. Since Chuck had last seen him, about five years ago, he'd donned a mustache and goatee, lost most of his hair, and gained about thirty pounds.

"Chuck, it's so good to see you," Bill greeted him as he reached out to grab Chuck's long, slender hand in a two-handed grip. "How long has it been, five years? You haven't changed a bit. It must be that good California weather treating you right."

Blathering as usual, Chuck thought as he summoned a smile anyway while returning Bill's slightly overbearing grip. "Hi, Bill. It's good to see you, too." Chuck wasn't much for platitudes or small talk, but he'd learned over the years the value of a few moments of useless chatter. It seemed to put everyone at ease.

"How's the family?"

"Oh, they're great. Carol is busy with the kids, as usual, keeping up with school functions, and Lisa and Toby both have straight A's. Is there anyone new in your life?"

Chuck's grin withered a bit. All he'd been able to think of for days, that wasn't associated with Kohler Leporidae, was Louise, and that just made him sad. "No, Bill, I don't really have the time these days even if I had the desire."

Bill was now following Chuck toward baggage claim as he continued to talk. He had no problem being heard over the general bustle of loudspeakers and people in the terminal, "Aw Chuck, it's not good for you to be alone like that all the time."

"I'm not really alone. The observatory always has people coming and going."

"Yeah, but that's different. You know what I mean?"

"So, any news with the shuttle or the asteroid?" Chuck hoped he wasn't being too abrupt, but the small talk was already annoying him.

Bill hesitated briefly at the change in topic, seemingly confused then picked up in a much more business-like tone. "Well, they've completed the huge arc around it as best they could and are matching its velocity, but they still haven't a clue where to plant the thing."

"Did they pick up any data when they made the loop?"

"Couldn't get in close enough and the instruments they planned to use weren't set up to be operated remotely. Nobody counted on the pilot dying."

"Yeah, really."

They reached the baggage belt which was just starting up. Chuck stood there in silence which was apparently more than Bill could take, "So what else new is going on at the observatory? Other than the asteroid, I mean."

Chuck managed not to roll his eyes. It was going to be a long drive back to NASA.

* * *

"Here we go," Valerie said as they stepped out of the car. The walk from the parking lot to the front door of the Space Center was in itself inspiring and daunting, not so much the chrome and glass of the ultra-modern looking entrance, but the array of former space craft that littered the grounds, some sitting upright and many lying horizontal on their gantries. It was a brisk trip back through time; the history of American space craft in three phases. Mercury capsules, Gemini rockets, then the long line of larger Apollo rockets that finally took America to the moon six times before further lunar trips were abandoned in favor of the reusable Space Shuttles. Jeremy couldn't help but wonder if all that technology had been enough. Had they learned enough to save Earth from the upcoming disaster?

Valerie had been taking in the sights as voraciously as Jeremy had. "Are you ready for this," he asked, riveting her eyes as he spoke.

"As ready as I'll ever be," she said.

"If our success depends on your looks, we're definitely ready."

He hoped his smile was all the reassurance she needed, because at the moment it was all he could offer. He held the glass door open as she breezed into the big building. The information counter was front and center with a smiling Hispanic lady manning the little space. Jeremy instantly had some misgivings. He really was hoping to use Val's looks to get them by some initial hurdles, but this lady wasn't going to be affected by them at all.

"May I help you?" she asked sweetly. She was a petite little thing with perfect skin, a slender face, and forever dark eyes that radiated a smile guaranteed to illicit a response.

"Yes," Valerie began, "My name is Amanda Hanson, and I'm from Linda Spinner's jet propulsion laboratory. We're here to see Arnold Shah."

The smile abruptly faded from the little lady's face as she perceived some gravity in what was normally a very casual post. "Do you have an appointment?"

"Actually, we don't. There simply wasn't enough time. We have some very important information for the director concerning the approaching Kohler/ Leporidae asteroid."

Now the woman's face took on a distinct pallor as she reached for the phone, "I'll see if he's available."

She talked quietly into the phone so Jeremy and Valerie could just hear enough to know she was giving the names they had given her. The only other snippet they could catch was the words *Kohler/Leporidae*. When she hung up, she turned back to them and tried vainly to regain her congenial smile.

"Follow me, please. I'll take you to his office, but he'll be a few minutes."

"That'll be fine," Valerie offered.

The lady walked rather briskly, causing them to initially fall behind and giving Valerie a chance to whisper to Jeremy, "OK, Champ, I did my part. It's about to be your turn."

The result of Jeremy's nervousness was a hard stare in response to Valerie's comment. How was he even going to pull this off? He'd rehearsed this speech fifty times in his head in fifty different ways, and each one sounded more ludicrous than the one before. He'd hit on what he thought was the best approach, but he still didn't like it. It was just the best shot he had.

They must have made at least half a dozen turns including one that paraded them past the big glass wall that overlooked the mission control center. Everyone in there either had their heads down working, had anxious looks on their faces, or both. Great, Jeremy thought.

The little lady made one last turn into a smaller corridor then stepped aside as she opened a door for them.

"This is Director Shah's office. He asked me to have you wait in here. He'll be in as soon as he can break away."

"Thank you so much," Valerie offered, but the woman was gone almost before she was through talking.

"You'd think we had the plague," Jeremy remarked.

"Wait until the director hears what we have to say. He'll most likely think we have something worse," Valerie responded as her eyes roved about the room. It was a modest eight by ten office, packed with decorum yet meticulously tidy.

"Thanks, Val. That's what I needed to hear," he murmured sarcastically. She didn't respond as Jeremy watched her inspect everything from the pictures of his family, to the model jets on his credenza, to the awards on his wall. When it seemed she had been scrutinizing a bit too long, he finally asked, "Something of particular interest holding your attention?"

She stopped and offered a condescending smile, "Haven't you ever been in sales?"

"What?"

"Everything in this room is a hint into the character and life of the man you're about to talk to. Wouldn't you like to learn everything you can before he comes in this room, and you attempt to tell him your crazy story?"

Jeremy was silent. She had an excellent point and on any other day it was a technique he might have thought of himself. Instead of answering, however, he let his attention roam around the room, too.

Valerie picked up a photo from his desk. "See from this we know he's East Indian and is married to a lovely woman and has two kids." She set the picture back down. "And look around Jeremy. A model of a plane I imagine he has flown along with the photos of him in uniform tells me he was a Navy pilot. Look at the walls. He's got a degree from MIT in Astrophysics with a minor in psychology."

That was an interesting combination, Jeremy thought. *Few people with technical degrees also have an interest in how people tick. Maybe that could be useful. On the other hand, this man is also very intelligent, so he wouldn't be very susceptible to, or have much tolerance, for what he perceived as bullshit.* Jeremy decided he would have to get to his point quickly.

Valerie picked up a golf trophy from a bookshelf. "Pretty good golfer too, apparently. Looks like he won this in Albuquerque on the same weekend as the balloon fest. Look at these photos of the annual mass ascension." She put the trophy back in its place. "Here is a man of many interests. Someone you can relate to, Jeremy."

Right then Jeremy realized that if he could connect with this man quickly on a personal level, his chances of gleaning a bit of belief in his crazy story would go up exponentially. It was valuable information indeed. Valerie had been absolutely right, and he was daring to have a smidgeon more confidence in their chances of success.

The thought caused him to turn to her, only to be greeted with a huge grin.

"See what I mean?" She said.

Jeremy grinned back. "Yes, I do, and thank you for pointing it out."

The minutes seemed to stretch into eternity, and Jeremy began to be concerned if Director Shah was making them wait intentionally. He had to dismiss that thought. Shah thought he was coming to see a fellow scientist. What reason would he have for intentionally making them wait? It was a useless line of thought, and Jeremy chided himself for dwelling on it.

To distract himself, he continued to look around the room for more clues into the director. There was a small bookshelf on the back wall by the door, and Jeremy turned his head sideways to read the titles.

To his surprise there were, amongst the hard core textbooks, a number of books dealing with spiritual experiences. *Embraced by the Light,* by

Betty J. Eadie, and *The Celestine Prophecy: A spiritual adventure* by James Redfield, were two that stood out, as well as a number of books about research concerning Jesus Christ. This man wasn't only spiritual, he was a Christian. It was a bit unusual for a scientist, and more unusual for an East Indian, but Jeremy was ecstatic. A little bit of faith was exactly what he was going to need.

"What do you think is keeping him?" Valerie asked.

"Valerie, he is trying to direct a space shuttle mission with a dead pilot going further than any space shuttle has ever gone, toward an asteroid that's on course to wipe out planet Earth. It's possible we're not at the tip top of his to-do list."

"Yeah, but we told him our information had to do with that mission. Shouldn't that raise our importance up a notch or two?"

"I imagine it did, or he wouldn't have agreed to see us at all."

They had been waiting for over forty-five minutes when the door finally burst open, nearly scaring Valerie out of her chair.

Director Shah's eyes locked with Jeremy first as Valerie was noticeably off to the side, and he was already apologizing in a rush before he even released the door.

"I'm so sorry I'm late, but I was in a meeting trying to decide if it was worth the risk to try to have the Shuttle orbit the asteroid one more time in the hopes of getting the data we need to . . ."

His eyes had finally shifted to Valerie, and his words stopped abruptly. The ensuing moment of silence felt like a black hole. Jeremy watched as the apologetic demeanor faded off Shah's face, and his eyes became flinty. This was going to be the moment of truth.

"You're not Amanda Hanson," he said flatly, "I met Amanda when I was briefed on the Cassini project. What the hell are you doing in my office?"

Jeremy took a deep breath and began. "You're right, Director Shah, we needed to get in to see you. I believe I might have the answer you're looking for with regard to the shuttle placement if you're open enough to listen to information coming from an unusual source.

At the very least you should hear me out, if for no other reason than the fact that I am not in your field, and I came by this information just a few days before Kohler/Leporidae was spotted. The chances of that happening are, should I say, astronomical? Getting this information to you nearly got me killed. Literally. I think it at least warrants a moment of faith to hear me out."

Jeremy clamped his mouth shut. He'd given it his best shot, and now he had to stay quiet. Jeremy watched as Shah's features softened ever so slightly, and his eyes moved again to Valerie who was evincing a barely perceptible nod in the affirmative. Another sales tool, Jeremy noticed, then thought how much he must have underestimated this woman's abilities at the job she did. Who could refuse her?

Shah seemed to be struggling with a decision but finally asked, "So, what *are* your real names?"

"Jeremy Andrews," he offered without hesitation.

"Valerie Latham." Like Jeremy, Valerie seemed to sense that less was better at this point.

"And what is your background?" He asked as his gaze locked briefly on the scar around his neck.

"I'm a pilot, a real estate investor, and a musical events producer and promoter." Jeremy intentionally put the "pilot" attribute first in the hopes of gleaning a bit of plausibility.

Director Shah frowned and shifted his gaze to Valerie "And you?"

"I'm a lobbyist for the digital rights industry, but before that I did some pro-NASA lobbying."

The smile she wore as she answered his question probably helped their cause more than her words themselves.

"Will you hear us out, Director Shah? I have a very unusual story to tell beginning with this scar around my neck."

Shah's eyes narrowed as they shifted again to the still-wicked looking trail left by the parachute line. "Very well, I'll listen," he said, "because you're already here, but I won't promise anything, and you had better make it relatively quick. And please call me Arnie." As he spoke, he finally moved past them and took a seat at his desk, his exhaustion evident in every detail including his request for familiarity.

Jeremy inwardly released a sigh of relief. He had a chance. Without wasting any more time, Jeremy started in as clearly and quickly as he could. He couldn't help but be impressed with the man. His mind was fast and nimble, and he was obviously able to adapt to a rapidly changing situation. Someone had chosen well when they had picked him to run this branch of NASA.

* * *

When they pulled into the parking lot at the Space Center, Bill was still chatting away. He was now onto the topic of golf and was completely oblivious to the fact that not only was Chuck not commenting, he hadn't even been paying attention for the last twenty minutes. His token to civility had merely been the occasional head nod, smile or the even less frequent, "uh huh," but even that had faded. None of it seemed to matter to Bill at all. Chuck couldn't help but wonder whether he continued these unmitigated tirades even when he was alone. Certainly, Chuck's presence seemed an unnecessary accoutrement.

"Here we are, Chuck. I have to get back into the situation room once we get in, but the girl at the front desk can take you to Director Shah's office."

Thank God, Chuck thought. He was afraid he was going to have to make some excuse to get away, but Bill had just made it unnecessary. "Thank you so much for the lift, Bill."

"Not a problem. It was good to get out of the office for a while. It seems like I'm glued to that place, and any chance to get a little fresh air is . . ."

The patter continued right up until they got into the building, and Bill excused himself as he pointed out the receptionist.

"Thanks again, Bill," Chuck said as he turned away, surprising himself by abruptly smiling at the pretty Hispanic girl.

"I'm here to see Arnold Shah. Could you direct me to his office?"

The girl looked a little flustered, "I'm afraid he might still be in a meeting, but I can call and ask him. Who shall I say is here?"

"Tell him it's Chuck Kohler, from the Palomar Observatory."

Her eyes got a little wider if that was possible. The name obviously rang a bell. "Yes sir, I'll tell him."

212

* * *

"At least he listened," Jeremy said as they navigated the corridors to the exit, "Maybe he'll call us back."

Valerie's eyes looked sad, "I wouldn't hold my breath, Jeremy. Isn't there anything else we can do?"

Jeremy had been asking himself the same question, but he wasn't coming up with any answers. They approached the last door that led into the huge foyer for the main entrance.

Both their heads had been down, but as they approached the information counter a deep rolling voice caught his attention.

"I think I can find it," the voice said. "And thank you very much."

Jeremy and Valerie's heads both popped up at the resonant tones, and Valerie's eyes shot wide open. "Oh my God. That's Chuck Kohler. I recognize his face from the television interview we saw."

"That's the guy Joel said we should try to contact. You've met him?"

"Well, sort of . . . He probably doesn't remember me, but I was introduced to him at a lobbyist function in DC. Maybe we can . . ."

~

Chuck stepped around the little kiosk and looked up. His eyes instantly locked with Valerie's, and his heart skipped a beat. Before he could even stop himself, a word escaped his mouth: "Louise?" Instantly he realized the absurdity of the question that had slipped from his lips, but the woman in front of him was an absolute doppelganger for his lovely wife, at least for what she looked like twenty years ago. He was already breathing heavily and had involuntarily taken another step in her direction. The sight of her was so amazing that it very nearly broke the remaining fragments of his heart.

~

Valerie wasn't sure what it was she was seeing in Dr. Kohler's eyes, but it was profound, and it was a chance they hadn't had a moment before. "Dr. Kohler?" she asked as she took another step toward him.

213

"Louise?" he repeated realizing how ludicrous the notion was even as the word left his mouth again. He couldn't seem to help himself. The last few days' worth of reminiscences combined with this unusual coincidence was taking its toll.

~

"No, sir. I'm Valerie Latham, and I met you a few years ago at a congressional committee meeting. You were laying out the advantages of the NASA program in general and the Hubble Space Telescope in particular. We were both trying to get the same funding bill passed."

Chuck's head was nodding, but he wasn't speaking, and he still had a vacant look on his face.

"Are you okay, Dr. Kohler? You look a bit ill."

~

Chuck did feel a bit ill. He couldn't tear his eyes away from Valerie. It was as if his dreams of the last couple of weeks had taken on life in the waking world. Memories of Louise were flooding back to him in such vivid cascades that he couldn't sort them out. Each and every one of them carried its own load of emotion, and for a moment he could only let them wash over him and relish the sensation.

He teetered a bit and Jeremy and Valerie were instantly at his side.

"Why don't we sit down over here for a moment, Dr. Kohler. You're looking pale."

"Yes. I think I need to sit down, and please . . . call me Chuck."

This comment was obviously directed at Valerie, as was Chuck's attention. As a matter of fact, Jeremy had never felt quite so superfluous to a human interaction for which he was present in his entire life. But in this case that was just fine. Chuck's attention was positively riveted on Valerie and maybe it was something they could use.

They moved to a line of chairs against the wall, halfway across the foyer, and everyone seemed to be waiting on someone else to say something. Jeremy broke the silence.

"Dr. Koh...Chuck. Are you feeling any better?"

Chuck lifted his head seeing Jeremy for the first time. "Yes, I'm feeling much better now. It's just that . . ." He couldn't bring himself to say it. Not yet.

Valerie had been watching him intently when she abruptly asked, "Who is Louise?"

You would have thought she had stuck Chuck with a pin, so sharp was his flinch to her question. His eyes got big again as he stared at her for a moment before answering.

"She was my wife. Pardon me for staring, but you could easily be her twin— at least her twin from a couple of decades or so ago, when I saw her last."

"I'm truly sorry if the likeness brings you any pain," she answered slowly, the wave of emotion evident on her face at the admission of his loss.

A tear was actually forcing its way from one eye, and the realization embarrassed him further, "Actually, it's wonderful. Thank you."

There was something surreal about hearing those soft emotions issuing from that weather-worn face on the wings of that deep, resonating voice. It held both Jeremy and Valerie transfixed in their seats beside him.

Finally, Chuck spoke again, "What brings you two here?"

Valerie and Jeremy's eyes locked briefly, and they both knew who was going to answer this question. This was their chance.

It's funny you should ask that, sir," Jeremy began.

"Chuck, please."

"Chuck, then. Would you be willing to take a few minutes and let us share our story?"

The initial look in Chuck's eyes as he watched Valerie was very close to love. It was the shadow of remembered love, and there was no way he was going to refuse anything that allowed him to hold on to this tiny piece of rapture just a bit longer. Nevertheless, at the recognition of Jeremy's question, that look morphed slightly into a combination of curiosity and suspicion.

"I'd be glad to," he said.

The moments passed as Jeremy related the story, while Chuck's eyes continually flickered back to Valerie. She smiled sweetly at him every time she caught him looking.

The story did seem to have an impact on him though, and Jeremy saw a real spark of interest when he related his near-death experience. When he finished, silence hung between them until, with one last glance at Valerie, Chuck finally responded.

"I believe you. And what's more, even if I didn't, your possibility is as good as anything else we've got except for one little twist I want to add. And that twist is the reason I came here to talk to Arnie Shah."

Jeremy's expression conveyed his shock at Chuck's simple acceptance, but he still took the opportunity to continue, "One more thing, Chuck. We just got through relating this story to Mr. Shah, and although he listened, he was somewhat less than receptive, so I wouldn't mention us when you talk to him."

Chuck turned the full weight of his gaze on Jeremy, and his bushy brows furrowed. Jeremy felt as though any thought he'd ever had was available to this man's penetrating intellect. "He'll listen to me. Besides I'm quite certain they don't have any better ideas, and I know Arnie very well."

"Thank you so much for listening to us," Valerie added.

"No. Thank you, Valerie, for a number of things."

~

It was an eerie sensation for Valerie to feel the weight of this man's emotions settling on her. It felt so much like what she sensed from Jeremy on a regular basis, but with an overlay of pain. It made the sincerity she hoped to convey that much more real and prompted her to interject one more question.

~

"Chuck, do you mind if I ask you something personal?"

"Not at all."

Jeremy again registered shock and took a sharp breath lifting a finger into the air, presumably to stall Valerie's next words, but she didn't hesitate.

"What happened to Louise?" A wistful look of pain overtook Chuck's features before he spoke.

"She died from an unusually sudden onset of Leukemia."

Valerie's face twisted with pain and tears promptly filled her eyes, "I'm so sorry. And let me apologize for bringing up such a painful memory."

The sorrow on Chuck's face had a different quality, though. It was laced with the peace of acceptance of a heartbreaking life's tragedy and was followed by a soft smile. "That's okay, young lady. It was a long time ago, but your face has brought me a few moments of remembered happiness and for that, I thank you."

The little receptionist at the front desk called over to Chuck, "Dr. Kohler, Director Shah is waiting in his office to see you."

"It looks like this is my cue," Chuck said, rising from the chair, "Would you two like to join me for dinner later and discuss the result of this meeting?"

Jeremy didn't even glance at Valerie before he responded, "That would be wonderful. We're staying at the Holiday Inn Express across the street. Here's my card. You can call us when you're ready."

"I'll do that."

"Again, thank you sir," Valerie added as he took a deep breath and turned resolutely away from them.

* * *

"Now what do we do?" Valerie asked, turning to Jeremy with a shrug.

Jeremy was grinning like a guilty kid, "Now we go sightseeing."

Jeremy made a game out of not telling Valerie where they were going, but it ended up being a simple jaunt to the bay to watch the boats, have a cocktail, and watch the sunset. It was romantic, exhilarating, and, as it turned out, the perfect formula for chewing up a bit of unplanned time.

A chill breeze was beginning to freshen from the bay as Jeremy and Valerie sat on the upstairs deck of The Turtle Club and watched a deep red sun dip slowly into the water. Clouds in the distance hovering just above the horizon gave the impression of steam boiling up from the sun's touch.

Valerie shivered.

"Cold?" Jeremy asked reaching his arm around her shoulder.

"Not really. More like apprehensive."

"Are you afraid Chuck won't convince them?"

"No. I'm afraid that even if he does, it won't do any good."

Jeremy's wan smile seemed to soothe her. "So, you're worrying about a little thing like the end of the world?"

"Yeah—silly, huh?" Now her grin was matching his.

"Yeah, I think so. Do you remember the Serenity Prayer? 'God grant me the serenity to accept the things I cannot change; courage to change the things I can; and the wisdom to know the difference.'"

"Yes, I know that one. I guess it does apply here."

"Yeah it does, but you know what I've always found to be the most difficult part of that little trinity?"

"No. What?"

"The wisdom to know the difference. Valerie, we're doing everything we can right now. I think after our meeting with Chuck tonight, we should focus on enjoying each other," he paused, and a mischievous grin bloomed across his face. Do you like to camp?"

~

Valerie was pretty certain she knew where this was going, and she was more than happy to follow along, "So are we back to Tarzan and Jane?"

"Sounds fun, doesn't it?"

"As long as it's with you it does."

The sun was just a glow below the horizon now, and the chill wind was getting uncomfortable when Jeremy's phone rang.

Mimicking Chuck's earlier words, Jeremy glanced at Valerie, "Well, here's our cue, then answered, "Hello?"

Valerie sat patiently and listened to Jeremy's side of the conversation. "Sounds good to me. Do you have a place in mind? I was thinking of Mexican. There's a Ninfas on Bay Area Boulevard and it's great Mexican . . . great. Seven it is then. See you soon."

"Time to go?" Valerie offered.

"Time to go," Jeremy agreed.

* * *

Ninfa's was a Texas tradition, and arguably one of the best Mexican restaurants around. Jeremy and Valerie arrived before Chuck and sat enjoying the engaging old-world Mexican décor that surrounded them.

Nibbling on chips and avocado salsa, they ordered a large Margarita for two and settled in comfortably.

They didn't have to wait for long before they saw Chuck's thinning grey-haired head towering above the hostess at the door. He was scanning the room while she attempted to talk, and Jeremy waived him over. With a quick word to the little hostess he moved in their direction.

"Margaritas, huh? Sounds like a good idea to me." He pointed to the glass as the waitress approached. She nodded before reaching the table and turned back to the bar.

"So how did it go?" Jeremy asked. Chuck's eyes were again focused on Valerie, and it occurred to Jeremy that if any other man gawked at her like that in his presence, he'd be motivated to say something. In this case, however, it only made him vaguely sad, and induced thoughts of how he might feel if he lost her someday. A small shudder rippled through him. Considering the state of the world right now, that possibility was all too real.

"In a nutshell, he agreed. I focused more on my idea of slamming the first shuttle into that same hole; it was an idea that the European Space Agency thought of first. They called it the 'Don Quixote project'.

The particular point of impact is still due to your information though, Jeremy. I didn't really have a better idea for a location. It was actually harder to get them to agree to that than it was to get them to place the second shuttle there. I didn't describe how I'd come up with that location, and surprisingly he didn't ask. He did look at me funny though. Anyway, I'm just hoping that the force of the impact might initiate the movement we hope to accomplish with the second shuttle."

"Wow," Valerie breathed, "They didn't even question your choice of sites? That's incredible."

"I think it was a combination of things. First, that he'd just had that site suggested from another source, even if he was skeptical, and second,

I had his thoughts focused on the ramifications of sacrificing a second 1.7 billion dollar shuttle on the project."

All Jeremy could do was shake his head. He couldn't quite believe they had succeeded.

They all sat in silence for a few moments enjoying their drinks, until Valerie broke the silence, "What are you going to do now, Chuck?"

Chuck's head was bent over his plate, but he was shaking it even before he looked up at Valerie to answer. "I'm not entirely sure, Valerie. The director asked me to stick around, and frankly the publicity back home has made it next to impossible for me to work or get any peace. I might just take him up on his offer. What about you two?"

It was Jeremy that answered, "We haven't really gotten that far. I think we'll head back toward Austin and maybe into the Hill Country.

"Hide from the escalating madness?" There was a smile on Chuck's face, but his eyes were still locked on Valerie.

"It seems like as good a plan as any."

Jeremy couldn't help it. Watching Chuck focus on Valerie like that fostered tiny slivers of jealousy that seeped into his mind, even as he let himself imagine what it would be like to lose someone you love and later be confronted with her exact look-a-like. Then, like a cleansing rain, the rush of sadness that image invoked washed away any residual jealousy, leaving Jeremy with a ridiculous desire to hug the man.

Jeremy's thoughts returned to the table only to find both Chuck and Valerie staring him. Apparently, his feelings had been playing across his face. Valerie's stare was sheer curiosity, but Chuck's held a degree of understanding. Both made him feel like he'd been caught with his hand in the cookie jar. He felt his face redden.

"Yeah, and I have plenty of supplies at my house we can take with us. Things I've been saving for a long time." Jeremy's diversion seemed welcome to everyone.

"You a survivalist of some sort?" Chuck asked.

"I call myself a closet survivalist. I've only stored a few things over the years."

"I think he just wants to play Tarzan," Valerie chimed in embarrassing Jeremy even further.

"Chuck, is there anything else we could do for you?" Jeremy asked, taking a deep draft of his margarita.

"No. I think I can handle things here, kids. You find a place to be safe, and I'll see if I can't help these NASA folks save the world. On the other hand, you might want to hang around a TV for the next day or two. NASA has quite a challenge to overcome."

"What's that?" Jeremy asked reflexively before surmising the answer.

"First they have to separate the two shuttles and make sure the second one is in a stable position above the asteroid. Then they have to aim and slam the first one into the Rabbit's eye, wait for the dust to settle and ever-so-gently set the second one down virtually on top of the wreckage. It's going to be quite a feat in itself to do remotely. It's never been done before, much less at such a great distance. There are cameras on both shuttles so the world will get to watch at least some of it."

The idea of remote controlling aircraft was not unfamiliar to Jeremy, and he wasn't so sure that it should be as difficult as Chuck was making it sound. "Chuck we've had all sorts of unmanned aircraft available for years. We take them off, land them, and basically pilot them completely by remote control like a video game. What makes this attempt so difficult?"

"You're right Jeremy, but you're not thinking about the distance. At their current distance it is going to take about five minutes for the shuttle to respond to a single command given to it from Earth, then another five to observe the result. That one fact is probably the main reason for having this be a manned mission from the beginning."

"Oh my God," Valerie exclaimed realizing the extent of the problem, "That sounds impossible." Her tone was heavy with fear and Jeremy could sympathize. When Chuck put it that way, it brought the odds of succeeding into sharp focus.

"Chuck, is that even possible?"

Chuck's slow smile and sleepy gaze were reassuring. "They practice these kinds of things a lot, Jeremy, with computer simulations, and have been doing so for years. The odds aren't quite as bad as you think."

Silence reigned at the table for a few minutes.

"Well, I think you have me convinced. I'm going to hang around the TV for a day or so."

"Ditto," Valerie echoed.

Jeremy and Valerie turned and smiled at each other.

"They are set to make the attempt in the next day or so. I don't think they've determined a specific time yet."

32

Everyone in the NASA Control Center was sweating as they watched the cameras on the shuttle—Jonathan Regis most of all. The giant image of the double shuttle floating peacefully alongside the Rabbit's Revenge asteroid depicted a serenity that was in stark contrast to the nervous systems observing it.

Jonathan had not only been trained as a shuttle pilot, but also to pilot the shuttles on remote control, and as such had been practicing some very specific maneuvers on the simulator at NASA for days, but he was still scared.

Back in June of 2006, as a result of an incident with the shuttle Discovery, NASA began working on a means to remote control the shuttles. Their first configuration was a twenty-eight-foot-long braided cable that was attached in space to the controls of Discovery increasing the distance to receive signals and giving Houston Center control of the landing gear, drag chutes and auxiliary power units. This was believed to give them the control to land the shuttles remotely. Since then the entire apparatus had been enhanced and permanently installed in all the shuttles. It now offered remote control of not only the landing systems but virtually every system aboard the shuttle including all the external thrusters as well as the main engines.

Up to this day none of those systems had ever been used—tested in the lab, yes, actually used in space, no. NASA began reconsidering these controls a day or two after the death of Eric Jensen, but the bigger concern had not been how well those controls would perform, it had been the delay involved in sending commands and receiving the visual results of those commands at such a great distance. The delay was now slightly more than five minutes each way.

The current necessity, however, had spurred NASA to task an entire team of programmers to write a program that would, in essence, turn the remote control of the Space Shuttle into an interactive video game that the double shuttle, Prometheus, would mimic exactly.

Jonathan was going to initiate a series of commands with the remote-control apparatus and the computer would display an instant depiction of the calculated results of his actions. Depending on the number of actions and the delay between them, it could take many, many, minutes before the actual results of his actions could be viewed. He also had a limited number of actions he could perform at once before the actual results returned. The program had been checked and rechecked and NASA was as certain as they could be of its effectiveness. In just a few more minutes they would know for sure.

Jonathan watched the simulated shuttle on the screen, and the simulated asteroid in its relative position next to it. From where he sat, he couldn't see the image of the real shuttles being sent back from their on-board cameras.

That view was determined to be too confusing for the pilot. There were separate controls for piloting each of the shuttles, but since both shuttles were ultimately going to the same spot, Jonathan was supposed to maneuver the double shuttle into place and then NASA would disconnect the two. The thrusting shuttle (named Atlas) would remain in position to be deployed after the piloting shuttle (named Ulysses) consummated its impact.

Everything *should* work, but with the literal, fate-of-the-world hanging in the balance the volume of cold sweat in the control room could fill buckets. Also, in an unprecedented decision, the entire operation was being viewed live on worldwide television. No program in history had ever received such coverage, and no program in history had ever had such an extensive audience.

Virtually the entire planet, anyone with access to a television screen, was standing by to watch this crucial step in NASA's bid to save Earth.

Jonathan took one last look down at the joystick in his hand and took a deep breath. "Well, here goes," he sighed. The broadcast to the entire planet was spared this audio transmission, but one could almost feel the planet taking a deep breath in unison as Jonathan began his first maneuver.

The world watched the simulated screen, many not understanding that they were watching a simulation even after the repeated explanations, as Prometheus began to rotate slowly to point its double nose at the eye of Rabbit's Revenge.

* * *

Jeremy realized he was holding his breath only when he heard Valerie release hers. They were both staring at the TV like the majority of the rest of the planet.

Their drive home had been uneventful other than an even more apparent stillness on the highways and in the cities. It seemed that wherever people wanted to go to wait out the remaining days before the anticipated impact of Rabbit's Revenge, they were already there. Normal business was grinding to a halt.

The TV was constantly reporting on the fact that although many people were trying to go through their days as though nothing was happening, an equal number had decided to abandon their daily activities in favor of remaining or leaving with their families.

Jeremy had watched with interest, trying to determine the best time for them to leave.

"It looks just like a video game," Valerie said clinging to Jeremy's arm on the couch.

"What we're actually seeing *is* just like a video game, but with about ten systems that have never been tried before, much less tried together."

"Thanks for that reassurance," she said. Jeremy just smiled.

The pilot, Jonathan, had completed the first maneuver. He had rotated the shuttle, so it was facing back in the direction of the asteroid. They were pausing before he made any additional adjustments to verify that the ship had in fact done what the computer said it had done from his manipulations.

It was an odd sensation to watch television and see dead spaces in time with no commercials. The announcer attempted to fill up as much of the space as he could, but finally ran out of useless drivel and simply let the still screen speak for itself.

As a result, whole segments consisted entirely of the regular beeping and faint background static of the equipment in the control room at Johnson Space Center. Having an inactive screen like that wasn't unprecedented, just unprecedented to this generation. Decades before when the shots were sent back from the Apollo moon missions, tens of minutes would go by watching almost no motion as those early astronauts went through their studied maneuvers on and near the surface of the moon.

As they waited, the announcer finally came back on and began talking about his recent interview with someone about how much money had been spent on the space program over the years. Many politicians over the years had decried that money as a waste of resources—the same resources that were currently being utilized in an attempt to save the planet. The greatest detractor was the current president who had recently slashed NASA's budget. He droned on for a while before being abruptly interrupted by the screen flashing back to the shuttle.

"What you are seeing is not the simulation screen, but the actual view from the shuttle cameras. As you can see the reversing maneuver has been achieved successfully. The next action will be to fine tune the direction and point the noses of both shuttles directly at the little crater referred to as the Rabbit's eye. In just a moment we will switch back to the simulation screen as pilot Jonathan Regis begins this maneuver."

Right then the screen switched back to the shuttle simulation screen. The world watched in rapt attention as the nose of the shuttle, visible via simulated cameras inside the cockpit looking out its front windshield, slowly lined up with the dark indentation on the asteroid that was being referred to as the Rabbit's Eye. As near as scientists could determine the valley itself was about three hundred feet below the remainder of the asteroid's surface. This image, however, was just the simulated one, and it would be another twenty minutes or so before the world could view the actual result of pilot Regis's actions.

Time marched on as the world waited.

Valerie leaned over to Jeremy, "Jeremy how strong do you feel about going and hiding somewhere in the hills?"

Jeremy pulled her in a little closer and turned to her. "I don't know. I just figure it'll be safer."

"Really? We're not exactly *in* the city out here by the lake."

The tone of her voice caught him more than the words, "Do you not want to go?"

"I want to be with you, and I'll follow whatever you decide, but if we don't have that much time left, I'd rather spend it someplace comfortable with you. Do you really think you couldn't protect us here?"

Jeremy thought about it. His instincts to run really were just that, instincts, and he probably could protect them just as well here at his house. It would give them access to his plane, too, which could be a plus. Now that he was weighing the options seriously, he realized that another part of his motivation was that sensation he'd had all his life of living during the end of civilization. The more he thought about it, the more he realized the benefits of staying. His house was already energy efficient and could be made more so. He had access to fresh water from the lake if all else failed, and he also had a generator and a fuel tank in the hangar, not to mention the large aviation fuel tanks on the field. He could fill up his personal tank and the aircraft's tanks and have quite a reserve of fuel.

As far as the terrain, they *were* more on the outskirts of a city than in the middle of one, despite what the map lines said. For that matter, even the lay of the land reduced the number of directions that anyone could come at them. There was really only a couple of roads in or out of their subdivision and beyond that the only access was by water.

Valerie waited patiently while he sifted through these details.

"No, actually Val, I think I could protect us just fine here. Would you rather do that?"

Her smile answered him even before the nod of her head confirmed the answer.

"Then that's what we'll do."

"I love you," she said.

"Ditto," he answered.

The announcer's voice interrupted the moment, "NASA has confirmed that the movements to position the shuttles have been successful. The next sound you hear from the shuttle itself should be the sound of the explosive docking bolts separating the two shuttles."

The announcer's voice faded again leaving just the occasional background static and rhythmic beeping of the control room itself.

There was nothing else to say and no verbal commands to give. Jonathan Regis had already initiated the action; the wait was for the shuttle to receive it and the sound to return to Earth. When it came it was abrupt and loud. Jeremy had a mental image of seven billion people around the world jumping just as he and Valerie did.

"Separation has occurred," came a stiff voice from the television. It wasn't the announcer but someone in the Space Center. That same voice continued,

"Initiating ignition of Ulysses engines."

That was all they heard then silence. Another ten minutes was going to have to pass as the commands raced at the speed of light half-way to and then back from the sun before the result of those actions could be seen by the world.

If it had been possible to measure the number of breaths taken around the world in that next ten minutes, it would have certainly proven that the entire world held its breath for the next announcement. But there wasn't a next announcement.

The next image the world saw was a view from the Shuttle Atlas' camera of Shuttle Ulysses slamming directly into the eye of Rabbit's Revenge, its engines still flaming brightly for many moments before extinguishing.

If seven billion people jumping up and down around the world at the same instant could have affected the Earth's orbit, then that orbit would certainly have adjusted at the instant that image flashed onto TV screens worldwide.

The celebration included Jeremy and Valerie in their den by Lake Travis.

"We did it. We did it!" Valerie yelled as she grabbed Jeremy's neck with both arms.

"Well we've done the first part of it," Jeremy answered enjoying her embrace but not nearly as exuberant.

Valerie heard the reticence in his voice and pushed back from him, "What's wrong?"

"We still have a long way to go, is all I'm thinking. I believe they will get the Atlas shuttle in place, but even then, we have to wait and see if it works."

His words were like water on her flame, and she sat back beside him on the couch to stare at the view of the destroyed Ulysses Shuttle that was lingering on the screen.

It would be there until the next images of Atlas accelerating toward the surface of the asteroid replaced it.

"Do you think it will work?" She asked.

Now it was Jeremy's turn to recognize the emotion in her voice. Fear this time, and he immediately felt guilty for fostering it. "The scientists sure think it will, and then there's my dream. Sure, it will. And you know what Valerie, even if it doesn't, I'll be happy to just die in your arms."

"Die in each other's arms," she corrected, her voice trembling as she hugged him again.

The hug turned into a kiss and fear was replaced with passion. The couch was wide and long, and while the world waited for the Shuttle Atlas to make its own controlled plunge to the surface of the planet killer, Jeremy and Valerie made love.

~

Some preparations were required to shift the earthbound remote controls from the Ulysses to the Atlas, so by the time the announcer came back on to tell the world that the Atlas Shuttle was ready to be deployed, Valerie and Jeremy were snuggled together under a big fuzzy blanket. Their act of life had temporarily displaced any fear, and they joined the rest of the world once more to watch.

"The Shuttle Atlas has been ignited," the announcer said then the moments slipped by. The next change on the screen was once more from the Atlas' nose camera and the world again held their collective breath as the eye of Rabbit's Revenge slowly grew on the screen. The images were now constant even though the world was receiving them ten minutes after the action was initiated and five minutes after they actually happened. With a stately quietness the Atlas approached Rabbit's Revenge like a tentative lover. Closer and closer it approached until the Eye filled the entire screen, framing the wreckage of the Ulysses—the tomb of Eric Jensen.

Closer and still closer.

The process must have gone on for twenty minutes or more before the slender needles of the forward thrusters became visible in the view of the nose camera. NASA was slowing Atlas for its contact with the asteroid.

The Atlas was aiming in, just to the relative right of the Ulysses wreckage and that wreckage was looming progressively larger on the screen. Watchers could clearly see the entire shuttle crushed completely into the surface of the asteroid.

The only recognizable portions left were the vertical tail and the cylinders of the three main engines; the rest had virtually disintegrated on impact. Presently, even that view disappeared leaving just a dark void ahead of the Atlas. Lights flashed on suddenly which could have only come from the shuttle itself and the proximity of the asteroid could be clearly seen. They were almost there.

Finally, a loud crunching sound caused the world to jump as the nose of the Atlas settled into a deep cavity in the crater.

"Shuttle Atlas has been successfully placed," came the voice from the control room at Johnson Space Center. Around the world the cheers started again.

"And now we wait," Jeremy said, getting up from the couch and reaching for his clothes.

"Wait," Valerie said rising from the couch herself, "Don't put on your clothes yet. Let's go take a hot tub." Even if her body hadn't been irresistible to Jeremy, her smile certainly was, so while the Atlas was prepared to begin its mighty battle with the mass of the asteroid, two people abandoned the TV to enjoy the pleasures of hot water and loving company.

* * *

David rose from the couch. He had been watching the TV as well. He finally believed that the entire asteroid story was true, but he didn't care. Ever since his failed attempt to have Jeremy killed, (he was finally willing to use his name) he had been seething. Something had snapped. The money no longer mattered. Sex no longer mattered. His practice no longer mattered. The Earth coming to an end wasn't even a consideration anymore. All that mattered to him was vengeance. Jeremy was the one that had caused his problems, and he wanted that man dead. Then nothing would stand in the way of his having Valerie. He could no longer even think of it as some kind of twisted love. At this point it was an insatiable lust for possession. He *wanted* her. That was all that mattered. And he *was* going to have her.

He'd actually driven by Jeremy's house a few times, but he hadn't seen any signs of anyone home. It was almost time to drive by again and check.

33

Chuck's idea had been to have the Atlas sustain a slow steady burn rather than a more forceful short burn, so the engines aboard Atlas had been burning on and off at regular intervals for four days now. Its fuel was nearly spent. He had decided to slow down the frequency of the pulses and spread them out over the next several days. Eight or ten more pulses would exhaust it completely, and then they could only hope.

It was puzzling Chuck though; the amount of force they had exerted on Kohler/Leporiade should have had more effect by now. *What is the back of that thing made of?* The amount of mass needed to resist that much force was incredible and in his mind, he had been trying to think of substances with enough density to do that. The more he thought about it the more he began to believe that possibly the back side of that meteor was made of some heavy metal like gold, lead, or possibly something radioactive like uranium. Wouldn't that be something if the back side of that meteor was made of Uranium? That would make its impact with Earth an interesting mixed blessing. Not only would the asteroid's impact do the damage, but if a large chunk of it was radioactive then even small bits could be deadly. On the other hand, if it *was* radioactive uranium that much uranium could fuel all the reactors in the world for the next thousand years.

Chuck had been helping to do the trajectory calculations, and it wasn't looking as good as he had hoped. Any change their efforts had accomplished was so small as to be barely detectable. It wasn't that they needed any great change, even a small course correction could do the job with the amount of time they had left, but he just wasn't seeing it

34

November 24th, 2016
Thanksgiving

Thanksgiving Day took on a new meaning for the people of America as everyone considered the fate that loomed heavy on the Earth. Turkeys were bought by the millions, and all the preparations for a Thanksgiving feast were made ready across the country. But a curious thing was happening around America. This Thanksgiving the size of the gatherings went dramatically up. Family members who hadn't spoken to each other in years turned up to spend the holiday with their extended families, and friends who didn't have families were invited to spend it with other families. Around the country, gatherings that might traditionally consist of four or five immediate family members had grown to ten and twenty, and relatives that might have left quickly just stayed.

People talked about their memories and experiences with each other as they enjoyed the closeness of the ones they loved. Not surprisingly, this Thanksgiving very few people spent time discussing plans for the future. It was a topic that was avoided with an unspoken mutual agreement. And in almost every household, in addition to the holiday football games and advertisements for Christmas gifts that were continuing to run, every household had a television or radio tuned in to follow the progress of Rabbit's Revenge.

Later in the day, the final burst of fuel from the Shuttle Atlas would be spent and sometime after that, maybe another day or so, the scientists would confirm whether or not their efforts to save Earth would be enough. The anticipation affected every human on the planet and prayers were voiced not only from American families celebrating their several hundred-year-old traditions, but from families around the world who together offered words of hope for the success of the mission.

Jeremy and Valerie woke up early that morning, and even before they got out of bed, Valerie was all full of energy.

"Jeremy, we ought to be around other people today." Her eyes were bright with child-like excitement, but Jeremy's response was subdued.

Both of them were only children and all four of their parents had passed away. It was a sad coincidence that Valerie found a bit remarkable. Now as she mentioned being around people, Jeremy's reaction caught her by surprise. Sadness wasn't what she was trying to achieve so, before Jeremy had a chance to answer, she decided to change the subject.

"Why don't we invite Chuck to dinner, and Joel?" This at least got a more positive response.

"Joel and his whole band would be fun actually. As far as Chuck, you think he'd drive up here from NASA?"

"Sure. I don't think he has any family either, and I bet he's had about enough of those number heads at the Space Center. And you're right, Joel's band would be fun, and I bet he'd come in a heartbeat." There was a brief pause and Valerie was certain it was connected to her reference to not having family either, rather than the notion of having guests up for dinner. She could sense the air of sadness around him and was preparing to interject something else when he responded.

"I think that might be a good idea. Don't get your hopes up about Chuck saying yes though. It's a three-hour drive one way, and we'll have to give him directions."

Valerie's smile blossomed at his response, "It's still early. You've got his card, right?"

"Sure. Just a sec." Jeremy got out of bed and walked to the dresser. "Here it is," he said holding up the card.

"Well, what are you waiting for? Dial the number!"

"Valerie, it's 7:30 in the morning."

"So what? It's a long drive and we don't want him to have to hurry. Now Joel is a different story. We'll try him later."

A slow grin spread over Jeremy's face. "You call him. I have a feeling we're much more likely to be dining with him this afternoon if you make the call. I'll make the call to Joel in a little while."

Valerie returned his sly smile. She knew exactly to what he was referring. She may not have mentioned it or even overtly responded to it, but she remembered the way Chuck had responded to her in their previous meeting.

"Fine, hand me my phone."

Chuck tried to resist when she got him on the phone, citing his work at NASA and the fact that the last burst of thrust was scheduled for later in the day, but in the end he knew he wasn't really needed there, and he had no will to resist Valerie anyway. Still, Valerie would have bet he surprised even himself when he finally agreed.

"He said he can be here by one," Valerie said, pressing the end button on the phone.

"I guess we better see if there are any groceries left at the store, huh?"

"Not a bad idea," she replied.

"Why don't we fool around for a while longer and take a nice long shower. Then we can go to the store, and I can call Joel."

"Jeremy Andrews, I like the way you think." She punctuated the remark with a prolonged kiss, which led to more intimate kisses, then tactile oblivion. The time raced by.

"Hell yes. I'd love to come," Joel said. "I don't know about the rest of the band, but I know Joan doesn't have anywhere else to go. What time do you want us there?"

Jeremy grinned. This was going to be fun. "Maybe around 1:00 or a little earlier?"

"Perfect. Sounds mmm mmm good. We might bring our instruments, too."

"You better. A little music for Thanksgiving and the end of the world."

Jeremy hung up feeling the warm sensation of camaraderie. It would be good to have friends around.

By 12:30 Jeremy and Valerie were beginning to pull things out of the oven. Chuck had already called from South Austin saying he should be there by about 12:45. An air of anticipation filled the house as the preparations were finished one by one.

True to his word Chuck walked in the door at 12:45 with a huge grin on his face and a bottle of champagne in his hand. The invitation had come as such a shock that it had taken him a moment to absorb it. He hadn't been to a Thanksgiving dinner with family or friends in years, and he was finding that it was something that he'd sorely missed. Setting aside the striking resemblance to his lost wife, he found he really enjoyed the company of these two. All in all, it was already a wonderful Thanksgiving, regardless of the dinner.

~

"Welcome to our home and thanks for coming," Jeremy said with a warm two handed handshake. Valerie added a hug to his greeting.

"Thank you for inviting me," Chuck replied a bit stiffly. He spent very little time in social interactions of any kind, and he felt a bit out of his element. The warmth of their reception, however, quickly dispelled any vestiges of awkwardness.

"I noticed the runway in the subdivision, and it looks like your property backs up to it. I assume you're a pilot?"

"Anything that gets off the ground makes me happy," Jeremy replied, beaming.

"I'm a pilot too," Chuck said.

"I'm thinking I hear the beginning of a conversation that won't involve me," Valerie piped in, "Would anyone like some spiked eggnog? I'm going to make myself one and work on getting the table set."

"Sounds wonderful," Chuck announced. He continually struggled with maintaining a more neutral demeanor toward Valerie. Her striking likeness to Louise still tugged at his heart, affecting him on a number of levels, and he knew it had to present a bit of discomfort to Jeremy. He was doing the best he could, however, and Jeremy seemed to be handling the unusual situation just fine.

"Count me in," Jeremy added, before turning to Chuck. "So, what kind of planes have you flown?" Chuck was answering as they moved off into the den, and Valerie faded towards the kitchen with a contented smile on her face.

Valerie had barely started on the eggnogs when the doorbell rang. She was in such high spirits she practically skipped to the front door.

"Hi, Joel," Valerie said as she opened the door.

"Hi, Val. I don't know if you've actually met Joan. Joan Akers this

Valerie Latham."

"Nice to meet you, Joan." Joan and Joel were both wearing T-shirts and ragged jeans. As a matter of fact, it occurred to Valerie that they looked exactly like they had when she last saw them on stage at The Hole in the Wall.

"Hi there," Joan answered. They shook hands awkwardly as Joan had something strapped over her shoulder and didn't seem interested in adding any more verbal interaction.

"Turns out Joan is the only other member that's free today. She brought her keyboard though, and I have my guitar. We might even try out a few of our new songs on you. Joan has written a couple, and I have a few too that I'm still tweaking."

"Great," Valerie answered as she moved backwards. Joel was already coming in the door anyway with Joan following.

"Where is Jeremy?"

"He's in the hangar discussing planes with Chuck Kohler."

"Chuck Kohler? THE Chuck Kohler? The astronomer that's all over the news? Joel suddenly looked like a kid at Christmas. "Oh man. I've got to go talk to him! I shook his hand once at a space conference he was speaking at. Man, that guy is a genius. But what is he doing here?" Joel didn't wait for an answer; however, he had already set his guitar down and headed for the hangar. Joan looked like she didn't quite know what to do.

"Want some spiked eggnog?" Valerie asked as she moved back toward the kitchen, hoping to make Joan feel comfortable.

"Sounds good," Joan said as she unshouldered the case across her back.

"So that's your keyboard?" Valerie asked.

"Yep. Has its own speaker too. Sounds pretty good by itself, but great when you hook it up to some real sound."

The conversation went quite well but then again Valerie was in the business of making conversation with strangers. Joan, fortunately, was surprisingly open and intelligent, too.

It was forty-five minutes before they sat down to dinner and another forty-five after that before everyone was groaning and pushing back from the table. Chuck was the first to plant himself firmly on the couch and announce, "I'm stuffed."

"Me too," Joel replied, "So I think it's a good time for Joan and me to play a little music while we digest."

"Sounds like a great idea," Jeremy answered as he found a seat. "Are you taking requests?"

"Maybe after another eggnog or two," Joel said grinning.

Joel slung his guitar strap over his shoulder while Joan was still rigging the legs on her keyboard and he promptly started playing an old tune that Karen Carpenter made famous but this time with a whole new meaning

"Don't they know it's the end of the world? It ended when . . ."

Jeremy and Chuck started cracking up immediately

"You've got to be kidding me," Jeremy finally got out.

"I thought it was appropriate. How about this one...Then I looked in space, now I'm a believer. Not a trace, of doubt in mind. We've been had, OOOO I can't believe it, we couldn't beat it we're screwed so bad."

The parody of the old Monkees song cracked Valerie up as well. "Dang, Joel if you're going to make up lyrics to old songs at least pick something from the last two or three decades."

Joel grinned again and he and Joan glanced at each other and started into a set of their new material. One of them actually was about the end of the world. The playing lasted another few drinks before everyone decided they were tired, and the impromptu party broke up.

35

A beautiful rose color bloomed over the eastern horizon of another in-credibly clear, cool, Lakeway morning. Jeremy and Valerie had awoken early. Neither of them felt like sleeping in, so they decided to go for a walk and watch the sun come up. The air was a crisp forty degrees when they left the house, but their clothes were warm, and the air was still.

The world had been waiting restlessly to hear the verdict from the scientists. The news had reported that the fuel on the shuttle had run out days ago, and supposedly the scientific community was waiting to take secondary measurements to determine the course change their efforts had wrought.

Both holding hands with one hand and a coffee cup with the other, Jeremy and Valerie strolled under the morning sky.

"Valerie, I don't care what those scientists say; I think they're stalling, and if they are stalling then it's bad news."

"What about what Chuck said about the delay to determine the course change being plausible." Chuck hadn't left until everyone else had and both Jeremy and Valerie had not only delighted in his stay, but they had invited him back anytime. Chuck had actually blushed when Valerie had said for him to think of their house as his Texas home, and that they'd decided to stay regardless of the outcome of the Rabbit's Revenge project.

"I don't know. I think he was trying to comfort us, too. Not that I blame him. It doesn't matter really. We're supposed to hear the word from NASA on the news tonight anyway."

"I can't decide if I'm afraid anymore or not," Valerie responded, glancing up at Jeremy's eyes.

"I guess I'm not, Val. It's either going to hit us or it's not and now that I have you, I guess my biggest fear is that we might be separated."

They were both quiet for a moment, slowly strolling steps seeming to underline their mutual awareness of the import of his words. Separation meant only one of them dying. It was a thought neither of them wanted to consider and the train of thought led Valerie to another topic.

"The police haven't contacted me about David. I wonder if they found enough evidence to act."

"You'd think we'd have heard one way or another," Jeremy answered, "On the other hand, these are unusual times and I'm wondering if the police aren't too busy with other matters to pursue it too energetically."

"Well that's a scary thought, seeing as it was an attempted murder. I think I'll call them today and see if they've made any progress. I'd hate to think he was still out there stalking us."

"I just wish he'd try something in person," Jeremy stated in a quiet voice. His meaning was clear. He'd had too many years in martial arts to be afraid of a physical confrontation. "If the police aren't on to him by now though, maybe he's made a run for the hills too."

"I'd just rather *know* something," Valerie answered.

Their conversation flagged as the morning sun peeked over the hills. It was going to be a glorious day by the lake. Silence enveloped them for the rest of their walk.

~

Back at home, Valerie and Jeremy sat snuggled together on the couch waiting for the news to come on. The day had been uneventful other than Valerie confirming that the police hadn't been able to take any action against David. It left her with a cold feeling, but with the broadcast about to start, there were bigger things to worry about.

"Well, here we go," Jeremy said as the familiar news reporter's face appeared on the screen.

"Good evening ladies and gentlemen. It has been days since the last of the fuel was used up aboard the Atlas, and we have all waited to hear what NASA had to say with regard to the asteroid's path and the fate of the world. In moments we will switch to the command center at

Johnson Space Center and hear the verdict from Director Shah himself."

Someone had had the bright idea to cancel commercials during events surrounding the asteroid, so television broadcasts had taken on a new format; when the reporter quit speaking, he turned his head away from the camera apparently staring off at another monitor. A moment went by in silence before he turned back.

"And now to NASA."

The screen shifted and the face of Director Shah filled the view. Jeremy immediately disliked the somber look on his face. He felt his pulse begin to accelerate even before the Director began.

"Ladies and gentlemen of the world, after a brief time to observe any possible changes in trajectory, we now have the final calculations.

We did manage to change the course of Kohler/Leporidae and to slow it down slightly. The slowing was inadvertent and was a result of the imprecise angle of thrust delivered by the Atlas shuttle. Unfortunately, the energy expended to slow the asteroid was some of what was needed to adequately deflect it. Therefore, the Kohler/Leporidae asteroid is still on course to strike earth."

The entire planet gasped at the sound of these words from the director of NASA. There was just the briefest of pauses as the director let his words sink in then he continued.

"It was deflected enough, however, to prevent a direct strike. The current expectation is that the asteroid will, instead, have a glancing impact, which in their estimation will not devastate the entire planet. Depending on final calculations as to the precise point of impact, it is estimated that deaths resulting directly from and then indirectly from subsequent earthquakes, tsunamis and dust cloud cover, could lay waste to approximately one-to two-thirds of the world's population." The director paused there to move some notes around in front of him.

"No," Jeremy heard himself say, "It just can't be." Somehow Jeremy couldn't believe that his vision had been for nothing. It just didn't make sense to have had it at all, if not to divert the disaster. The fact that his vision had at least saved the planet from total annihilation seemed a small consolation at that moment.

Valerie was already snuggled into his arm and now he realized that she was quietly sobbing. All he could do was pull her in even closer.

There was nothing to say, and Director Shaw was speaking again.

"Current expectations subject to verification are that the Kohler/ Leporidae asteroid will strike somewhere off the eastern coast of North America, on or about the 21st of December. More precise information will be available in a few days. Thank you. God help us, and I'm sorry."

The television screen switched back to the reporter who had his head turned, apparently staring at another screen and was slow to react to the fact that he was back on camera.

"Um, well . . . there you have it ladies and gentlemen of the world. Apparently, the strike is still occurring. We'll bring you any updates as we get them. Good night."

The announcer seemed in a hurry to get off camera and the broadcast ended abruptly. Jeremy wondered if it had anything to do with the fact that it was being broadcast from a New York newsroom—a city that was now apparently in the path of the imminent disaster.

"What are we going to do Jeremy?" Valerie asked, with a slight tremble still in her voice.

"I think we are going to very carefully decide what other supplies we might need and do the best we can to prepare."

"I'm glad I'm with you," she responded.

"Me too."

~

The next morning, the world came apart.

36

Worldwide panic became the news of the day, but nowhere was it worse than on the eastern shore of the United States. Millions of people were evacuating the eastern seaboard in an attempt to find a better chance at survival. U-Haul lots were quickly emptied, and any place that sold trailers of any sort, was sold out.

The only saving grace that kept the mass exodus from becoming brutal was the small blessing of having three weeks and three days to get away, though many people still acted as though the inevitable was occurring tomorrow.

The worst scene of havoc was New York City. Due to the concentration of people in that city, and owing to the fact that such a high percentage of them didn't even own a car, much less a truck, the scramble to find a method of taking yourself and your belongings out of the city turned ugly.

People who owned trucks were renting or selling them at exorbitant prices with a huge contingent of people only too glad to get them. Those who weren't willing to sell were being brutalized and having those vehicles stolen from them. The death toll around the city had already taken a horrendous jump, as the strong predictably began to victimize the weak. Blood ran in the streets.

37

November 28th, 2016
Miami, FL

Greg Ormond's piercing blue eyes were a perfect match for the ocean that he most often surveyed. He was the Captain of the Coast Guard Cutter Argus and had been the captain now for four years. His love of the ocean was the core of his soul, and days spent off duty were often still on the water in his own thirty-eight-foot Hunter sailboat. It was his pride and joy as well as a refuge for him and his lovely wife Sarah.

Today, however, those eyes were trying to discern low lying boats on the southern horizon. For the last few days since the announcement of the Shuttle's failure, boats had been coming in from all the Caribbean Islands. From as far away as Martinique to as close as the Bahamas, hundreds of boats of all different shapes and sizes had plied the waters of the US eastern seaboard and the Gulf of Mexico in an attempt to gain entry into what was seen as a safe refuge in the central United States. It was Greg's job to keep them out. Interdiction was the formal term. Sad, useless and selfish was what Greg called it.

Greg had launched from Miami with the sunrise, cruised under the bridge north of Key Largo, and passed between the Oyster Keys and the southern tip of the Everglades National Park. The Gulf was calm this morning and the blue-green waters sparkled in the morning sun.

Many boats seemed to be trying the route past the west coast of Florida as it was somewhat less patrolled than the area south and east.

When he'd kissed his wife Sarah goodbye this morning, it was with a heavy heart and a mild sense of foreboding. They had only been married for six years and with the looming disaster, every morning he left her now, felt wrong. He'd repeatedly imagined just scooping her and his son up, taking them with him and ordering the cutter to the Mexican coast. His honor, however, wouldn't let him.

He had gone much further out to sea than he normally did, and now as he surveyed the horizon, he spied a few of the boats he had already halted. A number of them had responded to his warnings by simply backing off a few miles into international waters and staying there. Apparently, they would prefer to try to just live on their boats looking for an opening in the hopes that the U.S. policies would change or the resources to enforce them would wane, rather than return and hope for the best in their own countries.

Greg didn't have any problems sympathizing with them. He had been tasked with the interdiction of illegal aliens into the U.S. for years now and had proudly done his job. He agreed that the U.S. had the right to at least curtail the masses who wished to enter its soil illegally, but this was different. With a massive asteroid on a path to strike the earth somewhere in the Atlantic and a prognosis of death to a significant portion of the world's population, his job was beginning to feel more and more like murder by inaction. He had been relaying his growing unease to Sarah who could only tell him that she trusted his heart and that he should guide his actions by it.

Now, here he was again on the open sea, watching for invaders. All he saw at the moment were some poor islanders who appeared to be attempting to fish from the sides of the barge that had become their self-imposed home. Frightened faces gazed across the water at him as he ordered his cutter to slowly approach. Their fishing was of the simplest kind, and in the hands of these simple folk it appeared totally natural and efficient. They didn't require 6' polycarbonate fishing poles or thousand-dollar, high-tech spinning reels, or amazingly realistic looking lures. Their efforts to draw sustenance from the sea required only some line, a hook, and some bait that he imagined was also drawn from the sea, probably with nets, and simple patience.

Greg stood there on the bow as his boat slowly glided past and watched. Even though he knew why they were waiting here, he currently had no business with these simple fishermen as they were in international waters; but he still liked to scan their faces. Their simplicity and industriousness seemed to carry with it its own brand of peace. It was the bliss of a simpler time when man was more in touch with nature and higher desires such as wealth were a bare distant dream. These poor fishermen weren't trying to find entrance into America for government benefits, and maybe not even for the vaunted "American Dream." These people were merely hoping to survive. His heart went out to them, and he desperately wanted to just escort them to safety on the nearest shore, if there still was such a thing.

"Speed boat approaching off the stern, Captain. Looks like they're in a hurry." The call echoed from the ship's speaker. It was from his first mate on the bridge, Lieutenant Watson.

"Bring her about on an intercept course, lieutenant, and all ahead full." The captain's bellow from the foredeck was amply loud even without a microphone. The Argus was wheeling about even before Greg made it back to the stairs of his upper deck.

The Argus was a Cyclone class patrol boat, one of fifteen that had been transferred from the Navy. They were relatively well armed with missiles, grenade launchers, and three machine gun mounts. Most of the Cyclone class could hit thirty-five knots already, but the Argus had been retrofitted as an interdiction boat and as such had been given the ability to match the speed of the open sea racers, at least for short distances.

Greg Ormond smiled at the rising whine of the additional turbofan engine as the Argus rapidly gathered speed. He only wished he could see the faces onboard the speedboat they were approaching. Their shock at seeing the Argus gaining on them would be a great satisfaction. This was a part of his job that he *did* enjoy.

The Argus quickly began to close the gap and Captain Ormond recognized the boat as a fifty-foot Donzi. It was slim and sleek with an extended V nose that, at its current speed, was mostly out of the water. The Argus was approaching at a forty-five-degree angle and Greg was mildly surprised that the boat's occupants hadn't noticed his approach yet. No sooner had the thought crossed his mind, however, than he saw the boat's pilot turn to him and point.

He appeared to be yelling too, but any voices were easily drowned out by the scream of both boat's engines and the race of the wind. The Argus was closing the gap nicely and Greg was reaching for his microphone. It was connected to bull horn devices mounted on both sides of the bow and would easily be heard by the speed boat's occupants.

"You are entering United States waters; stand down and prepare for boarders," he spoke into the microphone. For an answer, a second man appeared from the cabin below the pilot of the speed boat with a long slender object he was quickly raising to his shoulder. Captain Ormond was surprised but not too surprised to recognize the threat.

"Hard a starboard, Mr. Simmons," he calmly said to his pilot beside him. Simmons knew his captain well and although the words were spoken calmly and almost softly, he recognized the urgency in the tone and reacted instantly. All of Captain Ormond's men both liked and trusted him implicitly. The pilot's quick response saved their lives. A trail of smoke originated from the speeding Donzi as a missile raced in their direction, but the Argus was already turning. Greg had just a moment to wonder if the missile had heat seeking capabilities, before giving the next order into his microphone. The pilot was already correcting the intercept course when Greg spoke again.

"Ensign James, man the forward Fifty."

Greg watched his ensign race across the deck of the speeding cutter at the same moment he realized with a sigh of relief that the missile wasn't a heat seeker. The hiss of its' passing off their port bow was audible even inside the cabin.

Greg called out through the bull horns one more time. "This is your last chance to stand down or you will be fired upon," They were close enough now to see that the man with the missile launcher was desperately trying to reload and that was something Greg didn't intend to wait and see. "Ensign James, open fire," he called, still through the bull horns.

The deck-mounted fifty-caliber machine gun had an awesome rate of fire, and Greg watched as Ensign James stitched a short path of bullets in the water to the port of the Donzi which he quickly walked straight to the boat and straight at the man who was about to raise the rocket launcher for a second shot.

He never made it. The massive spray of bullets from the deck-mounted gun cut him and the Donzi virtually in half. There was just a brief instant when Greg thought he saw the two halves of the speed-boat begin to separate before the entire craft erupted in a ball of flame. Whether they had hit the gas tanks, or the boat had more explosives below, Greg would never know; his pilot abruptly turned to starboard again, this time to avoid the flying debris.

A surge of sadness washed over Greg at the sight. Killing was not something he relished, and he'd only done it twice before in his four years as a captain. Once with drug runners, as the ones he'd just destroyed probably were, and once with some pirates that had kidnapped a luxury sailboat and killed its owners.

"All ahead slow. All hands-on deck to search for survivors." Not that there were likely to be any, but he wouldn't sleep well if he didn't even make the attempt.

As they idled by the scattered debris, Captain Ormond saw a few white plastic bags float to the surface. It had been a drug boat.

"Ensign, get the grappling hook and retrieve that contraband."

The entire episode was making Greg more and more tired. He was bone weary of all the evil in the world. *Maybe we need this asteroid*, he thought absently, *or deserved it.* Those thoughts led him back to the fishing boats anchored in international waters and all those sad peaceful faces. Maybe when the time came, he would gather up his lovely wife and son, and just escort those poor people to shore. The idea lit his heart and raised his spirits. Yes, that would be the right thing to do.

38

For Susan Hummel the last couple of weeks had been an opportunity to live out a dream. As a sixth grade schoolteacher she had always lived one of her dreams, to work with kids, but with people's reactions to the approach of the Rabbit's Revenge asteroid, she had been given a different, very unique opportunity. In her life she had recognized that helping others brought a peace to her that she couldn't get anywhere else.

She was a very attractive, light eyed, brunette, and her looks alone had garnered her quite a lot of attention throughout her life. Unfortunately, the men that had been drawn to her had all seemed to be men of stone with desires as blatant as their egos. She had walked down that path a time or two in her youth only to receive the disillusionment she should have expected in the first place. As compensation, she had thrown herself into her work with the kids and into her hobbies, reading and martial arts, and had filled her time up fully enough to at least keep the lingering loneliness at bay.

Today, she was on her way to the grocery store just a few blocks away. It was grey, cold and the clouds looked like snow.

In just the past week she had already witnessed the world coming apart. She had seen handbags stolen from the handicapped, bloody fights in the alleys, people racing down the streets with TVs in their hands, and children running down sidewalks screaming in terror. The impending disaster seemed to be bringing out all the very worst in the human spirit. It saddened her heart, but in each instance, she had been too far away to be of any help.

As she walked these days, her awareness of what was going on around her was dramatically heightened, her thoughts always on others. It was a skill she'd learned in martial arts, but now she honed it to a fine edge. A brittle scream behind her rang on cue with her thoughts, though any unusual event these days would have seemed on cue.

"Stop that man! My purse!"

It was a little old lady using a walker. When the thief had snatched her purse, it had caused her to fall down, and a note of pain rode with the rage in the little lady's quaky voice.

Susan spun around at the sound, surprised to see the miscreant racing directly toward her. In broad daylight! It was more than she could bear.

She effected a cringe as the man approached at a dead run, not wanting to alert him, then, at the last minute, she stepped out, squared her shoulders leaning forward with her arm extended, and smoothly clotheslined the man with her forearm.

"Not today, buster," she heard herself say. The force of her blow was not that great, but it was so totally unexpected, that the racing felon's own velocity became his undoing. His legs flew out in front of him from the sudden deceleration of his head, landing him squarely on his back on the concrete. There was a sickening crunch from the impact, and his entire body went completely limp, releasing the purse.

The sound, more than anything else, caused Susan to wince. She had never heard bones crunching before, but in her heart, she was pretty certain that the noise she had just heard was it.

She reached down to pick up the purse and as an afterthought checked the pulse of the man on the ground. Nothing. Blood began to slowly trickle from the purse snatcher's nose and beneath his head.

"Oh my God," she whispered, "He's dead." Very few people were even stopping; as such incidences were becoming too common to let oneself become involved. The elderly woman finally limped up, leaning heavily on the walker. Susan absently handed her the purse.

"Thank you, sweetie," she said, then paused, gazing first down at her attacker then up at Susan's eyes. "It's OK, honey. I know you didn't mean to kill him, and I'm sure he had it coming. You probably saved someone else's life."

Susan's head slowly adjusted as her eyes focused on the little lady, shocked at her nonchalance, "But I killed him."

"Missy, he nearly killed me. I know it's harsh, but that's the way it is these days. And thank you so much for your help."

The woman's smile and heartfelt thanks did little to mitigate the way she felt. "I should call the police," she said in a distant, vacant tone, but what she was thinking was *'that's the way it is these days?'* Had that much changed that fast? The little lady's words haunted her.

"Missy, the police, I am sure, have already been notified, but it might well be hours before they arrive. Why don't you just come with me? I don't live far, and I'll make you some tea. It's the least I can do."

Susan stared at her like she'd lost her mind, but the logical side of her kicked in, and she began analyzing the situation. The woman was right. "Thank you for the offer but I should go, I guess."

Susan couldn't shake the feeling of wrongness associated with just leaving the body there on the concrete. Wouldn't there be repercussions? Probably not, she decided. Not with *things the way they are these days*. It was such a sad statement.

The sound of police sirens in the distance startled her into action. With so little time left for the world, she wasn't about to spend it explaining herself in some local jail.

"Take care of yourself ma . . ." She began, turning back around. The lady was gone. Where could she have gotten to so quickly? It didn't matter. With her gone, Susan *really* didn't want to try to explain herself. She turned and ran.

The dead man's face haunted her, and her sleep was full of dreams of the thief opening his eyes again to take revenge. When she finally relinquished her bed at 4:30a.m., the image of his face was still lingering in her mind's eye.

Susan almost surprised herself by showing up at her classroom the next morning. Attempting normalcy was the only thing she knew to do. Even so, her classroom was dwindling by the day as people took their children from school to leave for the central United States and a greater chance of survival. Soon there would be no reason for her to even pretend that things were normal, or show up, for that matter.

Looking around, she could only wonder why these kids were still here, and if maybe she should be following the example of so many others and leave. But where would she go? She had nobody and no place to run to. What would she even do if she did leave? She had a little money, but how long would that last? Many people had already been taking their money out of the banks, and as the days progressed the banks were beginning to be hard pressed to meet the rising demands for cash. It was a similar situation to what caused the bank run just prior to the Great Depression. This wasn't a case of the banks being insolvent, however, like had happened with some large institutions a few years ago.

This was just a matter of cash-on-hand, which banks only kept a certain amount of, but which their customers were now demanding.

The television news had been attempting to counteract this trend, giving the banks free airtime to reassure people that they were nationwide organizations, and that the asteroid destroying cities wasn't going to destroy the people's ability to access their funds. The strategy was at least partially working.

Susan trudged through the day. As a sixth-grade teacher, she found herself daily answering more and more questions about the coming asteroid.

"Ms. Hummel, how do they know if the asteroid is going to destroy this city?"

Susan smiled. This question was from Abe Arends. He was a bright young boy and very well mannered, and one of the more curious little children she had ever encountered. "They don't know that for sure, Abe. So far, they have only been able to tell us that the asteroid should hit somewhere in the Atlantic Ocean, probably near the North American coast."

"So how come they don't know?"

Susan hadn't thought much about it. She had simply listened to the news reports and accepted what they said. "That's a very good question, Abe, and I don't really know the answer. Maybe things like the sun and the moon might still affect exactly where it lands."

"I heard on TV that it could send a wave from the ocean that is as tall as a skyscraper."

Abe seemed particularly fascinated with the topic, and Susan decided it was as good a topic as any to be teaching them today. "That's true, Abe.

They are called tsunamis or sometimes tidal waves. It could also cause earthquakes or, more likely, both."

"If it could do all that, why are you staying here, Ms. Hummel?"

Susan was surprised that some of her other students hadn't chimed in yet, but their faces certainly showed interest, so she went with it, "Well, since we don't know exactly where it's going to hit, I haven't been in any great hurry to go. If it lands up closer to Maine, for instance, then maybe there is no reason for us to leave."

"My daddy says that they don't really know where it's going to land, so we might as well stay here. He says if they're wrong, and we head west we might be heading straight for it, or it might hit way far away, and we would have all moved for nothing."

"Well, I guess that's possible, Abe, but what if they are right?"

Now it was Abe's turn to smile. "Then I guess we get to see God a little bit sooner."

The depth of that simple response stunned Susan. Where did an eleven-year-old get that kind of peace in the face of death? She felt a bit shamed that she hadn't been able to face the issue with the same sort of serenity. The face of the purse snatcher drifted into her mind again. Was that something she could be forgiven for?

Her own faith in the afterlife was obviously not as firm as this little boy's. Instead she answered simply, "I guess that's right, Abe."

Susan finally managed to get the conversation on to other topics, but the boy's insight lurked in the back of her mind all day. The day's activities had kept her from brooding about either the asteroid or the man she had killed yesterday, but the moment she watched the children leave the classroom after the final bell, foreboding and indecision pounced on her like a hungry bear.

She left her classroom feeling as shaken as she had the day before. Why *was* she staying? Maybe it was simply because she couldn't find the will to abandon the life she knew, all by herself. She was a brave woman, but *that* thought was still a bridge too far.

On her way home she decided to stop for gas. She still had half a tank, but these were not times to let your tank run low and trust that the next pump could fill you up, so she pulled off the road at the first station she saw.

The wind was cold when she stepped out of her Ford crossover and walked around to the passenger side. Filling up reminded her again about leaving town. At some point she knew that it would be safer if she did leave. She rather figured she wouldn't have a job left anyway in about two weeks, so what did it matter? A pang of guilt grabbed her as she considered the look on her student's faces when she didn't show up. Could she do that? How much longer would those kids be in class anyway? She was already down to about eight. By tomorrow it might be six. The thoughts carried her as she slid her credit card in the pump and pulled the nozzle out. The actions required virtually none of her attention, and her hand rested needlessly on the gas nozzle. She thought about cute little Abe and his insightful questions until a curt voice startled her.

"Step away from the car lady," the terse voice said.

Merely the tone of the man's voice told her that this was trouble. A wave of anger welled up inside.

Not so much at her potential assailant, but at her own inattentiveness that had allowed him to get so close. She'd had way too much training to let something like this happen, and her temporary inattention infuriated her. Cautiously, she turned to face the voice leaving her left hand casually on the pump handle.

"What do you want?" She asked in her very best scared damsel voice, all the while considering that her loose-fitting slacks wouldn't slow her down in a fight. She followed it with a tentative smile hoping that either her feigned timidity or her attractive smile would cause a momentary lapse of attention. The man held a heavy caliber pistol low by his waist and kept his ten-foot distance. He knew what he was doing, she decided.

She finished turning to face him very slowly, withdrawing the pump handle even more slowly with her left hand.

"Put the nozzle away," he said as he inched closer to her, "I want your purse and your keys."

Susan felt that she should be getting an Oscar for her scared-little-female rendition. She kept her eyes glued to the ground, however, gauging the small slope in his direction. She even managed to jump when he barked a repeat of his command.

"I said put it away!"

As she jumped, she cringed, and squeezed the lever on the handle as though that too were a reflex. The result was a spraying of gasoline on his pants and shoes.

She immediately stood erect, dropping all pretense, "If you squeeze that trigger now, the odds are that you'll be burned alive, Mister. And frankly, it might be worth being shot just to watch it."

The sudden change in her demeanor caused astonishment and rage to do battle on the man's features. He was virtually shaking from the power of his emotions before he managed to mutter the next syllable.

"Bitch," he said and turned to run.

He'd only taken three steps when something came flying through the air and connected with his skull. He nearly cart-wheeled to the ground from the force of the impact, his gun skittering across the concrete followed by the baseball that had snagged him. He didn't move.

Susan whirled in the direction of the object's flight and saw a tall dark-haired man standing by a Range Rover grinning like a kid at a clown act.

"Hi," he said, "I'm Johnnie Oliver."

39

December 10th, 2016

The constant news surrounding the asteroid had effectively taken the world's eyes off any other event. However, as the date of the impact approached, the earth was still inexorably marching its way away from the plane of the Milky Way galaxy that it had so recently crossed for the first time in twenty-six thousand years. Other forces were at work in the galaxy; tremendous forces that were largely not understood by either the scientific community and certainly not the media.

The accident of the asteroid's path was only peripherally related to the predictions of the Mayan calendar and Earth's passage through the Milky Way's plane. This was due to the fact that a much larger number of celestial bodies had been trapped in that plane, increasing the chances of one making a bullseye of Earth. What the world seemed to be forgetting in the wake of the asteroid's news was the fact that the gravitational force created by that intersection had affected Earth in more direct ways. That un-measureable force had exerted pressures on the Earth's crust; it was nothing so obvious as a planet-killer asteroid but monumental, nonetheless. The results were just now, four years later, reaching their tipping point, but compared to the impending asteroid approach were on a smaller scale and therefore went unnoticed for what they were.

Now earthquakes began serious rumbling around the world. In the course of just a few days an 8.9 rippled through Lop Nur in China, leaving a 17-foot rent in a section of the historic Great Wall.

Another 6.8 temblor opened a crack in the ring of mountains comprising Lake Tahoe causing the 1,500-foot-deep lake to promptly drain out hundreds of millions of gallons of water somewhere into underground caverns, lowering its level by 150 feet in less than an hour.

Astounded onlookers said they could actually see the lake level descend as they watched. Yet another quake somewhere in the South Pacific caused a 300-foot Tsunami to race southwest across the great ocean and slam into the Solomon Islands east of Australia. The ridge in the ocean floor that was the basis for those islands acted as a breakwater for the coast of Australia, but the islands themselves were devastated.

News on the asteroid's path was momentarily unchanging, so by the third massive quake the media finally shifted its attention to the more immediate catastrophes.

40

It was almost time to leave. Billy Mason paused to watch the smoke trail through the air as he exhaled. He never touched cigarettes. This was a trick of the cold early evening air, yet he watched it thoughtfully. Watching his visible breath made him think of life, and lately he had been having *such* a life. In fact, he had been having a heyday.

Ever since the announcement of the asteroid's impact, the police had been too busy to be effective, and Billy had seen his chance. He felt his pocket reassuring himself that the cash he'd just absconded with was still there. He gave no thought whatsoever for the little old lady that lay unconscious in her bed nearly smothered with her own pillow by Billy's hands.

That had been his brilliant idea. Old people. Most of them weren't inclined to try to run from the asteroid even if they were physically able, and so many of them kept valuables in their homes. To make things easier, the Lock Aid lock-picking gun he'd acquired from a police officer's car during a gang fight had allowed him to enter any door quietly and take whatever he wanted.

And what fools all these other people were, trying to bail out of town as quickly as possible, when everyone already knew that the asteroid wouldn't be here for another week. Stupid! By that time, he'd have enough cash to live the good life somewhere out in the Midwest, maybe Arkansas or Illinois. It never once occurred to him that after the impact the cash he was stealing may have no value at all.

He didn't have any worries about getting out of town. When the time came, he'd get a vehicle from somewhere even if he had to fix a broken one someone had left behind. Not to mention many of these old folks had some antique in their garage that they hadn't driven in twenty years. Most of those were in pristine condition and wouldn't need more than a quick battery charge, and he'd be off. Billy didn't need anything big. He wasn't taking anything with him when he left except a few clothes and his stolen money.

Dark was closing in. It was time to get to work. He knew all the areas where older people lived in the nearby neighborhoods, and the night was his time. Another huge puff of smoky vapor left his body as he turned to go, as though his actions had caused his entire insides to combust with the heat of his malicious self-interest.

* * *

The infrastructure of New York City was crumbling. Many of the city employees who worked at the utility companies began to simply not show up for work. No call. No explanation. They just didn't show. No one really needed to ask why but knowing didn't help the situation.

The already undermanned, under-maintained, and under-expanded city power grid groaned on a regular basis at the demands put upon it.

Now transformer explosions and fires that were a constant source of concern and an additional need for manpower were going unattended.

People may visualize the eighty thousand plus miles of wires snaking below the surface of New York City as a pristine arrangement of gleaming, labeled conduits of power, but in fact those aging strings of metal wind through old concrete tunnels that are subject to occasional rain run-off, sewage and water main breakage, corrosion by the invasion of salt used to coat the snowy winter streets, and even the occasional nick from construction crews that got too close. These conditions, plus the vibration of the wires themselves from the passage of electrical current, required a constant effort to repair, replace, and reattach.

The manpower to do so is significant, and with people abandoning their jobs on a daily basis the overburdened system, which had already failed before when fully manned, had been inching closer to a total meltdown with each passing day. At 5:00p.m., during the massive rush to get home from work, the cascade finally began. One medium sized power line in a non-descript tunnel gave out. When it released, both ends snapped back to wind around several other lines causing them to arc, short and snap. In turn, yet other poorly maintained lines began receiving the burden of the extra voltage load as they had been programmed to do, but when laden with the extra load they too snapped or melted. Section after section of the grid began to fail, until by 7:30 p.m. a large portion of Manhattan, the Bronx and most of Queens had gone dark.

Billy was already well into the South Bronx when the lights went out, causing him to flinch momentarily. Listening carefully, he could hear the pop of transformers. "Power grid," he murmured to himself smiling, "Perfect."

He knew this area had a high percentage of elderly people, so it was perfect for his purposes, and now with the power out, his job just got easier. With the lights out, maybe this could be his last night.

There was a trick to picking out the right houses. Just about one out of two people in this neighborhood were elderly and those could typically be spotted by the trappings on the exterior of their homes. Picking out the right one after that, typically became more of a matter of chance than anything else. In this case though, it wasn't chance.

Billy had been in this neighborhood for weeks now, and he'd seen this little old man coming and going. He'd made it a point to notice where he lived. The old guy was skinny as a rail and got around in a motorized wheelchair. He would be an easy target. Billy had a feeling the man was loaded, too. He wasn't sure what made him feel that way, but he just knew that if he could find this guy's stash, he would have enough to blow this town and head for Illinois. Billy understood survival enough to realize that if the world was going to come apart, it was a good idea to be near fresh water, and Illinois certainly fit that description. Besides, if it didn't get blasted or something, Chicago was a big town, and he'd feel more at home there than in some Podunk, hick town with more gravesites than people. He'd heard a lot of his friends talking about going there, too. Hell, it might be like an old home reunion when he got there, not that he gave a damn about seeing any of those losers again. But first he had to knock off this last guy and grab some major cash.

With the lights out the town was seriously dark, and if he paused to listen, he could hear the sounds of many muted screams and fighting in the distance. He wasn't the only one planning on taking advantage of the lights being out. As a matter of fact, it was others like himself that had him packing a Glock behind his back. He wasn't going to waste a bullet on the old man though. He'd rather hoped he wouldn't have to kill anyone. Still, he carried a nine-inch black K-Bar military blade as additional protection. Some people were too squeamish to use a knife, but Billy liked the idea of it; he'd never had to use it, but it made him feel like some sort of predator cat or something striking in the night.

Billy's eyes were wide open and his ears on high alert as he covered the last few yards to the old man's front porch. The little house was skinny and deep and looked like it might have a second floor. Not that the old man could use a second floor unless he had some kind of a lift thing or a ramp like the one on the porch. So, that meant that he'd be easier to find, and since the ramp on the porch was newer, Billy decided to use it. It was much less likely to creak than those old wooden steps.

Billy eased up the ramp smiling to himself at the lack of noise as he moved. He was a good predator. The front door was only three steps away from the far end of the ramp when he reached for his Lock Aid gun.

Once up at the door, he tried the knob on a whim and was shocked to find it unlocked. There wasn't another keyhole but there must be a dead bolt on the inside. *Damn,* he thought. *So much for silence.* Still, Billy pushed on the old door anyway. He was greeted with another surprise when it slid open smoothly. *Is this guy some sort of idiot? Maybe he has that brain disease where you forget stuff.* No one left their door unlocked in this part of town. Hell, not in any part of this city for that matter.

Putting the Lock Aid back in its little holster, Billy closed the door, and reached for his knife with his right hand and his little Maglite with the other.

"I'd be real still right about now if I was you."

It was a steady voice coming from off to his right. Billy was proud of himself that he'd managed not to jump, but he inched to his right anyway. He was too far away to use his knife unless he could throw it, which he couldn't. A small light flipped on from that direction and Billy could see the outline of the wheelchair.

"If you think I'm kidding, boy, take one more step and you'll get to hear what a Colt .45 sounds like when it's fired inside. It'll leave my ears ringing for days so I'd rather not have to fire it, but you won't have to worry about that because with these hollow point slugs it'll blow out most of your midsection so you'll be dead before you notice the ringing."

At that point the silence became deafening. The man's voice was so steady that Billy believed him, even though he couldn't actually see the gun being held behind the flashlight. He was trying to decide what his next move might be when the man spoke again.

"So, you've got enough brains to know when to shut up and listen. That's a good start. Why don't you go ahead and put that pig sticker back in its sheath, too."

Billy couldn't think of a better idea at the moment, but he was confident that if he just played it cool, he'd get his chance to snuff this old fart and get what he came for. Then the old man's next sentence caught him so off guard that he forgot about any plans he'd ever made.

"So, you came here to rob me I imagine. And kill me too most likely. Well, neither one would make much difference. I might just let you. We'll see. Boy, why don't you take two steps back and light that lantern on the sideboard. There's a lighter beside it. I want to have a better look at you."

Billy found himself doing as the old man asked while he tried to decide if he'd just heard the old man right. He was going to let Billy rob and kill him? Was that what he'd said? Surely, he must have heard him wrong. The old man's flashlight beam was pointing right at the lighter on the sideboard by the lamp making it easy for Billy to follow his instructions. After having his eyes adjusted to the inky blackness of the city night the glow from the lamp seemed brilliant and lit up even past the confines of the small room they were in.

Sure enough, the old man was sitting there in his motorized wheelchair with a pearl-handled Colt .45 trained on him. He clicked off the flashlight.

"That's better," he said, "Now tell me boy, why shouldn't I just shoot you where you stand, other than the fact that I would have to wait quite a while to get anyone to haul your dead carcass out of my living room, and the blood would ruin my rug. Not that I care about that old damn rug, though it was Ruth's favorite. It'd be the smell that I'm not fond of. It reminds me of having to lie in a damn foxhole in Nam next to my best buddy who'd just had his face blown off. We were pinned down, so it was almost a day and half before air support came in to let us make a break for it. At first, I was sure that I'd never get the picture of Larry's face out of my mind, but as the years have gone by it's the smell I still remember."

Billy's shock kept finding new levels of profound as the moments passed, and a cold feeling was creeping through him. This man was no stranger to killing, and he was talking about killing him with less emotion than you would discuss squashing a roach. Even as cold as he was, Billy didn't think he could be *that* cold about killing someone. He was beginning to truly believe he was about to die.

"Are you mute boy, or just still too surprised at being cornered by an old bag of bones in a wheelchair? Speak up!"

Billy wasn't sure what to say. Not only were the old man's words shocking, and not only did he feel like he was about to die, but there was a calm surety in the old man's voice. That voice still sounded young too, and Billy would have bet anything that this man had been one that gave the orders, not took them. The next moment he heard words coming out of his own mouth that surprised him almost as much as the man's.

"I'm sorry, sir. Yes, I did come here to rob you . . . and probably kill you too. I was hoping you'd have enough money for me to leave this town tomorrow and be away before the asteroid hits." Billy wasn't certain if he'd ever told that much truth in three consecutive sentences in his entire life, and he was certain that the next sound, the last sound he would ever hear, would be the explosion from that cannon the old man was holding.

"Well I'll be damned," the old man began, "You told the truth. I'll bet that surprised you as much as it did me. You just bought yourself a few more minutes to live. Now tell me, what's your name, boy?"

"Billy, sir." Billy couldn't remember the last time he'd addressed anyone as sir, and he didn't really think it was just the gun that was making him do it. This old man simply commanded respect somehow.

"Billy. Hello, Billy. My name is Jackson, Andrew Jackson, and yes, my parents had a sense of humor. You can call me Andy."

Billy had almost laughed but caught himself. "Uh, nice to meet you, Mr. Jackson."

Andy did start laughing then, and even though the gun waivered wildly, Billy had no desire to attempt to rush the old man. He was intrigued like he had never been before. He also found himself respecting the old man, something else he'd never done before.

"Andy'll be fine, Billy. Sit down over there and tell me about yourself. It's going to be a long night and neither one of us has anything better to do."

The last thing on the planet Billy had expected to be doing this evening was sitting in a chair held at gunpoint by an old man and telling him his miserable life story, but that's exactly what Billy did. And Andy listened with an intent, quiet, interest that somehow made it easy for Billy to keep talking.

There was nothing unusual in Billy's story. He'd grown up poor, and never met his dad, some damn doctor named David according to his mother, though she was probably lying. That left him and his half-brother alone with their mother. They had both started working young until his brother was killed by a gang and his mother shot herself.

Billy had managed to kill several of those gang members later before moving to another part of town and had been getting along as best he could ever since. When he finished, he looked up at Andy and was quiet.

"I'm sorry son. That is a sad tale, to be sure, though not one that's so unusual in this city." Andy put the gun on a little end table as casually as you'd set down a glass of tea and looked back up at Billy, riveting his gaze. "Now tell me Billy, if I let you live what would you be willing to do different with your life?"

Billy was only vaguely aware that Andy had set the gun down, but he felt no compulsion to do anything other than answer the old man's question, "I don't know sir. I was thinking about going to Chicago if I could get the money."

"And what would you do there, Billy. Rob and kill people still?"

Billy hesitated, thinking about the man's words. The truth was, what he might actually *do* when he got to Chicago was at least one step further than he'd ever thought.

"I don't know, sir. I guess I haven't thought that far. Maybe it would depend on how much money I had. I've always been good at fixing things, especially cars."

Andy's blue eyes were a bit clouded with age, but they seemed to stare right into Billy's soul as they both sat there for a moment in silence.

"Do you think you could do something honest if you had the chance, Billy?"

Billy started to answer quickly but instead paused to consider the possibility. It wasn't something he'd ever considered before because it wasn't an option he'd ever believed possible. Now he truly considered it.

Andy continued, "If this old world survives at all, Billy, they're going to need people who are good with their hands, good at fixing things. Is that something you could do? Maybe even help people instead of hurting them?"

The possibility was like a tiny light approaching from down the neck of a long dark cave growing brighter as it approached. The closer it got, the better he felt, and for the first time in a long, long time, Billy smiled.

"Yes sir. I believe I could do that if I ever got the chance."

Andy smiled as he continued to hold Billy's gaze. "I think maybe you could, boy. I think maybe you could."

Andy went quiet then and Billy wasn't sure what to do. The idea of starting a new, better life had warmed him like he'd never felt before, but reality was setting back in. That was never going to happen, and if he ever even got the money to get to Chicago, his life would probably just be more of the same. The only difference was that now, after having really considered it, and for the first time in his life, he really wanted to change. He must have been sitting quietly, thinking about the possibility for a few minutes when Andy finally spoke again.

"Billy, do you see that globe over there on the stand?"

"Yes, sir."

"Go move that over and use that pig sticker of yours to pry up the board closest to the wall. It fits real tight but it's not nailed."

Billy was mystified with the instructions from Andy, but he got up to obey, nonetheless. As he moved the globe over and reached for his knife, he glanced back at Andy who had his arms folded over his chest and an odd smile on his face.

The board resisted but finally popped out. There was something down in the recess.

"Now pull back that second board, Billy, and grab that little strong box."

Billy did as he was told.

"Now, take it and go have a seat. I have a couple of more things I want to tell you."

Again, Billy did as he was told and sat back in the chair with the box in his lap. He was too stunned to speak. All he could do was watch as Andy's smug smile turned serious again, and the old man leaned forward in his wheelchair.

"Billy, there's fifty thousand in that box. I would like you to take it and promise me that you will make a new life for yourself, something that does some good for someone other than you. If you want to fix things then do that, but do something good with it, will you? Will you promise me that?"

Billy would have sworn he couldn't have been any more shocked than he already was, but Andy's words shook him more than anything else he had ever heard in his life. For several moments he couldn't speak.

He didn't even move to open the box. If Andy said it was in there, then it was. When he did finally answer, his own words were no less of a shock to him than Andy's had been, but he found that he truly meant them.

"Sir, I came here to rob and probably kill you, like I said. Why would you give me this money? Is this all you have?"

Andy smiled. "Because, boy, I'd rather give it to you with a promise that you'll do something good with it than have you take it and never change. I don't need it anymore. I do have a little more. A lot more than I'll need for the time I have left. You see if you didn't kill me, or someone else, or the asteroid, I'll be dead in another year anyway. I don't have anyone left in the world to leave it to, and I would like to try to make that little bit of money mean something before I die, Billy. Will you make me the promise I'm asking?"

Billy felt his eyes watering before he started to speak, "You have my word, sir. I'll make a new life for myself and do something good for others with it."

Billy was stunned all over again to realize that he really meant what he was saying. Nothing else in his entire life had affected him so profoundly. He'd keep his promise to Andrew Jackson. He looked up at the old man and hesitated. The next words were another surprise, but he couldn't help himself.

"I could take you with me, sir."

"Quit calling me sir, and no you can't. I don't want to go anywhere else. My life has been lived, and I'd prefer to spend what little that's left of it right here. As a matter of fact, why don't you go ahead and take that box and get on out of here. There is a car in the garage. It needs some work, but it should start. I haven't needed it in a long time."

"Yes, sir," Billy heard himself say.

Fifteen minutes later Billy was driving an old Chevy Trailblazer out of the neighborhoods he'd grown up in and away from New York City. He had fifty thousand in a box under the seat and a whole new life to think about. More importantly he had a brand-new perspective on people in general, courtesy of Andrew Jackson and an asteroid named Rabbit's Revenge.

41

David Coulson was alone in the world. He had been a bright young boy and very sweet. He was an only child and the apple of his Alabama parent's eyes. It was difficult not to overindulge such a sweet-natured, cherub-faced, intelligent youngster, and David's parents did not manage to resist the temptation. His sweet disposition slowly morphed into an expectation of getting his way, and with the onset of puberty his own self-indulgence garnered a rather ugly patina of demand. Those who didn't easily bend to his will were quickly discarded, which eventually included even his parents. David's ample intellect carried him even further down the path of success and self-promotion, when his personality alone no longer could. As a result, any relatives or friends he still had were either dead or had long since given up on having anything to do with him.

Though he had learned the technique of exhibiting a personality that attracted people, one didn't have to know him for long to slide past that veneer. His arrogant self-centeredness fostered a temper that was frightening to behold. That, in itself, could have driven away anyone who might have ever had any desire to be close, and it did except the one girl in New York he had seduced, impregnated, then shortly thereafter, left. David had deduced that amiability was conducive to getting people to accommodate him with the least amount of effort, therefore in public that was how he acted, but in one on one situations, he had difficulty maintaining the façade.

The only bright spot in his personal life had been Valerie. With Valerie for the first time in his life he actually *felt* like he was in love, and he had tried desperately to be the kind of person she could love, But by that time in his life it was too late for any real change.

He'd managed it for a while, but it was like exerting too much pressure on a sphere from the inside, eventually cracks began to show and each one weakened the whole until after just a few months, too much of his true heart was showing. It was at that point that Valerie had begun to recoil, and with each tiny step away from him, he began to fight harder to force her to stay. It was as effective as herding cats. Once she saw his true personality, she only needed an excuse to end it. David's angry abandonment of her in Jamaica when she had refused his rushed marriage proposal had been her chance. *That thankless bitch!*

Since then, she had become his obsession. Nothing else mattered, not his possessions, nor his business. He thought about her morning and night and everything else in his life became just another tool to further his burning desire to have her. Every little success only promoted his resolve to stay involved in her life in some fashion, even if it was from the perspective of a stalker.

Having her followed had resulted in his knowing when she had moved to Austin, which in turn offered him the opportunity to follow her. Repeating the process once he had moved there, had allowed him to know just when she began to see another man seriously.

His resulting solitary lifestyle and the upcoming demise of the planet only brought into sharp focus this self-imposed loneliness and a new fear of dying alone. Now the jealousy and envy surrounding Valerie and her new boyfriend had combined with his newfound fear to become a seething hate.

He knew they were staying at Jeremy Andrew's house now. He had driven by a hundred times. In his cold empty heart, however, also resided cowardice, and without anyone else to hire to do his dirty work, his own fear had kept him from the revenge that had become his last reason to live.

The television stations were sizzling with reports and even videos of the approaching asteroid. It seemed a foregone conclusion that the world as we currently knew it only had one more day to live. Scientists had pinned the projected impact point as 200 miles east of Philadelphia out in the Atlantic. This wasn't as bad as a land strike might be, but it would wipe out the eastern seaboard of the United States as well as marching across the entire Atlantic to inundate the west coasts of Europe and Africa.

The broadcasts said one-third to one-half of the world would die but they were probably lying to give the masses hope. They couldn't even predict how far inland the resulting tsunami would march before dissipating its energy. The world was done for, so if he was ever going to exact his revenge, today must be the day. Circumstances had finally overridden his fear.

He had been planning the deed for weeks, designing and discarding a dozen different ideas, but it wasn't until yesterday that he had realized that subterfuge was merely an effort to prevent being discovered and with the asteroid arriving tomorrow that was an issue that needn't be considered.

As a result, David followed the simplest plan. He drove his Jag over to Valerie's apparent new residence with that boy in Lakeway, parked in front of a house a couple down from them, and waited. It was late morning, and no one would question a high dollar car parked in that neighborhood.

While he waited, he fantasized about having Valerie all to himself. It was a pleasurable fantasy.

Even though his plan was simple, it had been thought out, none-theless. He wasn't interested in a physical confrontation with her boy-friend. Physical confrontations were never his bailiwick, and though he had had enough boxing instruction in his lifetime to defend himself, he already knew of the boy's martial arts expertise from his PI reports. So, he waited. He was willing to wait most of the day, and if the boy didn't leave the house on some errand or another, he would have to resort to plan "B". He smiled glancing down at the syringes on the seat beside him. He had a special one planned for her. It was a temporary paralytic that would leave her fully conscious, just unable to access her body for about fifteen minutes. The other one was a different matter. That one was reserved for the boy if he didn't leave the house of his own accord. There was enough morphine in that syringe to induce a permanent coma at worst or death at best. There were advantages to being a doctor after all, and he was more than comfortable with availing himself of them for his own purposes.

42

"Holy shit!" Darius yelled from his station in the control room as he bolted upright knocking his chair against the filing cabinet behind him, "Why hasn't anyone thought of this! Where is Director Shah?"

It was the morning before the impact and the control room was unusually full for this time of the day. Darius' sharp exclamation had made everyone jump and turn in his direction, even more so because Darius Gordon was an intellectual genius who wasn't given to bursts of emotion. Fifteen curious heads followed his actions as he raced toward the door even before the echoes of his outburst faded.

The looks of shock lingered on the faces of the rest of the staff for quiet moments after Darius left. One other physicist, after observing his hasty exit, casually got up and walked over to his terminal. He stared for a moment then sat down and studied for a moment longer.

"Oh my God," he finally breathed. By this point every eye in the control room was on him. Even though he was talking in hushed tones, his voice carried in the suddenly still room, "It's going to clip the moon first!" He turned to face the room and seemed surprised to realize every eye was on him. "Atlas slowed Kohler/Leporidae down, and the change in velocity effected the relative position of the moon at the time that it approaches us. I have no idea why it didn't occur to anyone to check the moon's position once Atlas had affected the change, but according to Darius' calculations, and they look correct to me, the moon is going to act as a shield. Earth isn't going to receive the direct impact." The words came rushing out of him in what seemed like one continuous breath.

The rest of the room continued in their shocked silence as he revealed this fresh piece of momentous news. It was at that moment that Director Shah burst into the room.

"Ok folks, judging by the looks on your faces, I'm guessing you have the news. So, let's not just stand here looking shocked. Let's start contacting the other scientist groups and begin to model the results of this new discovery. Maybe Earth is saved and maybe not. Surely something dramatic is going to happen. Will it shatter the moon completely? Will we still get hit with fragments? Will it push the moon at us? What is going to happen? Come on! Let's get some answers!"

Motion reignited in the room as everyone began talking at once. They turned to each other and picked up their phones or plopped back at their stations. For the first time in weeks they felt there was something they could do.

43

December 21st, 2016
5:00a.m. Central Time

"Jeremy?" It was Chuck's voice on the phone and Jeremy was struggling to clear his head. He glanced at the clock and was frankly surprised that he'd even heard the call. The emotions of the previous evening had drained him.

"Chuck? Is that you?" Not that anyone could have mistaken Chuck's voice.

"Yes, Jeremy. It's me. Clear your head. I have some important news for you."

Those words went a long way toward dissipating the cobwebs, and now Valerie was awake as well and leaning over to him.

"What is it, Jeremy. Why is Chuck calling?"

"I don't know yet . . . What's going on Chuck? Something happen with the asteroid?"

"Yes. Well, no. I mean. Jeremy you were right. It was your info that saved us."

"Saved us. What do you mean? It's still going to hit."

"The moon. We forgot the moon! Our efforts to move Rabbit's Revenge may not have deflected it, but they did slow it down. The moon is now going to be in the path of the asteroid. We don't know what will happen when they collide, but it most certainly isn't going to make a direct strike on Earth."

"Oh my God!"

"Exactly."

"Jeremy, what is it?" Valerie had skooched in as close as she could, trying to overhear the conversation, but it wasn't working, and her curiosity was spiking off the charts.

"My information was right, Val. Just a sec and I'll tell you the whole story. Chuck, what are you going to do?"

"I was going to stay here, but now I'm not so sure. They don't need me here anymore, or if they do it won't be anything I couldn't answer from elsewhere."

"Would you like to come here again? We'd love to have you." As the words left his mouth, Jeremy realized he should have asked Valerie first. He cast a guilty glance in her direction only to see her smiling and nodding. There was a bit more of a pause before Chuck answered.

"Yes. I think I will, if you don't mind."

"Great. We'll see you when you get here."

"It'll be about three hours or so," Chuck replied casually.

"That's fine."

"Wait. Chuck?" But it was too late. Jeremy wanted to ask him when the impact was supposed to happen, but now he'd have to wait until Chuck arrived to find out, unless the news got a hold of it first, which they probably would.

Jeremy hung up and Valerie was all over him. "So, what's the news? What did he say?"

"Rabbit's Revenge is going to strike the moon."

"What?!"

"Yeah, apparently my information *did* help. They didn't manage to deflect the asteroid, but their efforts slowed it down. No one thought to recalculate the orbit of the moon in conjunction with the arrival of the asteroid."

"Oh my God."

"Exactly," Jeremy smiled as he echoed Chuck's words.

"So, when is he going to be here," Valerie asked, the excitement evident in her tone.

"About three hours or so."

"Then we still have enough time to celebrate," she said as she crawled on top of him.

44

December 21ˢᵗ, 2016
6:00a.m. Central Time

David woke up to a horrible crick in his neck. It was morning and he was cold. He glanced at his watch, *Damn!* How many hours had he been asleep? He was certain no one had passed him in the night; he wasn't that heavy of a sleeper.

He'd waited long enough. It was time to do something. David did a twist of his neck that looked more like an owl imitation than a healthy maneuver to loosen it. It did work out the kink, however, and also served to let him see if anyone else was up and about. Nobody was. He grabbed the two syringes off the seat, put them in his jacket pocket, and got out of the car. All semblance of humanity seemed to fall from his countenance as he strode with determined steps toward Jeremy's front door, and his date with destiny.

The morning was clear and cold, and there was an eerie calm on the air, almost as if the world was holding its breath. Such a stillness this close to the lake was a rarity, but the only awareness that flitted across David's mind was the fact that his steps through the grass sounded like a herd of elephants.

This was his moment. Envy, jealousy, lust, and his profound sense of entitlement all rose to the surface augmenting his nerve and clouding his mind from any other thoughts. They seemed to warm him from the inside so the thirty-degree weather went unnoticed.

He had on a dark brown sports jacket and jeans; the first syringe was clutched in his hand inside his right pocket. The more he considered it, the more he felt certain that Jeremy would open the door if he knocked, and it had occurred to him that knocking was the simplest expedient; He wouldn't have to worry about breaking in, and when the boy answered, as suspected, he had the syringe ready and could be done with him quickly.

Twenty more paces to go.

David's thoughts flashed back to that horrible moment in Jamaica when he had asked Valerie to marry him. He had opened his heart for one time in his life. He had bought her a ring that would have pleased the First Lady. The setting in the beach house was nothing if not romantic. David could never forget that look on her face when he knelt down to give her the ring. The look of delight he had expected from her was instead replaced by one of doubt and concern and maybe even a twinge of fear. Fear? How could she be afraid of him? Then the atrocity of atrocities had occurred. She had asked him why he wanted to marry her. It took fifteen seconds for the confusion to turn to embarrassment and about the same interval for that to turn to rage.

All he could think of was retribution, and it just so happened that his sensation to escape served both purposes. So, he packed his bag as quickly as he could and checked out, leaving her there in the room. He remembered grinning as he left the hotel thinking of the look on her face and that if she didn't have any money with her that was just tough. Hah, serve her right, the bitch.

It hadn't ended there though. He wasn't even back in the states before he found himself wanting her again. However, his sexual desire was now borne from a desire to exert power over her as a means of retribution. He'd tried to call her back at the hotel the moment he'd landed, but the hotel clerk said she was no longer there. He'd tried for days after that to get her to return his calls but to no avail. Finally, one day he had determined that he wasn't going to give up until he reached her. He must have called her fifty times leaving messages about every third try until, by late evening, she had relented and answered his call. When she finally answered, he had only been able to laugh. "I knew I could make you answer. You have to answer when I call, Val, or I'll never give up." And with that he had hung up. He'd felt good for the rest of the day.

Very little else went well after that, and she had done a masterful job of avoiding him until the time when she finally moved. It had taken him weeks to find out where she'd gone so he could follow. Now it was all coming to an end. He would have her one last time. She'd be tied and, in his control, and he'd do whatever he wanted with her. And then what? He hadn't really thought things that far through. The memories faded quickly in an adrenaline rush.

Three more steps.

David tightened his grip on the syringe and listened to the sound of his shoes scraping on the walkway leading to the door. Stepping onto the doormat, he rang the doorbell. All of the sudden the absurdity of what he was doing struck him. Here he was with a few hours left until God knows how much of the world was wiped out, and he was about to wreak some vengeance on an ex-girlfriend. He almost turned away from the door, but the image of her telling him "no" and the hatred it had fostered rose up again in his mind. NO. That bitch is going to pay for what she did to me if it's my last action on Earth! The seconds danced into infinity with no answer. He was about to ring again when he heard a scraping on the other side of the door. Then the door boldly opened, and there was the boyfriend, wearing an undershirt. The guys' muscles momentarily daunted David, but the pause only served to lend credibility to the story he was about to lay out.

"Hi there. I'm sorry to bother you, but I was having some trouble with my car and . . ."

As David spoke, he pointed back to his car causing Jeremy to lean out and look in the direction he was pointing.

Valerie was standing behind Jeremy and the sound of the voice she heard sent chills down her spine. She knew that voice.

"Jeremy! Watch out! That's . . ."

At the sound of her voice David knew his only chance had arrived. He yanked the syringe out of his pocket and swung it up to Jeremy's left shoulder. The syringe hit home briefly but before he could finish depressing the plunger, Jeremy rotated his hand up in a blocking motion, knocking the hand and syringe away from him. In one more smooth movement Jeremy struck out with the palm of his other hand and struck David hard in the chest.

He'd meant to aim higher into his face, but his balance was off, lowering the point of impact. Instead of crushing his nose the blow merely knocked David backwards, albeit forcefully. As Jeremy watched David fall, his vision seemed to retreat along a tunnel and the world fell away from him.

"Run Valerie," he heard himself say as his knees began to buckle.

The blow left David feeling like his chest had been crushed. He was still trying to catch his breath as he watched Jeremy slowly sag to the ground. He was reaching in his left pocket for the other syringe when, much to his surprise, Valerie came screaming out of the house. The sound was enough to wake the dead and absolutely stunned David. Nevertheless, by the time she moved around Jeremy, he was ready.

Valerie virtually threw herself at him, mindlessly going for his throat in her rage. This was the same crazy asshole that had left her in Jamaica, followed her here and, she was sure, nearly succeeded in having Jeremy killed. As her hands closed on the flesh of his neck, she felt a sharp stick in her side.

"What the . . ." She got out before she had to refocus on his attempts to loosen her grip on his throat. Another few seconds of struggle passed before she rather suddenly lost the use of her body, falling painfully on the concrete walkway. It was a strange sensation. She felt the pain of landing. She was completely alert, but no matter how hard she tried, her body wouldn't respond to her frantic commands to move. It felt like the sensors coming to her brain from her body were working just fine but the ones going from her brain out no longer existed. She couldn't even move her eyes to shift her gaze back to David.

"Feeling a little out of it are we?" David said through a wicked laugh. He took one quick glance over his shoulder then pulled her limp body inside, followed by Jeremy's.

At the sound of his voice, Valerie's fear ratcheted up several notches, not only for herself but also for Jeremy. *What did that maniac do to him? Is he paralyzed like she was, or worse? Oh God help us!* She couldn't think about it. She had to find a way out. But how? She literally couldn't lift a finger on her own.

David simply left Jeremy on the floor where he was. He started to lean down and check his pulse but stopped. If the fool wasn't dead yet, he soon would be, and either way he didn't care. He had more pressing business with Valerie. The thought made him smile. He turned to look at her on the floor. It was odd seeing someone in that state, paralyzed, especially looking at their eyes and knowing that they were seeing and alert just incapable of movement.

"Well, I guess we have some business to attend to, don't we Valerie?" Instead of trying to lift her David merely grabbed a wrist and began to drag her across the carpet toward the bedroom.

~

From her angle, Valerie could see where she was being drug, past the kitchen and down the hall. He was taking her to a bedroom, probably the master. *What a surprise*, she thought. She could feel her heart begin to race even more. It seemed strange to be able to feel her heart accelerate when nothing else was under her control. She blinked and surprised herself again. How was that possible if she was paralyzed? For that matter, why didn't the same drug paralyze her heart muscle? Was it only affecting voluntary movement? Not autonomic functions? That must be it or her lungs wouldn't be working either, would they? Or maybe the drug hadn't reached its full effect yet. She could feel the burning of the carpet across the side of her leg. They were getting close.

If she could even speak, she felt she might have some chance to reason with him, however small it might be, but she couldn't. She was helpless. She saw the doorframe go by. It was the master bedroom, where she had just been with Jeremy only a few minutes ago. Was it only a few minutes ago? It seemed like a lifetime. Suddenly, she was aware of her clothing, or rather lack of it. She was wearing a pair of sweats and a T-shirt. No underwear. David leaned down to pick her up and began talking. She wished she didn't have to listen.

"My, my, this bed is in quite the disarray. Were we frolicking this morning? You slut!" Her eyes landed on him as he spoke and the expression she saw was a nightmare from a horror movie. He had lost his mind.

He dropped her on the bed and slapped her then. The stinging sensation seemed to pulse in time with the ringing in her ears. Tears formed and began to leak unbidden down her face. The response made the sick bastard smile.

"Hurts, huh? Well that's just the beginning."

Valerie wasn't a person who was used to the sensation of helplessness in any situation. To be immobilized and limp in the presence of this lunatic was beyond her worst nightmares. As the thought sunk in, he reached down and yanked off her sweats, then as an afterthought, spread her legs. More tears found their way from her eyes. He raised her arms above her head and left them there, seeming to derive some pleasure from being able to move her limbs like a rag doll.

~

Jeremy was running in the woods. The dark canopy of trees closed above him, a great tunnel of vegetation. Somewhere in front of him was a light, and he knew he had to get to it, but the harder he ran, the more it seemed to slip away. And why couldn't he feel the weight of his footfalls on the forest floor? It felt as though he were racing across a cloud, each step landing on some sort of cushion. Still he pushed harder. He had to get to that light, but why? Onward and onward he ran, each passing step felt as though it was moving him across countless yards of green canopy. The limbs overhead seemed to be lowering the further he went, and he had the sudden fear that if he didn't reach the light soon the limbs might block him altogether. He felt his heart pound in his chest, and he pushed himself even harder. He had to get to the light. He just had to…

Jeremy's eyelids rose ever so slowly. His first sensation was the cold of the entry hall tile against his cheek. His second sensation was the fuzziness of his thoughts. Had he been running? No that was a dream, wasn't it? He tried to move his arms and was almost surprised to find them answer his command, albeit sluggishly. Why was his head so fuzzy? Then he remembered, David. That son of a bitch had stabbed him with a syringe. What had been in it? It felt like some sort of narcotic. But he had blocked the arm and must have kept the prick from administering the entire dose. Jeremy placed the palms of his hands on the cool tile beside him and pushed himself up. It felt like the air had congealed around him and his head was in some sort of a cloud. It took all his will just to push himself up onto his knees, where he sat momentarily, swaying.

Think. He had to think. Maybe the best thing he could do was listen. He swiveled his head slowly to both reassure himself he was alone in the room and to give his ears the best chance to pick any sound.

There. Down the hall. Some sort of shuffling that sounded like clothes.

That thought propelled an additional dose of adrenaline into his system and enabled him to find the required balance and effort to lean forward onto his hands and knees then pull his feet beneath him. As he reached his full height, a dizzy spell snagged him, and he had to lean against the nearest wall.

"Can't rest," he told himself. Valerie was in trouble, and he might be her only chance. Tentatively he began to take steps down the hall, slowly drawing in deep breaths as he did and releasing them, a calming regimen he'd learned in martial arts. The additional rush of oxygen to his system helped clear the fog slightly, but he kept one hand on the wall at every opportunity, nevertheless.

~

David had pulled Valerie's T-shirt up over her head and was just standing there enjoying the view and her helplessness.

"Now you're going to get to feel as embarrassed as I felt when you refused to marry me," David heard himself say. For one brief instant the words rang in his ears like the sound of a grade school bully taunting a smaller kid, but the thought slipped away as quickly as it had appeared. He wasn't going to be deterred by some useless manifestation of conscience. Not now. Not when he was about to realize his dreams of revenge. Besides, conscience was a worthless convention that only served to hold back the intellectually unenlightened. He didn't need it, or care about it. What he wanted right now was satisfaction, and he was going to get it. On several levels.

Jeremy wasn't staggering as much. Each labored step down the hall seemed to be chipping away at the fog surrounding his head. He continued to breathe deeply. The voice from the television news reporter seemed a million miles away. He tried not to think about what he might find when he encountered David and Valerie. He just prayed he wasn't too late. One more step. One more step. He was almost to the end of the hall. He sagged against the doorframe fighting the dizziness, but when he lifted his gaze and saw Valerie naked on the bed with David undressing, another jolt of adrenaline rocketed through him like a firestorm clearing away even more of the fog.

David abruptly turned his head back to the room entrance. "What the hell?" He grumbled angrily. He wasted no time reacting to the new circumstances, however. He bolted to the bedside grabbing the heavy crystal lamp and turned to face Jeremy.

Jeremy had moved into the room, now feigning more dizziness than he was actually feeling. The less threatening he seemed to this fool, the better. David barreled toward him in a mindless rage. *Perfect*, Jeremy thought, planning the best way to end this contest quickly. Another wave of dizziness took him as David approached, and that was the deciding factor for his next move. Rather than fight the off-balance sensation Jeremy merely twisted his body, dropped onto his side and let his momentum continue sliding him forward. Simultaneously he aimed a vicious kick at a forty-five degree up angle. He let David's rage do the rest.

David was in the act of lunging forward and swinging the lamp when the boy suddenly slipped out of his view. It took just a fraction of a second to adjust his gaze, but he was already committed to the lunge. Pain exploded in his groin.

Jeremy felt the contact through his socked foot and knew the fight would be over. This guy may never have lustful thoughts again. Ever. Jeremy managed to smile as he heard the exclamation of pain from David. Then another dizzy spell rocked him almost to unconsciousness.

The wave cleared and a bolt of fear shot through Jeremy. That kick wouldn't keep David down forever. How long had it been? Forcing himself up he saw that David was already attempting to stand and reaching for the lamp. Jeremy levered himself to his feet and roundhouse kicked David in the head. He collapsed in a heap. Jeremy thought for a moment. Duct tape. He needed duct tape. Then he caught a glimpse of Valerie lying naked on the bed, and his heart froze.

"Are you alright?" He asked as he slid her legs together and covered her before sitting down by her side. Her eyes just stared fixed off into space. No response.

"Valerie?" Jeremy frantically checked her pulse. It was a little fast but steady. What the hell had he done to her? It must have been some kind of paralytic. Presumably it would wear off. "I'll be right back sweetie." He took a second to draw the blanket up over the sheet and made for the kitchen.

Ten minutes later he had David's still unconscious body taped to a chair in the kitchen then he was back with Valerie.

"Valerie, can you hear me?" There was still no response. He tried to move her arms and face and it was like moving a lifelike doll. The eeriest thing was her unblinking eyes. The way they just stared, more than anything else, gave the illusion of death. If it wasn't for her regular breathing and pulse, he could have believed she was dead. He didn't know what he could do for her other than . . . her eyes must be so dry…

"Hang on just a second Hon, I'll get you some eye drops," he murmured as he gently closed her eyes. It seemed like such a small thing to do, and he was still feeling a bit woozy from whatever drug he'd been given, but at least he was doing something. When he returned, he was almost surprised to find that her eyes were open again and following him. This was a whole different kind of eerie—to have her eyes follow his movements with no expression whatsoever on her face or movement from her head.

As he moved toward her with the eye drops, she blinked. "Aha! I saw that. I guess whatever he gave you is wearing off."

"Let me off this chair, you Neanderthal."

Jeremy's head whipped around. He took two steps toward David and slapped him hard. "I'd tell you to shut up, you Jackass, but it's not worth the effort or nearly as satisfying as another solution." With that, he unceremoniously taped David's mouth shut with noticeably more duct tape than was necessary for the job, then turned back to Valerie. There was just a hint of a smile on her face.

"You liked that did you?" The smile widened perceptibly.

45

December, 21ˢᵗ, 2016
7:00 a.m. Central Time

Billy had been in Chicago now for about eight days and things were settling in nicely. The pace and scenery reminded him a lot of New York. He thought of Andy every day, and the life that had so abruptly changed his.

Billy had decided to go back to New York and drag him out of that old house at least ten times, and each time he stopped himself knowing that it wasn't what Andy wanted.

He had, however, been living up to his word to the old man. Billy had taken Twenty thousand of the fifty he had gotten from Andy and bought a small automotive shop from a guy who was certain the world was ending and therefore in a dead hurry to get to the mountains. He'd taken another five thousand and paid first and last month's rent and a security deposit on a one-year lease for a place three miles away from the shop. Another three thousand had gone to basic furniture and kitchen stuff. It had been the best Christmas gift of Billy's whole life. The rest went into a bank account. A bank account, imagine that. Billy was twenty-eight years old and this was the first bank account he had ever needed. This whole *normal* life thing had to be the strangest experience he'd ever felt. Still, he listened to the TV and radio enough to know that the normal part wasn't going to last much longer. It didn't matter. What mattered was that he was keeping his word to someone, another new experience for him.

The little car shop had a decent business already and two mechanics that worked there, Jason and James. The little place was basically an overgrown brick garage with two of the type of lifts that didn't require excavation, just a large "U" shaped frame that the cars drive onto and got lifted by the arms on both sides. It was typically dirty but well stocked. Just the tools the guy had left were probably worth the money Billy had paid.

From the first day he had walked in and told James and Jason he now owned the place, they had both been stepping around the shop like cats on a hot tin roof. Both of them were uncertain what Billy's plans were, and whether or not those plans included them. For that matter Billy wasn't too sure himself. He had never had an employee before and wasn't exactly certain how to act around them. What he did know was cars though, and a few days of watching the two guys work, helped him decide that they knew what they were doing and weren't lazy.

So, he kept them, and just trusted for now that they weren't thieves. If they were, he'd catch them soon enough, in the meantime he needed them. The place was swamped with business—mostly people trying to get service or repairs done so they could bolt town.

Billy had been at the shop this morning since 5:30 reading through the ledgers and books that the former owner had left him in such a hurry. It was all very confusing, and not what he wanted to be doing, which was to be out in the garage working on cars, but he figured that he better learn something fast or he'd probably lose his ass, and that *wasn't* what he'd promised Andy.

46

December 21ˢᵗ, 2016
8:00a.m. Central Time

Susan couldn't quit smiling. The morning sun was beaming in the back window of the car, and she was sitting on the seat next to Johnnie Oliver. They were driving west. It was their third day on the road together and the fifteenth since he had beaned her would-be assailant with a baseball in a filling station. Not that she had needed the help. The guy was already running from her but that didn't do anything to lessen the impact of the gesture from the handsome stranger. She remembered the conversation as she watched him drive.

~

"Nice heater, Johnnie Oliver," she'd said, answering his introduction as she watched the baseball roll into the gasoline beside the unconscious thief.

"More of a curve ball, actually. Do you think we ought to pull his face from that puddle of gasoline?"

She'd glanced casually back down at the thug's still form, "Probably. Drowning in gasoline is most likely a really bad way to go, even if he does deserve it."

"Agreed on both counts," he said with a mischievous grin. They both moved over to the guy, and in silent unison picked him up by his arms and drug him over closer to the station itself. Once there, they both released him as though they'd discussed a plan, which they hadn't.

"So, what's your name, if you don't mind my asking?'

"Susan Hummel," she heard herself say, surprising herself at her lack of distrust.

"Nice to meet you, Susan," he said moving toward her, extending a hand.

"Well, thank you for your help, Johnnie."

"Yeah, right. More like a little target practice. It didn't look to me like you really needed any help."

"Yeah, but it was a nice gesture anyway."

"Well, speaking of nice gestures, how would you like to go to dinner?" Johnnie's abrupt invitation had caught her as much off guard as had his left field curve ball, but it was no less welcome for all that.

"I think I'd like that," she said smiling broadly.

~

Things had proceeded rather fast from there, and they hadn't been apart since. Johnnie was an attorney who'd decided that law was for the birds under the current set of circumstances, and he was trying to figure out what he wanted to do next, and where, assuming the world even survived.

Susan had finally given up trying to teach, as her class had dwindled down to two students. She'd spent every night and much of the days with Johnnie since they'd met and one morning they'd decided to head west together.

They'd been up and gone since 5:30 and were now making their way across Missouri toward Kansas City and then maybe western Kansas. They hadn't really decided on a specific destination, just that maybe the mountains would be a better place to be when the world started to come apart. The day was a crystal clear, crisp, Fall morning. The sun was shining, and the temperature was in the high thirties. When Susan had opened the hotel room door this morning the air had been dead calm. With an effort she managed to subdue thoughts of Earth's impending doom.

Their first day out of DC Johnnie had driven them all the way to Louisville Kentucky, about 450 miles. The next day they had driven about half that far and decided to stop and see the sights in St. Louis.

Susan couldn't help but focus on her brand-new whirlwind relationship. There was a part of her that felt stupid, but those feelings only applied if the world was going to go on with business as usual. Still, she did find herself wondering if the accelerated pace of her feelings was the result of the impending catastrophes. She didn't know what the result of the coming asteroid impact or all these huge earthquakes was going to be, but she was pretty certain that "business as usual" wasn't on the menu.

In that light, she was down-right thrilled to be driving across the country with a wonderful man she had only known for two weeks, especially since she didn't have any other family, except her uncle Chuck. She'd been surprised to hear his name on the news, and she'd even tried to call him a couple of times, but she only had his home phone and he didn't seem to be answering or checking that one. Since then she'd quit checking the news at all. If it wasn't for Johnnie, she really would feel completely alone in the world. She turned to look at him. He was watching the road and his thoughts appeared to be wandering until he felt the weight of her gaze and turned to her.

"You know, Susan, if it wasn't for you, I'd be feeling like the last man on the planet today. Hell, for the last several days for that matter."

Initially she could only smile at his voicing the thoughts that had just been going through her mind. Then she leaned over and gave him a quick peck on the lips, "I'm glad I'm with you, too."

Silence reigned in the car for a few moments before Susan spoke again. Her words came as a surprise to both of them.

"Johnnie, why don't we head down through Texas instead?"

"Any particular reason?"

"Not really. I've just never been to Texas, and it seems like a good idea."

"Works for me. We can swing south when we get to Kansas City." He paused for a moment, hesitating to bring up the next topic, "You know, Susan, it might be a good idea to turn on the radio, too. Today is the day after all."

They had been pointedly avoiding listening to any news on their trip out, but the asteroid strike was supposed to happen today, and they should at least have some idea of where the initial impact would be. It might possibly be useful information. So, with a silent nod and a smile she reached for the radio button.

Neither one of them could have been prepared for what they heard next.

"... to our music in just a moment, but we wanted to take a moment to repeat the momentous news. The Rabbit's Revenge asteroid is not going to make a direct strike on Earth. Scientists just revealed early this morning that the moon is going to act as a shield, and they suspect that the asteroid is going to glance off of it and either shatter or angle away altogether. Scientists do, however, still believe that the Earth is going to be exposed to a tremendous meteor shower. Other news from around the world is less encouraging. The earthquakes and volcanoes that have continued to increase for the last several weeks are continuing to swell in intensity and frequency. Mt. St. Helen is threatening to blow again, and severe earthquakes continue to rock San Francisco and Los Angeles as well as hundreds of other locations around the U.S. and the world. Across Europe ..."

Susan turned the radio back off. "Oh my God," she breathed, unsure as to which of the news to react to first.

47

It was a beautiful day at sea and Greg Ormond was feeling warm inside, despite the cooler winter temperatures and the stiff breeze in his face. He had decided to take the Argus out on his regular patrol despite the impending asteroid strike, but with one difference. Today his wife, Sarah was with him and their young son, Jacob. That by itself could account for his unrelenting warmth.

The seas were calm, and the breeze was a gentle breath from the south. Gulls hovered in pockets over schools of tiny fish beneath a glorious blue morning sky.

Greg stared off into the horizons, but as yet there was nothing to see. No drug boats to interdict and at this distance from shore, no lingering barges or scows with their masses of the poor.

Weeks had gone by since his run in with that last drug boat, the destruction of which was still haunting him, despite its necessity. With the asteroid scheduled to strike later today and the growing number of other catastrophes around the world, drug smuggling apparently had dwindled away. A temporary condition no doubt, should the earth survive the day.

Survive the day. What a thought, Greg mused and how was it that he could be so complacent on a day that could be the end of the world? But he knew the answer as he glanced down at Jacob, then up at Sarah. Jacob's smile was stretched from ear to ear. He loved getting to go on patrol with his dad, and Sarah's answering gaze was one of peace. Whatever happened today, they would be together. He smiled at that, and at the fact that everyone on board, including his family, had been conspicuously *not* discussing the event that was scheduled to take place in a few hours.

The Argus had tiptoed through the reefs surrounding the upper keys and was now approaching open water. It was her mission this morning to cruise up the western side of Florida before heading down to Key West and the outer territorial waters. "All ahead full," Greg called from the railed walkway just afore of the helm. The Argus' big engines wound up, and Greg couldn't resist looking at Jacob again. If there was anything Jacob enjoyed more than riding with his dad, it was when he got to do it while the boat was moving fast. That smile was worth more than life itself.

"So, do you think we're going to make it?" Sarah asked.

The smile had slipped from her face slightly as she asked the sober question that was haunting her.

"I think we will," Greg offered, "I'm not sure how I know that, but I do think we will. But you know what? No matter what happens at least we're together." That statement put the smile back on Sarah's face, and she put her arm around Greg's waist.

"And that's no small blessing," she added, tilting her head into his chest as her long dark hair blew back from the wind of the Argus' acceleration.

No one on board had tuned into the news since leaving port. As a result, it was 8:00a.m. Eastern Time and no one on board the Argus knew yet that the asteroid wasn't making a full strike on Earth.

48

Chuck hadn't made it away from NASA as early as he had hoped, but he was on the road now and heading to Austin. Beyond what the newscasters were saying, Chuck was certain that the meteor shower would occur, and occur in a big way. The exact time the shower was going to hit this area was impossible to determine. The Rabbit's Revenge had not yet struck by the time he left the Space Center, but he suspected the meteor shower would begin to fall in the Atlantic Ocean before he arrived in Austin at the very latest. His mind was calculating. The velocity of the various particles after they collided with the moon was an unknown as well as the width of the band of particle fall. The only thing Chuck knew for certain was that it was going to march its way across the United States and would be over Texas in the next few hours. It might even arrive in Austin before he did. He rather hoped not.

His thoughts wandered from considering the density of the falling particles and therefore their ability to penetrate various materials, to thoughts of Jeremy and Valerie and their kindness in inviting him back to their home. He found that his concerns hovered more toward their well-being than to his own. It was the closest sensation he had had to *family* since Louise had passed. That thought caused him to think of Susan. She was the only family he had left in the world, and he hadn't even talked to her in over a year.

A pang of worry and regret suddenly spread through him. How was she faring during this holocaust? Was she still in Virginia? It occurred to him that the meteor shower might already be over Virginia, and his concern deepened. He didn't have her number memorized, but he did have at least her home phone number programmed into his phone. Glancing down from the road he looked up the number and pushed the button. He didn't have a lot of hope that she might be sitting in her home waiting for events to happen, but he didn't know what else to do, and all of a sudden he *really* wanted to hear her voice. The phone rang several times before the voicemail picked up.

"Hello, this is Susan. I'm away from the phone. Please leave your name and number and I'll get back to you as soon as possible."

Chuck's heart sank. On the other hand, if the voice mail was still working maybe the Virginia area hadn't been pummeled too seriously by the meteor shower or any earthquakes or maybe she'd already left.

"Susan," he began slowly, with a hollow feeling in his heart. "This is Uncle Chuck. I wanted to call and see if you are alright. I don't believe you have my new cell number, but this is it, and you can reach me at any time. Please call if you get the message. I'm worried about you. And . . . I miss you."

As he punched the End button on the phone, Chuck's sense of loneliness increased. Those last words had been difficult for him to say. It felt very strange. Voicing emotions was not a natural part of his character, he was sad to realize.

He focused on the road noises and watched the scenery go by for a few minutes while he sifted through his memories of Susan. There weren't that many, and it caused him to feel more than a little guilt. Still, there was nothing more he could do, so he let those thoughts wind down and focused on the road ahead of him. The highway was surprisingly empty. The Texas sky was a gorgeous crystal blue. It was difficult to imagine the fire that would soon be raining from the heavens.

49

At that instant, while people scurried about on Earth, Rabbit's Revenge careened through the blackness of space racing toward its fateful rendezvous. It was roughly twenty-five thousand miles away from the moon or a bit less than forty-five minutes.

For all the efforts of mankind, it had only slowed down a few thousand miles per hour and varied from its original course less than a degree. The remnants of the space shuttles, Atlas in particular, still clung to its side like a parody of Ahab, dead and bound to the flank of his great white whale. But the tiny changes Man had affected on the asteroid were significant. Now, as it blazed through the void with bare minutes left before impact, the moon rose like a great white shield in the sky, and today, that's exactly what it would be.

Scientists raced to calculate the exact instant of impact so they could begin to model the effects, but Rabbit's Revenge was still defying them. It had begun to accelerate again as it approached its cataclysmic collision, reacting to the gravity of the Earth and the moon itself, but for some inexplicable reason it wasn't changing velocity in a linear fashion. Instead, it was accelerating, then holding constant briefly, then accelerating again. From the scientist's perspective, its velocity change was literally impossible, and the inconsistencies were effectively foiling their best efforts to be precise.

Their frenzied attempts to calculate the time of impact were due more to its effect on the magnitude of the resulting kinetic explosion, than a need to know the exact time.

When the two celestial bodies collided, there was going to be a detonation of monumental proportions, never before witnessed this close to Earth, and they wanted it recorded. Also, what the exact result to the earth would be from that explosion was the all-important result they were trying *not* to have to conjecture.

Any information they could glean prior to the cataclysmic event could mean hundreds of thousands of lives saved, and they were scurrying frantically to gain as much as they could.

At the moment, the best estimate of the time of impact with the moon was 9:44a.m. Central time, and by now that number was not likely to vary more than a minute either way. How long after that before anything entered Earth's atmosphere was anybody's guess, some particles might accelerate some decelerate, but it was going to be a few hours anyway.

Virtually every telescope in the world that could see the moon that morning was focused on the impending cataclysm. When it finally happened, they weren't disappointed. A million eyes glued to a million eyepieces flinched back as the careening celestial body plowed into the side of the moon. It was an eerie, soundless detonation and the sensation for the watchers was one of abject awe. To see an impact of this magnitude in total silence seemed to defy the senses of its earthborn spectators. The video recordings being taken of the event would be studied endlessly for generations to come.

The asteroid seemed to force its way further and further into the moon's surface like a baseball into a sphere of water until the moon lost a huge chunk of itself and Rabbit's revenge broke nearly in half, sending its largest fragment at a tangent away from the collision and also away from Earth. But the collision not only broke off a huge mass of the moon, it also left a substantial portion of the asteroid itself, embedded in the impact crater.

To the watchers, it was as if a giant had used a broom to swat a gargantuan nest of bees. Millions and millions of fragments raced away from the colossal collision and were drawn directly into Earth's gravity like a great, dark cloud. These fragments fell, not in the form of a single curtain racing toward Earth, but in wave after wave of particles. Celestial bullets of every size from pea gravel pellets that never made it past the atmosphere, to a few chunks a hundred feet wide emanated from the impact with lethal velocity.

Scientists had neither the data nor the time to predict the landfall of such a massive amount of meteorites, but of one thing they were certain, the earth was going to have the opportunity to do quite a bit of rotating from the time of the initial meteorite strike until the last particle finally landed.

This meant that although the initial strikes might be off the Atlantic coast of the United States, as predicted, this meteor shower was going to walk across a good portion of North America before it finished. The celestial onslaught was essentially going to be following the path of all the East coast refugees as they fled toward the central U.S.

Hundreds of thousands of eyes pulled back from eyepieces with mouths sagging and eyes wide. Their minds continued to tell them their ears should be ringing from the concussion of the vast detonation their eyes had just witnessed, but as there is no sound in space, the entire spectacle had taken place in mime. All that was left to see was a slightly smaller moon with an oddly ragged edge shrouded in dust, and a cloud of not-yet fiery particles racing directly for Earth.

People scrambled, and scientists calculated, as they desperately tried to not only log and record but analyze what they had just seen. The several hour interim saw every astronomical and geophysical scientist on the face of the planet busier than a trampled ant hill until the report came; at 12:45p.m. Eastern Time the leading edge of the deadly shower of rocks began to touch the Earth's atmosphere and turn into an easily traceable fire storm. Hundreds of satellites were obliterated as the storm passed just before touching the outer reaches of the atmosphere. All eyes were again glued to the telescopes of the world to watch the onslaught firsthand.

50

When the doorbell rang Valerie actually jumped in Jeremy's arms.

"Easy girl, that's probably just Chuck." Jeremy rose from the couch and moved toward the door, making a point to slap David on the back of the head as he went by.

David could barely react. He was seriously duct taped to the heavy wooden chair facing a corner of the room and had been for hours. By seriously duct taped, I mean that Jeremy must have found a special on duct tape at some point in the past because David was just a few strands shot of looking like a duct tape mummy.

They had struggled with what to do with him. Calling the police seemed a bit futile given the day's events, but they didn't really want to have anything to do with him either. The stopgap measure with the duct tape had been Jeremy's idea. Even more so after he saw how the suggestion made Valerie smile.

"Good morning," Jeremy said, as he swung open the heavy front door.

"It is a good morning," Chuck answered in his big booming voice. Chuck caught Jeremy by surprise by bypassing his offered hand and instead giving him a big hug.

"It is *such* a good morning," Chuck repeated, "when you find out the world isn't going to end today."

Valerie had come up off the couch and now came over to also give Chuck a warm hug. "Well that's a pretty hard statement to argue with. Come on in and tell us what we don't know."

The three of them moved into the hall toward the kitchen until

Chuck caught sight of the person taped to the chair. To watch his gaze, you would assume Chuck was seeing a new piece of furniture, judging from his apparent lack of surprise.

"Is this some sort of Egyptian ritual you have going on over here?"

Jeremy just smiled as if it was nothing unusual, "Don't they *wish* they had duct tape? No, this is just Valerie's ex-fiancée who has tried to kill me twice now and her once."

"He was not my fiancé. I refused him," she quickly interjected.

"Hmmm," Chuck began, "I guess you've had an interesting morning too then."

"Yeah, sort of . . . We're just having a heck of a time deciding what to do with him," Jeremy offered casually.

Chuck didn't exhibit the slightest surprise to the odd situation and promptly offered a suggestion, "Well, why don't we move him to the garage? At least there we won't have to look at him. Judging by the tape, I'm guessing that hearing him isn't much of a problem."

"Oh, he grunts and groans occasionally, but I like your idea. Will you help me drag the chair?"

"Certainly," Chuck answered.

"I think I'll go make us some mimosas." Valerie offered turning back toward the kitchen.

As he and Chuck drug the chair into his hangar, Jeremy was struck by the surrealism of it all. Here he was with a scientist he barely knew but felt like he'd known forever, helping him drag some doctor who'd try to kill him twice but was now taped to a chair, out to his hangar while his girlfriend made mimosas as they waited to see how many millions of people might be killed by a variety of world-class upheavals. It had to be fantasy, didn't it?

"So, this is the guy that shot you?" Chuck asked.

"No, but we're pretty certain he's the one who had it done. And he's damn sure the one who drugged me, no doubt with the intent to kill had I not deflected him before he emptied the syringe in me."

Chuck frowned deeply at this information, "What did he give you?"

"I don't really know but judging by the effects I'd have to say it was morphine or something pretty close to it."

"But you're feeling ok now?"

"Yeah, I was out for a bit then woozy and dizzy, but it seems to be gone."

"Well, if he gave you a narcotic, I'd go easy on the mimosa's for a while and maybe focus on a cappuccino or two."

"Point taken, thanks," Jeremy answered.

They reached the oversized door to the hangar and Chuck and Jeremy plopped David back down onto all four chair legs while Jeremy opened it. They both turned and silently drug David into the expansive place. David's eyes had a wild animal look to them, maybe layered with a patina of hate. Jeremy quit looking at him.

"I sure like your Saratoga." Chuck said as he gazed lovingly at the sleek aircraft.

"That's my baby."

"I know I told you I was a pilot too," Chuck mentioned, "But did I mention I have quite a few hours in a Cherokee six?"

"Then you'd feel right at home in this one. It flies the same only a little less payload and about 20 knots more speed. Maybe you can fly with me sometime?"

"I'd love that."

They turned back into the house as if they had just come in there to look at the plane and weren't leaving a human out there taped to a chair. David attempted to make some noises as they left. He was ignored.

51

The Argus had cruised up another hundred miles of the western Florida coast before turning back south and widening her course further west and away from the coastline. The radio had been on most of the trip and all on board had been straining to hear the news since the impact. They had only found out a couple of hours ago that the massive strike they had been mentally preparing for had now become thousands of little strikes. Greg had been angling away from western Florida and toward the west side of Key West for almost an hour now looking for anything unusual. What Jacob pointed out shortly, certainly qualified.

"Look, Daddy!" Came Jacob's excited voice.

Greg's eyes followed the pointing finger of his son and memories of his Boy Scout days sprang into his mind. What he saw in the sky was more reminiscent to those nighttime campfires when one of the older kids would drop a log on the fire sending a shower of sparks racing into the night sky than it was to their late-night observations of meteor showers.

But either way, these sparks weren't harmless, and they weren't racing away from view but right toward them.

"Oh my God," Greg breathed, "Jacob, sit down behind me."

His immediate thought was to turn his boat away from the onslaught, but he couldn't fathom what direction that might be, instead he turned to his first mate.

"All ahead full." Key West was his closest landfall and if something struck the Argus, he wanted to be closer to land.

The sky continued to fill with the fiery specks and all hands including his wife stared at the spectacle as the Argus lifted her bow and raced across the calm blue water. It was another five minutes before the crew saw the first meteorite strike the ocean with a hissing thump about a hundred yards off to their starboard. It was another several minutes before they saw another one strike even closer off their stern, the exact spot where the Argus had been just seconds before.

"My God, Greg, are we going to make it?" It was Sarah's voice, and it was as full of fear as he had ever heard from her in all their years of marriage.

He wanted badly to comfort her, but Greg couldn't bring himself to lie. "I don't know, Honey, just pray."

Even as he spoke Greg was trying to visualize what the outcome would be if one of those fragments struck the Argus. She did have some armor plating and it's possible that the rocks would simply bounce off. The thought died aborning when another meteor the size of a trash can struck the ocean's surface two hundred yards off their bow. Unlike the hissing thumps of the smaller particles, this monster packed an explosion like a large caliber cannon shell, or a depth charge for submarines, sending a geyser of ocean hurtling a hundred feet into the air. Greg didn't have to wonder what would happen if *that* size chunk impacted the Argus. It would shear off the bow and send them to the bottom. A feeling of helplessness overtook him. There was no reason to slow the Argus or veer her because he had no idea where the next strike would hit. His best course was the one he was on, Key West, and it was just a few more miles.

Moments went by without any further strikes, and the crew was beginning to have hope that they had passed out of danger. In reality they had just been outrunning the leading edge of the main fall and were now making themselves a target for an extended period of time as they tried to return.

"Sir, contact off the starboard bow."

All eyes on deck turned in the direction of the crewmember's shout. In the distance and closing fast was another ship. Greg strained his eyes, then reached for his binoculars.

It was another one of the refugee barges he had seen lingering in international waters, but this one was bigger than most. It was at least a hundred feet in length and as the Argus approached, he could see that it was overloaded with people and making way in the opposite direction.

Greg was briefly at a loss as to what to do. The boat grew rapidly larger in his view as he tried to decide. On any other day his duty would be clear, but with deadly missiles raining from the sky, today's decision wasn't such a simple one. Ten seconds later the decision was made for him when the entire crew watched in awe and horror as a meteor the size of a basketball rocketed from the sky and punched straight through the slow-moving freighter just fore of the stern. The big boat reacted as if a giant hand had slapped down on its stern. It sunk down then popped up, throwing a number of the stern passengers high into the air. When it regained the surface, it immediately began to settle lower in the water.

"Greg, that boat is sinking," Sarah yelled.

"I know," Greg responded in an eerily calm voice, looking at the many refugees who were now swimming as a result of the strike, "And we don't have the room to take her people onboard." Two more seconds was all it took for Greg to make a decision. "Prepare to come about and match that freighter's course," he yelled to his first mate. "Johnson, prepare to pay out the aft mooring line and drop one of the starboard lifeboats for those swimmers as we pass by."

He knew the refugees would have a tough time surviving if he left them with just the lifeboat, but he didn't have time to do more for them and still hope to save the others and the Argus.

People scurried across the deck to carry out Greg's orders, and the Argus was passing alongside the doomed freighter in moments. The rear of the barge was already settling very low in the water and would slip under in moments if he couldn't get his plan carried out quickly. The crewmen threw the end of the mooring line to waiting hands on the bow of the freighter.

"Tie it to your bow cleats," one of his men yelled to the frightened people on the deck. Apparently, a few of them spoke English because they didn't waste any time complying with Greg's crewman's request. Survivors clamored back on board as they did. Seconds later the sinking freighter was tied to the Argus.

"All ahead one third," Greg bellowed, "And Jimmy, bring it up slowly, then keep accelerating."

"What are you doing?" Sarah asked, "Won't that freighter drag us down?"

"Watch," was all Greg answered.

"Johnson, stand ready at the stern with the fire ax. If she's too heavy for us be ready to sever that line."

"Aye, Sir." Johnson scampered to obey.

Greg watched as the line came taught and Jimmy continued to ease on the power of the Argus' massive engines. It was slow going at first, but inch by inch the Argus picked up speed. Greg knew that if that mooring line didn't snap right away then it would probably hold for the whole pull.

Every mouth on both boats was silent and every eye was glued to the mooring line as the Argus slowly picked up speed. The forward motion that the Argus was generating for the freighter began to act like a siphon for the water that had been flooding the stern. With each passing second more and more of the water was being sucked out of the very hole that had been sinking her. Each passing moment saw the freighter's stern rise higher and higher and the drag against the Argus lessened.

Smaller meteors continued to hiss into the ocean all around, and Sarah screamed when she happened to see one strike a helpless swimmer. Greg turned sharply to her, followed her gaze then gently put a hand on her back as he returned his attention to the sinking ship. At about fifteen knots Greg called back to his first mate at the helm.

"Ease her up, Jimmy. I think that's fast enough."

As Jimmy complied, Greg had to make another decision. Where was he going to take these people? The front line of the meteor shower was apparently marching from East to West so reason told him that West was the shortest route from beneath the deadly deluge, unfortunately there was nothing but Gulf of Mexico to the west for hundreds of miles and he didn't have the fuel to get anywhere even if he wasn't dragging another boat all the way to the nearest coast line.

Even before the conclusion formed clearly, the foray of meteors resumed hissing and thumping into the water around them and onto the freighter making his decision for him. He was about to shout the course change to Jimmy when a scream from the Argus' stern cut him off. Johnson had been hit. This was followed by a host of answering screams from the freighter behind him.

Greg grabbed his bull horn and keyed his mike at the same time.

"Evans, pick up Johnson's axe. Everyone else below deck!" he yelled.

Greg's crew responded immediately, but there was some translation necessary which was passing among the refugees. While it happened quickly, the relaying of Greg's warning was dotted with intermittent screams as others fell prey to the fire from the sky.

Moments later, both decks were cleared as much as possible and the hissing and pinging of the rocks on the Argus' armor was all Greg could hear above the drone of its hefty engines and the intermittent screams of victims from the freighter that couldn't fit below deck. If they made it, America was about to have a small increase in its population. He'd made his decision.

Sarah, sensing both his quandary and his decision, hugged his arm. "You're giving these people quite a wonderful Christmas gift I think, and it's a good decision Greg."

That was all the reassurance he needed.

The strikes continued as Greg watched from the glass enclosed control room. One direct hit spidered the glass on the left side. It was a bit of a surprise to Greg because that glass was virtually bullet proof. He gave it little thought however as the little balls of fire continued to strike the two vessels and hiss into the ocean around them. They had been travelling now toward the western shore of Florida for about forty-five minutes without any more loss of life or major damage to either boat, and Greg was daring to entertain a bit of optimism about their chances of making it to shore alive when he heard a tremendous roar followed shortly by a chunk the size of a minivan exploding into the ocean about a half mile ahead of them and promptly raising a huge wave. Greg reacted instinctively when he shouted to the helmsman.

"All ahead two thirds."

"But sir that might shear the line to the refugee's boat."

"You heard me," Greg answered grimly; "We have to save ourselves first if we are going to be around to help them." As he spoke, Greg silently turned the Argus' wheel to a course straight at the explosion.

"Aye aye, sir," the helmsman answered as he eased the throttles of the Argus' tremendous engines forward.

It seemed like minutes before the geysering water fell back into the ocean, but the resulting wave was continuing to climb as they approached. Greg had correctly judged that their best chance for survival was to take the Argus straight into the turbulent water. He was hoping against hope that either the Argus would arrive before the wave reached its apex, or he had one more trick up his sleeve to coax the Argus into knifing through the growing wave before it reached tsunami proportions.

He grabbed his microphone as they lurched forward, "Wilson, prepare both forward cannons with the high yield shells, and have someone use the bullhorn to tell the refugees to hang on tight. We're in for a rough few minutes."

"Aye, aye, Captain," Wilson had no idea what the Captain had in mind, but he trusted him implicitly.

Greg knew that his only hope was to go straight into the building tsunami. As the seconds passed it would only get bigger and if it hit them broadside or broke over them from the back, the Argus would be finished. By racing straight to the building wave, he was putting the best possible portion of the Argus, her bow, straight into it and was diminishing the time the wave had to grow in size. The problem was climbing the crest of the wave. Greg had seen the movie "A Perfect Storm" and he had no intention of forcing the Argus to try to climb the vertical mountain of water that was growing before them. He had other plans.

Charlie Lynden was manning the helm beside Greg. Greg had him take over for Jimmy a few minutes back. He was a rake thin man with a lopsided grin and a great sense of humor, but Greg had chosen him for this position for his nerves of steel. The man was absolutely unflappable. When he'd promoted Charlie to helm, he felt that he couldn't imagine a situation that could ruffle Charlie's nerves. But then again, he was about to attempt a maneuver that had never been done before and that he couldn't have ever imagined having to try. He hoped that his intuition about Charlie had been correct.

The Argus was almost to the base of the great wave when Greg spoke, "OK Charlie here's what I want you to do. You keep edging those throttles up as much as you think the tow line behind us will take. When I give Wilson the command on the forward cannons, I want you to pull the throttles to idle, count to two and rev 'em up again. You got it?"

Charlie could only guess what the captain had in mind but to his credit he didn't even blink in his response, "Aye, Captain, back to idle, count to two then fire 'em back up."

The Argus' bow was beginning to climb, and time was running out.

"Wilson, Fire the bow guns! Charlie, now!"

These two cannons, as they called them, didn't fire single shells but 120mm cannon shells at the rate of fifteen per second if needed. The high yield shells Greg had ordered loaded were explosive and designed to detonate on impact. As the volley of shells hit the rising wall of water in front of the Argus, the surface of the wall exploded from the concussion of the shells, making a tremendous disruption in the surface of the wall. When Charlie cut the throttles momentarily it dropped the Argus' nose into that disruption and when Charlie reengaged the engines, they effectively pushed the Argus through the wall. The sensation was of launching the battle cruiser into a tunnel for a brief instant that seemed to last forever before the tons of water came crashing down on top of the Argus. Greg held his breath then released it as his brave little ship poked her bow through to the other side.

It was seconds later before it occurred to Greg to see if the refugee barge was still connected, and he turned almost guiltily to find, to his delight, that it was still there. Swinging his gaze again across the bow Greg watched in wonder as the matching wave from the meteor crash raced away in the distance. Greg had a brief thought of falling through the looking glass. An instant calm fell over the water and all voices on both boats were stilled. He'd done it. Yells of exultation erupted everywhere.

In the aftermath, it was yet another moment before it occurred to Greg that no more meteorites were falling. They were in the clear. Home was just an hour of clear sailing away.

52

Billy had just come back from lunch when all hell broke loose. Buildings were beginning to shake all over the downtown area, and Chicago was on the verge of having the dubious distinction of being the only city in the world to receive the disaster triple-crown. It looked like Chicago was about to be hit with an 8.8 Richter earthquake at the same moment that the meteor showers began to pass over it and then get flooded.

The gravitational forces being exerted on the earth by its passing through the plane of the Milky Way Galaxy and causing worldwide earthquakes, had taken their toll on a very old fault zone the northern edge of which runs right under Chicago. It's called the New Madrid fault zone, and it was giving way. One gigantic rent in the earth's surface was actually running west to east, most likely stretching toward another weakness, the Wabash Valley fault line. This conjunction was about to have a most unusual reaction, it was about to cause a partial draining of Lake Michigan . . . into downtown Chicago. The doomed city was about to be the nexus of three of the greatest natural disasters to hit the earth in modern times and they were going to happen within moments of each other.

Tremors were still shaking under Billy's feet as he approached his shop, when suddenly a bus careened around the corner and crashed into the truck parked on the curb beside him. It was a school bus and it was full of kids, who at this point, were all screaming. They were all in danger of being struck by oncoming traffic and when Billy glanced up, he couldn't see a driver. He reacted without thinking and ran for the door of the bus. It was sagging open a crack and he pushed himself through. The driver was an elderly man and he was sagging to the side. Billy couldn't tell what had happened to him, but he quickly unclipped his seatbelt and removed him from the driver's seat. Then he took his place. With only a quick backward glance,

Billy shifted the old bus into reverse and swung the wheel. He wasn't sure where he was going to take the bus but at least he could get it out of the line of fire of the onrushing traffic. He pulled into the flow of traffic right as the meteor shower began to rain down. *It's finally here,* he thought.

That motivated him to take the next left. There was a bus station parking garage there, and it was covered parking. Concrete above and tall enough to admit the bus, it was perfect. A small meteor smacked onto the edge of the bus's hood and Billy watched in awe as it punched right through the edge of the fender, followed by another one that tapped onto the center of the hood and slowly burned its way through the metal. Billy almost sideswiped a row of cars as he returned his attention to the road. He had to pay attention to what he was doing.

"Don't worry, kids, it'll be alright. I'll find a place to park this thing where we will be safe." He only partially turned his head as he spoke, taking care not to take his eyes off the road again and as he did so he wondered where all these heroics were coming from. He had never said three words to any kids in his life and here he was trying to save a bus load of them and keep them calm at the same time. Billy smiled to himself. Andy would be proud.

Two more blocks and he'd be there. The traffic was heavy but sporadic, and Billy was considering the possibility of having to push other cars out of his way with the bus when the street in front of him began to dance. It was an amazing site to watch the road in front of him bow up. It reminded Billy of the old news reels he'd seen of Galloping Gertie, the Tacoma Narrows suspension bridge that had shaken so violently in the earthquake of 1940. But this wasn't a bridge and didn't have the flexibility to move like Gertie had. As he found himself downshifting to climb the new hill in the road, Billy saw a fracture in the concrete tear open and he swung to the right barley missing the danger and knocking a parked car out of the way in the process. Several kids began screaming again from the back of the bus. Billy swung back onto the road and down the back side of the newly formed hill and saw the garage ahead. He was going to make it.

He arrived at the garage entrance during a break in the traffic and immediately swung the big bus to the left toward the entrance. His front wheels had entered into the garage when another huge tremor tore the concrete underneath him.

The meteors were pinging consistently off the roof of the bus now and several more kids joined the chorus of screams as a few of the tiny fireballs made their way into the bus and onto or through its floor.

The hard thud of the bus's frame slamming down onto the concrete as its rear wheels dropped into the crevasse only augmented the scream-ing of the children. Billy kept his foot on the accelerator as he felt the bus frame skid along the concrete. The entrance in front of him was bowing up as well, and he was hoping he would get some traction again before the bus began to slide backwards. Then the tires grabbed, and Billy felt the bus begin to lurch forward...

He felt the white-hot pain as the particle from another galaxy seared its way through his lung. He knew he was a dead man by the time he actually glanced down for a second to see the hole in the bus floor the particle had left. But even with just moments left Billy forced his body to obey him for another few seconds and in those seconds, he could still make a difference . . . and keep his promise to Andy.

Billy focused with his rapidly diminishing strength and mashed the accelerator to the floor. The tires on the big bus actually screeched and spun in their effort to bite the increasingly tilted pavement. But as the last few seconds of Billy's awareness drained away, he felt the bus begin to move. He'd done it. Billy's head drooped down on the steering wheel, but the weight of his foot kept the pedal to the floor. The bus clawed its way up the incline and under the protection of the garage overhang until the big double wheels slid into another newly formed break in the concrete and dropped two feet down, stealing the bus's last remaining traction and virtually anchoring the entire undercarriage on the black-top. The engine on the bus, now freed of any load, over-revved briefly until the engine froze and with a loud thunk, went silent.

The stunned children sat still for just a moment until one of them realized that the barrage from the sky was no longer striking the bus or the pavement outside and the bus was no longer in danger of sliding into the crevasse.

"Let's get out of here," one of them yelled and acted on his own suggestion. The other kids were quick to follow, and the bus quickly emptied.

Once back on the tilted street, however, they again froze. None of them had any idea where to go. They weren't sure where they were or how many of the roads home were either destroyed or underwater.

Many were already reaching for their cell phones, but the network of towers supporting those devices had been destroyed in the catastrophic violence. For a thirty-mile radius around what used to be Chicago, all remote communication was gone.

Marley Holmes, a bus station employee, had witnessed the dramatic entrance of the school bus and without a single thought ran out of the safety of her office enclosure to gather the children in with her.

"This way, kids!" Her voice boomed from her petite frame and spurred the group into action. As one they bolted her direction.

Chicago continued to disintegrate.

53

December 21ˢᵗ, 2016
1:45p.m. Central Time

Jeremy and Chuck were talking amiably in the den with the television nearly muted when the first particles began to strike, and the front door burst open.

"Feel like a little company guys?" Joel said as he and Joan scampered inside with Joan slamming the door shut behind her.

"Hi, guys!" Jeremy said as Valerie came into the den from the kitchen, "What a great surprise. What's the occasion?"

"Are you kidding me?" Joel asked.

The hissing thumps and whumps that had initially gone unnoticed by the small group now became the focus of everyone's attention as Jeremy, Chuck, Joel, and Joan moved back over to the couch and chairs and sat. Valerie however was already glued to the TV.

"Guys, you have to come see this."

Jeremy hadn't even sat down before his eyes too were glued to the set along with everyone else. Chuck slowly lowered himself into an adjacent seat. The news *wasn't* about the asteroid.

~

"Several monumental non-asteroid events are happening simultaneously around the world. Scientists are extrapolating that they are possibly the result of the extraordinary gravitational forces exerted on the earth when it passed through the plane of the Milky Way galaxy several years ago around the end of the Mayan calendar. An earthquake in western Africa seems to have lowered a portion of the continent and water is now flowing back up the Niger and overflowing into the Sahara Desert.

The entire Island of Japan is convulsing with earthquakes and seems to be sinking. The population is evacuating as quickly as possible by any means available but there are just too many people to remove from the island in a short space of time. In further news the . . . "

It was at that point the TV went out, followed seconds later by the power.

"Well," said Jeremy, "that's interesting." As he moved from the couch to the window, he immediately saw a number of meteorites striking in the front yard. A wave of fear passed over him and was gone. He turned to Valerie.

"It seems as though the weather report is mostly clear with a 70 percent chance of meteor showers. At least we know what happened to the power."

The fear in Valerie's eyes however didn't dissipate, "Can they come through the house?"

That look triggered Jeremy's protective instincts, and he unconsciously moved closer to Valerie, but it was Chuck that answered the question.

"Some might be able to. I noticed that the roof is slate and that should stop most of the smaller particles, but the bigger ones—I don't know. It rather depends on the size of the particles. The larger ones have more mass, and they will certainly have the velocity to penetrate asphalt shingles. It's much less likely with a slate roof like this though."

The words were barely out of his mouth when an explosion rocked the house. Chuck fell back down on the chair beside him as every head swung back toward the kitchen and the hangar door.

"The garage," Jeremy shouted, as he bolted back in that direction.

Chuck was right behind him. When they reached the garage, the site was both shocking and gruesome.

A meteor had pummeled its way through the slate roof and sheared the top half of David's body from the bottom before careening into the concrete floor of the garage. Shards of the slate roof littered the floor and the remnant of meteor was still visible in the bottom of the small crater that was rapidly filling with blood. Everyone was struck dumb by the sight as the dull thuds of the impacts and the hissing sounds from the massive meteor shower continued.

Beyond the small puddle, there was very little blood to be seen relative to the damage as the meteor fragment had apparently cauterized most of his flesh as it passed through him. Due to all the duct tape, even his lower half still taped to the chair was intact with the remainder of his arms and fingers hanging limp in place beside his body. With so little blood it was almost like someone had dressed a manikin then cut it in half and dumped some mixed red colors on the top.

Chuck stared at the body with them for a moment then commented.

"The heat required to do that much cauterization must have been tremendous."

His eyes shifted from the body to the smoking hole in the floor and he stepped over closer to look down in the hole. Folding his arms, he spoke again in a tone that sounded far away, as if merely thinking out loud.

"I'm thinking that we are going to get some interesting answers when scientists get a chance to study these fragments."

Jeremy was still riveted to the scene, but Valerie had looked away. Jeremy's hand unconsciously drifted up to his neck and the cauterized skin remaining from his own incident.

"What are we going to do with the body? Should we call the police?" Joel's questions lingered as everyone considered.

Another tiny meteorite sizzled through the air next to Valerie and tinked on the smooth concrete floor causing her to jump violently

"For starters, I think we step away from this hole in the roof until the storm passes." She had already taken her own advice as the others moved to follow.

They all stood there in silence for a few minutes listening to the varied noises of the meteors striking outside.

"I think we should just dump his remains in the lake somewhere," Chuck suggested off-handedly.

Jeremy gave Chuck a quizzical look and Valerie appeared stunned, "You really think that would be the right thing to do?"

"Look," Chuck said, "we can call the police anyway, but you can imagine what's going on out there with this meteor shower hitting the city. I doubt anyone would rush out here to inspect one more dead guy. And frankly, these remains are going to begin to stink in about four to six hours so we certainly can't leave it in the house. We really don't have a better place to put the corpse. You want to drop it in a dumpster? Leave it on the front lawn? Our choices are pretty limited."

The look on Valerie's face spoke her thoughts easily enough. Shock had shifted to revulsion as her main reaction. Jeremy on the other hand was simply considering Chuck's words. Joel and Joan, who had remained mostly silent since entering the house, continued to stare in shock.

"How long do you think this meteor shower will continue?" he asked, cocking his head to meet Chuck's eyes.

"Hard to say. Maybe an hour, maybe three. I'd be amazed if the band of particle fall is consistent in width."

At that moment the ground beneath their feet began to tremble.

"What the hell is that?" Valerie asked, "Is that from the meteors?"

"No," Chuck answered promptly, "*That* is an earthquake albeit a mild one."

"But we don't have earthquakes in Texas," Valerie replied.

"You do now."

Jeremy spoke up as though the ground hadn't just shaken beneath their feet, "I guess I agree with you. I don't really want to dump it too near the shore, though. After the meteors stop falling let's go see if my boat is sunk. If not, we'll just go out to a deep place and dump it." Jeremy's words sounded rather matter of fact but his automatic use of the word "it" rather than "him" wasn't lost to his ears. This was no longer a person but just a thing.

Valerie stared at him like he was crazy, but said nothing

Chuck nodded quietly. Jeremy's gaze refocused on her as he moved beside her and put a protective arm on her waist. "Let's go get a drink."

54

Susan and Johnnie had turned south on the outskirts of Kansas City and taken highway 71 to I-40 and from there west to Oklahoma City. Wrecks and abandoned cars littered the highways, and more than once Johnnie was forced to use the Range Rover's 4-wheel drive capabilities to circumvent cars blocking their way.

It was a beautiful blue sky when they entered the outskirts of the City and the first meteors began to fall.

At the first few taps on the roof Johnnie thought it was hail, but the clear blue skies and a couple seconds of thought corrected his misperception.

"Oh Lord, it's the meteor shower, Susan. I think we should find some cover."

Before he could finish his sentence, the sound changed. More taps began to hit the hood of the Rover and these were much more solid—too solid to be mistaken for hail even with your eyes closed.

Cars began to swerve off the road around them as Susan recognized the distinct tap of metal on metal.

"I think you're right," Susan answered as a small particle struck the hood of the Rover and sat there sizzling. Johnnie's gaze lingered a bit too long on that particle burning into the hood of his car, so Susan had to redirect his gaze.

"Johnnie, the road." Her voice was just urgent enough to garner Johnnie's attention to the overturned pickup in front of them.

The truck exploded, rocking the Rover, causing Johnnie to widen his arc as he swerved around the burning vehicle. "That does it. I'm making for the downtown spaghetti bowl and parking underneath one of those overpasses. It's just a few miles ahead."

Susan just nodded. She was brave by nature, but her face was draining of color as she continued to watch the particle that had fixated Johnnie's gaze. It had almost burned through the hood.

Johnnie glanced back at her expression and wondered if she was considering what would happen when it dropped into the engine compartment.

The meteors were coming down harder, but most of them either missed the Rover or bounced off. The traffic was not only getting heavier but crazier as people were struck by more particles or shifted their attention to cars that had already been struck. Vehicles were leaving the road left and right and the sense of rampant panic was apparent everywhere. Johnnie had to stomp his brakes or swerve several times more before they reached an overpass he liked on I–35. Other cars had already had his same idea and when he parked the Rover, it was only about ten feet under the shadow of the overpass.

"Come on," Johnnie urged as he slammed the Rover into park, "Let's get out of here and further under the road."

Susan didn't need any more urging as she grabbed her purse and jumped out of her door. Johnnie met her in front of the SUV and caught one last glimpse of the hole the little meteor had burned in its hood before grabbing her hand and beginning to run.

Another thunderous explosion shook them as they ran and a person in front of them whispered, "Oh my God," while staring off to the west. Johnnie turned his gaze to follow hers in time to see a burning semi crash through the overhead guardrail on the other side of the freeway followed shortly by the sound of its impact. He pulled Susan along quicker.

There was a small crowd huddled near the middle of the underpass. Susan and Johnnie stopped when they reached them. None of the group seemed interested in talking, so Johnnie and Susan just mimicked everyone else by staring back toward the Rover and the havoc the meteor shower was creating beyond it.

It was several minutes into the incredible display before Johnnie realized how close he was holding Susan, and how much he valued this new sense of closeness. He sensed she felt it too, and his protective instincts flared even more.

"What do you think's going to happen, Johnnie?"

"I think this is going to pass in a little while, and we're going to wait right here until it does."

"But what about after that?"

Johnnie paused to look into her eyes. The fear there was apparent, and his expression softened to match his feelings.

"Susan, after that…we'll still have each other, and we'll figure something out."

He pulled her in even closer as he spoke. He was a bit surprised to see tears welling in her eyes. She didn't seem like the crying kind, but then again this was anything but the typical situation. She squeezed his waist harder in unspoken response.

In the distance more explosions could be heard from the impact of larger particles laced intermittently with the increasing hissing and thumping of the smaller ones, not to mention the vehicles that were detonating. Tongues of flame rose higher into the air from the smoke tinged sky over downtown. The air itself was filled with an acrid smell that neither of them recognized. Susan and Johnnie could both feel the rising swell of terror as the whimpering and crying grew from the others gathered beneath the bridge.

Moments seemed like hours and the general din of noise continued to increase. More and more fires could be seen cropping up in the distance. The entire group of refugees just stared in rising awe and shock.

An augmented sizzling sound drew everyone's attention fractions of a second before a meteor slammed into the back of the Range Rover. It must have angled directly into the gas tank for the next instant the rear of the Rover bucked into the air accompanied by a tremendous explosion. Johnnie dove to the ground, forcibly taking Susan with him, as others from the group with slower reflexes were propelled backwards by the concussion.

Pieces of metal and glass shot everywhere as the vehicle continued to rotate in the air until it crashed on its roof in flames. It was several minutes before any of the group got up off the ground where they'd either ducked or been blown. Now all eyes stared dumbly at the flames from the burning vehicle.

"We didn't want that stuff anyway," Johnnie said as he calmly stared at the burning ruins. Susan stood huddled next to him.

Susan didn't miss a beat falling in with his sarcasm, "Yeah, those clothes were old anyway and I *like* hiking."

Johnnie seemed to come out of a daze at her words and turned to look at her. Suddenly they both started cracking up as the rest of the group stared, no doubt assuming they had lost their minds.

Johnnie's laughing stopped abruptly when he realized there was screaming and crying going on around him, and he caught a glimpse of blood running down Susan's fingers.

"Damn Susan, some of that shrapnel must have hit you."

He reached for her arm as she looked down.

"I thought I felt a sting there. Looks like some other people were hit as well," she observed as she glanced around her.

"I think you need stitches," he said while he examined the four-inch slash across her forearm.

Susan flexed her fingers then looked away. "Well, everything is still working. We can just jog on over to the hospital when the meteor shower stops."

Johnnie smiled grimly as he took his shirt off, then his undershirt. He put his over-shirt back on and began tearing the undershirt into wide strips he then used it to partially close and bandage the wound.

"Wait," someone called from further under the bridge, "I at least have some antibiotic crème."

The speaker was a middle-aged woman with long dark hair, dark eyes and a face that suggested she spent most of her time outdoors.

"Give me just a second and I'll get it."

Johnnie stopped his bandaging and he and Susan watched while she sauntered back to her beat up old Ford Bronco.

"Thank you Ms . . ." Susan began when the lady returned.

"Beverly. You can call me Beverly," she answered as she handed the tube to Johnnie.

"We'll give this right back to you," he said.

The woman looked like she might be shaking.

"Are you alright," Johnnie asked noticing her demeanor.

"Yeah. Well, no," she stammered, "My house was destroyed, and my husband was killed by a meteor, but the kids are alright."

"Do you have a place to go," he asked.

"Yeah, we're going to my sister's place outside of Norman. She had a storm shelter, so I know they'll be there."

Johnnie had been undoing Susan's bandage while he spoke and applied the ointment. He now handed it back to Beverly.

"Well thanks again, Beverly, and good luck."

"You're welcome. Eh, do you and the lady have a place to go?"

The question prompted both Susan and Johnnie to glance back at the still burning Range Rover.

"Was that your car?" She continued.

"Uh, yes it was and as to your other question, we don't know yet," Susan answered while Johnnie finished re-bandaging her wound.

"Well, if you don't have any place to go, you can come with me if you want."

"Thank you very much, Beverly. We'll keep that in mind," Johnnie answered.

With that Beverly turned and walked off. Johnnie turned to Susan. She was staring at the burning Rover.

"Whatcha thinking?" He asked.

"I was wondering where we were going now. Which made me wonder if my place is still standing," her voice faded to a faraway note as she finished.

"As to your first thought, I agree with you. I'm wondering where we go now too, as to the last part, call your answerphone," Johnnie suggested.

A look of confusion overtook her features as she turned to him. "No one's calling me these days. I'm sure of that."

"Doesn't matter," Johnnie replied. "If your answering machine picks up there's a good chance your place is still intact."

"That's good thinking."

Susan unslung her purse from her shoulder and dialed the number. On the third ring it answered, and she hit the button to retrieve the messages before she even thought about it. Realizing what she had done, she was about to hang up when she heard her machine state that she had one missed call.

She listened for a moment then a dumbfounded look settled on her face as she hung up and typed something into her phone. Her gaze shifted to Johnnie's eyes.

"What?" He asked.

"It was my Uncle Chuck. I haven't heard from him in years. He left me a message. He's in Texas."

"Is that the astronomer guy you told me about that has been on the news about discovering the asteroid?"

"Same one."

"Wow. What else did he say?"

"He said that he loved me and asked me to call him to let him know I'm OK."

"So, call him."

Susan was nodding as she pushed the call button on her phone to dial the number she had just entered. The phone began to ring and at the same moment the meteor shower stopped.

~

It took three rings before Chuck even heard his phone ring. They were all sitting on the couch watching the TV, which surprisingly had come back on and was still working. Many of the stations, most notice-ably WGN in Chicago, were off the air, though.

"Do you hear that?" Valerie asked.

"Hear what?" Jeremy answered as he muted the TV.

"The meteors have stopped," she whispered. The sudden cessation produced an almost hypnotic quiet that halted all conversation.

It was at that instant that Chuck heard his phone ring and they all jumped simultaneously.

Everyone stared at him as he fumbled for the device.

"Hello?" he answered his big voice deepening slightly.

"Uncle Chuck?"

"Susan?" he responded at once, "Where are you? Are you all right?"

"Well, that's a good story, Uncle. We left Virginia a couple of days ago headed for Colorado but decided to come to Texas instead. At the moment we're under an overpass in Oklahoma City watching our car burn after a meteor hit the gas tank."

"Oklahoma City? Good Lord, were you hurt? Has the meteor shower stopped? Wait a minute, who's "we"?"

Susan smiled into the phone at her Uncle's flustered questions. "No, we're not hurt, and "we" is me and my boyfriend, Johnnie." She turned to Johnnie as she spoke his name to see him smiling at her broadly. It was the first time she had had a chance to introduce him to anyone.

"But what are you going to do now with your car destroyed?"

Jeremy tapped Chuck on the shoulder.

"I don't know, Uncle Chuck. The meteors have stopped but we haven't had a chance to think about it yet."

"Well, I . . . just a sec Susan," Chuck turned to Jeremy who was in the midst of tapping him on the shoulder a third time.

"We can take my plane and pick them up first thing in the morning. We couldn't make it there and back before dark today and I'd rather not try it in the dark. But early tomorrow . . ." Jeremy didn't finish the sentence as Chuck was nodding furiously and grinning.

"Susan, I'm with some friends in Austin, and he has a plane. Jeremy-Air can come pick you up in the morning. Where exactly are you?"

"A plane? Um, wait, eh we're at the underpass where I-35 runs under I-44 just south of downtown OKC. Uncle Chuck we're nowhere near an airport."

"I can get you to the Norman airport easy enough." It was Beverly, the lady with the antibiotic ointment.

Susan turned her head sharply toward the lady, "Are you sure?"

"Am I sure of what?" Chuck asked.

"No not you, Uncle Chuck. Just one second."

"Are you really sure?" She asked again of Beverly as she continued walking in their direction.

"It'll be no problem. I was going to head that way shortly anyway. I'm glad to help."

"That would be wonderful. Thank you so much Beverly." Susan put her mouth back to the phone, "Uncle Chuck, we have a ride to the Norman airport."

"That's wonderful, honey. Just keep your phone with you and we'll call you early in the morning."

"I will. Thank you so much. I love you."

"I love you too, honey. It'll be good to see you again."

Susan ended the call and turned to Johnnie, "So, I guess we have a plane picking us up at the Norman airport in the morning. Ever been to Austin?"

"Nope. But I'm looking forward to it."

"Come on folks," Beverly began, "The meteors have stopped, and I'd just as soon get out of here."

Beverly was walking back to her truck as she spoke, and Susan and Johnnie just fell in behind her.

Chuck was looking a little sheepish, and Jeremy supposed it wasn't a sensation he was used to.

"Are you sure you don't mind flying to pick them up?"

"Are you kidding? It sounds like an adventure and I *love* adventures." Jeremy's grin was an ear-to-ear, little-kid expression that left no doubt in anyone's mind.

Chuck nodded silently. "In that case, I think we have some trash to dump in the lake if your boat's still afloat.

When they checked, Jeremy's boat was still floating so Joel helped him wheelbarrow the grotesque half a corpse down to the dock and onto the boat. It was a brief but gruesome task which Valerie decided to forego.

"I guess this guy is now at the corner of Dead and Decaying," Joel offered with a straight face.

Jeremy chuckled and Chuck grinned as he carried the rest of the remains in a black plastic bag following them.

"Really, Joel? That is some dark humor."

"Might be the only kind we get for a while," he responded.

That comment turned everyone's face somber.

The lower remains were still taped to the chair and both Chuck and Jeremy had agreed that it would be simpler and easier just to transport it as it was.

Jeremy couldn't decide whether he was surprised or not that nobody was outside as he fired up the engine on his Invader inboard/outboard runabout. Jeremy knew the lake well, and he knew the spots where it was the deepest. The closest one was just a few hundred yards away from his dock and since they weren't all that concerned about hiding anything, they made for that one.

Chuck found an extra anchor in one of the storage compartments and suggested he tie it with the other remains to the chair. Jeremy quickly agreed, and Joel helped.

Ten minutes later they were heading back to the dock as if nothing unusual had just happened. Certainly no one was mourning David and in light of recent events this really was just taking out the trash.

They were already discussing tomorrow's flight.

* * *

The drive to Norman was relatively uneventful, albeit slow, if cars and car pile ups littering the road, dead bodies, and fires everywhere could be considered uneventful. To Susan the most surprising thing was that as they approached the heart of Norman, she saw several buildings that had fallen down. It appeared that everything over three stories had toppled.

"Look at that," she began, pointing to a fallen building.

Beverly barely turned her head as she needed to focus on the numerous obstacles in the road, but her two kids and Johnnie turned to look.

"Are you talking about the fallen buildings?" Johnnie asked.

"Yeah. Could the meteors have done that?"

"I don't think so. I'm guessing they had an earthquake here, and a good one at that."

"An earthquake in Oklahoma?"

"Sure. Didn't you read about the 5.1 Richter they had southeast of here in October 2010? It made all the news. And they've had a bunch of smaller ones since then."

"Come to think of it, I do remember that. I've just never thought much about earthquakes that far inland."

"Plenty of them this time. And all over the world too, I'd bet."

Susan went quiet and the kids remained eerily silent the entire trip. They were probably eight and ten and their continued silence must have been a symptom of shock.

What should have taken twenty minutes ended up taking an hour and a half because of all the obstacles in the road.

Beverly finally took the Hwy 77 cutoff which promptly turned into N. Flood Ave as it passed through Norman. The airport was only a mile or two up and off to the right.

"Thank you so much for the lift," Susan said as Beverly pulled the Bronco up to the tiny little terminal at the airport. "I hope your sister and her family are all right."

"I'm sure they're fine," Beverly answered casting a concerned eye on the terminal. "You sure you two will be OK here? It looks deserted."

"Just let me check the door," Johnnie volunteered. He had similar concerns after seeing the apparent desolation of the place. Ruined aircraft littered the ramp. Presumably some of the aircraft in the hangars were intact but none were visible.

The door opened easily and he quickly spotted a couch and a couple of vending machines.

"We'll be fine," he yelled as he waved back at Beverly.

Susan said one more goodbye then waved as she followed Johnnie into the building.

Susan was looking around at the sparse furniture and considering their sleeping options while Johnnie walked over to the big windows past the service counter and stared out at the ramp. There were a few planes still intact. The sight prompted him to open the door to the ramp.

"Where you going?" Susan asked.

"I'm going to go check the runway for potholes. I don't want your uncle and his friends to get a bad surprise when they try to land here."

He came back about twenty-five minutes later. "Long runway," he said smiling. "Well, there is one nasty pothole about a third of the way down from here on the terminal side of the runway, but it should be easy enough to miss once we tell them about it."

Susan met Johnnie as he came back in and grabbed him in a fierce hug before he finished speaking. "I'm so glad I have you with me," she said.

"I'm glad to be with you too, Susan. Does that mean I get to sleep on the couch?"

That got him a playful punch in the stomach before she answered.

"I think we can both fit," she said, smiling shamelessly.

55

December 22nd, 2016

The history books would record that by 3:00p.m. Central time on the 21st of December the meteor shower stopped. The final particles of Rabbit's Revenge never made it as far west as El Paso, Texas. Newscasters were so excited to report the cessation of the asteroid's particles that they neglected, for nearly an hour, to update the even bigger story. The earthquakes around the world were still increasing. The great passage through the plane of the Milky Way galaxy had pulled and stretched mother earth like a soft rubber ball, but the final straw had been the Earth's new moon. It was slightly bigger and (as they found out later) more massive, effecting an additional tug on an already destabilized earth. All over the world tectonic plates were shifting, volcanoes were erupting, and tsunamis were forming.

Due to the more visible and immediate fear of Rabbit's Revenge the media failed to focus on other dangers. That is until the meteor shower passed and Mt. Fuji blew. Tokyo began to sink. Suddenly, every news station in the world that was still functioning began to report the inundation of tectonic and volcanic disturbances around the world and the massive evacuations that were fleeing these catastrophes.

The fault-line that had given way near Chicago causing it to flood was neither the first nor the worst, even in the United States. Kilauea, the most active volcano in the world was continuing to live up to her reputation and had begun spewing lava into the sky even before the meteors had stopped falling. So much material was flowing down her slopes that scientists were estimating that Hawaii was gaining about 600 acres of new land per hour. And increasing.

Another newscast reported:

High rise buildings from LA to Dubai have fallen like so many houses of cards and the death toll is mounting by the hundreds of thousands. The San Andreas Fault line actually held together better than expected.

It only separated by about thirty feet and sank ten, rather than breaking off completely and dropping the western half of California into the Pacific. The Aleutian island chain has risen up out of the Arctic and, according to scientists, in two days' time the land bridge from Alaska to Russia will once again be passable on foot; an occurrence that hasn't happened in fifty thousand years.

Guatemala, Nicaragua and Costa Rica have also felt the effects of the Pacific Ring of fire as their volcanoes are erupting as well. So many volcanoes in so many areas have taken so many people by surprise that in many cases whole cities have been buried before any major evacuation could even begin. It will ultimately be like the ravages of Pompeii, times a thousand.

Millions and millions of tons of volcanic ash and dust have been thrust up into the upper reaches of the atmosphere to be snagged by the jet stream and flung around the world. Global warming is going to be a thing of the past for some years to come.

In another unusual twist, some tectonic activity shifted the plates beneath Northern Italy. Buildings in many areas toppled, but Venice, the city that was already sinking, got a boost of pressure from the movement, and the entire city has actually risen a foot. It will be months before scientists can confirm if that boost is permanent and if the sinking of the city has been, for the foreseeable future, arrested.

Jeremy, Valerie, Joel, Joan and Chuck were oblivious to all these happenings, however. They weren't receiving that broadcast. They would find out later, but at the moment they were busy preparing for a flight up to Norman.

It was 6:00a.m. and Valerie began preparing breakfast with Joan while Jeremy, Joel and Chuck worked in the garage. The meteor that had killed David had passed through the roof and grazed one of the rails for the garage door before embedding itself in the concrete floor. The passage had shifted the rail just enough to stop the door from going up fully. When Jeremy tried the button to open it the door only rose about two feet before the torque caused the motor to stop and reverse.

"Looks like we have a little work to do on this near rail," Joel suggested.

Jeremy followed his gaze, "Yep. I guess that meteor came a little too close. I'm just glad it didn't hit the rail directly."

Chuck was still nodding agreement as Jeremy found his ladder, and Chuck held it while he did his best to pull the rail back into line. It took him a few tries of delicate application of pressure, but Jeremy managed to realign the rail without ripping any brackets loose.

"I think that does it, Chuck. Why don't you try the button again before I get down from the ladder?"

"Sure thing," Chuck answered.

Joel took over holding the ladder as Chuck moved over to the wall and pushed the button. The rumbling of the motor immediately sounded less strained than it had on the first try and the door slid up smoothly, almost knocking Jeremy off the ladder before he remembered to lean back.

"Great," Jeremy said, glancing out the expansive opening and up to the sky. "It looks like we have clear skies too . . . except...does it look a little hazy to you?"

"Yeah, it does," Chuck agreed.

"Well, we can worry about that later. Let's go get some breakfast so we can get airborne," Jeremy said as he put the ladder away.

"Sounds great to me," Joel responded, releasing the ladder so Jeremy could step down, "I can smell it from here."

Valerie had scrounged around and found blueberry muffin mix and sausage. When the three of them walked back into the kitchen the coffee was ready. Joan was setting the table, and Valerie was just pulling the muffins out of the oven.

"Sit down boys. Breakfast is ready."

"Is this the first time you've ever cooked for me?" There was a sly little grin on Jeremy's face that Valerie caught immediately.

"Why, yes, I think it is, and if you don't say nice things it will probably be the last."

"Boy it smells wonderful," he retorted immediately, seating himself as ordered.

"It truly does," Chuck echoed following Jeremy's example.

"Amazing," Joel offered grinning.

Joan just smiled. Her continued silence was quite the counterpoint to her flamboyant on-stage presence. She had barely said ten words the entire time she had been there other than a few tidbits Valerie had drug out of her while they were in the kitchen. She was pleasant, just quiet. Nevertheless, Valerie now knew she was an only child from a middle-class family in Memphis, Tennessee and had no living relatives.

Valerie set the steaming muffins on a hot plate on the table and sat next to Jeremy. For a few moments there was silence at the table as the food was served and everyone dug in.

"So, what time do you think we can be off the ground?" Chuck asked.

"I'm shooting for 7:30," Jeremy answered. "I checked the mileage last night and it's about 350 air miles. I'm thinking we can be there by 9:30 or so if the winds aren't against us.

"Great. As soon as we're done eating, I'll call Susan and tell them when to expect us."

* * *

Susan's eyes opened at 6:30 from a combination of the cramped position she was in on the couch both beside and on-top-of Johnnie and the morning light streaming through the windows of the airport.

No one had appeared at the place since they had arrived, and it was kind of an eerie feeling to be in a public place that seemed abandoned. She wondered if anyone would even show up today.

"You awake?" Johnnie asked in a gruff husky voice.

"More than you," she said looking back at him and smiling.

"Well, we're still here. I guess that's a good thing," he said.

"It's certainly better than the alternative."

Bones creaked and both groaned as they untangled themselves from the couch and stretched a bit. Johnnie stumbled over to the bank of vending machines and was thrilled to not only find one that would brew coffee on demand but also that he actually had some change in his pocket.

He came back over to the couch a minute later with two cups of coffee and some powdered sugar donuts. Susan was still sitting on the couch twisting her neck left and right trying to get out the kinks.

"Oh, thank you," she said releasing her neck and leaning back on the couch.

"Don't get too comfortable. Why don't we walk outside for a moment and smell the fresh air?"

Susan knitted her eyebrows in a mock frown, "It's cold for one reason."

"Oh, come on. We have hot coffee and we don't have to stay out there very long."

She huffed a groan of complaint but reluctantly followed him as he walked through the double glass doors out onto the tie-down parking area.

"Do you smell that?" Johnnie asked.

"Yeah, it smells like smoke. Damn, Johnnie it's freezing out here!"

"It is smoke, I think. I wonder how many places are burning as a result of the meteor shower, and it's not freezing. I saw the thermometer behind the desk on the way out. It's forty-two degrees."

"That *is* freezing in my book."

Right then her phone rang. "Ah, saved by the bell," She pulled her phone from her pocket as she moved to go back in. Johnnie followed her.

"Uncle Chuck, good morning."

Johnnie walked up behind her putting his arm around her waist and listening to her side of the conversation. He could almost hear Chuck speaking, too, but he didn't try very hard.

"Oh, we were fine. The whole place is deserted but we slept on a couch and they have vending machines for coffee and food . . ."

Um, the weather is clear and just a little breezy here. Looks a little hazy, though . . . The wind? Just a sec."

Johnnie was already moving over to the customer counter where wind speed and direction dials were displayed on the walls along with barometric pressure and temperature.

"Tell them the wind is 010 at 5 and the pressure is three-zero, zero-zero," Johnnie called to her.

She relayed the information.

"Sure, 9:30 will be fine. Yeah, we have some stories to tell too. Oh, and Johnnie wanted me to tell you there is one large pothole in the runway. It's about two-thirds of the way down the north runway on the west side. Johnnie says it's runway 03 . . ."

"Sure . . . OK . . . You guys stay safe. We'll see you then."

"So, 9:30 then?" Johnnie asked.

"That's what they said. And you sounded like you spoke the lingo. Are you a pilot?"

"Nah. I just took a few lessons and I've always been interested. So, we have two hours to kill. Hmmm...Susan, have you ever made love in an airport?"

Susan just smiled.

* * *

Valerie and Chuck cleaned up the kitchen while Jeremy did a preflight on the plane where it sat in the hangar. He was thinking about the flight and glad to get the information about the pothole on the runway in Norman. The information prompted him to grab his bike and make a trip down his own runway. There were a number of little divots in the pavement, but, much to his surprise, there were no chunks missing. Nothing larger than a quarter. When he got back to the hangar Valerie and Chuck were waiting there.

"Just checking this runway for potholes," he said to their quizzical looks.

"Good idea," Chuck said, "Have you already done the preflight?"

"Yep, and she's unscathed and full of fuel too. I think we're ready."

Jeremy set his bike against the wall and picked up the tow bar. While he pulled, Chuck helped by pushing on the back of the propeller to ease the plane out of the hangar.

"Go ahead and climb in, Valerie. I think we'll have to have the big guy up front with me."

Joel and Joan had readily agreed to stay behind. The little aircraft would only hold six, so rather than leave one of them, they both just stayed. Joel quipped that he'd have the entertainment prepared for when they got back.

Valerie smiled and opened the door and a half on the left side of the fuselage. The extra opening was a luxury on a plane this small and made it easy to load cargo behind the front seats or the other four seats that faced each other. Valerie picked the one behind Chuck where she would be facing backwards, but at least it would make it easier to see Jeremy. They all had headsets so hearing their conversation wouldn't be a problem.

When they were all in, Jeremy pushed the remote to close the hangar door and fired up engine. He had attempted to call flight service earlier to get a weather briefing and wasn't too surprised when they didn't answer. At least he knew the winds locally from the windsock, and he knew what they were in Norman. *Nothing like eyes on the ground at your destination.* Most likely there wouldn't be much change between now and the next few hours.

He had, however, looked up the airport in his flight manual and had the elevation at Norman which was 1,182 feet. At least he'd be at the right pattern altitude when he got there since no one was apparently there to answer the Unicom.

Jeremy did his run-up and engine check just off the end of the runway, then pulled the throttle back.

"Everyone ready to go?"

"You bet," Valerie answered. Chuck just smiled at him and nodded.

"Lakeway traffic, this Saratoga 2887-Mike departing runway three four, Lakeway."

Jeremy eased the throttle forward all the way to the stops and the throaty Continental engine roared in response. Jeremy began easing back ever so slightly on the yoke as they gathered speed. He wasn't actually pulling to lift off, he just wasn't pushing as much. When the airspeed indicator read 80 knots, he actually did begin to pull on the yoke and the sturdy little plane gently lifted into the skies.

They were at 500 feet above the ground and Jeremy was still checking engine gauges and preparing for his first turn when he heard Valerie's voice over the mike.

"Oh my God, Jeremy."

Jeremy lifted his gaze from the cockpit and immediately saw what she was commenting on.

The world was burning.

Fires raged in every direction. The newscasts they had watched had been blathering incessantly about the meteor shower then the earthquakes and volcanoes, but they had failed to mention the extent of the fires. The burning meteorite fragments had apparently found dry fodder everywhere.

Several fires were burning in the woods around Lake Travis and as he climbed higher, he could see even larger flames in and around downtown Austin. Now he understood the hazy cast to the air. Jeremy was frankly astonished that the smoke smell had not been accosting them at his home. It must have been a trick of the wind.

After turning north, he continued to climb to 5,500 feet before finally leveling off. Easing the throttle back, he adjusted the fuel mixture and the propeller pitch to maximize his cruise speed and fuel efficiency. When he finished, he watched his airspeed level out at 158 knots or about 180 miles an hour.

No one else was talking, being too engrossed in the spectacle below them. The little fireballs that fell from the sky for about six hours as they marched halfway across the United States had met ground conditions that had been pretty dry since early September.

Jeremy, Valerie and Chuck hadn't given much thought as to what they might see once they were airborne but based on the television broadcasts of earthquakes and tsunamis they might have anticipated great rents in the earth beneath them or flooding everywhere. They hadn't been expecting to see raging fires in every direction.

Heading north they were basically tracking I-35 and Jeremy varied his course from one side of the highway to the other to allow everyone to see the major thoroughfare below.

"There doesn't seem to be very much traffic," Chuck commented.

"And what *is* there isn't moving very quickly," Valerie added.

"Yeah, you can see all the pile-ups and cars on the side of the road," Jeremy said.

"A lot of those cars don't look like they've been wrecked, Jeremy. What do you think is happening?"

"Valerie, it's like when Hurricane Ike hit Houston a few years ago.

The roads are so littered with damage and wrecks that the fuel trucks are having a tough time reaching their deliveries, so even the cars that could get off the highway and to a filling station might have had a tough time finding fuel. I'm betting a whole lot of those cars got stuck on the highway and are simply out of gas. At least this time they didn't have the mass exodus issues too. I don't think anyone really had a good idea of where to go that might be safer, so they just stayed put."

Everyone was silent for a while as all eyes were focused on the dreadful scenes below. The more Jeremy thought about it, the more surprised he became that he wasn't seeing even more fires than he was. Casting his eyes to the west, he figured he could count fifty or more, but given the vastness and length of the meteor storm that wasn't near as bad as it could have been.

The terrain moved swiftly beneath them and the air was almost unnaturally smooth. Except for the haze from the fires, there wasn't a cloud in the sky.

"Jeremy, look up there." It was Chuck's deep voice and Valerie loosened her seatbelt so she could turn to see as well.

It was downtown Dallas approaching in the distance.

Or what was left of it.

Jeremy knew this skyline well and he recognized immediately that it had changed. He was finally seeing the effects of the earthquakes. Fires were also raging throughout the city but the first thing he noticed in the distance was that Reunion Tower that was known for its distinctive golf ball shaped top wasn't there, or at least the top wasn't.

Without really intending to, Jeremy had shifted their course a bit to the east to have them flying closer to Dallas than Ft Worth even though the Ft. Worth route was the more direct path.

The view of the devastation was so incredible that Jeremy had to force himself to pay attention to his flying. He had nearly forgotten to report in to Flight Service that he was approaching the business metro area.

"Fort Worth center this is Saratoga 2887-Mike inbound from the south over Waxahachie at 5,500 squawking VFR requesting permission to traverse airspace."

There was a brief delay, and he was just about to repeat his request when a female voice came on the radio. The voice sounded way past exhaustion. His first clue was the fact that she spoke much slower than was the norm for flight traffic controllers. But the weariness was apparent in her tone too.

"Saratoga 2887-Mike cleared to traverse airspace. Turn right heading 040, squawk 0145 and descend to 4,000. Expect further clearance over downtown Dallas."

Jeremy repeated the instructions back to her and followed them with an uncharacteristic, "Thank you Ma'am." He was surprised when she responded to him again.

"You're welcome 87-Mike and best of luck to you."

It was a measure of the extraordinary situation that the lady controller had either the time or the inclination to add such a personal note to her required responses.

The new course took them directly over downtown Dallas and the physical damage to the city was ghastly. Numerous overpasses had collapsed, and the trio could see myriads of cars sticking out from those fallen ruins.

Fully half of the Dallas skyline exhibited some form of damage and cars seemed to be either stalled or in ruins everywhere in the downtown area. The huge ball Jeremy had noticed as missing from the Reunion Tower he now found smashed in the streets below. He tried not to consider how many people might have been in or under that structure when it came down. Smoke billowed everywhere from skyscraper windows, reminiscent of the videos of the World Trade Center attacks, though this damage was much more widespread.

"It's like civilization is coming to an end," Valerie whispered into her microphone.

Jeremy wasn't sure whether she was talking to herself or not, but he decided to answer anyway, "No. I think we just barely missed out on that one, but I'm not sure I want to know how many people died today."

"Me neither," she replied.

The controller returned to direct them back to a due north course. They were already past downtown by this time and most of the way to Denton. A few moments later she cleared them to return to VFR frequency and altitudes and wished them luck again.

There seemed to be noticeably less fires as they crossed the Red River into Oklahoma. Jeremy was wondering about the change when Chuck spoke up. It was the first time he'd spoken since before they crossed the Dallas Metro area. His remark was an eerie reply to Jeremy's unspoken thought.

"I believe they have received more rain in this area lately."

"Less fires, huh?"

Chuck just nodded his head at Jeremy's comment. All conversation subsided as the little plane droned on northward. It was much less depressing being away from the cities where the visible damage, barring the fires, was greatly reduced.

Jeremy continued to scan his instruments while Valerie and Chuck kept watching the terrain pass below them, but no one spoke again until they approached Norman about forty-five minutes later.

"I've got the runway, Jeremy. Do you see it?"

Chuck was on the right as was the runway, but it was far enough ahead so that Jeremy didn't have to dip a wing to see what Chuck had already spotted.

"Got it," he said then keyed his mic. "Norman traffic this is Saratoga 2887-Mike ten miles south of Norman airport inbound to land. Intend crossing midfield to enter left downwind for runway 03."

After releasing the microphone key, Jeremy reached up and pulled the throttle back, adjusted the fuel flow and prop, and pointed the nose down.

When they crossed midfield, Jeremy was looking diligently out of his side window and just ahead of the wing.

"Wow that really is a pothole. We could have disappeared into that one. I'm glad they gave us a heads up. I don't see anything else though."

They touched down just past the pothole and rolled to a gentle stop far short of the end of the runway. Jeremy maneuvered the plane around and taxied back down the runway to the terminal where Johnnie and Susan were waving from the ramp near the double front doors.

Jeremy parked the plane near the self-service fuel tank and killed the engine. By the time he had switched all the electronics off and set the brakes, Chuck was already clambering out of the cockpit. Jeremy listened to the navigational gyro slowly spin down as he waited for Chuck to finish climbing out. There was no door on his side, but he didn't mind the wait, and it was interesting to see the excitement in Chuck's demeanor.

"Uncle Chuck," Susan shouted as she jogged across the tarmac.

"Susie," he answered as he swept her up in his long arms, "It's been so long."

"Too long," she answered, tears of joy clouding her voice, "Where did you ever happen to find people with their own airplane?"

Chuck gently set her down and held her shoulders so he could look into her face. His face was plastered with an ear-to-ear grin. "That's an interesting story but it's pretty long. Why don't we wait on that one until we get back? Right now, I'd like to introduce you to my two new friends."

They both turned to Valerie and Jeremy who were slowly walking up to the pair.

"Jeremy, Valerie, this is my niece Susan Hummel."

"So nice to meet you," Valerie offered.

"And this is my boyfriend, Johnnie. Johnnie, this is Valerie, Jeremy, and my Uncle Chuck," Susan answered, pointing to each as Johnnie came up beside her.

"Nice to meet all of you," Johnnie replied, "Uh, will that plane hold all of us?"

"With one seat to spare," Jeremy said smiling, "Unless of course you have more than 100 pounds of baggage."

"Only what we're wearing," Johnnie answered with a rueful smile. "Everything else blew up when a meteor struck my Range Rover."

"You have a Range Rover, too?" Jeremy responded.

"Had . . . I think would be the correct term. It's now a burned-out clump of metal under an overpass south of downtown Oklahoma City."

"I'm sorry to hear that."

"I'm just glad we weren't in it when it blew."

Johnnie's smile was sincere, and Jeremy could tell right away that this guy wasn't overly enamored with his own belongings. It was a characteristic that Jeremy valued and he right away decided that he was going to like this guy.

"OK. Well, let me get a little bit of fuel and we can be on our way out of here."

Ten minutes later they were lifting off the runway and heading back south.

"Good Lord," everyone heard Johnnie say as they reached altitude. He and Susan were just now seeing what everyone else had experienced on the flight up.

"Pretty horrible isn't it?" Valerie answered.

"I'll say," Susan responded. "There is a part of me that refuses to believe all this has happened. It just seems like a dream or a movie."

"And I don't think we were hit as hard as some other places in the world," Chuck added, "I'm guessing the earthquakes, volcanoes, and tsunamis did much worse to other parts of the world than the meteor shower did in the States."

There were a number of gasps and "Oh my God" exclamations coming from the two new passengers as they later passed back over the Dallas/Ft. Worth area. This time, however, flight service directed them more over Ft. Worth, but the scene was the same. Smoke, fires, and building and bridge collapses.

No one really had much else to say until Jeremy decided to descend as they approached Waco.

"Why are we going down, Jeremy?" Valerie asked.

"I just thought we'd get a closer look for this last leg."

"I'm not so sure I want a closer look," Valerie mumbled.

"Look at that," Johnnie exclaimed. Johnnie was in the forward-facing seat at the back of the plane on Jeremy's side. He was facing Susan and she and Valerie looked out the windows on their side of the plane.

"Wow," Jeremy breathed.

"What is it?" Chuck asked.

The two passengers on the right side of the plane couldn't see what the other ones were looking at out of their windows.

"Just a second, I'll let ya'll look," Jeremy said as he banked the plane to the east.

When he had maneuvered the Saratoga to the east side of I-35 he leveled it again.

"Ah," Chuck said, "That's quite a chasm." A yawning crevasse ran for several miles along the eastern side of interstate 35. Though it didn't quite extend to the interstate itself, a number of cars could be seen protruding from it.

"There was a fault line around here?" Johnnie asked.

"Yes, there is. It is called the Balcones fault zone, but it hasn't been active in recorded history," Chuck answered casually, as though addressing a class.

"I guess it has now," Valerie responded. "I wonder how we missed that coming up?"

"I'm not so sure we did, Val. It might have happened since we flew over here last." While he spoke Jeremy again swung the plane this time back to the west so the rift could be seen from his side.

"You mean things are still moving?" There was just a hint of frantic in her tone.

"I'm sure they are," Chuck answered again, "It may be awhile before the movement stops completely."

"How long is a while, Uncle Chuck?"

"I'm not sure, honey. A few more days, maybe. It all depends."

The fires were still raging over downtown Austin as they approached, but the ones around Lake Travis seemed to have subsided. Everyone just watched in silence as Jeremy made his radio calls and lined up the Saratoga for landing back at Lakeway.

They were back-taxing to Jeremy's house when Johnnie finally broke the silence.

"Well, all in all I'd have to say that was a pretty smooth ride, Jeremy. Thank you. It makes me wish I'd finished my flying lessons."

"Don't thank me. We just happened to catch smooth air this time."

Jeremy pushed the remote and the huge hangar door began to rise as he approached. "Home sweet home," he said as he swung the nose around and killed the engine.

56

By Christmas Eve, all of Earth's upheavals had been calm for two days. The devastation from the passage of the Rabbit's Revenge meteor shower and the dancing of the Earth's crust had finally stopped. Tsunamis subsided, earthquakes calmed, and most of the fires in the United States had been quenched by the passage of a massive rainstorm that came down from the north and swept across the Midwest. The volcanoes around the world had reverted to a rumbling downward slide back toward dormancy. Even more suddenly than they had begun, the Earth's crust simply ceased its terrible dance in response to extraordinary cosmic forces and seemed to breathe a sigh as its pieces and parts were finally allowed to settle once again into a relatively static state. Cities were gone, new land had been formed and well over a billion and a half human lives were absent from planet Earth.

The Earth had been luckier than most yet realized. Many of the volcanoes that blew did so with only a fraction of their potential power. Had every one of them blown with the force of the previous Mt. St. Helen's blast in the 1980's the world would have surely retreated into another Ice Age. The fortuitous eruption of Mt. Rainer had acted as a pressure release valve for the Yellowstone super-volcano. There are six worldwide super-volcanoes that have the potential to erupt with 1,000 times the power of a regular volcano. Had Yellowstone blown, most of the United States would have been obliterated. An eruption of any of the super-volcanoes would have sent enough dust and ash spewing into the air to have promptly caused a dramatic return of the Ice Age, leaving the continued existence of mankind an unanswered question for years to come. Instead the skies across the earth offered a slightly dingy blue as the dust and ash from fifty-one volcanoes swirled through the jet stream and quickly encircled the entire planet.

~

The little group of seven at Jeremy's home had spent the last two days being quite industrious. It was determined that everyone should just stay while they found out what services were still available and what was going to be difficult. A foray into the fringes of town proved that food was more available and fuel less available than any of them would have guessed. Fuel was obviously in short supply as a result of a partial disruption of the trucking industry, but the grocery stores had already stocked up for the Christmas Holiday and there were substantially less people available to buy that food.

Joel and Joan had only left long enough to retrieve the rest of their instruments which were now set up in one side of the den. They periodically played which cheered everyone up. Again, they not only played cover tunes but a smattering of some of their new stuff including a couple they wrote while there in Jeremy's house. It was a subconscious reminder of what it was to be human and that the world was going to go on. The electricity had gone out again, but Jeremy simply fired up his commercial grade generator that resided in a small building attached to the back of the garage along with a bank of batteries on shelves connected to solar panels on the roof.

"You are a survivalist," Chuck had commented upon seeing the inside of the shed.

"Maybe a little bit," Jeremy had answered with a slightly embarrassed grin, "But we're still going to need gasoline. I do have the extra tank in the garage that I used to store some fuel for the plane but that will only last a few days."

"Don't you have natural gas to this place?" Chuck asked.

"Sure, why?"

"Let's see if we can get a little piping at the hardware store and I believe I can solve the electric problem."

Johnnie had turned out to be quite a handyman and had taken it upon himself to repair the hole in the roof. Jeremy already had a little spare lumber and a few extra slate shingles, so he set himself to the task while Jeremy and Chuck went to the hardware store.

They had to drive around a while to find one that was open, but they did and got not only the plumbing supplies but also a few bags of concrete to repair the hole in the garage floor.

Susan and Joan had hit it off immediately and decided to work with Valerie on preparations for a big Christmas dinner.

The weather was turning colder by mid-afternoon and the skies were looking threatening. The little group had themselves quite busy when the girls heard the doorbell ring.

They looked a question at each other, and curiosity mixed with a twinge of fear as they all three made for the door. Once there, they all paused in unspoken agreement.

"Jeremy," Valerie yelled toward the garage, "Someone's at the door."

When Jeremy didn't answer Valerie hesitated, "Maybe I should go get him. We have no idea who that could be."

"Don't worry about it, Val. I think we can handle 'em," Joan smiled at Susan then crossed the den to the fireplace and calmly picked up the poker.

"OK," she said, "Let's see who our visitors might be."

The doorbell rang a second time just as Valerie was reaching for the knob. She pulled on the door and opened it to a small group of smiling faces. There were three women and two men all of whom looked a bit tired but happy.

"Hi there. I'm Margaret," the nearest lady said.

She was a diminutive blond with a trim figure and an engaging face.

"We saw your lights come back on and thought we'd come by and say 'hi.' Actually, we've been scouring the neighborhood to see who is still around and if anyone needs anything. With Christmas coming tomorrow, we thought it would be the Christian thing to do. Are ya'll doing alright here?"

"We're doing fine," Valerie answered, "Are you finding very many people?"

"Not too many," Margaret answered sadly, "And we've found a few dead, but mostly it seems everyone just left."

"Why don't you come in for a moment and you can meet the guys.

My name is Valerie by the way, and this is Susan and Joan."

Joan surreptitiously leaned the poker against the wall next to her.

"Nice to meet you," Margaret said. "This is Phillip and Allison, and that's Carl behind them, and Sherry."

"Nice to meet all of you," Valerie replied sweetly.

Susan went and got the boys and after introductions all around, it was determined that Jeremy's was currently the only house in the neighborhood with electricity.

"Well in that case," Jeremy offered, "I think everyone should come over here for Christmas. We can all make a huge meal and just enjoy each other's company. I can't think of a better way to spend it than with new friends."

Jeremy hadn't been known as being a neighbor who interacts with his other neighbors. In fact, he was gone way too much to get to know anyone, so the surprise on everyone's faces was completely genuine. It was a member of the new group who spoke up first.

"I think that's a great idea," Margaret said, "We'll find whoever we can and have everyone bring some food for a big dinner."

"You don't have to wait for dinner either. I'd be glad to have people come over whenever they like. We'll be up in the morning working on the house," Jeremy continued.

Valerie moved in closer and snaked her arm around Jeremy's waist. "That's very generous of you, Jer. I like the idea, and I like that you thought of it."

Jeremy spared her a quick kiss on the mouth, which she returned, a fact that frankly shocked Jeremy when he thought about it later; public displays of affection were not exactly high on Valerie's list of "likes".

"Hi, my name is Chuck Kohler. Does everyone have a warm place to sleep?" Chuck asked out of the blue as he walked up from the garage.

"My group does," Margaret answered. Her eyes widened a bit and she hesitated. "Are you the Chuck Kohler we saw on TV that found Rabbit's Revenge?"

Chuck looked a little sheepish, "Yes ma'am that's me. But I'm not the one that gave it that ridiculous moniker."

Everyone laughed, if a bit nervously.

"How did you happen to be here?" Margaret asked.

"That's a long story," Chuck replied, "and one we can get into after dinner."

"OK. Well, in answer to your other question, I have a big fireplace with a natural heater built in and lots of wood. This group is staying with me."

"Great," Jeremy said, "Let us finish repairs on the house then, and we'll see all of you tomorrow. Come over whenever you like. We'll have coffee on in the morning and bring whoever you can find."

The entire group was nodding and smiling as Margaret again answered, "Thanks, Jeremy that is very generous of you. Given the circumstances, I think that'll make for a great Christmas. We'll see you tomorrow."

The group shuffled back out the door and a few seconds later the seven of them were still standing there as if not sure what to do next.

"I think we have some repairs to finish," Johnnie offered. His words galvanized the group into action. All of a sudden, they all had a lot to do.

57

December 25th, 2016
Christmas Day

The sun rose behind the clouds the next morning and the temperatures were well below freezing. Chuck had already been up for an hour and had just finished his piping to the generator. When he made the final connection to his flexible hose he would have natural gas available to the little generator.

He had slept like a rock the night before and when he awoke at 5:00a.m. his first thought was that he couldn't remember the last time he'd slept so well. For the first time in so many years he felt like he was part of a family, and he was relishing the sensation. *How ironic*, he thought, *to feel part of a family now when so many have just been destroyed.*

Tightening down the last clamp, Chuck flipped the switch, and the generator sputtered twice then caught. The house had steady electricity again.

Chuck stepped out of the power shed, as he called it, and closed the door. The air felt damp as he opened the other door into the garage-hangar. It was probably going to snow today, he thought. He hadn't seen snow in years and the idea of it tickled him.

The next thing on his list was making coffee. So, he quietly moved down the hall to the kitchen and was surprised to see Susan already there just turning on the coffee pot.

"You're up early," she said.

"So are you," Chuck answered with a grin, "It must be genetic."

"It's wonderful to see you again, Uncle Chuck."

"You, too. Why don't you let me build the fire back up and we can drink our coffee and catch up?"

Chuck had the fire crackling in the fireplace by the time Susan brought the two cups of coffee over and set them on the coffee table. With grins on their faces that really looked like two kids on Christmas morning they began to talk.

* * *

Valerie's voice was soft and warm as she murmured into his ear, "Merry Christmas." Jeremy's eyes slowly opened up. The bed clothes were warm and snuggly.

A smile slid onto his face through the sleep as he answered, "Merry Christmas to you too, sweetie."

"That really was a nice thing you did yesterday offering everyone a place to meet."

"Thanks. It just felt right. After all the disasters I think we are all going to need to practice thinking of others more, and what better time to start than Christmas Day."

"I know, I'm already thinking of you more," Valerie answered playfully as she rolled on top of him.

Jeremy's arms went up and around her chest. "I love you, Valerie. I'm glad we made it together."

"I love you too. There's no one else in the world I would rather survive with."

Her next actions gave a new meaning to the term survive, but Jeremy didn't complain.

* * *

Judging by the sound, everyone was already up when Johnnie came shuffling into the kitchen looking for the coffee pot. Joel and Joan staggered in shortly thereafter.

"Merry Christmas, sleepy head," Susan called from the couch where she was still sitting by Chuck.

"Sleepy head? It's just 8:30," Johnnie replied.

"OK. It's a relative term. Come here and give me a hug."

345

Johnnie's head was still obviously heavy with sleep, and he was still shuffling when he took his coffee cup over to Susan by the fire and gave her a big hug.

"Anyone mind if I turn on the TV?" Chuck asked, "First I want to see if there is a station functioning and then I'd like to hear how much of the world is left."

His words had a sobering effect. They had nearly managed to force the worldwide catastrophe out of their immediate thoughts. Now it all came crashing back in and a patina of gloom settled over the little group.

"Fine by me," Jeremy said.

Chuck took a quick glance around the room and realized the result of his words. "I'm sorry to depress everyone. I didn't mean to." He was having familiar feelings of social inadequacy as he reached for the remote.

"It's OK, Uncle Chuck," Susan said making a point of leaning over to give him a hug, "You didn't make the problem. As a matter of fact, according to Valerie, you're one of the two people in the world who did the most to fix the problem. Which reminds me, Jeremy, I'd like to hear the story of your vision about the asteroid, and while you're at it how about the story of that scar around your neck?"

Jeremy smiled. "Why don't we wait on that till a little later? I have a feeling someone else might want to hear those stories too and I'd rather just tell them once."

"It's a great story too," Joel interjected.

~

Joan was sitting close to Joel on one of the couches and Jeremy seemed to notice for the first time that the two were acting much more connected than they had been. He wrote it off to the disasters. It was a pretty common response.

~

Susan was nodding when the voice from the TV interrupted. A somber faced CNN reporter was standing in front of the capital in Washington...

"... the events continue to unfold. Reports are slowly coming in

346

from around the world as communication systems are slowly restored. A substantial number of the satellites in geostationary orbit above the United States were destroyed by the passage of the meteor shower, and it has taken quite an effort to reroute that traffic to other functioning towers and satellites. However, ladies and gentlemen, let me tell you, the face of our planet has changed. From the few reports we have been able to assemble, here are some of the most dramatic changes: several deserts including the Great Victorian and Gibson deserts in Australia, the Sahara in Africa and portions of the Gobi desert in Asia are now inland seas, the long-sunken land bridge between Russia and Alaska has once again resurfaced, sections of the Nile have been cut off and several new paths have been formed, and there are now two new islands in the Hawaiian chain but Oahu has disappeared completely.

"Fires continue to rage in various areas throughout the world. Those that were not caused by the meteor shower were caused by earthquakes and volcanoes. The body count continues . . . "

"Oh, my Lord," Valerie gasped, raising her hand to cover her mouth.

Jeremy drifted over to her, taking her by the waist and pulling her close. Her head sank onto his shoulder.

"The resurfacing of that land bridge to Alaska ought to have some interesting political ramifications," Chuck observed.

"I think this entire experience is going to have significant political ramifications," Jeremy commented, "For the first time in modern history, Man has had to consider the possibility of extinction. I believe our new president is going to have a lot on his hands."

"There were almost 400 thousand people on Oahu alone," Joel murmured distantly. "I wonder how many might have escaped."

"To where?" Chuck added matter-of-factly. "Some surely made it to the other islands but how many boats could there have possibly been on short notice that weren't already destroyed? It's one of the things people are not used to considering. What are the escape routes in the event of an emergency? Islands like Hawaii are particularly vulnerable."

The tone of the conversation was apparently irritating Valerie. The iron in her next words caught everyone's attention.

"Hundreds of millions of people die, and you discuss it like it's some kind of science experiment? What is wrong with you people?"

Joel shrugged it off, but Chuck evinced a look somewhere between shock and embarrassment.

"I don't mean to sound cold, Valerie. It's just that in the past hundred years or so people have become so accustomed to their civilized lives that they seem to have forgotten that some of the danger they face is a result of their own choices. People that live on coastal areas or islands or in the shadow of dormant volcanoes really do run greater risks with their lives, but people want to live in those places so they take those risks and just because these disasters don't happen frequently people let themselves believe they won't happen. I do care about the people though."

~

Valerie could plainly hear the conciliatory tone in Chuck's voice and the look of mortification on his features softened her response, "I know, Chuck and I'm sorry I sounded so angry. I'm just so devastated by the incredible loss of 1 . . ."

The doorbell interrupted her words and Chuck's thoughts. Jeremy moved quickly to the door. It was several of the neighbors including Margaret from the previous night.

"Good morning and Merry Christmas," she said. Her hands were full with two serving dishes as were the hands of the two others with her.

Chuck eyed the group as they flowed in the door. They had smiles on their faces but there was a haunted look behind their eyes. They weren't immune to the tragedy, just hiding it as best they could. His social deficiencies didn't prohibit him from recognizing other's feelings when he saw them.

He was still feeling the inadvertent sting of Valerie's words as he watched their little group grow. He was about to turn his attention back to the TV and tune out the rest of the group when Valerie appeared at his side and draped an arm on his shoulder.

"Hey there. I wanted to apologize again. I had no right to be short with you. I am just unnerved by all this death, and I think I'm feeling a little guilty that I'm still alive. Isn't that stupid?"

Chuck smiled at her. Her words were more soothing than she could have possibly imagined, and he wanted her to know it.

"No, Valerie. It's not stupid. In the face of tragedy such as this it is a common reaction to feel guilty to be alive. It's called survivor's syndrome and I want to truly thank you for your apology. I most often feel ill at ease in social settings because it seems that sooner or later, I make someone angry, and I think the world of you and Jeremy. I especially didn't intend to make either of you uncomfortable. You two and Susan are the only family I have."

Tears seeped into Valerie's eyes and for a frightful moment Chuck was afraid he'd said something else wrong. "We love you too, Chuck, and I know you didn't mean to be callous. I've known enough scientists to understand that a part of them is always analyzing data and at those moments emotions aren't in the equation. I should have thought before I ran my mouth. By the way, you're welcome to stay here with us for as long as you care to."

Now it was Chuck's turn to have tears seep into his eyes, a sensation with which he was most unfamiliar. "That might be the kindest offer I've had since Louise said yes to my marriage proposal. I've been wondering where I might go next. I saw on the news that one of the quakes cracked Mt. Palomar. The telescopes and the structure were destroyed, so I guess I don't have a job anymore."

Valerie hugged him tighter. "You don't have to go anywhere and for that matter Susan and Johnnie are welcome here as well."

Chuck managed a crooked little smile. "Don't you want to check with Jeremy before offering his house up to a bunch of strangers?"

Valerie certainly didn't miss the teasing tone in his question and wasted no time responding in kind, "Are you kidding? He's going to marry me, so it's my house too, and you know men don't get a say in these things with their wives."

"I think I heard my name over there along with a couple of other interesting words. Maybe I should stand over here with you two and defend myself."

The group he had just welcomed into the house was busy putting away and preparing things in the kitchen.

Valerie and Chuck stared at each other for a moment and then burst out laughing.

"You tell him," Valerie said between laughs.

"Oh no. I would never give a man that kind of news. That's your job. You tell him."

"Tell me what?" Jeremy replied with mock annoyance.

Chuck and Valerie cracked up again. "I'll tell you later," Valerie finally answered.

"Typical," Jeremy responded, grinning broadly.

~

About thirty minutes later the doorbell rang again and more people filed into the house. Introductions continued all around, but this time Chuck stayed seated in front of the television. The growing size of this get together had long since outstripped his interaction skills. He did manage a wave from his seat when his name was included in the introductions, but that was about it.

He continued watching the TV and his analytical mind sifted through the data. No one had ventured a global death toll yet, but he had been keeping a running total in his mind based on what he knew of world populations.

The number was moving way past the several hundred million number he had thrown out to Valerie. His best guess at this point was more in the range of a billion and a half dead. A billion and a half bodies. That meant a billion and a half bodies to dispose of in some fashion. Had anyone even considered that yet? There weren't enough people in the world to provide burials for that many and it had to be done quickly before the decaying bodies began to spread disease. Something more radical was going to be required. Would people dump them in the ocean? Burn them? He could barely imagine the social outrage at that thought. That many bodies could be used as fuel for furnaces to generate electricity but that would be perceived as even more cold hearted.

The more he thought about it the more Chuck realized what a serious challenge this new president had laid out for him. At least the United States had managed to elect a man of quality and character this time. In Chuck's mind it was the first time the country had done so since Ronald Reagan, and it was none too soon. Carl Iverson, the Colorado cattle rancher, Republican, and a real-life hero, was the new president of the United States, it was an incredible thought. It wasn't just the United States either. All the other countries would be faced with the same challenges of rebuilding the world and dealing with the loss and changes.

Chuck's rambling thoughts were interrupted when a little kid sat next to him on the couch.

"Aren't you the man I saw on TV last week?" The young fellow was probably about nine years old and his blue eyes held a world of curiosity that Chuck couldn't resist.

"What's your name, young man?"

"You *are* the man I saw on TV. I remember your big deep voice. You sound like Santa Claus. My name is Chuck just like you."

Chuck smiled. This he could handle. "Just like mine, huh?"

"Yes, sir. Aren't you the man that discovered the asteroid that hit us?"

"Well, it didn't really hit us. It hit the moon, but yes I'm the one that found it."

"It did too hit us. Parts of it did."

Chuck had to smile again at this young critical thinker, "Why yes, you're absolutely right. We certainly did get hit with pieces of it. You're a pretty smart young man."

The compliment didn't even faze little Chuck. "And momma said Mrs. Margaret told her the guy that had the dream that saved us from the asteroid lives here. Is that true?"

"Right again. You're pretty well informed."

"How did it happen that you two are in the same house at the same time?" Little Chuck asked, eyes growing wider by the second.

"Chuck, what do you want to be when you grow up?"

"Mr. Kohler, I want to be an astronomer just like you."

"Really?"

"Yes, Sir. Maybe you could teach me some things."

The excitement in the boy's voice was rising with every sentence issuing from his mouth and Chuck found the boy's enthusiasm contagious.

"Maybe I could at that. I gather you live around here?"

"Yes, sir. Just a couple of blocks away. Do you have a telescope here?"

"Well, no. I used to live in California, so not many of my things are here with me."

"So, you live here now?"

Chuck smiled as he considered the boys words. He hadn't had much time to think about the future, at least not the future beyond the world's recent disasters.

It was a little bewildering and a little exciting, but the overwhelming feeling was one of belonging and of having a family. It was something he hadn't felt in many years and it was a warming sensation.

"Actually, I guess I do," he finally said and proceeded to lecture the young astronomer on the rudiments of astronomy as the house continued to fill with guests.

~

Most of the women were in the kitchen making preparations for what looked to be a tremendous feast and Johnnie was over by the bar talking to Jeremy. They had hit it off famously and had apparently decided that on this Christmas Day there was no time too early to begin to drink. Joel and Joan had joined them when they both began sipping on heavily spiked eggnogs. Valerie caught Jeremy's eyes and decided to make a pass over to the bar as well.

"Quite the little shindig we have here, don't you think?" She asked, smiling at Jeremy as she slipped her arms around his waist and buried her cheek against his chest.

"Yep. There's nothing quite like a the-world-didn't-actually-end-Christmas party."

Valerie's actions seemed to have attracted Susan who stepped away from the kitchen and moved in their direction with eyes locked on Johnnie. She put her arms on his shoulders and gave him a quick kiss before assuming a place beside him. At that point Joan slipped an arm around Joel. It was the first overt show of affection they had shown.

By now the group had grown to probably thirty-five including about eight children, and people were milling everywhere enjoying the company. Maybe everyone was more thankful than usual to be alive. Maybe catastrophe had reminded everyone how important relationships truly were. In that room and maybe on the entire planet there was no one who hadn't lost someone in the last few days and it was a sobering thought.

Once kitchen preparations were mostly finished, people began to move into the large den where Jeremy's big screen TV and the crackling fireplace became the centers of attention. Everyone was sipping or munching and the smiles all around seemed somewhat out of place in the light of recent events.

Jeremy didn't know half of the people that were there and still the doorbell would ring from time to time. By noon his house was full, and it began to snow. Big fluffy flakes floated like butterflies all through the air and quickly generated a patina of white on all the ground visible from Jeremy's huge windows.

"A white Christmas!" One of the children yelled, "Yea!"

~

The afternoon drifted on, and the camaraderie and general closeness only seemed to grow. The snow continued to fall, so by late afternoon there was a very unusual accumulation for the Texas Hill Country. Most of the kids went out to play in it.

The TV droned on with a litany of the losses the world had suffered, but by this time most people received the news a mild grimace or no reaction at all to further revelations.

One plump reporter was particularly lucid, ". . . that as this Christmas Day continues the world is forced to endure such horrible losses as well as such incredible changes. This just in; the Grand Canyon is mostly gone. Many of the sheer walls have collapsed as a result of the tremendous upheaval of the Earth's crust.

Also, it is now confirmed that although the San Andreas fault did give way today, the movement wasn't nearly as much as scientists projected; however, there is a separation between east and west California now and the chasm that formed promptly filled with water so we have a new river in the United States. People are speculating that this new body of water might well be called the California Chasm River. We are now hearing from Hawaii again, since their communications were cut off two days ago by the eruption of the volcano on the Big Island. More stories continue as more and more locations manage to restore . . ."

"Ah turn it off, Jeremy," Joel said, "We've heard enough for one day.

Let's enjoy each other and our food."

"Good idea," someone from the crowd echoed.

"Jeremy, tell us the story about your scar and the vision." This came from one of the few neighbors that Jeremy did know. Everyone began to gather around even before Jeremy had a chance to reply.

"Chuck, we want to hear your story too, about how you discovered Rabbit's Revenge." This came from another child. Little Chuck, sitting beside him, had just heard the story, but he smiled and nodded agreement anyway.

"Hey, wait a minute," Joel interrupted, "We still have a video to watch."

"Oh yeah," Jeremy responded. "The Go-Pro video!"

Jeremy promptly went out into the garage and grabbed the camera. It took him a few minutes to hook the connections up to the TV, but everyone waited patiently.

"This is the video from the camera I had on my wrist the day I got this scar on my neck." While Jeremy began his narration, you could hear a pin drop in the room.

At first the video showed Jeremy's legs out in front of him sitting in the bow of the ski boat, and beyond that the ski rope and the jet boat in the distance. Next you could see Jeremy's legs begin to flex.

"Hey Lance, could you inch it up a bit? That turkey has sped up some, and I'm getting compressed up here." Jeremy's voice sounded clear but a bit distant

"Sure thing, Jeremy." Lance's response was almost unintelligible.

At this point the camera jumped around a bit and all you could see were flashes of Jeremy's legs, the water, and the sky. Then a muffled "Oh shit" from Jeremy.

The next image was of the sky and then a thin flash of cord, before the camera hit the water.

"Did you see that?" Jeremy exclaimed, "That was the parachute line going around my neck before I hit the water!" Just seeing the brief image gave Jeremy the chills and made his neck itch.

The next image was mostly bubbles underwater which seemed to go on forever. Then the sun again and the camera suddenly seemed to make a quick panorama of the lake. The group was still holding their breath as

Jeremy paused the playback.

"That must have been me removing the rope from around my neck. I don't remember that at all."

"Wow," Joel replied in a far-away voice. He was the only one that said anything at that moment.

The next flash or two simply consisted of Jeremy swimming back to the boat. As Jeremy hoisted himself into the boat, the camera caught one quick glimpse of Jeremy's neck.

"Oh my God," Margaret exclaimed. The collective intake of breath in the room echoed her words.

Jeremy turned off the recording at that point.

"Tell us the whole story!" The excited voice came from little Chuck, but the muted nod from around the room signaled everyone's agreement with the little guy's sentiment.

After Jeremy recounted the entire story, Joel and Joan picked up their instruments and began to play to the applause of a delighted group. They started off with their own music and a few cover tunes then with a grin to each other, Joan broke into a rock and roll rendition of White Christmas and everyone went nuts clapping.

~

There was a magical quality to the day as the survivors unconsciously reveled in the fact that they were alive. Christmas seemed to be the perfect day to thank God for an Earth that still existed.

58

January 1ˢᵗ, 2017 AD

Chuck remained with Valerie and Jeremy through New Year's Day. That morning he was up early as he had imbibed significantly less than his hosts. As he sat and sipped a mimosa, he turned on the TV. A lovely blonde newscaster appeared with a particularly thoughtful and compelling story:

~

"The mourning all over the world has only abated slightly for the celebration of the New Year. Even though this new year is not only a celebration of the march of time, but also a rejoicing of the Earth's survival, the billions of deaths are still too near.

"The impact to the ecological system of the Earth has been dramatic. As the dust began to settle from the volcanoes, man's footprint on the planet has retreated enough to allow many of Earth's resources to begin recovering.

A great haze, as scientists are calling it, circles the earth. They have assured us it is not enough to bring on another Ice Age, but it is enough to dramatically affect the climate around the world. And millions of survivors in the northern climes are already seeking refuge in the warmer areas nearer to the equator. We are being told that the poles are refreezing at a dramatic rate, and to that extent the world's oceans are lowering proportionally.

"We are told that it will be months before worldwide communications can be completely restored and world leaders and scientists can easily confer. One ironic twist, however, to the collision of Kohler/ Leporidae and the moon is a change in the landscape of the moon's surface which we have a picture of for you." The screen switched to an image of the moon with the lovely blonde shrunken and confined to the lower left-hand corner. She continued her report, "You are currently looking at the side where the collision occurred, as you can see a great mountain has risen on the moon's surface and one astronomer jokingly made reference to another reporter that the new, great lunar mountain resembled a rabbit's cotton tail. The reference seems to be catching on and we wouldn't be surprised if the scientific community eventually names the new protuberance Mount Leporidae."

"Or Mount Bunny," Chuck snorted dismissively as he changed the channel.

Another dark haired, slender, male reporter appeared on the screen with a different sort of interesting tidbit.

"I have recently gone back and read some of the old prophecies concerning the time near the end of the Mayan calendar and found this quote from the ancient Roman prophet 'The Sybil'.

"In her prophecies she predicted that the world would last for nine periods of 800 years each and that the tenth generation would begin approximately in the year 2000 and it would be the last. Her words were, 'These things in the tenth generation shall come to pass. The earth shall be shaken by a great earthquake that throws many cities into the sea. There shall be war. Fire shall come flashing forth from the heavens, and many cities will burn. Black ashes shall fill the great sky. Then know the anger of the Gods.'"

"As it turns out," the reporter said, "her words from almost 2000 years ago were strikingly accurate."

~

In the following days Chuck discussed going back to California and leaving Jeremy and Valerie alone. Valerie wouldn't hear of it and said they had plenty of room.

"You can't leave now, Chuck," Valerie stated.

"Why not?" Chuck replied.

"Because you have to stay around for the wedding. Jeremy asked me to marry him."

"Well congratulations! When is this event supposed to take place?"

"Probably another month and we want you in the wedding."

"I'm flattered," Chuck answered with a slight tremble in his voice, "In that case I'll have to stay."

* * *

To fill his time Chuck followed closely the continued reports filling the media from the scientific community regarding the aftermath of the collision.

One such significant event came after the discovery that the meteorite particles were extremely rich in the mineral ruthenium. Several scientists in the U.S. where the vast majority of these particles had fallen had already been working on the concept of artificial photosynthesis as a way to improve air quality and to generate energy.

Ruthenium was the key mineral in the process but was so rare in the Earth's crust that the entire line of study had been set aside until another substance could be found to replace the ruthenium. Now, as a result of the asteroid collision, the United States had an abundance of the mineral and before the end of the New Year the United States was well on its way to producing both cleaner air and an abundant energy source to replace fossil fuels. To brighten the picture even further, the scientists were well aware of the amount of asteroid that had imbedded itself in the surface of the moon. If they ever needed any more ruthenium than what had already impacted the earth, they certainly knew where to get it.

But maybe most significant of all the developments was the earth's recognition that we are not immune to the projectiles of space and cosmic forces that could potentially destroy us. As a result of this new realization two things occurred. First, renewed interest in space exploration and space technology reasserted itself like never before in the history of mankind.

As a first step, tremendous attention was poured into the new NASA WISE (Wide-field Infrared Survey Explorer) telescope. It had been launched in early December and given the task of hunting new asteroids that were previously undetectable because they shine only in the infra-red range of the light spectrum. It had already been discovering dozens of new asteroids on a daily basis, but now the entire Earth was interested in studying its results. Billions were again being poured into space and space travel technology.

We as a species had finally come to the realization that if we don't find a way to settle other planets, our continued existence has a very uncertain termination date.

Lastly, a conference of scientists proposed a change that was accepted by the remaining rulers of the world. Our calendar would be changed.

As of the end of 2017 the world's calendar would no longer con-tinue forward. It would now begin to march backward in recognition of the billions of lives lost and the dramatic changes made to the Earth. Therefore, the New Year after the end of the catastrophe was renamed from 2017AD to 2015ADm. It was the end of the old calendar as we knew it.

Chuck smiled as he turned off the TV and went out to the back deck of Val and Jeremy's home.

Thinking about what he had just seen he decided that in a very real sense, the events that caused this upheaval were due to the celestial align-ment predicted by the end of the Mayan Calendar four years previously. Therefore, at the end of their 26,000-year cycle, the prophecy came true.

The Mayan Legacy was fulfilled.

THE END

ABOUT THE AUTHOR

The adopted son of a prominent Texas restaurateur, Jody grew up in New Orleans, Memphis and then Houston, learning the restaurant business while he built a career as a competitive gymnast that propelled him to a scholarship at the University of Kansas.

After college, Jody followed in his father's footsteps owning, at one point, three 24-hour restaurant franchises along with four tanning salons in Tulsa. Finally leaving that business, he turned his entrepreneurial skills to everything from a patent in the Pet Industry to a Single's website.

A restaurateur, a gymnast, a stunt man, an entrepreneur, a pilot, skydiver, scuba diver, and an accomplished martial artist for twenty-five years, Jody Summers has tried it all. Now he brings all those experiences to paper in his books.

Don't miss the upcoming release of the third book in his supernatural thriller series, *The Art of the Dead*.

www.ingramcontent.com/pod-product-compliance
Lightning Source LLC
Chambersburg PA
CBHW050538260626
47157CB00002B/345